ONE SUMMER IN PARIS

This Large Print Book carries the
Seal of Approval of N.A.V.H.

ONE SUMMER IN PARIS

SARAH MORGAN

THORNDIKE PRESS
A part of Gale, a Cengage Company

Farmington Hills, Mich • San Francisco • New York • Waterville, Maine
Meriden, Conn • Mason, Ohio • Chicago

LIBRARY OF CONGRESS CIP DATA ON FILE.
CATALOGUING IN PUBLICATION FOR THIS BOOK
IS AVAILABLE FROM THE LIBRARY OF CONGRESS

ISBN-13: 978-1-4328-7058-4 (hardcover alk. paper)

Published in 2019 by arrangement with Harlequin Books S. A.

Printed in Mexico
2 3 4 5 6 7 23 22 21 20 19

For Susan Swinwood,
with love and thanks.

"The real voyage of discovery consists not in seeking new landscapes, but in having new eyes."

MARCEL PROUST

GRACE

Grace Porter woke on Valentine's Day, happily married and blissfully unaware that was about to change.

Downstairs in the kitchen she added slices of cheese to the bread she'd baked fresh the day before, put fruit and raw vegetables into lunch boxes and then checked her list.

Number four on today's list: *remind Sophie about dinner.*

She glanced up. "Don't forget Dad and I are out tonight. Your dinner is in the fridge."

Her daughter, Sophie, was messaging a friend. "Mmm . . ."

"Sophie!"

"I know! *No phones at the table* — but this is urgent. Amy and I are writing a letter to the paper about that development they're going to build on the edge of town. Dad promised he'd publish it. Can you believe they want to close the dog shelter? Those dogs are going to *die* if someone doesn't do

9

something, and that someone is me. There. *Done.*" Sophie finally looked up. "Mom, I can make my own lunch."

"Would you include fresh fruit and veg?"

"No. Which is why I'd rather make my own." Sophie gave a smile that didn't just light her up, it lit Grace up, too. "And you're starting to sound like Monica, which is a little scary."

Her daughter was like sunshine. She made the world a brighter place. For years Grace had been braced for her to rebel, take drugs, or roll in drunk after an illicit party with friends, but it hadn't happened. It seemed that Sophie's genetic makeup favored David's side of the family, which was a relief. If Sophie had an addiction it was causes. She hated injustice, inequality and anything she deemed unfair — particularly when it related to animals. She was the champion of all dogs, especially the underdog.

Grace was quick to defend her friend. "Monica is a wonderful mother."

"Maybe, but I can tell you that the first thing Chrissie is going to do when we get to Europe this summer is feast on a ton of fries to make up for all the years her mom wouldn't let her touch them." Sophie finished her oatmeal. "Did you say something about dinner?"

"Have you forgotten what day it is?" Grace closed the lunch boxes and put one next to Sophie. The other she slid into her own bag.

"Valentine's Day." Sophie slid off her chair and picked up her empty bowl. "The day it becomes public knowledge that nobody loves me."

"Dad and I love you."

"No offense, but you're not young, cool and athletic."

Grace took a mouthful of coffee. How much should she say? "It's still Sam?"

Sophie's smile faded as if someone had hit the dimmer switch. "He's seeing Callie. They walk around together holding hands. She keeps giving me these smug smiles. I've known Callie since I was three, so I don't understand why she's doing this. I mean, date him, sure. That sucks, but it's life. But it's like she's *trying* to hurt me."

Grace felt a burning in her chest. Not heartburn, but parenthood. As a mother, her role was to support from the sidelines. It was like being forced to watch a really bad play without the consolation of knowing you could leave in the interval.

"I'm sorry, honey."

"Don't be." Sophie put her bowl in the dishwasher and then added the one her

11

father had left on the side. "It would never have worked out. Sophie and Sam sounds pretty lame, don't you think?"

Her hurt slid into Grace and settled deep in her gut.

"You're going to college soon. After a month in California you won't even remember Sam exists. You have your whole life ahead of you, and all the time in the world to meet someone special."

"I'm going to study, graduate top of my class and go to law school where I can learn how to sue people who are assho—"

"Sophie!"

"Er . . . not very nice people." Sophie grinned, slung her backpack over one shoulder and stroked her long ponytail over the other. "Don't worry, Mom. Boys drive me insane. I don't want a relationship."

That will change, Grace thought.

"Have a great day, Mom, and happy anniversary. Twenty-five years of not yelling at Dad when he leaves his socks on the floor and his dirty plate on top of the dishwasher. Major achievement. Are you seeing Mimi today?"

"This afternoon." Grace slid her laptop into her bag. "I made macarons, like the ones she used to buy in Paris. You know

12

what a sweet tooth your great-grandmother has."

"Because she lived in Paris during the war and she had no food. Sometimes she was too weak to dance. Can you even imagine that?"

"That's probably why she talks to you about it. She doesn't want you to take things for granted." She opened the box she'd carefully packed that morning, revealing pastel macarons lined up in neat rows of rainbow perfection.

Sophie made a sound that was almost a purr. "Wow. I don't suppose I could . . . ?"

"No." Grace closed the box. "But I might have packed a couple for your lunch." She tried not to think about the sugar, or how Monica would react to the inclusion of empty calories in a lunch box.

"You're the best, Mom." Sophie kissed her cheek and Grace felt warmth flood through her.

"Do you need a favor or something?"

"Don't be cynical." Sophie grabbed her coat. "Not many people would teach French at an assisted-living center, that's all. I think you're amazing."

Grace felt like a fraud. She didn't do it out of any sense of charity, but because she liked the people. They were always so

13

pleased to see her. They made her feel valued.

It was embarrassing to think she could still be needy at her age.

"Their French Club is the best part of my week. Today being Valentine's Day, I've allowed myself to be creative." She picked up the stack of menus she'd designed. "The staff are laying the tables in the restaurant with red-and-white tablecloths. We're eating French food, I'm playing music . . . Knowing your great-grandmother, there will be dancing. What do you think?"

"*Ooh là là,* I think it sounds great." Sophie grinned. "Just remember that the average age of Mimi's friends is ninety. Don't give them all heart attacks."

"I'm pretty sure Robert has his eye on Mimi."

"Mimi is a minx. I hope I'm like her when I'm ninety. She has this wicked twinkle in her eye . . . It must have been fun having her living with you when you were growing up."

It had been lifesaving. And that, of course, was why Mimi had moved in.

It was a time she'd never discussed with her daughter. "She's one in a million. You'll be okay tonight?" She checked the kitchen was tidy. "There's casserole in the fridge.

14

All you need to do is heat it up."

"I'm eighteen, Mom. You don't have to worry about me." Sophie glanced out the window as a car pulled up outside. "Karen is here. I need to run. Bye."

Telling Grace not to worry was like asking a fish not to swim.

Two minutes after Sophie had left, she slid on her coat, picked up her keys and walked to the car.

Turning the heat up, she focused on the drive.

Four mornings a week, Grace taught French and Spanish at the local middle school. She also tutored children who were struggling and occasionally gave lessons to adults keen to improve their language skills.

She took the same route she always took, seeing the same houses, the same trees, the same stores. Her view only changed when the seasons changed. Grace didn't mind. She savored routine and predictability. She found comfort and security in knowing what was going to happen next.

Today the snow lay deep on the ground, coating roofs and gardens in thick slabs of white. In this little corner of Connecticut the snow was likely to linger for many weeks. Some people embraced it. Grace wasn't one of them. By March, winter felt like a guest who had outstayed her welcome. She longed for sunshine and summer dresses, bare legs and iced drinks.

She was still dreaming of summer when the phone rang.

It was David.

"Hi, Gracie." That voice of his still made her insides melt. Deep and gravelly, but smooth enough to soothe life's hurts.

"Hi, handsome. You had an early start today." *And you left your breakfast plate on top of the dishwasher.*

"Things are busy at work."

David was editor of the local newspaper, the *Woodbrook Post,* and had been kept busy lately thanks to the astonishing success of the girls' tennis team, the formation of a county children's choir and a robbery at the local gas station during which the only things stolen were a box of doughnuts and a bottle of rum. By the time the local police had located the man responsible, the evidence had been consumed.

Whenever Grace read the paper it reminded her of all the reasons she lived in this quaint town with a population of only 2,498.

Unlike other journalists, whose sights might have been set on bigger targets, David had never shown a desire to work

16

anywhere but this small town they'd both fallen in love with.

The way he saw it, he was the voice of the community. He was obsessed with the news, but he also believed that it was what happened right here in their hometown that mattered to people. He often joked that all he needed to fill the entire newspaper was to spend an afternoon at a backyard barbecue listening to the gossip. He was friends with the police chief and the fire chief, which ensured that he was given all the major scoops.

Of course in Woodbrook, a place most people had never heard of, there were more scoops in the ice cream parlor than there were in the local community, and that suited Grace.

"Happy Valentine's and happy anniversary." She slowed as she approached an intersection. "I'm already looking forward to dinner tonight."

"Shall I book somewhere?"

Only a man would think it possible to get a table on Valentine's Day without forward planning. "Already done, honey."

"Right. I should be home early. I'll fix something for Sophie to eat so you don't have to bother."

"I've handled that. The fridge is full of

17

food. You can relax."

There was a pause. "You're superwoman, Grace."

She glowed. "I love you."

Her family was the most important thing in the world to her.

"I'll drop by the store and pick out something for Stephen's birthday on my way home. He says he doesn't want a fuss, but I feel we should buy him something, don't you?"

"I do — which is why I bought him a gift when I was shopping last week." Grace waited for a gap in the traffic and turned into the school. "You'll find it under the bed in the spare room."

"You've already bought something?"

"I didn't want you having to think about it. Remember that great photo of Stephen with Beth and the kids?"

"The one I took at the Summer Fair?"

She pulled into a space and undid her seat belt. "I had a print made and bought a frame. It looks great."

"That's . . . thoughtful . . . ."

"I've wrapped it. All you have to do is sign your name." She reached across and gathered her coat and bag. "I'm at school, so I'll call you later. You sound tired. *Are* you tired?"

18

"A little."

She paused with one leg out of the car. "You've been working long hours lately. You need to slow down. There's nothing for you to do at home, so maybe you should lie down and rest before we go out."

"I'm not geriatric, Grace."

There was a sharpness to his tone that was unusual.

"I was trying to spoil you, that's all."

"Sorry." The sharpness vanished. "Didn't mean to snap. There's been a lot going on lately. I'll call a cab for tonight, so we can have a drink without worrying about driving."

"Cab is already booked for seven."

"Do you ever forget anything?"

"It's all down to lists — you know that. If I lose my lists, my life is over."

It occurred to her that if she died someone would be able to pick up her "To Do" lists and carry on with her life as if she'd never inhabited it.

What did that say about her? A life should be individual, surely? Would someone looking at the lists be able to learn anything about *her*? Would they know that she loved the smell of roses and indulged her love of French movies when no one was home? Would they know she listened to Mozart

19

piano concertos while she cooked?

"Is there *anything* you need me for?"

Grace gave a smile that her daughter would have said was very like Mimi's minxy look. "I can think of a few things . . . I plan on showing you later."

David ended the call and she walked into school, waving at a couple of parents who were delivering their precious cargo.

Twenty-five years. She'd been married for twenty-five years.

She felt a glow of pride.

Take that, universe.

She and David were a perfect team. They'd had their ups and downs like any couple, but they'd handled everything together. Grace had become the person she wanted to be, and if a tiny voice occasionally reminded her that underneath she was someone quite different, she ignored it. She had the marriage she wanted. The life she wanted.

The day deserved a special celebration, and she'd made a reservation for dinner at Bistro Claude, the upmarket French restaurant in the next town. Claude himself was from Texas, but he'd seen a gap in the market, cultivated an accent and modeled his restaurant on something he'd once seen in a French movie.

20

Even Grace, a purist and Francophile, had to admit the place was charming. She would have loved to take Mimi there, but her grandmother no longer enjoyed eating out.

Bistro Claude was the perfect setting for tonight, because Grace had planned a big surprise. Organizing it had been a major undertaking, but she'd been careful to leave no clues or hints.

Fortunately David had worked long hours over the past couple of months, or it would have been impossible to keep her research a secret.

She pushed open the doors and headed into school.

The children in her class were at that age where anything to do with sex or romance was treated as either hilarious or awkward, so she was fairly sure Valentine's Day would evoke plenty of giggles.

She wasn't wrong.

"We've written you a poem, miss, to celebrate your anniversary."

"A poem? Lucky me." Grace hoped they'd give her the PG version. "Who's going to read it?"

Darren clambered onto his chair and cleared his throat. "Twenty-five years, that's a very long time. More than you get for a life of crime."

21

Grace wasn't sure whether to laugh or put her head in her hands.

By the time she headed back to the parking lot at lunchtime she felt exhausted, and relieved she only worked mornings. Fortunately the drive to the assisted-living center where her grandmother lived would give her time to decompress.

It was a scenic route that wound through woodland and sleepy villages. In the fall the road was clogged with tourists admiring the sunset colors of the foliage, but now the trees and the rolling hills were coated in snow. The road followed the curve of the river, which had a tendency to flood as the snow melted.

Grace drove past the wildlife sanctuary, turned right into the road that led to Rushing River Senior Living and parked the car.

When Mimi had first announced her decision to move here Grace had been horrified.

As well as having a love of dance and all things hedonistic, her grandmother was a celebrated photographer. She'd traveled the world with her camera at a time when it had been rare for a single woman to do such a thing. She was famous for her photographs of postwar Paris, and Grace had always marveled at how her grandmother could capture people's personal struggles in a single frame. Mimi's vivid, exuberant personality was at odds with her dark, atmospheric photos of streets drenched by rain, or couples clinging together in a desperate embrace. The photographs told a story that her grandmother rarely shared in words. Of hunger and deprivation. Of fear and loss.

The last thing Grace had anticipated was that her well-traveled, worldly grandmother would choose to move somewhere like Rushing River. She'd tried to persuade her otherwise. If Mimi had reached the age when she could no longer manage alone, then she should live with Grace and David.

Mimi had insisted that she enjoyed her independence far too much to live with other people — even her beloved granddaughter. She'd gone ahead and paid the money without giving Grace any say in it.

That had been five years ago, but it had taken only a couple of visits for Grace to understand why her grandmother had chosen the place.

It was a haven. On busy days, Grace fantasized about living there, too. There was a fitness center, including a pool, a spa and salon facilities, which Mimi loved. But the best thing was the people. They were interesting, friendly and, thanks to excellent management, the place felt like a community.

Her grandmother lived in a two-bedroom garden cottage, with views across the lawns down to the river. In the summer, with the doors and windows open, you could hear the sound of the water. Mimi had turned one of the bedrooms into a darkroom, where she still developed her own photographs. The other room, her bedroom, looked like a dancer's dressing room, complete with a mirrored wall and a barre that her grandmother used for stretches.

The front door opened before Grace had lifted her hand to the buzzer.

"What do you think? *Je suis magnifique, non?*" Her grandmother did a twirl and then immediately reached out to steady herself. "Oops!"

"Careful!" Grace grabbed her hand. "Maybe it's time to stop dancing. You might lose your balance."

"If I'm going to fall, I'd rather do it while I'm dancing. Unless I fall out of bed having sex. That would also be acceptable — although unlikely, unless the men around here get their act together."

Grace laughed and put her bags down. She loved the mischievous look in her grandmother's eyes. "Don't ever change."

"I'm too old to change — and why would I want to? Being yourself is the one thing every person should excel at." Mimi smoothed her dress. "So, what do you think?"

"Is that the dress you wore when you were in the ballet in Paris?"

She'd seen photos of that time. Her grandmother, impossibly delicate, standing *en pointe* with her hair swept up. According to Mimi half of Paris had been in love with her, and Grace had no trouble believing it.

"I didn't know you still had it."

"I don't. This is a copy. Mirabelle made it for me. She has such a talent. Of course I was younger then and my legs weren't as scrawny as they are now, so she made it longer."

"I think you look incredible." Grace leaned down and kissed her grandmother's cheek. "I have everything ready for French Club. I need to go and help the staff set up, but I wanted to give you this first." She handed over the macaron box, which she'd tied with a beautiful bow. "I made them."

"A gift you make yourself is the best gift of all." Mimi slid her fingers over the silk ribbon. "I had a pair of ballet shoes with ribbon exactly this color." She opened the box with an enthusiasm that ninety years on the planet hadn't dimmed. "They look exactly like the ones I used to buy in Paris. They were there in the shop window like jewels. I remember a man once sneaking out of my apartment early in the morning to buy me a box for breakfast — we ate them in bed."

Grace loved hearing about her grandmother's colorful past. "What was his name?"

Could Mimi be talking about the man who had made her pregnant?

Grace had tried on numerous occasions to persuade her grandmother to talk about the mysterious man who was her grandfather, but she never would. *It was a fling,* was all she would say.

As usual, her grandmother was vague. "I don't remember his name. I only remember the macarons."

"You're a wicked woman, Mimi." Grace took the box from her and closed it. It felt odd to not know anything about her grandfather. Was he even still alive?

"Since when has it been wicked to enjoy oneself? And why are you closing the box? I was about to eat one."

"You'll have plenty to eat in French Club. There are more where these came from."

"I like to enjoy the moment." Mimi

opened the box again and helped herself. She took a delicate bite and closed her eyes. "If you focus on living well in the moment, you will never have regrets about yesterday."

Grace wondered if she was thinking of Paris, or of the man who had brought her macarons in bed. She knew her grandmother had stories she hadn't shared, and that there were times she didn't like to think about. Grace understood that. There were times she didn't like to think about, either.

"Good?"

"Excellent." Mimi opened her eyes and reached for her coat and a silk scarf. Today's choice was peacock blue. "How is Sophie?"

"Enraged about the plans to close the animal shelter. She's writing letters and calling anyone who will pick up the phone."

"I admire a person who is prepared to stand up and fight for a cause they believe in. Even more so when that person is my great-granddaughter. You should be proud, Grace."

"I am proud — although I'm not sure the way she is has much to do with me. She has David's genes."

Mimi read her mind. "Relax. She has nothing of your mother in her." She tucked her arm into Grace's as they stepped out of the apartment onto the covered walkway that led to the main house. "When is Sophie coming to see me?"

"On the weekend."

"And David?" Mimi's expression softened. "He popped in yesterday and fixed the broken handle on my door. That man is perfect. He has time for everyone. And did I mention that he gets more handsome by the day? That *smile.*"

"I know." She'd fallen in love with David's smile. "I'm lucky."

Mimi stopped walking. "No, honey. *He's* the one who is lucky. You went through so much and yet you have a family like this — well, I'm proud of you. You're the glue, Grace. And you're an excellent mother."

Her grandmother was her biggest supporter. Grace hugged her in full view of anyone who happened to be watching. It was only when she held her grandmother that she was aware of her frailty. It scared her. She couldn't imagine a life without Mimi.

"I love you."

"Of course you do. I'm the buttercream frosting on the stale cake that is life."

Grace let her go. "Twenty-five years today. Had you forgotten?"

"I have creaking bones and varicose veins, but my memory is fine. I know what day it is. Your anniversary! I am happy for you. Every woman should love deeply at least once in her lifetime."

"*You* didn't. Were you never tempted to get married? Not even when you discovered you were pregnant?"

Mimi flipped the scarf around her neck and slid her arm through Grace's. "I wasn't the marrying kind. You, however, always were. I hope you're wearing your sexiest underwear to celebrate."

"I refuse to discuss my underwear with you, but I *can* tell you that I've booked dinner. And that's when I'm giving him his gift."

"I'm envious. A whole month in Paris. Sunlight on cobbled streets, and the gardens . . . Paris has a special atmosphere — do you remember that? It slides under your skin and permeates the air you breathe . . ."

Mimi seemed to be talking to herself and Grace smiled.

"I remember — but I have only been once, and just for a short visit. You were born there. You lived there."

"I did. And I really did *live.*" Mimi was never so animated as when she talked about Paris. "I remember one night we stripped off our clothes and —"

"Mimi!" Grace paused at the door to the

dining room. "You're about to appear in public. Don't scandalize everyone. We don't want to shock them with your sinful stories."

"Boredom is a sin. You're never too old for a little excitement. I'm doing them a favor." Mimi snapped her fingers in the air. "Pierre! That's it." She looked at Grace, triumphant.

"Pierre?"

"The man who bought me the macarons. We'd made love all night."

Grace was intrigued. "Where did you meet him? What did he do for a living?"

"I met him when he came to watch me dance. I have no idea what he did for a living. We didn't talk. I wasn't interested in his prospects — just his stamina."

Grace shook her head and adjusted her grandmother's scarf. "You should go back."

"To Paris? I'm too old. Everything would be different. The people I loved — gone."

Her grandmother stared into the distance and then gave a shake of her head.

"Time to dance." She opened the door and sailed into the room like a prima ballerina making her entrance onstage.

They were greeted by a chorus of cheery voices, and Grace unloaded her bag onto the table. She'd stopped to pick up baguettes from the bakery on Main Street.

They weren't as crisp and perfect as the ones she'd eaten in France, but they were the closest thing she could find in rural Connecticut.

While the staff helped prepare the tables Grace selected the music.

"Edith Piaf!" Mimi glided gracefully to the center of the room and beckoned to Albert.

Several other people joined them and soon the room was filled with people swaying.

When they sat down to eat, they bombarded Grace with questions.

Did she have everything in place for David's surprise? How exactly was she going to tell him about the trip she had planned?

She'd shared her plans with them, knowing how much they enjoyed being part of a conspiracy.

It had been David's idea not to buy each other gifts for their anniversaries, but instead to treat themselves to experiences. He'd called it their "Happy Memory Project." He'd wanted to fill her memory bank with nice things to cancel out all the bad experiences of her childhood.

It was the most romantic thing anyone had ever said to her.

The previous year she'd booked a weekend at Niagara Falls. They'd had a good time, but Grace had been determined to go bigger and better this year.

The afternoon passed quickly, and she was clearing up when her friend Monica arrived to teach a yoga class.

Grace and Monica had met when pregnant. No one understood the anxieties of parenting like another mother, and it was good to talk to Monica, even though her friend often made her feel inferior.

Monica was obsessed with living a healthy lifestyle. She blamed red meat for at least half the wrongs in the world. She juiced, grew her own vegetables and taught yoga. She insisted the whole family were vegetarian, although David swore he'd once seen Monica's husband devouring a sixteen-ounce bone-in rib eye at a steak house in the neighboring town. They'd only socialized once as a couple — a dinner consisting almost entirely of lentils, after which David hadn't been able to leave the bathroom for twenty-four hours.

Never again, he'd yelled through the bathroom door. *She's your friend.*

Grace, whose own stomach was listing like the deck of a ship in a storm, had agreed.

From that point onward the friendship had been confined to the two women. They met for coffee, or lunch, or the occasional spa day.

Despite David's reservations, Grace loved Monica. She had a good heart and teaching yoga here at Rushing River was an example of that.

Grace helped Monica set out her equipment in the exercise studio. "How is Chrissie?"

"Anxious. Not sure what she'll do if she doesn't get her first choice of college. The waiting is driving us insane. I've been practicing meditation techniques, but they don't seem to be working."

"Sophie is stressed, too. They're not going to hear until next month."

Both girls were hoping for places at Ivy League colleges, and Grace and Monica knew there would be major disappointment if they didn't get in.

"Chrissie wants Brown because she loves their program, but I want it because it's close." Monica removed her sweatshirt, revealing perfectly toned arms. "I want to be able to visit sometimes." She sent Grace a guilty glance. "Sorry. That was tactless."

Grace would have loved her daughter to go to college on the east coast, too, but Sophie was desperate for Stanford and excited about going to California. Grace wouldn't have wanted to stop her, or try to

33

persuade her to pick a college closer to home. She was pleased that Sophie had the confidence to fly far from the nest.

"Do you think about it a lot? What life will be like when she leaves?" Monica dug out the microphone she used to teach her class. "Chrissie seems so young still. Todd is dreading her leaving, although at least we don't have to worry about her suddenly going off the rails. She's such a steady, sensible girl. How's David taking it?"

"He seems relaxed. We don't really talk about it." Grace didn't want to spoil the last few months of having Sophie at home by constantly focusing on her departure. She'd hidden her feelings of anxiety in case she somehow transmitted them to her daughter. She and David were *not* Sophie's responsibility.

She'd stuck to that resolution — even with friends. "It will be a change, of course, but we're both looking forward to having some time together."

Long summer days stretched ahead, just her and David . . . No Sophie bouncing into the kitchen and raiding the fridge. No clothes strewn around the house and open books on the furniture. No letters of outrage spread across the kitchen counter ready to be mailed.

When Sophie left there would be a big gaping hole in her life. There were moments when it scared her to think about it, but she knew it was up to her and David to fill it.

"You're both so well-adjusted." Monica clipped the microphone to her top. "When Chrissie first raised the possibility of going to Europe with Sophie this summer I thought Todd was going to explode. I keep telling him she's not a child anymore and that she wants to be with her friends. But I'm worrying a little, too. Do you think we should have encouraged them to do something less adventurous?"

"I was the same age when I first went to Paris. It was an unforgettable experience."

Memories flashed through her head. Rain-soaked Paris streets, sunshine filtering through the trees in the Jardin des Tuileries, her first proper kiss in the moonlight with the river Seine sparkling behind her. The glimpse of a life so far removed from hers, it made her dizzy. The excitement of knowing there was a whole world out there waiting for her.

Philippe.

First love.

And then the phone call that had changed everything.

It all seemed so long ago.

35

"But they're doing Rome and Florence, too." Monica wasn't reassured. "I've heard bad things about Florence. Donna's daughter had her purse stolen, and she said they didn't dare go out unless there were two of them — even in the day. They were groped all the time. And what if someone spikes their drinks? I don't want Chrissie introducing poisons to her system. She's never even had antibiotics."

Grace dragged herself out of the past. She was pretty sure that Chrissie would be poisoning her system plenty when she got to college. "They're sensible. If they do get into trouble — which they won't — they can call us. David and I will be in Paris for a month."

It sounded exotic, and suddenly it felt as if a door had opened just a crack. Part of her would always ache for those days when her daughter had been safely nestled in the protective cocoon of the family, but there were plenty of things to be excited about in the future.

Possibilities stretched before her.

David's parents had passed away early in their marriage and he had no other family. He'd often said that Grace and Sophie were his whole world, and Grace was happy with that because she felt the same way. And she had Mimi, too. She smiled. *Her buttercream frosting.*

The idea of a month in Europe, when every day would be completely their own, left her feeling almost light-headed. They'd lounge in bed, enjoy long breakfasts on the balcony of the hotel, do some sightseeing. They'd have the time and energy for sex, and wouldn't have to worry that Sophie might disturb them.

She'd miss Sophie, but the more she thought about it the more excited she was about spending more time with David.

She raised the subject later, when she and David were at dinner.

"I've been thinking of all the things we can do when Sophie has left for college."

The restaurant was full. They were surrounded by the low hum of conversation, the clink of glasses, the occasional sound of laughter. Candles flickered on tables and silverware gleamed.

"We don't know where she's going yet." He tucked into his *boeuf bourguignon.* The scent of herbs and red wine drifted across the table. "She might not get in."

"She will. She's smart. And she works hard. Our baby is grown-up."

From behind them there was a burst of applause. Grace turned her head. A man was on one knee behind them, holding out a ring to a weeping woman. Grace clapped, too, and then glanced back at David. She'd expected him to wink at her, or maybe roll his eyes at the clichéd public display, but David wasn't smiling. He was staring at the couple with an expression Grace couldn't quite interpret.

"It's going to be just the two of us," he said. He watched as the man slid a ring onto the woman's finger. "Do you ever think about that?"

Grace shifted in her seat so that her back was to the couple. She'd ordered the duck confit, and it was delicious. "Of course. I've also been thinking of all the things we can do. I'm looking forward to it, aren't you?"

She was so caught up in her own burst of positivity that it took a moment for her to realize he hadn't answered her. He was still staring past her to the couple.

"David?"

He put his fork down. "I feel old, Grace. As if the best days of my life are behind me."

"What? David, that's *insane*. You're in your prime! If it helps, Mimi thinks you're sexier than you've ever been."

She thought so, too. When you grew up alongside someone you didn't always see them the way a stranger did, but lately she'd found herself looking at the width of David's shoulders or the shadow on his jaw and thinking *nice.* Age had given him a gravitas that she found irresistible.

At the mention of Mimi, the tension left his features. His eyes crinkled at the corners — a precursor of the smile she loved so much. "You've been discussing my sex appeal with your grandmother?"

"You know what she's like. I swear if I weren't already married to you, *she'd* marry you. No, actually . . ." She frowned. "Marriage is too establishment for Mimi. She wouldn't want to be tied down. She'd sleep with you, and then discard you and not even remember your name. Paris is paved with the fragments of all the hearts Mimi broke there."

And soon they'd be going there. Maybe this was a good time to tell him.

He fiddled with his knife. "I still remember the day Sophie was born. I can't believe she's leaving home."

"It's natural to feel that way, but we should be proud. We've raised a smart, kind, independent adult. That was our job as parents. She thinks for herself, and now she's going to live by herself. It's the way things are supposed to be."

The fact that it hadn't been that way for

39

her had made her all the more determined to make it happen for her daughter.

David put his knife down. "A milestone like this really makes you take a good look at your life. I've been thinking about us, Grace."

She nodded, pleased. "I've been thinking about us, too. We should celebrate our fresh start. And our summer *won't* be empty, because I have the perfect way to fill it. Happy anniversary, David."

She handed over the parcel she'd kept hidden under her chair. The paper was covered in tiny pictures of Paris landmarks. The Eiffel Tower. The Arc de Triomphe. The Louvre. It had taken two hours of searching to find it on the internet.

"What's this?"

"It's my anniversary surprise. We always take a trip and make a new memory. This is a special one. And maybe you'll feel inspired to work on your novel." He'd been working on a book for as long as she'd known him, but had never finished it.

"A trip?" He removed the paper slowly, as if he wasn't sure he wanted to know what was underneath.

The couple at the next table glanced at them, intrigued. She knew them vaguely — in the way everyone knew everyone in a small town like this one. Faces were always familiar. Someone's cousin. Someone's aunt. Someone's husband.

David pulled out the street map of Paris she'd also ordered on the internet. "We're going to Paris?"

"Yes!" She was ridiculously pleased with herself. "It's all booked. We're going for a month, right through July. You're going to *love* it, David."

"A *month*?"

"If you're worried about taking the time off work, don't be. I already spoke to Stephen, and he thinks it's a great idea. You've been working hard, and July is a quiet month, and —"

"Wait. You spoke to my *boss*?" He rubbed his jaw, as if he'd suffered a physical blow. Streaks of color appeared on his cheekbones, and she couldn't work out if it was anger or embarrassment.

"I needed to know you could take the time off." Perhaps she shouldn't have done that — although Stephen had been charming about it.

"Grace, you don't have to handle every detail of my life."

"I thought you'd be thrilled." Wasn't he going to look at the other items in the box? There was a ticket for the Métro, the Paris

41

subway, a postcard of the Eiffel Tower and a glossy brochure for the hotel she'd booked. "This trip is for *us*. We'll have a month together in the summer, exploring the city. We can eat dinner outside in pavement cafés, watch the world go by and decide what we want our future to look like. Just the two of us."

She was determined to view this new phase of life as an adventure and a celebration, not as a time for regrets and nostalgia.

Would it feel weird being in Paris with David? No, of course it wouldn't. Her last visit had been decades ago. It was part of a past she didn't let herself think about.

"You should have talked to me about this, Grace."

"I wanted it to be a surprise."

He looked sick. She started to feel sick, too. The evening wasn't going the way she'd imagined it.

He closed the box. "You've booked everything already? Yes, of course you have. You're *you*."

"What's that supposed to mean?" Was she supposed to apologize for something that was one of her best qualities? Being organized was a *good* thing. She'd grown up with the opposite and she knew how bad that was.

42

"You do everything — even though I'm capable of doing things for myself. You don't have to buy my boss's gift, Grace. I can handle it."

"I know you can handle it, but I'm happy to do it so that you don't have to."

"You organize every single small detail of our lives."

"So nothing gets forgotten."

"I understand why that is important to you. Really, I do."

There was gentleness in his tone and the sympathy in his eyes made her squirm a little. It was like walking into a crowded room and discovering you'd forgotten to button your shirt.

"We don't need to talk about bad stuff on a night like tonight."

"Maybe we do. Maybe we should have talked about it a lot more than we have."

"It's our anniversary. This is a celebration. You're worried I'm doing too much? It's fine, David. I *like* to do it. It's not a problem."

She reached across the table but he moved his hand away.

"It's a problem for *me,* Grace."

"Why? You're busy, and I love spoiling you."

"You make me feel . . ." He rubbed his

jaw. "Incapable. Sometimes I wonder if you even need me."

Her insides swooped. She felt as if she'd stepped off a cliff. "How can you say that? You know it's not true."

"Do I? You plan every detail of our lives. You are the most independent woman I know. What exactly do *I* contribute to this marriage?"

At any other time she would have said *great sex,* and they both would have collapsed with laughter, but tonight David wasn't laughing, and she didn't feel like laughing, either.

The people at the table closest to them were staring.

Grace didn't care.

"You contribute plenty! David —"

"We have to talk, Grace." He pushed his plate to one side, his meal only half-eaten. "I wasn't going to say this tonight, but —"

"But what? What do you want to talk about?" Unease mushroomed inside her. He didn't sound like himself. David was always sure, confident and dependable. She almost always knew what he was thinking. "Why do you keep rubbing your jaw?"

"Because it aches."

"You should see the dentist. Maybe you have an abscess or something. I'll make you

44

an appointment in the morning —" She stopped in midsentence. "Or you can make it yourself if you prefer."

"I want a divorce, Grace."

There was a strange ringing in her ears. The background music and the clatter from the kitchen had distorted his words. He couldn't possibly have just said what she'd thought he'd said.

"Excuse me?"

"A divorce." He tugged at the collar of his shirt as if it was strangling him. "Saying those words makes me feel sick. I never wanted to hurt you, Gracie."

She hadn't misheard him.

"Is this because I bought Stephen a gift?"

"No." He muttered something and tugged at his collar again. "I shouldn't be doing this now. I didn't plan to. I should have —"

"Is it because of Sophie leaving? I know it's unsettling . . . ."

Panic gripped her heart. Squeezed. Squeezed some more. Her lungs. She couldn't breathe. She was going to pass out in her duck confit. She imagined the story appearing in the following day's edition of the *Woodbrook Post.*

A local woman was asphyxiated when she fell face-first into her meal.

"It's not because of Sophie. It's us. Things

45

haven't been right for a while."

There was something in David's eyes she'd never seen before.

Pity. Yes, there was sadness, and also guilt, but it was the pity that tore her to shreds.

This was David. *Her* David — who had cried on their wedding day because he loved her so much, who had held her while their daughter fought her way into the world and been there for Grace through thick and thin. David, her best friend and the only person who truly knew her.

He would never want to see her hurt, let alone hurt her himself. Knowing that, she felt her panic turn to fear. He didn't want to hurt her but he was doing it anyway — which meant this was serious. He'd decided he'd rather hurt her than stay with her.

"I don't understand." Surely if something hadn't been right, she'd have known? She and David had been a team for as long as she could remember. Without him she would have fallen apart all those years ago. "What hasn't been right, David?"

"Our lives have become . . . I don't know. Boring." His forehead glistened with sweat. "Predictable. I go to work in the same place, see the same people and I come home every day to —"

"To me." It was all too easy to finish his

46

sentence. "So what you're really saying is that *I'm* predictable. *I'm* boring." Her hands were shaking and she clasped them in her lap.

"It's not you, Grace. It's me."

The fact that he was shouldering the blame didn't help. "How can it be all you? I'm the one you're married to and you're unhappy — which means I'm doing something wrong." And the problem was that she *loved* the fact that their life was predictable. "I grew up with unpredictability, David. Believe me, it's overrated."

"I know what you grew up with."

Of course he did.

Was she boring? God, was it true?

It was true that she was a little obsessed about them being good parents to Sophie, but that was important to David, too.

He undid another button on his shirt and gestured to the waiter to bring more water. "Why is it so hot in here? I don't feel too good . . . I can't remember what I was saying . . ."

She didn't feel too good, either. "You were telling me you want a divorce."

She hadn't believed that word would ever come up in a conversation between her and David, and she wished it hadn't come up now, in a public place. At least two of the

47

people in the bistro had children in her class — which was unfortunate, given the nature of this conversation.

Mommy says you're getting divorced, Mrs. Porter, is that right?

"Grace —"

David took a sip of water, and she noticed there was a tremor in his hand. He was looking pale and ill.

She was pretty sure that if she looked in the mirror she'd think the same about herself.

What about Sophie? She'd be devastated. What if she was too upset to go away for the summer? It was terrible, awful timing.

Monica would probably blame red meat. *Too much testosterone.*

"We can talk to someone, if you think that would help. Whatever it is that needs working on, we'll work on it."

"Fixing our marriage isn't something you can add to your 'To Do' list, Grace."

She felt color flood into her cheeks, because mentally she'd been doing exactly that. "We've been married for twenty-five years. There is nothing — *nothing* — we can't fix."

"I'm having an affair."

The words were like a solid punch to her gut.

"No!" Her voice cracked. And that was how she felt. Cracked. Broken. As if she were a piece of fine china he'd flung against the cabinet. "Tell me that isn't true."

She was going to be sick. Right here in a pretty little French bistro, in front of an audience of around fifty people, she was going to be sick.

She could imagine how the kids in her class would react to *that*.

Did you barf, miss?

Yes, Connor. I barfed, but it had nothing to do with the duck.

David looked worse than she felt. "I didn't plan it, Grace."

"Is that supposed to make me feel better?"

She had a thousand questions.

Who is this woman? Do I know her? How long has it been going on?

In the end she asked only one. "Do you love her?"

David rubbed his fingers over his forehead. "I — Yes. I think so, yes."

She almost doubled over. Not just sex, then, but feelings. Strong feelings.

It was the ultimate betrayal.

She stood, although her legs didn't seem to agree with the decision. They felt like water. But she didn't want the local community to witness any more of this conversation — not for his sake but for hers and Sophie's. How much had people heard already? Was she going to be stopped in the supermarket?

I hear David doesn't love you? That must be tough.

"Let's go."

"Grace, wait!" David fumbled for some bills and dropped them on the table without counting them.

Grace was already halfway to the door, the box filled with her Paris plans tucked under her arm. She had no idea why it seemed so important to take it with her. Maybe she didn't want to leave her dreams lying around. The happy summer she'd spent months planning wasn't going to happen. Instead, they'd spend the time dividing up property and belongings and consulting lawyers.

The reality of it swamped her.

David was the love of her life. He was the solid foundation upon which she'd constructed her wonderfully safe, predictable world. Without him the whole thing would crumble.

She felt as if she was having an out-of-body experience. Her mind was elsewhere but her body was still here in this bistro, going through the motions. Smiling, leaving — *thank you, yes, the meal was delicious* — as if her life hadn't just been torn apart.

David pressed his hand to his chest again and shook his head when the waiter offered him his coat. "Grace, I'm not feeling too good —"

Seriously?

"Oddly enough, I'm not feeling too good, either."

Did he expect sympathy?

"I feel as if — I can't —"

David staggered and then collapsed, sending a trolley and a coat stand flying. The weight of him hit the floor with a sickening thud.

Grace couldn't move.

Was this what shock did to you? Did it freeze you into a useless object?

Silence had fallen across the restaurant. She was vaguely aware that a few diners were standing up, the better to see what was going on. Waiters had turned to look at her, panic and expectation in their eyes.

David was on the floor, sweat covering his brow and his eyes bulging.

He clawed at the collar of his shirt and pressed his hand to his chest.

His eyes met hers and she saw the terror there.

51

Help me . . . help me.

"Call the emergency services." She was fascinated by how normal she sounded.

She was trained in first aid, but her body and mind were paralyzed by the knowledge that her husband of twenty-five years didn't love her anymore.

He'd been unfaithful to her. He'd had sex with another woman. Probably multiple times. How long had it been going on? Where? In their bed or somewhere else?

David's throat made a rattling sound and Grace examined her response with a mixture of awe and curiosity. Was she seriously considering not resuscitating him?

My name is Grace Porter and I murdered my husband.

No, not murder. Murder was premeditated. This was more . . . opportunistic.

If he died she wouldn't even know who to call to break the news. She'd have to look around her at the funeral and try to identify the one woman who was crying as hard as she was.

Dimly registering the clattering and panic around her, Grace stared down at him for what felt like minutes but was in fact no more than a few seconds.

This was the man she loved. They'd had a child together. She'd assumed they'd grow old together.

If he was bored with his life, why hadn't he said something?

The injustice of it almost strangled her sense of duty. He hadn't even given her a chance to fix things. He'd made the decision for both of them. How could he *do* that?

As sirens sounded in the distance, David made a choking sound and then his eyes closed.

Grace woke from her inertia.

She couldn't let another person die even though it felt as if that person had stabbed her through the heart.

She knelt down beside him, felt for a pulse, checked his breathing and then put her hands on his chest and started compressions.

One, two, three — Damn you, David . . . damn you, David . . .

She counted as she pumped and then pinched his nose and breathed air into his mouth, trying not to think about those lips kissing another woman.

The first thing she was going to do when she got back home was change the sheets.

The sound of sirens grew louder. She willed them to hurry. She didn't *want* him to die. That would be the easy way out for him, and Grace didn't want to give him the easy way out.

She wanted answers.

AUDREY

Thousands of miles away in London, Audrey was in the middle of studying for a chemistry exam when her bedroom door burst open.

"Which dress? Green or pink?" There was a note of wild panic in her mother's voice. "The green shows more of my cleavage."

Audrey didn't turn her head from the screen. *Why didn't her mother ever knock?* "I'm working." And every word was a struggle. Whoever had put her brain together had done a crap job.

There were days when she totally hated her life and this was one of them.

"It's Valentine's Day. You should be out on a date. At your age I was already a party animal."

Audrey knew just how much of a party animal her mother was. "My exams start in May."

"You mean July."

"I'm done by the middle of June." Why did it bother her that her mother didn't know that? She should be used to it by now. "These exams are a big deal."

Audrey felt sick about them. She was terrible at exams. It didn't help that the teachers kept saying that the results would affect their whole future. If that was really the case then her life was already over.

Everyone else in her class had parents nagging them.

Are you doing enough work?

Should you be going out on a school night?

No, you don't need fizzy drinks and pizza.

Audrey longed for someone to show her that much care and attention. *Any* care and attention. She longed for her mother to stroke her hair, bring her a cup of tea and say a few encouraging words, but her mother did none of those things and she'd given up hoping for it.

She'd been six years old when she'd realized her mother was different from other mothers.

While her friends' parents hovered outside the school gate, Audrey stood alone, waiting for a mother who frequently didn't show up.

She hated being different, so she began making her own way home. The school had strict rules about only releasing a child into the care of a known adult, but Audrey found a way around that. If she smiled and waved a hand in the vague direction of a group of mothers, they'd assume hers was among them. She'd slip through the crowd and once she was out of sight she'd make her way home. It wasn't far and she'd memorized the route. Turn at the red post box. Turn again at the big tree.

Day after day Audrey let herself into the empty house, unzipped her schoolbag and struggled with her homework. Every time she pulled her book out of her bag, she had a sick feeling in her stomach. Her handwriting looked as if a demented spider had hurled itself across the paper and she could never quite organize her thoughts in a way that made sense written down. Teachers despaired. She'd despaired. She tried hard, achieved nothing, stopped trying. What was the point?

When she'd tried telling her mother she found reading difficult, the suggestion had been that she watch TV instead.

Finally, after years of handing in messy work and missing deadlines, a teacher who was new to the school had insisted Audrey was tested.

Those tests showed her to be severely

dyslexic. In a way the diagnosis was a relief. It meant she wasn't stupid. On the other hand, she still *felt* stupid and now she also had a label.

They gave her extra time in exams, but everything was still a struggle. She needed help, but when her mother came home from work she usually fell asleep on the sofa.

For years Audrey had believed her mother was just more tired than other mothers. As she'd grown older and more observant she'd noticed that other people's parents didn't drink a bottle of wine or two every evening. Sometimes her mother was late arriving home, and then Audrey would know she'd started her drinking early. She had no idea how her mother managed to hold down her job as an office manager, but was thankful that she did.

Functional alcoholic. She'd done an internet search once and found the perfect description of her mother.

Audrey told no one. It was too embarrassing.

The happiest days were when a school friend invited Audrey for tea or a sleepover. Audrey would watch other mothers, and occasionally fathers, fussing over home-cooked meals and homework and wonder why her mother didn't know that was the way it was supposed to be done. She tried not to think about their empty fridge, or the empty bottles stacked outside the back door. More embarrassing were the men her mother brought home from her after-work drinking sessions. Fortunately, since meeting Ron, that had stopped. Audrey was pinning all her hopes on Ron.

"Your exams are done by June?" Her mother leaned on the edge of the desk, creasing a stack of papers. "I had no idea. You should have told me."

You should have known. Audrey tugged at the papers and moved them out of harm's way. "I didn't think you'd be interested."

"What's that supposed to mean? Of course I'm interested. I'm your mother."

Audrey was careful not to react. "Right. Well —"

"You know I've been busy planning the wedding. If you're done by the middle of June, then that means you'll be around all summer."

Not if she had anything to do with it. "I won't be here in the summer. I'm going traveling."

It had been a spur of the moment decision, driven by a deep-seated horror of being at home.

She'd saved some money from her Saturday job at the hair salon and hidden it inside the soft toy she'd had since childhood. She didn't trust her mother not to use the money to buy drink, and that money was her hope for the future. Every time she felt herself sinking into darkness, she looked at the bear that she placed in the middle of her bed every day. He had a missing eye and discolored fur, but he felt like a friend to her. A coconspirator in her escape plan. She'd worked out that it should be enough to get her a ticket somewhere. Once she was there she'd find a job. Anything was better than being trapped here in the repetitive, exhausting cycle that was living with her mother.

"That's good. It's just that with Ron and I newly married, well — you know —" She nudged Audrey, woman to woman.

Audrey did know. The walls in their house were thin. She probably knew far too much for a person her age.

She noticed that her mother didn't ask where she was traveling, or with whom. All she cared about was that Audrey wouldn't be around to intrude on her romantic interlude.

It hurt even though it shouldn't, but Audrey was used to handling conflicting emotions. And to be honest she was relieved that her mother and Ron were getting married. Ron treated her mother well, and if the wedding went ahead, then Audrey would no longer feel responsible for her.

A whole new life was within reach.

"I'm spending the summer in Paris." The idea had come to her in a flash the week before. Paris was meant to be beautiful in the summer. The men were hot, the accent was sexy and if they talked crap, as most boys did in her experience, it wouldn't matter because she wouldn't understand them anyway. Best of all, she could get away from home.

The first thing she was going to do when she had her own place was put a lock on the door.

Her mother sank onto Audrey's bed, ignoring the piles of clothes that needed sorting. "Do you speak French?"

"No, which is why I want to live in France." In fact, it wasn't, but it was as plausible a reason as any and her mother wasn't a woman given to examining anything in greater depth. "I need a language."

"It will be good for you. You need to live a little! At your age —"

"Yeah, I know, you were having the time of your life."

"No need to use that tone. You're only

young once, Audie."

Most days she felt about a hundred. "I need to work now. I have a test tomorrow."

Her mother stood up and wrapped her arms around Audrey. "I love you. I'm proud of you. I probably don't tell you that enough."

Audrey sat so stiffly she wondered if a spine could snap. The fumes from her mother's perfume almost choked her.

Part of her wanted to sink into her mother's arms and let her take the worry for once, but she knew better than to lower her guard. Within minutes her mother could be screaming at her, throwing things and saying mean words.

Audrey had never understood why mean words sounded louder than kind ones.

"You're very tense." Her mother released her. "Would a drink help relax you?"

"No thanks." She knew her mother wouldn't be offering a cup of tea.

"I opened a bottle of wine. I could spare you a glass."

Wine explained the glittering eyes and the brittle mood. It also explained the perfume. "Have you eaten?"

"What? No." Linda smoothed the dress over her hips. "I don't want to get fat. What are you studying?"

Audrey blinked.

Her mother had never shown the slightest interest in what Audrey did with her life. At the open evening at school when they'd been invited in to discuss subject choices and university, Audrey had been the only student attending alone. As usual, she'd lied and said her mother was working. It sounded so much better than admitting that her mother couldn't be bothered and that the only time her father had been present in her life had been during her conception. She lied so much about her life that sometimes she forgot the truth herself.

She cleared her throat. "Organic chemistry." And she was going to fail. She'd picked sciences so that she could avoid essays and reading, but there was still a ton of reading and writing. After this she was never studying anything ever again.

"I think this fad for everything organic is nonsense." Her mother checked her reflection in the mirror on Audrey's desk. "It's just an excuse for the supermarkets to charge more."

Audrey sat with slumped shoulders, swamped in misery as she stared at her laptop screen. *Go away. Just go away!* She sometimes found it hard to believe she and her mother were related. Most days she felt as if she'd been dropped by a stork into the wrong house.

"Mum —"

"You've always been a slow learner, Audrey. You just have to accept that. But look on the bright side — you're pretty, and you have big —" her mother thrust her hands under her breasts to make her point "— get yourself a male boss and they'll never notice that you can't spell."

Audrey imagined the interview.

What do you consider to be your best qualities?

They're both attached to the front of my chest.

Not in her lifetime.

If a work colleague ever touched her boobs Audrey would break his arm.

"Mum —"

"I'm not saying that college isn't *fun,* but everyone gets a degree these days. It's nothing special. You pay a fortune for something that in the end means nothing. Life experience, that's what matters."

Audrey took a breath. "Wear the green dress."

She was exhausted. She wasn't sleeping. Her schoolwork was suffering.

Her friend Meena had helped her make a spreadsheet with all her exams on it. Then they'd set alerts on Audrey's phone, because she was terrified of misreading the spreadsheet and getting her timing wrong. They'd printed out an enlarged version and stuck it on her wall because every since the day her mother had drunk a bottle of whiskey and decided it would be a good idea to throw the computer in the trash, Audrey no longer dared risk storing things on her laptop.

You teenagers spend too long on screens.

On the calendar above her desk were crosses where Audrey marked the end of each day. Each cross took her closer to the day when she could leave school and home.

Her mother was still hovering. "You don't think Ron would prefer the pink? It shows a little hint of lingerie, and that's always good."

"It isn't good! It looks like you forgot to get dressed! It's called underwear for a reason. It's supposed to be worn *under* clothes." Bursting with exasperation, Audrey finally glanced away from the screen. Her mother's hair was wild from pulling dresses on and off. "Wear the dress *you* prefer. You can't live your life constantly trying to please another person." She couldn't for a moment imagine asking a man what she should wear. She wore what she liked. Her friends wore what they liked.

It was a roundabout of trying to fit in and trying to be different.

Linda's lip trembled. "I want him to think I'm pretty."

Audrey wanted Ron to think her mother was pretty, too. Audrey wanted Ron to take care of her mother, so she didn't have to.

"Green," she said. "Definitely green."

None of the men her mother had dated had stuck around as long as Ron.

Audrey liked Ron. His favorite response to everything was *As long as no one is dead, it will be fine.* Audrey wished she could believe it. "Stop drinking. Sober is sexy. Drunk isn't."

"What are you talking about? I've had a drink, yes, but I'm *not* drunk."

Audrey paused, her heart pounding. "You drink a lot, Mum. Too much." And her biggest dread was that Ron would grow tired of it. "Maybe you should talk to the doctor, or —"

"Why would I talk to a doctor?"

"Because you have a problem."

"You're the one with the problem, but I can't reason with you when you're in this mood." Her mother flounced out of the room, slamming the door.

Audrey stared at the door, feeling sick. This was why she rarely brought the subject up. How could her mother think she didn't have a problem? Someone in this house was crazy and Audrey was starting to think it must be her.

And now her mother was upset. What if she went off the deep end and she drank everything in the house? From time to time Audrey went through the place, room by room, hunting down hidden bottles. She hadn't done it in a while.

Stressed, she grabbed a chocolate bar from the stash she kept hidden behind her textbooks.

She tried to get back to work but she couldn't concentrate. Giving up, she left her room and stood listening.

She heard sounds of her mother crying noisily in the bathroom.

Crap. She knocked on the door. "Mum?"

The crying grew louder. Anxiety balled in Audrey's stomach. It felt as if she'd swallowed a stone. "Mum?"

She tried the handle and the door opened. Her mother was sitting on the floor leaning against the bath, a bottle of wine in her hand.

"I'm a bad mother. A terrible mother."

"Oh, Mum." Audrey's insides churned. She felt exasperated, anxious and a little desperate. Most of all she felt helpless and scared. She didn't know how to deal with this. Once, in a state of desperation, she'd called a help line for children of alcoholic parents but she'd lost her nerve and hung up without speaking to anyone. She didn't want to talk about it. She *couldn't* talk about it. It would be disloyal. Despite everything, she loved her mum.

She wasn't alone, but she felt alone.

Her mother looked at her, mascara smudged under her eyes. "I do love you, Audrey. Do you love me?"

"Of course." Despite her dry mouth, she managed to say the words. It was a routine that happened often. Her mother drank, told Audrey she loved her, sobered up and forgot all about it.

Audrey had given up hoping that one day her mother might say those words when she was sober.

"Give me the bottle, Mum." She eased it out of her mother's hand.

"What are you doing with that?"

Audrey poured it down the sink before she could change her mind, bracing her shoulders against her mother's distressed wail.

"I can't believe you did that! I was having one drink, that's all, to give me confidence for tonight. What did I do to deserve a daughter like you?" She started sobbing again, apparently forgetting that a moment before she'd loved Audrey. "You don't understand. I don't want to lose Ron. I'm no good on my own."

"Of course you are." Audrey put the empty bottle down on the floor. "You have a good job." Which she was afraid her mother might lose if she didn't sober up.

What would happen then? Did Ron know her mother was an alcoholic? Would he walk out once he found out?

She clung to the idea that he wouldn't. Hope, she'd discovered, was the light that guided you through dark places. You had to believe there was something better ahead.

Audrey grabbed a packet of wipes and gently erased the streaked mascara. "You have pretty eyes."

Her mother gave a tremulous smile, her earlier nastiness no longer in evidence. "You think so?"

The vulnerability made Audrey queasy. Most of the time she was the adult, and the responsibility terrified her. She didn't feel qualified for the role. "Definitely. People wear contact lenses to get this shade of green."

Linda touched Audrey's hair. "I hated having red hair when I was your age. I was

69

teased all the time. I wanted to be blonde. You don't get teased?"

"Sometimes." Audrey reapplied her mother's makeup, her approach subtler than Linda's.

"How do you handle it?"

"I can take care of myself." Audrey styled her mother's hair and stood back and admired her handiwork. "There. You look good."

"You're so much stronger than I was."

"You're strong, too. You've just forgotten it." *And if you stopped drinking it would help.*

She didn't say it again. Her mother was calm now, and Audrey didn't want to do or say anything that might change that. They lived on a knife edge. One slip, and they'd all be cut.

Her mother studied herself in the mirror, touching her cheekbones with the tips of her fingers. "You'd better get back to studying. Thanks for your help."

It was as if the emotional explosion had never happened.

Audrey returned to her bedroom and closed the door.

She wanted to cry, but she knew that if she cried she'd get a headache and then she'd fail her test. If she failed her test, she might fail her exams and she hadn't come this far to fall at the last fence. A few more months and she'd never have to study again.

Half an hour later a deep rumble of laughter announced that Ron had returned home.

Audrey covered her ears with her head-phones, turned up the volume on pounding rock music and drowned out whatever was going on in the room above her.

Only when she glanced out of the window and saw her mother and Ron heading out of the house together, hand in hand, did she finally relax.

Don't blow it, Mum.

When she was sure the coast was clear and that her mother wasn't about to return for a bag, a coat or any other number of things, she ventured downstairs.

She could hear a dog barking in the street outside, and one of her neighbors shouting at another. She didn't know them. It wasn't that kind of street. In this particular London suburb, people came and went and never spoke to their neighbors. You could die, and no one would know. It was one of the cheaper areas of the city, which basically meant you paid twice what you would anywhere else in the country and got half as much for your money.

Rain was sheeting down, obscuring the

71

view from the window.

Hardy, their rescue dog, was curled up in the warmth of the kitchen but when he saw Audrey he greeted her like a long-lost friend.

Audrey dropped to her knees and hugged him. "You are the only thing about this place I'm going to miss. You're my best friend, and I wish I could take you with me when I go." She giggled as he licked her face. "I hope she gets out of bed long enough to feed you when I'm gone. If not, scratch at the door. Or bite Ron on the ankles." She stood up. "Food?"

Hardy wagged his tail.

She put food into his bowl, freshened his water and was wondering what to eat herself when her phone buzzed. It was Meena, asking if she could come over so they could study together.

Audrey and Meena had both moved to the school two years earlier, at an age when everyone else was already in groups and cliques.

Their friendship was one of the best things about the place for Audrey.

Given that she was likely to have the house to herself for hours, Audrey messaged back a yes. She would never, ever have contemplated having a friend around when her

72

mother was home, but she occasionally invited Meena, provided the house was empty. Her parents were both doctors and Meena had the kind of stable home life Audrey could only dream of. She had uncles, aunts and cousins and Audrey wanted to implant herself in her family.

She checked the fridge.

It was empty apart from two bottles of wine.

She'd asked her mother to buy milk and cheese, but instead she'd eaten the few things Audrey had stocked up on the day before.

Tired, Audrey grabbed the open bottle of wine and tipped it down the sink. It was like trying to bail out a sinking ship with an eggcup, but still she couldn't help trying to fix the situation.

There was no time for her to shop, so she headed for the freezer. Fortunately the frozen pizzas she'd bought the day before were still there. She threw them in the oven and retrieved a packet of chocolate biscuits she'd hidden for emergencies.

The moment she answered the door to her friend, she knew something was wrong.

"What?"

"Nothing." Meena pushed past her into the house. "Close the door fast."

"Why?" Audrey peered out into the street and saw two girls leaning against a wall. She recognized them immediately. They were in her year at school. "What do those hyenas want?"

"My carcass. For dinner. Close the door, Aud!"

"They followed you again?" Audrey felt something hot and uncontrollable burn inside her. "What did they say?"

"The usual." Despite the cold, Meena's face was sweaty. Her eyes looked huge behind her glasses. "It doesn't matter. It's just words. *Please* don't say anything."

"It matters." Audrey was out of the door and across the street before Meena could stop her, carrying all the extra emotion leftover from her encounter with her mother. "What is your problem?" She directed her question at the taller of the two girls because she knew she was the ring-leader. Her name was Rhonda and she and Audrey clashed regularly.

Rhonda folded her arms. "I'm not the one with the problem. But you should stop hanging out with that dumb bitch. You need to rethink your friends."

"Yeah." The smaller girl standing by her side sounded like an echo. "You need to rethink your friends."

Audrey glared at her. She couldn't even summon up the girl's name. She was a mouse who hid in Rhonda's shadow. "When you have an original opinion you can voice it, but until then shut up." She shifted her gaze back to Rhonda. "I don't need to rethink anything. And seeing as Meena gets top grades in everything, the only dumb bitch I see is standing right in front of me."

Rhonda lifted her jaw. "She should go back to wherever it is she came from."

"She comes from here, you brainless baboon. She was born half a mile down the road from you but you're too stupid to even know that, and who the hell cares anyway?"

"Why are you defending her? This isn't your business, Audrey."

"My friends aren't my business? Is that a joke?" Audrey felt the last threads of control unravel. She took a step forward and had the satisfaction of seeing the other girl take a step back.

"You shouldn't be here."

"It's you who shouldn't be here. This is my street. My wall. I don't need a bunch of mean girls leaning against it." Audrey stabbed Rhonda in the chest with her finger. "Get out of here, and if you come near Meena again I swear I'll hurt you."

"You and whose army?"

"I don't need an army. I'm my own army. Now fuck off back to wherever *you* came from, which is probably the sewer." With a threatening scowl that she'd spent hours perfecting in front of the mirror, she stalked away from them. They called something after her and she lifted her finger and kept walking.

She found Meena shaking like a baby fawn, her phone in her hand.

"I thought they were going to kill you."

"You have so little faith in me." Audrey glanced at the phone. "Why are you calling emergency services?"

"I thought you needed backup."

"We're not in an action film, Meena. Put the phone away. And stop shaking. You look like a kitten someone dropped in a puddle."

Meena rubbed her arms. "I wish I could be like you. You're funny and everyone likes you."

"Yeah? Well, I wish I was like you. You have a brain and a place at Oxford."

"I'd rather be popular and fit in. Pathetic, I know. Those girls say I just got the place to fill their diversity quota."

"Yeah, well, those girls are mean as snakes and dumb as shit. They've got to say something to make themselves feel better because their lives are crap. But *you* —" Audrey grabbed Meena and swung her around. "You're going to rule the world. And because you have me to do your hair, you're going to look good while you do it. Be proud! You're, like, *insanely* smart. I can't even spell engineering, let alone study it. I boast about you to everyone. *My friend Meena is going to Oxford.*"

"You don't hate me for it?"

"*What?* Don't be crazy. I'm proud of you. Why would I hate you?"

Meena looked sweetly anxious. "Because studying is so hard for you."

"Life is hard for you, too. I don't have to put up with the crap that's thrown in your direction on a daily basis." Audrey shrugged, trying not to think of her own life. "Everyone has something to deal with, right? I've got your back and you've got my back."

"No one will have my back at Oxford." Meena wiped the rain from her glasses. "I wish you were going, too."

"No, you don't. You'll be hanging out with smart people, saying smart things and doing smart things. Now stop letting them get to you. Be mad, not scared. And if you can't actually *be* mad, then act mad. You need to be meaner than they are. You need to be meaner-Meena." She collapsed, laughing, and Meena giggled, too.

"Meaner-Meena. I like that."

"Good. Because right now you're far-too-nice-Meena. Let's eat."

Meena followed her into the kitchen and sniffed. "Is that pizza?"

"Mushroom and olive."

"Bliss. Well, apart from the olives, but I can pick those off." Meena dumped her bags on the kitchen floor and stripped off her coat. Her long black hair was damp. She wore jeans and a black sweater that belonged to her sister. Audrey would have loved to have a sister to share clothes with, but mostly she would have loved to share the load of her mother.

She watched as Meena sent a text.

"Who are you texting?"

Meena flushed. "My mum. She made me promise to let her know I arrived safely."

"You live, like, two streets away."

"I know. It's embarrassing, but it's either that or she drives me here and that's more embarrassing."

Audrey felt a stab of envy. "It's great that she cares so much. You have the best family."

"Aud —"

"What?"

"I smell burning."

"Shit." Audrey sprinted across the kitchen

and opened the oven. "It's fine. A little burned maybe, but not totally charred. Can you grab plates?"

Meena opened a cupboard. "Are you nervous about leaving home and living alone?"

"No." Audrey dumped the pizza on a board. She virtually lived alone now. No one cared what she did. She didn't have a curfew or rules. She'd reached the point where she'd decided that genuinely living alone would be an improvement. "Are you?"

"A bit, but it will be nice to have some independence. Mum is determined to make sure I eat healthily while I'm revising so every hour she brings me a healthy snack."

The mere thought of someone thinking to bring her a snack, let alone a healthy one, almost made Audrey bleed with envy.

"And she's on my case the whole time." Meena unloaded her books and piled them on the table next to the plates. "We should get started. My uncle is coming at nine thirty to pick me up."

"I could walk home with you if you like."

"Then you'd have to walk back alone."

"So?" She walked everywhere alone. "What do you want to drink?"

"Anything." Meena walked to the fridge and opened it before Audrey could stop her.

"What happened here? Why is your fridge empty?"

"My mother was defrosting it. It was so full, it needed clearing out." The lie came easily, as lies always did to Audrey.

Yes, Miss Foster, everything is fine at home. My mother couldn't make parents' evening because she's working.

She could control the story she told. Less easy to control was the shame. It clung to her like sweat and she turned away, terrified it might be visible. "This pizza is getting cold. We should eat."

"You're lucky. Your mum gives you so much freedom."

Audrey switched on her habitual smile. "Yeah, it's great."

Why didn't she just tell Meena and her other friends the truth? It was partly because having started this story it was hard to untangle it, but mostly because it was embarrassing to admit that your own mother thought a bottle of wine was more important than you were. What did that say about her? At the very least, that she was unlovable.

"Have you decided what you're going to do this summer?"

"I'm going to Paris." Audrey snapped the top off a can of soda. They had no food in the house, but they always had mixers. "I'm going to find a job and somewhere to live."

"That's going to make Hayley sick with envy. You need to post photos that are cooler than hers. Have you seen her Instagram? *Spending a month by the pool in Saint-Tropez this summer. #lovemylife.*" Meena crunched her way through the overcooked pizza and licked her fingers.

"Yeah. I've got my own hashtags. *#yousmugbitch* or maybe *#hopethepoolturnsyourhairgreen* or *#hateyourguts.* Trouble is, I can't spell any of them."

"I'll spell them for you if you promise you'll post at least one smug photo of you in Paris. How are you going to communicate? You don't speak French."

Audrey nibbled her pizza. "I can say I'm hungry, and I know the words for *hot guy.* The rest is going to have to be body language. That's universal."

"Do you think you'll have sex?" Meena pulled at another slice of pizza, catching the cheese that trailed in strands. "You've done it, right?"

Audrey shrugged, not wanting to admit what a total letdown sex had been. She had no idea why so many books were written about love and passion. There was obviously something wrong with her. "It's like going

81

to the gym. You can get physical without having to engage the brain. Not that I exactly have a brain to engage."

"Stop it! You know that's not true. So you're saying sex is like being on the treadmill? What happened to romance? What about Romeo and Juliet?"

"They died. Not romantic." Audrey nibbled her pizza. "Also, that Juliet had no street smarts whatsoever."

"She was only thirteen."

"Well, I can tell you that even if she hadn't drunk that poison, she never would have made it to old age."

Meena giggled. "You should write that in your exam. So do you want to revise?"

"You don't mind? It's not like you exactly need to."

"I do need to. And I love being here with you. You always make me laugh. What do you want to start with? Physics? I know that's really hard for you because of all the symbols. It's hard for me, too, and I don't have dyslexia. Whenever I open my book I'm just one atom away from a brain explosion."

Audrey knew that wasn't true, but she was touched by her friend's attempts to make her feel better. "I think I'm getting there, but ask me some questions and we'll find out. Shall we have some music?" She finished her pizza and reached for her phone. "I revise better to music."

"I love coming to your house. Everything is so relaxed here. Where's your mum tonight?"

"Out."

"With Ron?" Meena watched as Audrey chose a track and pressed Play. "Now *that's* romantic. All those years widowed, missing your dad, and now she's in love again. It's like a movie."

"Widowed" sounded so much better than "divorced three times."

Losing a husband in tragic circumstances attracted sympathy and understanding. Being divorced three times attracted suspicion and incredulity.

Audrey figured that with the way her life was, she was allowed a little poetic license. And since she and her mother had moved to this part of London only two years before, no one was likely to find out the truth.

"I love this song. Revision can wait." She slid off her chair. "Let's dance. Come on, meaner-Meena, show me what you're made of."

She turned up the volume and danced around the kitchen. She swayed and bumped to the music, her hair flying around her face. Meena joined her, and soon they were whooping and laughing.

For ten glorious minutes Audrey was a teenager without a care in the world. It didn't matter that she was going to fail her exams and that the rest of her life would be ruined. It didn't matter that her mum preferred to drink than spend time with her daughter. All that mattered was the pump and flow of the music.

If only the rest of her life could be like this.

GRACE

"Do you want me to come in with you?" Monica pulled up outside the hospital. "You're shivering."

Was she? Grace felt removed from everything, even the reactions of her own body. It was hard to believe that three days had passed since that night in the restaurant. "I need to do this on my own, but thanks. You're a great friend." She stared down at her feet and realized she was wearing odd shoes. One navy. One black. Visible evidence that she was falling apart. "Losing it" as Sophie would say.

"I still can't believe it. I mean, *David.* You two are the perfect couple. And he's such a family man. He takes Sophie swimming every Saturday and does backyard barbecues."

"This isn't helping, Monica." Should she go home and change her shoes? They offended her sense of order.

"I'm just so angry. I could strangle David with my bare hands." Monica thumped the steering wheel with her fist. "How could he *do* this to you?"

How? Why? When? Her brain was stuck in a loop.

What had she done? What hadn't she done?

She'd thought she was the love of David's life. The one.

Finding out that she wasn't overturned her entire memory bank. What was real and what wasn't?

"Apparently, he's bored with his life." Her mouth felt dry. "And since I was a large part of his life, I guess that means —"

"Do *not* tell me you're boring," Monica spoke through her teeth, "because we both know that's not the case."

"He said I organize every part of our lives and it's true. I like predictability and order. I've always seen that as a good thing."

"It is a good thing! Who wants a life full of chaos? Don't do this to yourself, Grace. Don't make it about you. The truth is you're so competent, you've bruised his ego."

"I don't think so. David is very secure and sure of himself. I think I've made him feel — redundant. But it's not a manhood thing. He isn't like that."

"Don't you believe it. He's having a full-blown midlife crisis. His little girl is leaving home, and suddenly he feels old. He's faced his own mortality — literally, in the last few days — it's classic."

Grace stared out of the window, remembering David's face that night at dinner. "He hasn't bought a sports car or dyed his hair. He hasn't given up his job. The only thing he seems to have changed is the woman in his life."

Images played through her head, as if she'd accidentally clicked on a porn site on the internet. She wanted to cover her eyes. Reboot her brain. Cold, she tugged her coat around her.

Monica turned the heat up. "You have no idea who it is?"

"No." Grace looked at her friend. "How could I not have known this was going on?"

"Because David is the last man on the planet you'd suspect of having an affair, so you weren't looking. You need to ask him right out who it is."

"The hospital staff say he mustn't have any stress." And she knew, deep down, she was postponing the moment when she'd have to hear the details. A name would make it real.

Monica snorted. "*He* mustn't have stress?

87

How about you? He's a man who chose to tell his wife he wanted a divorce during a dinner to celebrate their twenty-fifth wedding anniversary. Any other woman probably wouldn't have resuscitated him when he collapsed."

"It crossed my mind not to." Perhaps she shouldn't have admitted that. "What does that say about me?"

Monica reached out and took her hand. "It says you're human, and thank goodness for that."

"I stood there and couldn't move — I don't know how long it was —" Her heart had been beating frantically while his had been failing. "I thought I couldn't do it."

"But you did," Monica said gently.

"What if I walk into his room and she's there?"

Monica swallowed. "Surely David wouldn't be that tactless?"

"He's in love with another woman. I think tact has gone out of the window." She twisted the edge of her coat with her fingers. "At dinner he kept rubbing his jaw. I thought he needed to see a dentist, but it turns out that can be a sign of a heart attack. I missed it."

"Please tell me you're not blaming yourself for that!"

"David was so stressed about hurting me, it brought on a heart attack. Even breaking up with me, he was inherently decent."

"Grace, *please*. He was a heartless rat bast—" Monica broke off and lifted her hands in apology. "Sorry, but I can't bear to hear you make excuses for him. How is Sophie taking it?"

Acid gnawed at her gut. Maybe she should see a doctor. "I haven't told her yet."

"What? Grace, she —"

"She needs to know. I'm aware. But telling her that her father had a heart attack and was in the hospital seemed like enough at the time. She's upset and worried sick. I couldn't bring myself to make it worse. She idolizes him. They've always been close."

"You have to tell her, Grace."

"I was hoping it might all get fixed and I wouldn't have to."

"He's had an affair with another woman. Would you fix it if you could?"

"I don't know." It was a question she'd never thought she'd have to ask herself.

"You can't, Grace. You'd never be able to trust him again. You need to boot him out. That's what I'd do if Todd ever had an affair."

Grace's head spun. This was an aspect she hadn't considered — that everyone around her would have an opinion. Whatever she did, she'd be the focus of gossip and judgment and she knew from experience that people tended to think that their way was the only way.

"I need to go."

"Tell him how much he has hurt you. Tell him how you're feeling."

She didn't want to be told what to do.

The fact that she felt the need to get away from Monica made her feel lonelier than she ever had in her life before. "If I cause him stress and then he dies, it's my fault."

Guilt. Blame. Responsibility.

An ugly sludge of emotions churned inside her, the same ones she'd felt when her parents had died. She knew you didn't have to be directly involved to feel responsible. She'd had to live with those feelings, and David was the only one who knew.

David, who was no longer there for her.

David, who would now share secrets with someone else.

Losing that particular intimacy was the most painful thing of all.

A steady stream of people flowed through the revolving door at the entrance to the hospital, and Grace watched, wondering what their stories were. Were they visitors? Patients?

After he collapsed in the restaurant, David had been taken to the nearest hospital and rushed straight to surgery to have a procedure on his coronary artery. Or was it arteries? She couldn't remember. Grace had sat on a cold, hard chair in a drafty corridor, feeling as if someone had lifted her out of her comfortable life and dropped her in a prison cell.

At some point during the night the doctor had found her, but his words had flowed past Grace like a river rushing over rocks. She'd heard *blockage* and a few other technical words that had meant nothing to her. She'd tried to pay attention, but her mind had refused to focus for more than a few minutes before wandering back to the fact that David wanted a divorce.

"David should tell Sophie," Monica said. "He's the one having the affair."

Grace forced herself to move. "I'll deal with that part later. He could be discharged tomorrow."

"So soon? Please tell me you're not thinking of taking him home."

Grace paused with her hand on the door. "I don't know. I'm taking this minute by minute."

"Do you think he'll want to stay —"

"— with her? I don't know that, either.

91

But if he wants to come home, I don't see that I have much choice."

"Of course you have a choice!" Monica exploded with rage and then subsided. "What can I do? I feel helpless."

"You are helping." In fact, she wasn't helping, but that wasn't Monica's fault. There was nothing anyone could do. "Thanks for the ride."

Grace slid out of the car and walked slowly into the hospital. It was the loneliest walk of her life.

Monica was right. They needed to tell Sophie. They couldn't put it off any longer.

"Hi, Mrs. Porter." The nurse in charge of the cardiac care ward greeted her from the desk. Grace had virtually lived at the hospital for the past few days. It was hardly surprising that they all knew her.

"Hi, Sally. How is he today?"

"Doing better. Dr. Morton saw him this morning, and she promised to drop by and talk to you both once you arrived. I'll let her know you're here." She reached for the phone, and Grace walked into David's room.

His eyes were closed, his skin pale but even a heart attack didn't stop him being handsome.

She remembered what he'd said about

feeling as if the best days of his life were behind him. The memory was like a sharp stab. What he'd really been saying was that there was nothing left to look forward to. The life with her wasn't enough for him.

Forcing herself forward, she walked to the chair next to his bed.

David opened his eyes. "Grace."

She put her bag on the floor. "How are you feeling?"

"Terrible. I guess you're thinking it's just punishment. They put in a stent, did they tell you?"

Had they? Maybe. She hoped he didn't ask her any other questions, but fortunately at that moment Dr. Morton walked in. Elizabeth Morton had a daughter in Grace's class, so they knew each other from school events.

"Hi, Grace. How are you?"

"I'm good, thanks." As well as can be expected for a woman who has just been dumped by her husband of twenty-five years. Did Dr. Morton know? How far had word spread? Grace tried to remember who had been in the restaurant that night.

"I'm the patient." David made a feeble attempt at a joke. "You're supposed to be asking me how I am."

Was it her imagination, or did Dr. Morton's smile cool slightly as she looked at him?

Oh God, Grace thought. *She knows.*

The thought of female solidarity should have cheered her, but it didn't. She hated the thought of people gossiping about her. It was so personal. Humiliating.

Everyone would be wondering why David Porter had chosen to leave his wife. They'd be looking at her and speculating. *Did she nag? Was she bad in bed?*

Maybe they all thought she was boring, too.

She could feel droplets of confidence evaporating like water in sunlight.

"You can go home tomorrow." Dr. Morton flipped through the notes. She was clinical. Efficient. "We'll send you a date for a follow-up." She gave some general advice and then added, "This is a question I find some patients are embarrassed to ask, so I always give the answer anyway. Sex." Her face was expressionless, but Grace knew she'd never be able to meet her at the school gates without remembering this conversation.

She didn't want Dr. Morton to talk about sex, but it seemed her wishes no longer counted for anything.

Grace gripped the edge of the chair until

the plastic dug into her hands.

"You should take it easy for the next month." Dr. Morton went on to elaborate, and Grace tried to shut it out.

She emerged from her trance to hear Dr. Morton saying, "After that, you're good to go."

Grace felt her anger rise. He was good to go, but what about her?

David squirmed. "Thank you."

"Don't look so gloomy. People recover well from this and go on to live good lives." The doctor outlined plans for his discharge, and then left the room with a final nod toward Grace.

"No sex for a month," Grace said. "I guess that's going to be tough on whoever it is you're sleeping with."

She saw the shock in David's eyes and then the spreading color in his cheeks.

"You're angry. I understand."

"You *understand*? You can't do this and still get to be the nice guy, David. This wasn't an accident, or some random thing that happened to us that you regret. You *chose* this path. You knew what this would do to us. To me. But you did it anyway."

Because he'd wanted it.

It wasn't the first time someone hadn't loved her enough to fight temptation.

Feelings she'd worked hard to subdue swirled to life inside her.

"I didn't plan it, Grace. I was unhappy, and she was there and — Well, it just happened."

It was the worst thing he could have said to her.

"What happened to self-control, David?"

He shifted in the bed. "You don't have to tell me how important self-control is to you. I already know."

"But I didn't know how unimportant it was to you."

"Grace —"

"You didn't tell me you were unhappy. You didn't give us a chance." The more she thought about it, the more she realized she wasn't just angry, she was furious. It was almost a relief. Anger was fuel, and easier to handle than grief and confusion.

"Everything you say is true, and I feel terrible."

"I feel terrible, too. The difference is that you deserve to feel terrible, and I don't." She stopped. He looked so pale she was afraid he might be having another heart attack.

How could she care so much about his welfare, when he'd given no thought to hers?

It seemed that love defied logic.

"Grace —"

"Do you know what it's like to be in love with someone, and to assume they feel the same way, and then to discover that it was all fake? It makes you question everything." She heard the catch in her own voice. "All those memories we made together, I'm wondering how many of them were real."

"They were real. They *are* real."

"What's real is that at some point you started feeling differently and you didn't share that with me. I made a chicken salad with low calorie dressing." She unloaded the bag and slapped the containers on the table next to the bed.

"You've had a few messages. Rick from the golf club called. He sent you his best wishes."

"Right."

He hadn't even mentioned the fact that she'd resuscitated him. Not that she wanted thanks exactly, but a small amount of praise for keeping a cool head in an emergency and saving his life might have been nice.

Thanks, Grace. It was kind of you to bring me back to life after I said you were boring. Glad you didn't exercise the option to leave me to die.

He watched her cautiously. "Did Stephen call?"

97

"Yes. He sends his best wishes and told you not to rush back to work. Lissa said she'd call around with a few things from your office. You left your bag there, and your laptop."

"That's kind of her."

"Yes." Grace was fond of Lissa. She'd been a few years ahead of Sophie in school and Grace had taught her French and Spanish. Lissa had struggled academically after her father walked out, and Grace had been delighted when she'd graduated high school and David had given her a job at the newspaper as a junior reporter. It was good to see her doing well.

She wondered if Stephen and Lissa knew about the affair.

"We need to talk to Sophie."

There was alarm and panic on his face. "I'm dreading that part. Do you think it would be better coming from you?"

"You said you were tired of me doing everything, so no, this is one thing you can do yourself. And you're the one who has given up on our marriage, so you're in a better position than I am to explain it to our daughter. Do it tonight, when she comes to visit. She needs to know we love her and that your decision has nothing to do with her."

"Tonight?" He lost more color. "I'm not feeling great, Grace."

"I don't care. I don't want her finding out from someone else."

"No one else knows."

"You're a journalist, David. You of all people should know how hard it is to hide information."

He gave her a long, meaningful look and in the end she was the one to look away.

Damn him.

Grace curled and uncurled her fingers. Damn him for choosing this moment to remind her of the information he'd kept hidden. To remind her what she owed him.

"No one knows," he said. "We've been careful."

"Careful?" She imagined him creeping around. "Were you sneaking into motel rooms and paying cash? Did you use condoms?"

His cheeks turned dark red. "That's a personal question."

"I'm your *wife*!"

"Yes, I used condoms. I'm not stupid."

Maybe not stupid, but thoughtless and careless with her feelings and their marriage? Definitely. She wanted to take a shower and scrub herself all over.

"Did you at any point think about me?"

He looked exhausted. "I thought about you all the time, Grace."

"Even while you were having sex with another woman? That's not a compliment." She took a deep breath. "What's her name?"

He closed his eyes briefly. "Grace —"

"Tell me! You owe me that much."

He looked away. Licked his lips. "It's Lissa."

"Lissa?" She stared at him and then felt a rush of relief. She didn't know a Lissa. It wasn't someone she knew personally or was going to bump into. "Where does she live?"

David turned his head, and his eyes were tired and sad. "You know where Lissa lives."

"I don't. The only Lissa I know is —" She stopped. "Wait. You don't mean — *Lissa*? *Our* Lissa?"

"Who else?"

"Oh God." Grace's legs suddenly refused to do their job and she sank onto the chair. "She's like a daughter to us. To me," she corrected herself. "Obviously to you she's something different."

Grace remembered the day Lissa had graduated from high school. After all the support Grace had given her, it felt like a double betrayal.

"She's a child!"

"She's twenty-three. Not a child."

She couldn't absorb it. She hadn't thought things could get worse, but this was so much worse.

Sick, she stood up and almost stumbled over the chair. She had to get away. "You need to find somewhere to go when you're discharged. I don't want you home."

"Where am I going to go?"

"I don't know. Where were you thinking that you'd go? Or were you planning on putting Lissa in our spare bedroom? One big happy family, is that it?"

He looked ill. "I'll find a hotel."

"Why? She doesn't want you in sickness? Only in health?" Grace snatched up her bag. "I'll drop Sophie here later. You can tell her the good news."

"It would be better to do this together. We need to keep this civilized."

"I don't feel civilized, David. And as for telling Sophie — you're sleeping with someone she considers a friend. You're on your own with that one."

She walked out of the room, managed to smile at the nurses at the desk and then dipped into the stairwell. Everyone else seemed to have taken the elevator and the echo of her footsteps somehow emphasized her loneliness. She made it as far as the first floor before control left her. She sank onto

101

the bottom stair, sobbing.

Lissa? *Lissa?*

Grace thought about Lissa's beaming smile and the way her ponytail swung when she walked. She wore jeans that looked as if they'd been painted on her, and tops that showed off her lush, full breasts.

It was so *sordid.* What would Lissa's parents say? Grace was on a charity committee with her mother. She'd never be able to look her in the eye again.

How could David do this to her? To them? They were a unit. A family. And he'd torn that apart.

She was so lost in a world of misery and memories it was a moment before she heard the sound of footsteps and realized someone was coming down the stairs toward her.

She stood up quickly, brushed her hand over her face and walked down the last flight of stairs.

Sophie would be home from school soon. Grace needed to be there to make her something to eat, and to support her when her father blew up her life.

AUDREY

"How did your exams go, Audrey, dear?"

Audrey adjusted the temperature of the water and directed the spray so that it ran over the hair and not near the eyes. If there was such a thing as an exam in hair washing, she'd ace it.

"They weren't great, Mrs. Bishop." She'd started working in the salon for a few hours on a Saturday when she was thirteen. She'd done it to give herself an excuse to leave the house and had been surprised by how much she enjoyed it. The best part was chatting with customers, and they were startlingly honest with her. After five years, many of them felt like family. "The thing I hate most is when you come out of the exam and the other kids are all talking about what they wrote for each question and you know you totally messed it up. Is that temperature right for you?"

"It's perfect, dear. And I'm sure you didn't

103

mess it up."

Audrey was sure she had. She knew for sure she'd gotten at least two of the questions muddled up on that last paper. She'd got confused between *discuss* and *define.*

Whichever way you looked at it, exams sucked but at least they were done now.

She pumped shampoo into her palm and started lathering Mrs. Bishop's hair. The woman's hair was thin on top, so Audrey was very gentle. "I'm not going to do a second shampoo, Mrs. Bishop, because your hair is a bit dry. I'm going to use a moisturizing treatment if that's okay."

"Whatever you think, pet. You're the expert."

"How is Pogo?" Audrey struggled with facts when they were in a textbook, but she had no trouble remembering the smallest detail of people's lives. She knew all about their pets, their kids and their illnesses. Pogo was Mrs. Bishop's Labrador, and the love of her life. "What did the vet say about the lump?"

"It was nothing serious, thank goodness. A cyst. He removed it."

"That's good. You must be relieved." Audrey rinsed carefully.

"What will you do now your exams are over? Will you work here full-time this summer? We're all hoping you do."

It was tempting. Audrey loved the people and she enjoyed the work. For some of the women who came to the salon, their ten minutes at the basin with Audrey was the only time they relaxed during the week. Her high point had been when customers started asking for her because her scalp massage was so good.

No one had ever said Audrey was good at anything before.

But staying at the salon would mean living at home, and Audrey couldn't wait to leave.

"I'm going traveling."

She sprayed the treatment onto Mrs. Bishop's hair and massaged gently.

"Oh, that's bliss, dear. You always use just the right amount of pressure. You should do a massage course."

Audrey used her fingertips on Mrs. Bishop's forehead. "The clients would probably all be dirty old men."

Mrs. Bishop tutted. "I don't mean that kind of massage. I mean real massage. For stressed people. There are plenty of those around."

"Yeah, I should probably start with myself."

"You'd be fantastic. You could do makeup,

too." Philippa Wyatt, who came in every six weeks to have her color done, joined in the conversation from her chair in front of the mirror. Her hair had been segmented and was currently wrapped in tinfoil. She looked like a chicken about to be roasted.

"How are the preparations going for the wedding, Mrs. Wyatt?"

"My daughter changes her mind every five minutes. One minute the cake is going to be fruit, and the next it's sponge."

"I love sponge." Audrey finished the head massage and rinsed off the product. She wrapped Alice Bishop's head in a warm towel, changed her gown and guided her back to the basin.

"Thank you, dear." The woman pressed a note into Audrey's hand.

"That's too much! You don't have to —"

"I want to. It's my way of saying thank you." She sat down in the chair, and Audrey pushed the note into her pocket and stuck her head around the staff room door.

"Ellen? Mrs. Bishop is ready for you."

Ellen owned the hair salon. There was a lot Audrey liked about her, not least the fact that she didn't make Audrey split her tips. *You earned it, you keep it,* she always said.

"Right." Ellen was finishing a cup of coffee. "Want to grab lunch together later?

Milly can cover for us."

"I thought I'd go for a quick walk. I need to clear my head after all those exams."

It was a half-truth. The other half of the truth was that the fridge had been empty again and Audrey hadn't realized until it was too late. Her mother, in a drunken state, had thrown everything away claiming it was "off."

It wouldn't hurt not to eat for a day, but she didn't want to draw attention to it.

An hour later she grabbed her bag and took a walk to the local park.

It was teeming with people enjoying the sunshine. Some sat on benches, others sprawled on the grass, shirtsleeves rolled back.

Several were eating lunch. Huge slabs of crusty bread, fresh ham, packets of crisps, chocolate bars.

Audrey's stomach growled.

Had anyone ever been mugged for a sandwich? There was a first time for everything. She could grab it and run. A whole new definition for fast food.

Maybe she should use the tip Mrs. Bishop had given her to buy food, but she was saving everything she earned to put toward her escape fund.

Trying to ignore the food around her, she

pulled out her phone and carried on her search for summer jobs in Paris.

That morning she'd narrowed it down to two.

A family who lived in Montmartre wanted an English-speaking au pair with childcare experience. Audrey had never looked after children, but she'd looked after her mother and she figured that more than qualified her for the job although she still had to work out how to convince a potential employer of that without revealing more than she wanted to.

She lifted her head and stared across the park. There was a faint hum in the distance and she could see someone cutting the grass. It was June and the air was sweet with the scent of flowers.

In the distance she could see the running track. Audrey used it sometimes. She liked running. Maybe it was because it felt as if she was getting away from her life.

She imagined herself wandering around Paris in the summer sunshine with two adorable children in tow. Or they might be two annoying children. Either way, the life she could see ahead of her was so much more appealing than the one she was living now.

No more wondering what state the house

would be in when she arrived home.

No more worrying about her mother. That would be Ron's job.

Audrey felt dizzy at the thought of handing over responsibility and being liberated from it all.

The man on the grass closest to her put his half-eaten cheese sandwich down.

Not reaching out to grab it required more willpower than Audrey knew she had.

She slipped her feet out of her shoes and turned back to her phone.

A dental surgery needed someone to answer the phones and book appointments. True, Audrey didn't speak French but there would be advantages to not understanding the inner workings of dentistry.

She was about to close the app when a photograph caught her eye.

She lifted the phone closer and peered at the text.

A bookshop on the Left Bank was looking for someone to help out part-time during the summer.

Audrey let out a snort of laughter. Working in a bookshop? If a worse job existed, she couldn't think of it. She hated books. She hated reading.

She was about to scroll past the job when something caught her eye.

Did that say accommodation included? Yes, it did.

Audrey stared at her phone. That side of things had been worrying her. How was she going to find somewhere to live when she didn't speak French, didn't know Paris and had limited funds?

Her pulse raced forward, taking her imagination with it.

A job with accommodation would solve all her problems. Still, a bookshop? She saw now that it was a used bookshop. Did that mean it was full of books people had given away? That was a concept she could get behind.

What sort of person would they be looking for?

Someone brainy and serious. Audrey was neither of those things, but she could fake it if necessary. She was used to presenting a fake self to the world. She'd tie her hair back. Maybe buy a pair of glasses to make herself look more intelligent. Try not to talk too much or crack jokes. That way she'd be less likely to reveal her real self.

"Hey! Audie!" Meena appeared in front of her. "I was wondering if you'd be here."

Meena worked at the supermarket in the high street and sometimes they managed to coincide their lunch break.

"You're late."

"I was being verbally abused by a customer who couldn't find his favorite brand of canned tomatoes."

Audrey didn't see how a can of tomatoes could be the cause of friction, but she did know people got all revved up about different things. "Tomato rage."

"Don't even joke about it. I was afraid he was going to throw it at me, and it was a multipack. That would have been the end of me." Meena sat down next to her and opened her lunch box. "Where's your lunch?"

"I ate it." Audrey put her phone on her lap. "What's that?"

"I don't know." Meena investigated. "Pakora, rice, yogurt — that's to absorb the heat from the chili."

"It smells good. What's in it?"

"Vegetables and love." Meena grinned. "That's what my mum told me. When I was little I thought you bought love in the market, along with carrots."

"I can't believe your mum makes all that for you every day and works as a doctor."

"Yeah, well, home-cooked food is a big deal in my house. Mum says she finds cooking calming. I do, too. Sometimes I think my whole family is glued together by food."

111

Audrey felt no envy that her friend had a place at Oxford University, but she envied Meena her family. "Is your sister still good at French?"

"My sister is okay but my cousin is better. She gets top marks in everything." Meena ate a spoonful of yogurt. "It's annoying how good she is at languages."

"There's a job I want to apply for, but my French isn't good enough. Do you think she'd help?"

"Yes. If she doesn't, I won't help her with physics." Meena leaned across, trying to read Audrey's phone. "What's the job?"

"It's a bookshop in Paris. The pay is crap, but it comes with a studio apartment."

With the money she'd saved from working in the hair salon she'd be able to afford to get herself to Paris and keep herself for two weeks, maybe three if she ate only one meal a day. Then she'd need to find a job.

True, she didn't know anything about the Left Bank or the Right Bank and would definitely get them muddled up because knowing her left from her right was one of her biggest struggles, but she'd find a way.

"Wait." Meena stopped chewing. "You're going to have your own apartment and a job in a bookshop? That's cool. But if your French isn't good enough to apply for the job, how are you going to manage when you get there?"

The same way she'd lived her whole life. "I'll muddle through."

"You're so brave. What do they want you to do?"

"I was hoping you could tell me that. Your French is pretty good, too." Audrey thrust the phone toward her friend, and Meena read it quickly.

"You need to write a piece on why books and reading are important."

"Crap."

Meena wiped her fingers. "I thought you hated books and reading."

"I do. I prefer movies." Her secret passion was watching animated movies, but she'd never admit to anything so childish. "Obviously I'm not going to tell them that. Does your cousin like books?"

"Yes. She's always reading."

"Great. So if she could write why she loves books, in French, I'll send that off. Can you ask her tonight?"

"Sure." Meena peered into her lunch box. "Why does my mum make me so much food? If I ate it all I'd be the size of a small office building. Every day I have to throw it away in case she finds out I didn't eat it all and gets offended. I don't suppose you want

113

some, do you?"

"Sure." Audrey had to stop herself from falling face-first into the lunch box like Hardy and his dog bowl. "Anything for a friend."

She consumed the rest of Meena's food and tried to figure out a way to persuade Meena's mother to adopt her.

She was on her way back to the salon when her mother texted.

Come home. It's an emergency.

Audrey stopped in the doorway. Ellen was cutting hair. Milly answering the phone. The salon was heaving with people. And there was Mrs. Dunmore, who always booked on a Saturday because she liked Audrey to wash her hair.

She glanced at her phone again, torn.

Her mother's idea of an emergency was running out of gin.

Saturday was the busiest day of the week at work. She was part of a team. She wasn't going to let them down.

She switched off her phone and walked into the salon.

By the time she eventually arrived home, her mother was waiting for her at the front door, her face ravaged by grief and her breath smelling of alcohol.

"Ron and I have broken up."

Audrey's heart hit the ground. "But the wedding is in a week. What happened?"

She walked into the house and closed the door, keen to keep their problems firmly inside.

"I drove him away. Everybody leaves me. No one loves me."

Audrey struggled to stay calm.

It was her worst nightmare. She'd put all her faith in Ron. "What did you fight about?"

"Nothing!"

"It must have been something."

"I can't even remember." Linda waved her hand. "Something small. I said it was obvious that he didn't love me and that he might as well just leave right now, so he did."

"Did he —" Audrey swallowed. "Did he actually *say* he wanted to break up? Maybe he just needed some air." She needed air all the time when she was around her mother. "Have you called him?"

"What's the point? He was always going to leave at some point, so maybe it's better that it's now." Her mother sank onto the sofa. "You're right, I have to take control of my life."

Audrey felt a flutter of hope. That was

something, at least. "Right. We'll make an appointment with the doctor. I'll come with you, and —"

"I started with your room."

"What?"

"Your room was a mess. Normally I overlook it, but I decided that from today we're both turning over a new leaf."

Audrey's heart started to pound. She wasn't the one who needed to turn over a new leaf.

"You tidied my room?"

"Not only tidied. I had a clear-out. You're an adult now, Audrey. You don't need all that rubbish around you. I filled two black sacks with things you should have thrown out years ago."

Audrey stared at her mother, and a horrible premonition washed over her.

Surely her mother wouldn't have —

She couldn't —

She left the room at a run, taking the stairs so fast she stumbled twice.

Please no, *no,* don't let her have done it.

She pushed open the door of her room and stared at her bed. "Mum?" Her voice was hoarse. "Where's my teddy bear?"

GRACE

When Grace's parents died, it had been impossible to escape the sympathy. It had wrapped around her like tentacles, squeezing and squeezing until she couldn't breathe. There was speculation, too, of course, about what exactly had happened on that night, but no one voiced their thoughts directly to her. Everyone had handled her carefully. They'd tiptoed, sent her anxious glances, whispered among themselves — *is she doing okay?*

It was the same now.

"One sourdough loaf?" Clemmie bagged it up and handed it to Grace with a pitying look. "How are you doing?"

"Great," Grace lied.

She'd learned a lot about herself since David had left. She'd learned it was possible to smile while crying inside and make cheerful conversation even when you wanted to tell someone to mind their own business.

"You've lost a bit of weight."

Grace paid for the bread. "Slimming down for the summer."

"It must be so hard."

She'd seen that same look in people's eyes ten times a day in the weeks since David had left her. She used to love this small town that she and David had made their home, but now she hated it. In a city she could have disappeared, but here she stood out like a red wine stain on a white carpet. Everyone knew, and each encounter left another tiny cut in her flesh and her feelings, until she felt as if she'd walked naked through a thornbush.

If David hadn't been the editor of the newspaper, his transgression probably would have made the headlines.

Editor leaves boring wife.

In the days after it had happened even the children in her class had avoided eye contact. None of them had asked her how her Valentine's date had gone. They'd been particularly well behaved, as if trying to avoid her attention.

Several of them probably had Lissa as a babysitter.

They all assumed the affair must be the worst thing about it, but for Grace the worst thing was losing David.

Being left wasn't a gentle thing. It was a vicious wrench, a tearing of flesh and feelings. Occasionally, she glanced down at herself and was surprised to discover she wasn't bleeding. Such a trauma should at least leave a bruise, surely?

She missed the sound of his voice, his familiar solid presence in the bed next to her. She even missed the parts that had annoyed her, like the fact he always forgot his door key. Most of all she missed his gentle humor and wise counsel. She felt like a climbing plant that had lost its support. Without something to lean on, she was lying in an unsightly tangle, unable to unravel herself.

Her thoughts were an endless conveyer belt of what-ifs. What if she'd worn sexier underwear? What if she'd arranged more nights away in hotels? No, that wouldn't have helped. He already thought she was too organizing. She could have encouraged *him* to arrange nights in hotels, except that then she knew it wouldn't have happened. Part of the reason she organized things was because David didn't. He preferred to be more relaxed and spontaneous, but Grace knew that didn't get you a hotel booking on a busy day.

Would Lissa remind him to take his cho-

119

lesterol medication?

She'd probably be too busy encouraging him to take Viagra.

"She was in here yesterday." Clemmie lowered her voice in that way people did when they were talking about something scandalous. "I still can't believe it. I mean *Lissa.* No offense, but there's something a bit disgusting about it."

Why was it that people said "no offense" before going on to say something clearly offensive?

"I have to go, Clemmie." If it hadn't been for the fact that Sophie was about to finish school, she would have contemplated moving.

"I mean, it's obvious what *he* saw in *her.*" Clemmie was undeterred by Grace's attempt to curtail the conversation. "She's a pretty girl and no guy is going to say no to that if it's on offer, is he? I blame her."

I blame him.

The David Grace had married never would have had an affair, but she no longer knew the man she was married to. He was a mystery to her.

It was depressing to be part of such a desperate cliché, and mortifying to think everyone was talking about her.

"Here —" Clemmie dropped two doughnuts into a bag and handed them to Grace. "No charge."

To top it off, she looked like a woman who needed to drown herself in sugar.

Sophie was sitting at the kitchen table doing her homework when Grace arrived home. "Hi, Mom." She'd lost that open, trusting happy smile that had been part of her personality. Now there was caution, as if she did a quick audit to check if life was about to slap her again or if it was safe to smile. "Did something happen? You look pale."

"Forgot to put my makeup on." Grace put the loaf and the doughnuts on the table. As a child she'd learned to hide her feelings. She'd been a master of secrecy. So why was she finding this so hard? "There's chicken in the fridge and I thought I'd put together a salad."

"Delicious."

The phone rang as Grace was rinsing tomatoes. She glanced at her phone and spilled half the tomatoes in the sink.

"It's your dad."

Sophie's jaw lifted. "I don't want to talk to him."

She'd always been a daddy's girl, which had made it harder when disillusionment took the shine off that relationship. Sophie hadn't cared much when she'd discovered Santa didn't exist, or the tooth fairy, but she'd almost broken when she'd found out her daddy wasn't the man she'd believed him to be.

Grace rescued the tomatoes and sliced them with more violence than was strictly necessary. "He's still your father, honey."

She remembered feeling the same shock when she'd discovered the truth about her own parents. The puzzlement and disappointment of realizing they were human and flawed. Somehow you expected your parents to know better than you did. To be able to rise above the failings that afflicted other people.

It was frightening to realize adults didn't have it figured out, because if your parents didn't have the answers, then who was a child supposed to rely on?

"I don't need reminding. It's all I think about." Sophie pushed her homework to one side and laid the table. Since that awful day when David had come out of the hospital, she'd hovered around Grace like a protective force field.

It was touching, but it also added stress because Grace had to watch her every move and every reaction. In front of Sophie she had to hold it together. No matter how

122

angry and upset she was with David, she couldn't share that with her daughter.

Sophie's reaction had been worse, far worse, than Grace had anticipated. Although David had told her the news, Grace had insisted on being there because she hadn't trusted David to handle Sophie's emotions in a sensitive way. In the end he'd stumbled his way through it, as clumsy as a drunk knocking over chairs in a bar. He'd mumbled something about how people changed over time, and had started to say that he and Grace had grown apart but then he'd seen something in Grace's expression and confessed that it had been his decision and his alone. When he'd started talking about Lissa, it had been hard to figure out who of the three of them was the most embarrassed. It had been excruciating.

For days afterward their daughter had raged around the house, ricocheting between anger and tears. *It was disgusting. Gross. She was going to have to leave school. Everyone would be talking about it. She never wanted to see her dad again.*

After a few days of continual sobbing, Sophie had returned to school, vowing never to trust a man in her life.

Together they'd stumbled and shivered their way through the next few months.

The only bright light in their dark days was that Sophie had been accepted into Stanford.

Grace showed only her pride and her joy. Dismay and fear she kept hidden.

How would she cope? What would she do when Sophie left, too? She was facing a life that looked nothing like the one she'd planned for herself. It was like hiking in the wilderness with no map.

David had moved in with Lissa the night he'd been discharged from hospital, and they were now sharing her small one-roomed apartment on the other side of town.

"I've decided I'm not going to travel this summer." Sophie mixed dressing for the salad.

"What? Why? You've been looking forward to it."

"I'm not leaving you." Sophie tossed the salad violently, as if each leaf had personally offended her. "Unless you'd consider still going to Paris?"

"Alone?"

"Why not?" Sophie rescued a leaf that had landed on the table. "People travel alone all the time."

Grace hadn't traveled alone since she was eighteen. All the trips she'd taken in the last twenty-five years had been with David.

Should she feel embarrassed about that? Maybe she *should* have traveled alone. But why would she when the thought of traveling with David was so much more appealing? And it wasn't as if they could afford multiple holidays.

"This trip was ridiculously expensive. Even if I cancel the hotel, I'll still lose a fortune on the flights."

"Then why cancel? You deserve a treat. I really think you should go, Mom."

But it wouldn't be a treat. It would be a cruel reminder of what she'd lost. She'd be imagining how it might have been if they'd done it together. She'd assumed they'd be making memories together. It hadn't occurred to her that those memories wouldn't include David.

"Maybe I'll do something else later in the summer."

Sophie put the salad in the center of the table. "If you don't go, I don't go."

When had Sophie become this stubborn? "You've been planning it for months. Things have changed for me, but they don't have to change for you."

"Seriously?" Sophie clattered plates. "My father is sleeping with my friend, and you think things haven't changed? Everyone at

125

school knows, and most people think it's disgusting and gross, which, by the way, it totally is. I mean, this is my *dad* and I'm having to think about —" She shuddered. "Never mind. Teachers keep asking me how I'm doing. Hello, humiliation."

Every word she spoke inflicted more damage to Grace's wounded heart.

For the first time in her life she came close to hating David.

"We'll get through this." She was surprised by how strong she sounded, and Sophie looked surprised, too.

"I don't get how you can be so *calm.*"

"I'm doing my best in difficult circumstances, and that's all anyone can do. You need to carry on and do all the things you were going to do before this happened."

Sophie slid into her seat and pushed the salad toward Grace. "No."

It was scary to acknowledge that a small, needy part of her *wanted* her daughter to stay home for the summer. *Don't leave me.* But she wasn't going to listen to her inner child.

"We'll argue about it another time."

They sat down to eat. Grace was relieved to see Sophie eating normally again. For weeks after David had left, she'd eaten almost nothing.

"I heard Sam is having a party. Are you going?"

"No." Sophie sliced into chicken. "He's still with Callie. And don't look like that, because I don't even care. I've chosen a career over relationships."

"You can have both." Grace helped herself to more salad and silently cursed David.

"A career is in your control. I am going to work my butt off in college and get a brilliant job. I am going to shatter that glass ceiling into so many pieces that all the men around me cut their feet on the shards."

Grace put her fork down. "Don't let what happened color your view on life. I don't want you to miss out on love and family because of this."

Sophie stabbed a piece of chicken. "Would you have married Dad if you'd known this was going to happen? I mean, you've been together *forever* and he's thrown that away like it's nothing. Was it even worth it?"

Grace thought back to the beginning of their relationship. The night that had brought them together. She and David were the only ones who knew the exact circumstances. She thought about the happiness they'd shared.

"I would. We had many happy years." One day, maybe, she'd be able to look back with fondness. "And if I hadn't met your dad, I wouldn't have you. Sometimes you're a pain, of course, but mostly you turned out pretty well." She was relieved when her daughter threw her a grin.

Sophie stood up to clear the plates and paused, her attention caught by movement outside the window. "Dad is here!"

"No!" Grace stood up, too, heart pounding. "Why?"

"Probably because we didn't answer the phone."

The last thing she needed was an impromptu visit from David. It felt as if the universe was testing her, to see how far it could go before she cracked. "Go upstairs and do your homework, Sophie."

Sophie folded her arms. "I'm not leaving you." Her father walking out had made her draw closer to her mother. She had chosen a side, even though Grace had been careful not to encourage it.

She didn't want Sophie to cut David from her life.

He hadn't mentioned divorce since that awful night back in February, but Grace assumed he was going to raise it again at some point. Whatever happened, he'd always be Sophie's father.

"Please, Sophie."

"Mom —"

"Sophie!"

"Fine." Sophie grabbed her laptop and headed for the stairs. "I don't want to see him anyway."

Grace thought about all the times Sophie had listened for her father coming home. She'd race through the house, filling it with her joyful yells, *Daddy, Daddy.*

She opened the door, hating the fact that she felt nervous. It seemed unjust that she should be the one feeling that way.

It had been weeks since she'd seen him, and her first thought was that he didn't look like himself.

David was always clean-shaven, but today his jaw was darkened by stubble. On another man it might have looked as if he hadn't bothered to shave, but on him it looked annoyingly good. The touches of gray in his hair looked good on him, too. He was broad shouldered and solid. The kind of man people leaned on in a crisis. *She'd* leaned on him. She wanted to lean on him now, but as he was the cause of this current crisis that impulse made no sense.

If he was suffering, it didn't show. She, on the other hand, was fairly sure that her suffering was as visible as a drop of blood on fresh snow.

If he looked closely he'd probably see the nights she hadn't slept, the tears she'd shed, the food she hadn't eaten.

She made a note to always wear makeup from now on, even in bed. That way she couldn't be caught out.

"Grace." His voice was gentle. He might have been speaking to the victim of a traffic accident. *I'm terribly sorry to be the bearer of bad news.* "Can we talk?"

"You should have called."

"I did. You didn't answer. Please, Grace." In that split second, she saw the old David. The David who had supported her through unspeakably tough times, the David who understood her.

She opened the door wider. "Five minutes."

He stepped through the door and had the good manners to pause, waiting for her to direct him even though he'd lived here with her for twenty-five years. They'd bought the house together and when they'd picked up the keys he'd carried her over the threshold. They'd had sex in every room in the house, including the bathtub.

"Kitchen," she said, and saw him glance into the living room as they passed the door. "You moved the sofa."

"The light was fading the fabric." She

didn't tell him that she'd moved things around in the hope that she wouldn't feel his absence every time she walked into a room.

He waited until she sat down before he sat, too.

"Where's Sophie?"

"Upstairs, working."

"How is she doing?"

"How do you think she is doing?"

"I don't know. She won't talk to me."

For the first time she noticed he looked tired, too.

Too much sex, she thought bitterly.

"It's been a shock for her. You have to give her time."

David stared at his hands. "Hurting you both was the last thing I wanted to do."

"And yet you did."

He lifted his gaze. "Were you honestly happy in our marriage?"

"Yes. I liked the life we had, David."

"Our life was safe and predictable, and I know you need that. But a marriage has to be more than a routine that doesn't change. Sometimes I felt you wanted me as a support and a crutch. Not as a man."

"You're saying this is my fault?"

He spread his hands. "I'm not attributing blame. I'm trying to get you to listen to me

131

and see that there are two sides."

"Why? The time to have this conversation would have been before you had an affair and walked out."

He rubbed his fingers over his forehead, as if he was trying to massage away the pain. She knew every one of his gestures. This one meant he was dealing with a situation for which there was no fix.

"Do you need anything?" He let his hand drop. "Money, or —"

Or what? The only thing she needed was sitting in front of her.

"I'm fine." She still didn't really know why he was here and then she saw him draw breath and knew she was about to find out.

He studied something on the kitchen counter. "Have you canceled the trip to Paris?"

"No." Canceling would be the final acknowledgment that her marriage was over. Also, the moment she did it she knew Sophie would also cancel her own trip. She was still figuring out how to handle that.

"Right. Good."

Good? Her heart skipped in her chest.

Had he changed his mind? *That* was why he'd come here tonight, to find a way to ask her forgiveness.

This was the first step toward reconciliation.

Would she be able to forgive him?

Yes, she probably would. They'd need to move away, of course. Leave this town and move to a place where no one knew them. They'd see a counselor. Find their way through this knotty mess. Rebuild their lives.

"You don't want me to cancel?"

"I'll pay you for my flight ticket. I don't want you to lose the money. And I'll take over the hotel reservation."

Grace felt as if her brain was working in slow motion. He didn't want to take her to Paris. He was offering her guilt money.

And suddenly she knew. God, she was so slow.

"You're taking Lissa."

He ran his hand over the back of his neck. "Grace —"

"You want the tickets so you can take the girl —" she emphasized *girl* "— you're having an affair with, on our anniversary trip."

He looked almost as sick as she felt.

"I know it's not the most tactful thing to ask you." He looked desperately uncomfortable. "But it does make financial sense. You already booked the whole trip, and I know you'll lose money when you cancel."

She could imagine how the discussion

133

might have gone with Lissa.

He would have fought it, she was sure of that.

I can't expect my wife to give me the tickets she booked to celebrate our anniversary so that I can take my lover.

Maybe Lissa had been testing him, checking how far he'd go for her.

A part of Grace wanted to know the answer to that, too.

He was a man at war on the inside. Good versus bad. David, the good guy, trying to slide into the skin of bad guy and finding it didn't fit comfortably.

"What have you turned into, David? What's happened to the man I married?" She stood up quickly, frightened that her emotions would tumble onto the table between them. "Go. I said five minutes, and you've had your five minutes."

His fingers curled and uncurled. "I know it's been stressful for you, but it's also been stressful for Lissa." He slid her a look. Wild. A little desperate. "Some of the people in town don't even speak to her anymore. She's finding it upsetting. She's young, Grace. She's struggling to handle all this."

Grace almost choked. "*She's* struggling?"

"I've lost a lot, too. I've lost my house, my standing in the community and also my

134

close relationship with my daughter."

"She isn't a pair of socks you've abandoned under the bed. You haven't lost her. You chose something different." Even as she said the words she was wondering *what about me*. Why wasn't she on that list? Hadn't she ever been important to him?

She looked more closely at him and saw that he looked haggard. Why hadn't she noticed that right away? If anything he looked worse than she did. Maybe having a girlfriend half his age was proving harder work than he'd imagined.

"You need to leave now." Before she picked up a skillet and clocked him over the head with it. That would give him the best headline he'd ever had in his time as editor. Shame he wouldn't be alive to read it.

He stood up. "Let me pay you, Grace. I don't want you to lose money."

"I won't lose money, because I'm not canceling."

It was difficult to know which of them was most surprised.

David couldn't have looked more dazed if she *had* clocked him over the head. "You're surely not planning on going?"

"Yes, I'm going. I've been looking forward to it for ages. Why would I cancel?"

"Because —" He seemed lost for words,

even though words were his job. "You don't — You never — You travel with me. I'm the one who takes care of the passports and —"

"I can carry my own passport, David. And yes, in the past we've traveled together but you now have a new traveling companion, so I'll travel alone. If Lissa needs a trip to Europe, you can arrange your own."

"I — This isn't like you."

"Maybe we don't know each other as well as we thought."

"Maybe we don't." He took a deep breath. "Can I see Sophie?"

"No." She'd discovered a layer of steel inside her that she didn't know she had. "You'll upset her and she has a test tomorrow."

"I was the one who always reassured her before tests."

"Maybe, but right now she doesn't find your presence reassuring. Call her tomorrow, and if she feels like seeing you then she can. It's her decision."

She stalked to the front door and was relieved when he followed.

She'd half expected him to make a dive for the stairs.

He paused in the doorway, and his eyes were sad. "I know you're never going to forgive me, but I didn't want it to be this

136

way, Grace."

She gave him a little shove and closed the door between them, not because she wanted to be rude, but because she didn't trust herself not to break down and cry.

She'd always believed she could control the things that happened in her life and keep her world in the shape she wanted it to be. Discovering that wasn't the case was as frightening and heartbreaking as losing David.

Tears poured down her cheeks. She couldn't let Sophie see her this upset.

She waited until David's car disappeared into the distance, called up to Sophie to tell her where she was going and then drove to the one person who always made her feel safe.

MIMI

Through her kitchen window, Mimi saw Grace flying down the path toward her cottage.

The edges of her coat flapped open and the rain had dampened her hair into curls so that each strand appeared to be fighting with the next, but what really caught Mimi's attention was her expression. Everything she felt showed on her face.

Instinctively Mimi reached for her camera but then put it down again. She'd recorded many things over her lifetime, but she wasn't going to record her granddaughter's pain.

As a child Grace had learned to hide it with most people, but never with Mimi. It was as if she'd given her grandmother the key that opened the door to her soul. In that moment she looked so like her mother that Mimi was immobilized, her memory transported to another time. It was like see-

138

ing Judy again, like being given a second chance.

Some women weren't meant to be mothers. Mimi was one of them.

It was all my fault, and I'm sorry.

Her silent apology to her daughter went unheard and when Grace lifted her fingers to brush tears from her cheek, Mimi saw only the differences. The nose was different. The mouth was different. Grace's face was oval and thinner than her mother's, although Judy's appearance had altered toward the end.

Mimi clutched at the kitchen counter, steadied herself.

Why did life come with so much tragedy?

Right now she felt every one of her ninety years, and for a fleeting second she wanted to lie down and curl into a ball and let life do whatever it needed to do.

And then Grace drew closer, and Mimi knew that while she was still able to function, she would never give up and let life do its worst. And she would never abandon Grace.

It was a relief to discover that the fight, the anger that she'd thought had maybe left her along with much of her hearing and her previously perfect eyesight, was still there.

She opened the door, heard the hiss of

the rain on tarmac and breathed in the smell of damp grass.

Winter had been nudged aside by spring, but the sun had yet to emerge from hibernation. Every day brought a dank wetness, and skies heavy with cloud. The cold made Mimi's bones ache. She longed for summer when she could fold away the extra blankets she kept close.

"Grace."

Grace tumbled through the door into her arms, and Mimi almost staggered. It was as if grief had made her heavier. She led her to the pretty blue sofa that made her think of Mediterranean skies and azure seas. She sat, and Grace slid to the floor and sobbed into Mimi's lap.

She'd done the same thing as a child, Mimi remembered. When her mother had rejected her, embarrassed her, frightened her.

It was painful to watch, and she stroked Grace's hair, feeling frightened herself.

She'd seen enough in her nine decades not to be shocked by much, but she was shocked by this.

Oh, David, how could you?

David, who she would have said was the most solid, predictable, dependable man she'd ever met. He'd almost made Mimi believe in marriage.

What would happen now?

Was this karma? Was Grace being punished for Mimi's sins?

Seeing Grace so safe and secure had given her joy. She hadn't anticipated this, even though she should have done because she knew how easily life could change direction.

"I hate him." Like a child she sobbed, her tears drenching the thin silk of Mimi's dress. "I truly hate him."

"No, you don't." Mimi held her, stroking her shoulder. "You hate what he's done."

"Same thing."

"It's not the same thing. At some point you'll see that, but it might take a while." David had been Grace's rock. He'd given her the emotional stability she'd craved. Protected by his love, she'd thrived.

"I am never going to forgive him. She's twenty-three. He has completely and *utterly* humiliated me. Everywhere I go, people are wondering about me. They're talking about what I did wrong."

"You did nothing wrong, Grace."

"Then why did he leave?"

Such a simple question for a complicated situation.

"I don't know."

"I'm not important. I'm never important."

"That's not true." Mimi knew this was about more than David. "Your mom was sick. It was different."

"Maybe the reasons, but not the result." Grace's words emerged in an uneven volley, between sobs. "I have to be cheerful and together for Sophie, and put on my best coping face whenever I leave the house." She blew her nose. "People are looking at me wondering what I did wrong."

"You didn't do anything wrong, Grace."

"I must have done something, or he wouldn't have left me for her."

"Men sometimes do selfish things." Mimi paused. "Women, too."

She'd been selfish, hadn't she?

It was something she didn't like to admit to herself, which was why she'd never discussed it with anyone. Not even Grace. Her family saw only the facts — that she'd had a child.

They didn't know the history of her heart.

Grace looked at her, her eyes bruised with grief. "He chose her over me."

Mimi's heart felt heavy in her chest. She knew this wasn't just about David. "It's not that simple."

"Isn't it? He is living with her. And now I have to go to Paris on my own." The words were barely distinguishable between the sobs.

"You're still going to Paris?" Mimi's heart gave a little lift, like a bird catching a thermal.

"I don't have any choice —" Grace hiccuped, sobbed, hiccuped again. "If I don't go, Sophie won't travel this summer. And I am not giving the tickets to David. I'm not that evolved."

"Did he ask for them?" Surely even a man blinded by a new infatuation — she refused to believe it was love — wouldn't do something so thoughtless and cruel?

"Yes. I told him I was using them." Grace blew her nose. "And I can't see a way out of it that doesn't involve ruining Sophie's summer."

She would do it, Mimi knew, because Grace was an excellent mother. A far better mother than Mimi had ever been.

"You might enjoy it."

"It would be a miserable trip. It feels like the wrong choice."

"Paris is never the wrong choice. And staying here would be worse."

Grace brushed her hand across her cheeks. "It was supposed to be a trip of a lifetime with the man I love."

Mimi ignored the ache in her chest. "It

can still be the trip of a lifetime."

"Memorable for the fact that I'm alone in the City of Lights? Paris is for lovers."

Mimi made an unladylike sound. "Paris is for everyone. Don't romanticize, Grace."

"I haven't traveled alone since I was eighteen, and even then I stayed with the French family you put me in touch with."

"Then it's time you traveled alone again."

"I booked an expensive hotel."

"*Quelle plasir,*" Mimi murmured. "I don't see the hardship. You will have to spell it out for me. Go! You might surprise yourself and have a good time."

Grace's expression said that the chances of that were zero. "You want me to do this for Sophie."

"I want you to do it for you. You will do it and send David pictures so that he can see for himself what a fool he is."

"I don't know how to live without him, Mimi." There was fear in her voice, and Mimi felt the same fear.

What if she couldn't help Grace through this? She'd failed her own daughter. What if she failed her granddaughter, too?

She punched her way through it.

"You know what I've always said — a man is icing on the cake, that's all. And with all the new research on the dangers of sugar, maybe you're better off without."

"You can't possibly understand. You've never been in love. You can't imagine what it feels like to lose it."

Mimi felt pain slice through her. She knew exactly how it felt. "Don't make the mistake of thinking you can't survive without David. Life might be tougher, and different, but you will find a way."

She'd found a way. There had been times when she'd thought that living without him might kill her, but it hadn't. A broken heart, she'd discovered, was rarely fatal. Instead, it inflicted a slow, painful torture.

Mimi was too old to do many things but remembering was one skill she hadn't lost. She often thought about him. Of dancing late into the night, strolls along cobbled streets wrapped in the darkness of Paris, long nights entwined together with the open window letting in the breath of wind and street noise.

Was he still alive? Did he ever think of her?

Did he consider her the love of his life or his biggest mistake?

Grace fumbled for her bag. "I'm sorry. I shouldn't be doing this to you. You shouldn't have to deal with this."

"I'm providing a sympathetic ear and a

shoulder, that's all."

Grace found a tissue and blew her nose. "It's everything. I have no one else I can talk to. I can't believe this has happened to us. To me. I feel helpless and out of control."

And feeling out of control, Mimi knew, would be the most frightening thing of all for her granddaughter.

It broke Mimi's heart to do it, but she did it anyway. "Get up, Grace."

Grace lifted her head, her eyes glazed with pain.

"Up!" Mimi said sharply. "Lying there howling never gives you anything but a headache, and the only good reason to get a headache is because you've drunk too much champagne." She patted Grace's shoulder in a brisk fashion. She wanted to stroke and soothe, but that would help neither of them.

Grace stumbled to her feet, confused, and Mimi nodded.

"You see? You can stand without him."

Grace looked wobbly and wounded. "You think I'm being pathetic."

"I think you're underestimating yourself. You didn't have a choice about your marriage ending, but you have the choice about what happens next."

"You think I should lift my head high and show David I'm fine without him?"

"No, I think you should hold your head high and show *yourself* that you're fine without him. You love David. You miss David. But he isn't necessary for your survival. You might want him, but you don't *need* him, honey. You can do this. *You.*"

"How?"

Mimi thought about herself. About those long, agonizing days when she'd had to push herself forward. The down moments of life when she'd had to struggle alone. "Discipline. You get up in the morning. You take a shower. You do one thing, and then another. It's tempting to lie down and give up, but you will resist it. You know everything there is to know about resisting temptation."

Grace sucked in a breath. "It's not the same."

"Yes, it is. You get through a second, and then a minute. And then another minute. You don't think about the length of the journey, you focus on each step. One at a time. And one day you'll pause and realize you're starting to enjoy the view."

Grace gave a watery smile. "You sound like one of those bad motivational posters."

"I love those posters," Mimi lied.

Grace paced to the window and looked

out onto the garden. "I don't think I can do it."

"Go to Paris, Grace. Stay in the luxury hotel. Sleep in the middle of the bed. Stroll through the Tuileries Garden and feel the sun on your face. Visit the little bookstore where I spent so much time."

"Bookstore? You?" Grace turned to look at her. "You've never had time for reading."

"I've been known to pick up a book in my time." Mimi was purposefully vague. "You go to Paris, Grace. And you smile."

"You expect me to do all that *and* smile?"

"Of course. And who knows —" Mimi shrugged, although her heart was breaking for her granddaughter "— you might find love in Paris."

After all, she had.

PARIS

PARIS

AUDREY

Why had she thought Paris would be a good idea?

Audrey carried her backpack along the cobbled street. Sweat glued her clothes to her body and made her shoes rub. She was going to have a massive blister.

She said, *"Excusez moi,"* for the thousandth time as she tried to push her way through the thick throng of tourists. Meena's cousin had taught her a few other phrases, but they were all rude and Audrey didn't want to spend her first night in Paris in a police cell.

The voice navigation on her phone told her that she'd reached her destination, but she couldn't see a bookshop anywhere.

She checked her phone again and then looked at the street name.

She was lost.

Irritated and overheated, she walked into a small shop selling handbags. The woman behind the counter gave her a suspicious look and stared hard at Audrey's hair. The heat and a day of traveling had turned it into something resembling a bird's nest, but there was nothing she could do about that until she had access to a shower and her hair products.

Audrey told herself that she didn't care what the woman thought of her. All her life she'd been on the receiving end of people who judged. People who judged her because she was a slow reader. People who judged her for having red hair. People who judged her because she had no wish to go to college. Why did everyone have to follow the same path and be the same? Audrey didn't understand it.

"*Bonjour.* I'm trying to find this place." Audrey thrust the phone at her, desperately hoping the woman spoke English. "Do you know where it is?"

The woman glanced at the address on Audrey's phone, nodded and gave directions in rapid French.

Audrey caught one word in four, and didn't understand even those.

Tout droit? What did that mean? And she couldn't even look it up because she couldn't spell it.

Too embarrassed to admit she didn't

understand what the woman was saying, she mumbled words of thanks and backed out of the shop. From the woman's arm gestures, she'd picked up that she was supposed to carry on straight up this street to begin with, so she did that.

It was hot and sticky and everyone around her was dressed in sundresses or shorts. They strolled slowly, pausing outside each store. They examined the baskets stuffed with goods, turning each product over in their hands, trying to work out if they were looking at a bargain. There was a shop selling the inevitable Paris memorabilia. Sketches of Montmartre that would look ridiculous on the wall of a cramped room in London, tiny Eiffel Towers that would dangle from keys for a month and then gather dust in a drawer until someone decided that they weren't even worth the memory.

People who hated shopping at home seemed happy to shop on holiday.

Audrey wasn't happy. She'd dreamed about this moment forever. But now she was here she didn't feel any better than she had in London.

She'd longed for freedom, but hadn't known freedom would feel as lonely as this.

She'd longed to pass over responsibility

for her mother, but hadn't realized that the hot burn of anxiety would stay in her stomach even after she'd arrived in France. She couldn't stop thinking about it.

In the end her mother and Ron had fixed whatever had gone wrong between them. Linda had told Audrey that his reaction to a fight was to seek some alone time, whereas she needed intimacy and reassurance, and automatically saw that need for space as a sign that the relationship was over.

Her mother had promised to try to be less insecure and Ron had promised never again to walk out without making it clear he planned on coming back.

The wedding had gone ahead, but Audrey had held her breath along with her posy of flowers, terrified that it wouldn't last.

What if her mother drank too much and he left for good? Would Linda even call Audrey? She could be lying on the bathroom floor right at this moment and Audrey wouldn't even know.

She paused when she reached a busy square.

The delicious smell of fresh pizza and herbs wafted toward her from a small pavement café, crowded with people. Everyone in the world seemed to be having fun, except her.

Her stomach growled. All she'd eaten since she left London was a squashed energy bar she'd found at the bottom of her bag.

Ignoring the pain in her feet, she shifted her backpack to ease her sore shoulders and carried on walking. Cobbled streets looked quaint and pretty in photos, but they were less charming when you were trying to walk over them.

Finally she found it, tucked away in a little courtyard and accessed by a narrow passageway. *Le Petit Livre* was close to the river and the charming cafés that lined the pavements.

The door was painted a bright, cheery blue and the windows on either side were filled with books of every description.

The name of the shop was stenciled onto the windows in a curve, and she pushed open the door, jumping as a bell jangled.

The place smelled of books, dust and leather but there were worse smells in her opinion. Alcohol. Smoke. Food past its sell-by date. She could name dozens.

Shelves reached to the ceiling, and she glanced upward, wondering what she was going to do if someone wanted a book from the top shelf.

"Entrez, entrez, j'arrive!" A woman emerged

from the back of the shop. Her hair was white and swept up in an elegant knot, and she wore a black dress that flowed around her slender frame.

Audrey stared, fascinated. Her mother's approach to glamour was to lower her neckline. This woman had almost no flesh on display, and yet she was the most glamorous creature Audrey had ever seen.

Confronted by such cool elegance, she was even more aware of how badly she needed a shower.

"Je m'appelle Audrey." It was the one phrase she'd practiced a million times.

She was feeling pretty proud of her pronunciation, particularly when the woman's face brightened.

She introduced herself as Elodie, stretched out her hands in welcome and kissed Audrey on both cheeks.

It felt bizarre to be kissed by a stranger but she had no time to dwell on that because the woman was talking in French, gesturing toward the books. She was obviously giving Audrey a summary of her responsibilities, which was awkward because Audrey didn't have a clue what she was saying.

The woman paused, and Audrey felt a rush of frustration.

She was usually quite chatty, but she had

no idea how to be chatty in French. She felt her cheeks grow hot.

"Er — I didn't actually understand all of that — *ne comprenez.*" What was the phrase for not understanding? Oh, this had been a seriously bad idea.

Puzzled, the woman switched to English. "The letter I received from you was written in excellent French." Her words were heavily accented, but it was clear that her language skills were vastly superior to Audrey's.

"I'm better at writing than speaking." Audrey beamed. She'd learned that a smile often distracted people from what was really going on. "I'll soon pick it up."

"You're going to go to language classes while you are here?"

"Definitely." She had no intention of signing up for classes. Not only because she had no money, but because she never wanted to study again in her life. She planned to find a local hair salon that would give her work. Maybe she'd learn a few words there.

"You will work mornings," Elodie told her, as she showed her around the shop, "and the occasional evening if Etienne is busy."

"Etienne?"

Elodie led her into the tiny kitchen where

they could make tea, and pointed out the cupboard where the first aid kit was kept.

"Etienne is studying French literature at the Sorbonne. He works here evenings, weekends and during the holidays for the past two years. Our regular customers love him."

Audrey could picture him. Glasses. Slightly pale because he spent too long indoors with only books for company. Probably skinny because books didn't weigh much and they were the only things he lifted. And superior. He'd look down his nose at someone like her.

She already knew she was going to loathe the saintly Etienne. Any boy whose idea of excitement was spending his evenings working in a bookshop wasn't her type. He wouldn't know the first thing about the hottest places to hang out in Paris.

"You have regular customers? So it's not all tourist trade, then?" She gazed around the shelves. She'd never seen so many books in one place outside a library.

"This bookshop has been here for over a hundred years. It was owned by my great-grandmother and has been in the family ever since. Even during the German occupation of Paris, my grandmother kept it running. She kept all the valuable books hidden."

"Cool." Audrey was interested. Hiding things was her specialty. Or it had been until she'd been stupid enough to hide her money inside her bear. She still couldn't think about that without wanting to cry. All the money she'd saved. Gone. If it hadn't been for the kindness of all the people in the hair salon, she wouldn't be here now. When she'd told them what had happened they'd all got together and given her a "leaving present." Ellen had made a speech and Doris had baked a cake. Then they'd handed her an envelope stuffed with enough notes to cover her ticket to Paris and a few meals. It had been the first and only time in her life that Audrey had cried in public.

She felt a sudden pang. What would they all be doing now?

Her throat thickened and she tried to focus on the bookstore.

"It's interesting. I like history." As long as she wasn't expected to write an essay on it. The past always seemed so much more interesting than the present, which in her life was pretty challenging.

"Let me show you your new home!" Elodie led her to the back of the shop and scooped up a key. "Your parents are happy for you to be in Paris this summer?"

159

"They're very supportive." Audrey looked at the till, wondering how often Elodie counted the money. Not that she intended to steal it exactly. Just borrow enough to tide her over until she found a job. Then she'd put it back. She had no idea how much money she'd need to survive here, but as the area was packed with tourists she assumed the answer was "a lot."

"The room is in the eaves. It's small, but I think you will find it comfortable. When my children were little, they used to fight to sleep up there."

Audrey hauled her backpack up the narrow staircase and paused by a doorway. "Is this it?"

"You're on the next floor up. I rent the other apartment for extra income, but for now it is empty. I have two people coming to see it tomorrow. Your apartment is smaller, but you have a view over the rooftops of Paris."

The rooftops of Paris sounded better than the backstreets of London, which had been her view for the past eighteen years.

By the time they reached the top of the stairs, Audrey was out of breath.

Elodie unlocked the door and handed over the key. "Welcome to your new home."

"Thanks. I mean, *merci.*" Audrey followed

her inside. She wasn't sure what she'd been expecting. The single small photo she'd seen had suggested something small and dark, but whoever had taken the photo hadn't done the place justice. Yes, it was small, but what the photo hadn't shown was the row of windows and the generous flood of light.

Her spirits lifted and her relief must have shown on her face because Elodie beamed.

"Perfect, no?"

"Totally perfect."

There was a bed against one wall. Not a narrow bed like the one she had at home but a generous double with an ornate frame that looked like something out of an old French movie. Against one wall was a large sofa, covered in a throw and heaped in cushions.

There was a tiny fridge in the corner of the room, a hot plate and a microwave. Since Audrey didn't intend to cook anything much, she knew she wouldn't need more than that.

Toast was her favorite food, and there was a toaster on top of the counter.

"The bathroom is here." Elodie waved her arm and Audrey poked her head around the door.

There was a shower, a toilet and a hand basin, crammed together in a space so small that Audrey would have to keep her elbows tucked in if she didn't want bruises. But it was all hers. Audrey had never had a bathroom that was all hers. She wouldn't have to wonder if she'd find her mother crying on the floor, or alcohol stashed behind the toilet. She closed her hand over the key. She'd never been able to lock her door before. Her mother barged in at any time that suited her. For the first time in her life, she'd have privacy. Right now that felt as valuable as cash.

She slid the key into her pocket, feeling grown-up. Maybe that was all it took. A key. A place of your own. The ability to decide what you did with your day. To make choices that weren't driven by compensating for other people's mistakes.

She closed the door on the bathroom and walked across to the windows. The floorboards creaked under her feet and she had to duck her head in the section of the room where the roof sloped, but from here she had a view across what seemed to be the whole of Paris.

She opened the window and leaned out. She heard the blare of car horns, shouts from the people below in the streets, the smell of cigarettes and sunbaked streets. Beyond the rooftops she could see the gentle curve of the river Seine, the golden stone of the Louvre and in the distance the bold jut of steel that was the Eiffel Tower.

Across the narrow street was another building, also full of apartments. Through one window Audrey could see bookshelves, tumbling plants and sofas. Through another, she could see into a bedroom.

It made her realize that she needed to close the shutters, particularly if she invited company back.

"It's great." She pulled her head back from the window. "Thanks."

"You can have the rest of the day to settle in and start tomorrow." Elodie walked to the door. "We open at 9:00 in the morning and stay open until 9:00 at night. Will you be able to handle an early start?"

Audrey had been getting herself out of bed in time for school for what felt like her whole life. She could handle 9:00 a.m., although she had to admit she'd been hoping for more of a lie-in now that she'd left school. Still, as long as she wasn't expected to actually read the books . . .

"Great. Can't wait."

She waited until the door had closed behind Elodie, and then finally, finally, she was alone.

Alone!

She stretched out her arms and spun on the spot, feeling the space and the silence.

Feeling restless and strange, she unloaded the contents of her backpack onto the bed. Everything was crumpled.

Suddenly exhausted, she sat down next to her clothes.

She'd been dreaming of leaving home for the best part of a year. Having her own place. Living far away from her mother. She'd expected to feel giddy and euphoric, and instead she felt —

How did she feel?

Lonely. She felt lonely. At least at home she'd been able to call Meena and ask her over for a pizza. Here, she knew no one except Elodie and she sensed they weren't likely to become besties.

She dug out her phone and checked her messages.

There were two from Meena. Sometimes she left voice mail because it was easier for Audrey, but mostly she forgot and typed.

Met anyone hot?

Are you in love yet?

Feeling a little better, Audrey grinned and texted back.

Only been here ten mins.

It was a moment before Meena replied.

Check out Hayley's FB page. Pics of her
by the pool. You need to post some cool
pics of Paris to make her jealous.

Audrey checked the page and saw a bunch
of photos of Hayley looking smug on a
beach with an azure sea sparkling in the
background. How many shots had it taken,
and how many filters, to achieve that look?

She flung her phone back into her bag and
forced herself upright.

*Fuck other people and their perfect virtual
lives.*

She needed to get out and get a job. Once
she had money, she could start living.

She rifled through her tops and jeans, trying to find something that might impress
the owner of a hair salon.

In the end she settled for a miniskirt
because there was less of that to crease, a
pair of boots and a strap top.

She twisted her hair into a messy knot on
the back of her head and carefully applied
her makeup.

Leaving the rest of her belongings piled
on the bed, she grabbed her purse and her

sunglasses and clomped her way down the stairs and into the Paris sunshine.

She didn't want a virtual perfect life, she wanted an *actual* perfect life. And the only way she was ever going to get that was if she got off her butt and went looking for it.

GRACE

Grace emerged from her taxi into bright Paris sunshine.

The Hotel Antoinette was a historic building dating back to 1750. Grace had chosen it carefully for its position, its views and its grandeur. Originally it had been a palace belonging to a member of the French aristocracy who had met a grisly end during the revolution. The building had been left to crumble until a large hotel group had taken over its renovation.

Close to the Tuileries Garden and the Louvre, it nestled near the banks of the Seine in newly restored splendor.

Perhaps she should be inspired that the building had survived a revolution and emerged looking so spectacular. Maybe there was hope for her.

The long flight left her feeling tired and dusty. She longed for a bath.

The receptionist was charming and

checked her in swiftly.

"Twenty-five years of marriage, madame." The girl flashed her a smile as she returned Grace's passport. "*Felicitations.* Here at the Hotel Antoinette we are pleased to play a part in your special celebrations."

She hadn't thought to tell them she was coming alone. What business was it of theirs?

"As this is a special occasion, it is our pleasure to offer you an upgrade." The girl handed over a glossy folder that included two credit card–shaped keys. "You are in the Tuileries Suite. You have also a balcony overlooking the gardens and the river. We have made a reservation for two for dinner in our restaurant."

"Thank you, but my husband has been delayed and won't arrive until tomorrow. Possibly later."

Or never.

Why didn't she just tell them the truth? That she was alone?

"I will amend your reservation for tonight," the receptionist said, tapping a couple of keys on her computer, "and we will give you a table for one by the window. If you cannot look at your husband, you can look at the view. We wish you a wonderful, romantic stay."

168

The one thing this wasn't going to be was a wonderfully romantic stay.

What was she supposed to do? Dance with herself on the balcony? Dine with a mirror in her hand so she could stare into her own eyes?

On the other hand, she did have to eat so she might as well eat in the restaurant tonight.

It was marginally less challenging than finding a restaurant in Paris in her jet-lagged state.

She smiled her thanks, muttered something about Monsieur Porter attending to some urgent business — namely the needs of his lover — and sailed across the elegant marble foyer toward the elevator.

Her suite was on the top floor, the French-style windows opening onto a balcony that offered enviable views of Paris.

Grace stepped onto the balcony and felt the sun on her face.

Happy anniversary, David.

Had he remembered that she'd be arriving in Paris today?

What was he doing now?

She turned away from the view.

She wasn't going to think about David.

To distract herself, she walked back into the suite. It was closer to an apartment than a room, a testament to good taste, decorated with neutral elegance, with no personal touches. Cream, pale peach, touches of gold blended together to create an atmosphere of calm. There was a rosewood chest and exquisite art on the walls. The place felt expensive, which of course it was. It was costing her a small fortune to stay here.

She closed the balcony doors and explored her temporary Paris home. If she was spending the money, then she might as well enjoy it.

The dressing room was larger than her bedroom back home.

She hadn't been looking forward to this, but now she realized how good it was to no longer be at home, surrounded by reminders of David.

She opened her suitcase and hung up her clothes. The silence unnerved her, so she walked back to the balcony and flung open the doors, letting the noise in. Car horns, shouts, street noise — the general cacophony that was Paris.

She closed her eyes, remembering the first time she'd come here.

Eighteen years old and her life so complicated she couldn't begin to untangle it. But she had. She'd created the life she'd always wanted and had never thought for a moment that her life would one day be a mess again.

She walked into the bathroom and gulped at the opulence. It was like something from the Palace of Versailles, all mirrors and gilt. She half expected to find Louis XIV lying in the bath.

There were twin basins and she unloaded her toiletries next to one of them.

The mirrors made it possible to see herself from every angle.

She stared at her reflection, noticing the dark smudges under her eyes. Her complexion was sallow, as if she'd been stored in a dark place for six months. Her hair was lank after the journey and she felt hot and tired. Old.

She'd ignored the years, but she saw them now in the fine lines etched into her skin and the streak of silver peeping between blond strands. She thought about Lissa with her perky breasts and dewy, perfect skin and instinctively stood up straighter.

She turned away, knowing she wouldn't be spending much time in the bathroom. Those mirrors forced reflection in more ways than one. It was tempting to spend her whole time ruminating on the past, but she knew she had to move forward.

It was early afternoon. All she wanted to

do was lie down and sleep, but she knew that if she did that she'd never adjust her sleep pattern.

Instead, she unpacked the rest of her clothes, folding them neatly into the drawers.

If David were here, he'd be watching her with one eyebrow arched.

You don't have to be so obsessively neat, Grace. You're allowed to leave a jacket on a chair or a shoe on the floor.

It had almost been a joke between them, her inability to have any disorder in the house.

It was a habit that had stayed with her long after her parents had died.

With a soft curse, she dragged open the drawer she'd just filled, pulled out a shirt and flung it on the bed.

Her heart started to beat faster. Her palms itched to pick it up and fold it back to neatness, but instead she reached into the drawer again and this time she flung a scarf.

"You see?" She spoke aloud. "I can let things go if I need to, but what's the point? What's so good about living in a mess?"

She stripped off the clothes she'd worn for traveling and dropped them on the floor.

The hotel staff would think she was a madwoman.

She walked into the bathroom and took a shower, washing away all the dirt of the journey.

She'd thought her life was clearly mapped out. Of course David's still was. He'd simply switched certain parts around, namely her. It was like selling one house and seamlessly buying another without the need to go into rental accommodation first.

Her future, however, was not sorted. Unlike him she didn't have a lover waiting in the wings.

How did women meet men when they reached her age? She imagined herself filling in an online profile. What would she say about herself?

Predictable, boring, organized.

Or perhaps she'd learn to relish her single status and travel the world alone. She'd read an article on the plane: You Don't Need a Man to Be Happy.

Grace didn't need a man. She needed David. Her best friend. But he, apparently, didn't need her.

What if he and Lissa had a child together? Sophie would have a stepfamily. What if she chose to spend holidays with her dad, Lissa and the new baby? Grace would hover around the edges of her life.

No! She wasn't going to do that. She

wasn't going to think ahead and make herself miserable.

Fighting her thoughts, she dried her hair, sent a message to both Mimi and Monica, letting them know she'd arrived safely, and then called Sophie.

She was trying hard not to be an intrusive parent, but she needed to hear her daughter's voice.

"Hi, Mom!" Sophie sounded bubbly and happy. There was the sound of chatter and laughter in the background.

Grace smiled. "Where are you?"

"In a bar. We met a bunch of really fun people. We're practicing our Spanish."

A bar? Grace checked her watch to see what time it was in Seville. "You're having fun?"

"It's awesome. We went to a great party last night."

Grace frowned. Sophie had never been a party animal. She'd always been quiet and studious. The only boy she'd ever been interested in was Sam. "Be careful, won't you?"

"Mom, this is *me* you're talking to. I don't know how to be anything but careful."

The noise in the background grew louder and Sophie had to shout to be heard.

"I'd better go, Mom. Talk to you soon."

"Okay! Love you." Grace hung up, missing David more than ever. She wished she had someone to share the anxiety with.

There was Monica, of course, but her friend worried more than she did.

To distract herself, she pulled out the map her grandmother had given her.

She wished Mimi had agreed to come to Paris with her, then she could have shown Grace all her favorite places in person instead of simply drawing them on a map.

Perhaps she'd go for a stroll before dinner, but first she'd lie down just for a few minutes.

She woke three hours later, disorientated and with less than fifteen minutes until her dinner reservation.

She sprang off the bed, ignoring the wave of dizziness that was a combination of jet lag and months of sleep deprivation.

She applied her makeup, slid into a dress that was smart but not too over-the-top, grabbed her bag and made her way to dinner. On her own.

She could read a book, but she'd left hers on the plane and hadn't yet bought another. After dinner she'd find that bookshop her grandmother had talked about, but for now she was going to have to stare out of the window and try hard not to look as if her husband had abandoned her.

The moment she entered the restaurant, she knew this had been a mistake.

This wasn't a place where single women came to gaze out of windows. This was a place for romance and fine dining.

She was about to turn around and head back to her room, when the headwaiter spotted her.

"Madame Porter."

How was it everyone knew who she was? She'd come here to disappear, but this hotel prided itself on personal service.

Grace followed him to the table laid for one in the window of the restaurant. Usually she loved traveling. She loved the sights and smells of new places, the discovery of local food, the sheer unfamiliarity of it all.

Right now she couldn't access the usual feelings of excitement.

Feeling conspicuous, she looked at the menu.

She ordered a steak, and refused the suggestion of red wine.

The couple next to her, both of them effortlessly elegant, were laughing at a shared joke.

Another couple nearby kept reaching across the table and clasping hands.

Grace picked up her water. Maybe she

should have made an exception and ordered wine. She needed something to numb her misery.

Some people loved solo travel. She was clearly doing it wrong.

At the end of the most excruciating evening of her life, Grace exited the restaurant and pulled out Mimi's map.

"Madame Porter." The concierge smiled at her. "Can I help you with something?"

Grace held out the map. "I'm trying to find a bookshop."

The concierge studied the marks on her map and gave her directions.

Stepping through the door of the hotel, she felt the warmth of the sun.

It was late evening, and the whole of Paris was bathed in a summer glow.

Grace still had that slightly fuzzy-headed feeling that followed a transatlantic flight, but she hoisted her bag onto her shoulder and followed the path along the river.

It was as busy as it had been in the middle of the day, and her spirits lifted slightly as she watched the evening river cruisers drift slowly past her. Music and laughter floated downstream along with the boats.

Philippe.

The memory was so vivid, she stopped walking.

It had been exactly this time of year. She'd been desperate to go on a river cruise. Neither she nor Philippe had the money so instead they'd taken the Batobus, the water taxi that stopped off at various points along the Seine.

It was from the river that she'd caught her first glimpse of the Musée d'Orsay, Notre Dame and the Louvre. From the water you could see the entire facade of the famous Grande Galerie and the Pavillon de Flore. There was no commentary, of course, but she hadn't needed one because she'd been with Philippe, a native Parisian, who had kept his arms wrapped around her as he'd volunteered his knowledge of Paris.

They'd jumped off so that he could show her the Eiffel Tower, and then caught the last boat back. He'd kissed her as the sun was setting over the famous Pont Neuf, the oldest standing bridge over the river Seine.

Grace blinked, surprised that the memory could still be so vivid after so many years.

What was Philippe doing now?

She'd never looked him up or tried to find him on social media. The past was a door she'd never wanted to walk back through. She was only thinking of him now because this was Paris.

Would she have thought of Philippe if she'd

been with David?

Focusing on the present, she strolled across the bridge as the concierge had instructed and followed the river on the other side toward the cathedral of Notre Dame. She ducked away from the river and here the streets were narrow, cobbled and shady. People were buying ice cream, browsing in boutique stores and strolling along enjoying the late-evening sunshine.

Grace glanced at the map and tried to orientate herself. Engrossed in working out where she was, she wasn't aware of the man approaching from behind until he shoved her.

She flew off balance and landed hard on the cobbles. Her ankle twisted under her and her shoulder smacked into concrete, followed by her head. There was an explosion of pain. *This is it. This is where I die.*

Even in her dazed state, she imagined the headline.

Body of jilted wife found in Paris.

A tug on her shoulder brought her back to the present and she realized the man had snatched her bag.

"No!" All her valuables were in her bag. Passport. Money. ID. A photo of Sophie smiling on a trip to the beach.

The man was already sprinting away.

"Stop!"

A few tourists turned their heads, but this wasn't Woodbrook, where the man's identity would have been known to all. No one knew who he was and no one cared. Grace had craved the anonymity of a big city, but right now the big city wasn't her friend.

Someone streaked past her. She heard the rhythmic thump of boots on cobbles and then a girl launched herself at the man, the weight of her and the surprise of the assault making him stagger. He collapsed onto the cobbles, howling and swearing. Grace watched in horror as he took a swing at the girl, but she grabbed his arm, twisted it behind his back and sat on him hard.

"Merde . . ." She fired off a volley of words, most of which Grace didn't understand.

She'd thought her French was fluent, but it seemed she still had a few curses to learn.

The girl glared down at him. She reminded Grace of a very angry tiger cub.

"You think you're so tough? Remember which one of us is lying facedown on the floor right now."

Grace struggled to a sitting position feeling bruised and inadequate. Here she was wondering if she had what it took to spend a month alone in Paris, and there was this girl who looked barely older than Sophie chasing down a criminal.

"Is this all he took?" The girl waved the bag at Grace and in doing so lost her balance.

The man took instant advantage, twisted away from underneath her and sprinted away before she could grab him again.

"Well, shit —" The girl clambered to her feet. "I should have punched him and had done with it. There's the proof that nonviolent solutions never work." Her eyes were fierce and her mouth set in a determined line. Her hair was a vibrant red and tumbled past her shoulders in crazy curls. She had to keep scooping it back to stop it falling over her eyes. Her skirt was the shortest Grace had ever seen, her legs were bare and she was wearing a pair of heavy boots.

"Lowlife." Scowling, the girl dusted off her legs and handed the bag to Grace. "You'd better check everything is there."

"I don't know what to say." Grace checked her bag, relieved to have it safely returned. She stood up, trying to assess the damage. Her head hurt and her shoulder hurt, but the worst damage was to her pride. "Are you injured?"

"Me? Nah. I landed on him. He'll probably feel it for a while, though." That thought obviously gave her satisfaction and it gave Grace satisfaction, too.

"I don't know how to thank you. I arrived in Paris today. Everything important is in my bag. If I'd lost it —"

The girl shrugged. "You didn't, so no biggie."

"We should probably find a gendarme and report it."

"Why? The police have bigger things to deal with. And anyway, I don't know enough French to report a crime. I can say my name, and I can say *I don't understand*. I have no idea what the French for *this asshole stole a bag* is. Do you?"

"I'd probably find a different way of saying it. My French is pretty good."

"Lucky for you. And if you don't hang on to your bag, you're going to need that French." The girl straightened her strap top. "Your head is bleeding. You'd better come into the shop. You can clean up inside and then get a cab back to wherever it is you're staying."

Her head was throbbing and so was her ankle.

"You've been kind. And I don't even know your name."

"Audrey."

"I'm Grace. You're British? Are you on holiday? Working in Paris for the summer?"

"Yeah. I live over the bookshop." The girl gestured along the street. "I was on my way home when I saw him grab your bag. You don't look good. Are you going to faint?"

"No." Grace analyzed her spinning head. "I'll be fine, but I will take up your offer of cleaning up before I go back to my hotel. I don't want to attract attention." She could just imagine the reaction of the staff if she limped in with her head bleeding and her hands skinned.

"It's down this street. It's closed now, but I have a key." Audrey slowed her pace so that Grace could keep up.

"You work in the bookshop?"

"Mornings. My payment is an apartment for the summer and enough money to buy one croissant a day. Unless I can find another job, I'm going to lose weight." She paused outside a door, and Grace realized that this was the bookshop she'd been looking for when she'd been assaulted.

"I was coming here." She gazed up at the windows, enchanted. "My grandmother is French. She used to visit this place when she lived in Paris." And she still didn't understand it. Why would Mimi have been interested in a bookshop?

"Well, I don't think they've cleaned since that time, so you're probably seeing the same dust bunnies she did. I hope you don't have asthma or anything, because if you do you're pretty much dead." Audrey unlocked the door and pushed it open. A bell jangled noisily.

The girl dumped her bag on the floor and grabbed a chair. "Sit. I'll clean up your head."

Feeling unsteady, Grace sat.

Audrey vanished through a door and reemerged with a first aid kit.

She poured something onto gauze and cleaned Grace's head. Her hands, if not exactly gentle, were quick and efficient. "So you don't travel much?"

"I travel, but not usually alone."

"The first rule is you've got to keep your bag close. Keep the strap across your body." Audrey threw away the gauze. "And don't stop in the middle of the street and look at the map. That shrieks tourist. Look up your route before you leave the hotel and if you have to check where you are, then do it discreetly. If you speak French, you can just ask for directions."

"Yes." What had she been thinking? It wasn't as if she'd never left Connecticut. "I can't believe you caught him."

"You can thank years of almost missing the school bus. That's my best running

184

distance." Audrey pressed a dressing to Grace's head and taped it down. "Now let's look at your ankle. Is it broken?"

Audrey was the most capable teenager Grace had ever encountered. What would Sophie have done in the same situation? She wouldn't have chased after a man and brought him down with a few moves.

"It's not broken. You brought him crashing to the ground. Where did you learn to do that?"

"I did martial arts at school. Can't throw a ball to save my life, but I have a great turning kick." Audrey ran her fingers over the bruising. "It's swelling up a bit. Same thing happened to one of my friends at Sports Day last year. You probably shouldn't walk on that for a few days. Put ice on it."

Feeling a little better, Grace looked around the bookshop. "This place is like paradise."

"I'm pretty sure paradise smells better than this. Also, shouldn't paradise be sunny and full of drinks with those cute umbrellas in them?"

"But to work in a bookshop — it's a dream, isn't it?"

"Maybe. I'm mostly doing it for the apartment."

"If you don't speak French, how are you

going to serve customers?"

Audrey shrugged. "Sign language? And I'm learning a few words. I'm using an app. It's pretty good."

"You seem to know plenty of swear words."

"Yeah, a friend taught me the useful stuff." The girl closed the first aid kit. "So how did you learn French?"

"I'm a teacher. I teach French and Spanish."

Audrey's expression blanked. It was like watching a door slamming shut. "We'd better get you back to wherever it is you're staying. Can you walk or do you want me to get you a cab?"

The thought of going back to the hotel didn't appeal to Grace at all. She would have liked to stay longer, but she sensed Audrey didn't want her. Had she somehow upset her? "I don't suppose I could buy a book while I'm here?"

"Go ahead. There's enough of them. Where are you staying?"

"At the Hotel Antoinette."

Audrey wrinkled her nose. "That's the expensive one that looks like a palace."

"That's the one." An idea came to her. "You should come over one evening and have dinner with me."

186

"Are you kidding?" Audrey shoved the first aid kit into the cupboard. "Your husband would love that, I'll bet. Me tagging along on a romantic break."

"My husband isn't with me. He's back home, with the woman he left me for." She couldn't believe she'd blurted it out to a stranger. She expected Audrey to shift uncomfortably and make some excuse that meant she could leave, but the girl didn't budge. She tilted her head, giving Grace her full attention.

"That sucks. So you're here on your own?"

"It was that or cancel it. And I can't believe I just told you that."

Audrey shrugged. "Friends and family all have opinions and feel they have to fix things, and sometimes all you want is someone to listen."

The girl had summarized the discomfort of it in a single sentence. "I don't normally discuss details of my private life with people I don't know."

"Don't worry about it. My old boss in the hair salon where I worked always said that we know more about people's problems than priests and psychologists." Audrey wiped her forehead with the back of her hand. "I'm glad you didn't cancel. The bastard. I mean, it happens a lot, of course.

People breaking up. Women come into the salon all the time wanting a makeover to make themselves feel better. But not after twenty-five years. You'd think after that long most people would know what they wanted."

"David knew what he wanted. Unfortunately, it wasn't me."

Oh, shut up, Grace!

To take her mind off it, Grace browsed the shelves.

"I hope you're posting happy pictures all over social media to make him jealous. *#lovemylife* or maybe *#greattobesingle* — that kind of thing."

"Right now I'm not sure I *do* love my life, and it doesn't feel so great to be single. I liked being married to him."

She selected a book and flicked through it, more as a way of hiding her emotion than because she was interested.

"I still think you should show him you're doing great. Living well is the best revenge, right?"

"I'm not sure I'm a particularly vengeful person." She put the book back. "Nor am I living well."

"So? The purpose of social media is to show everyone the life you *wish* you were living, not the one you're *actually* living.

Most people are living two lives. The one they let people see, and the real one."

David had been living two lives, hadn't he? With two women.

Grace wondered what Audrey's other life was like. She seemed both incredibly young, and unusually mature at the same time.

"I mean it about dinner. Please join me." She pulled a pretty edition of Madame Bovary off the shelf. "If not tomorrow, then any night."

"Dinner in that place costs, like, a million euros."

"My budget for this holiday included two people. Now there's just one of me."

"So what you're saying is that I'd be doing you a favor." Audrey grinned. "I guess I could choke down a prime steak if it would help you out, although I should warn you that I left my ball gown at home."

Grace thought about the stuffy restaurant. She didn't want Audrey to feel uncomfortable and she wasn't in a hurry to go back there herself. "We could order room service. The suite has a balcony. We can eat there." She opened her purse and handed Audrey enough money to cover the book.

"You're in a suite? You must be seriously rich." Audrey stuck the money in her pocket. "I probably should have swiped your

189

bag myself."

"I'm not rich. I've saved for this trip for a year and they gave me an upgrade. Shouldn't you put the money in the till?"

"I'll do it later. Dinner tomorrow." She pondered. "Shame to waste your upgrade. Thanks. I won't say no to a free meal."

Grace gazed around the bookshelves, wondering how much the place had changed since Mimi was here. She took a few photos to send to her grandmother. "How long have you been here?"

"Arrived today. Tomorrow is my first working day."

Grace scribbled down her phone number. "I hope it goes well, but if you need translation help — or anything at all — call me."

Audrey shrugged. "It's a load of old books. Books don't talk. How bad can it be?"

AUDREY

It was bad.

Hardly surprising really. Here she was, Audrey Hackett, the girl who everyone had agreed was least likely to succeed, working in a bookshop. Not only that, she was in *charge* of a bookshop. She had the keys in her pocket. She could hire and fire, although that power was limited by the fact she was the only person here.

Her and about a million old books.

If she sat here long enough, maybe the contents of the books would seep inside her brain and make her clever.

She spun around on the chair. It reminded her of the roundabout in the park where she'd often met Meena for lunch. She felt a pang. She didn't miss the chaos of home, but she missed Hardy, and Meena of course, and she missed the buzz of the hair salon.

The bookshop was eerily quiet.

As she was the only person here she stood

up, posed in front of one of the bookshelves and took a selfie while wearing her new glasses. Meena had typed some hashtags into the notes app on her phone, so Audrey pasted them next to her picture. *#bookish Audrey #loveParis*

She wondered if she should add *#bored rigid* but decided it had too many letters.

Also, there was no way she was admitting that her life was less than perfect.

With luck her old English teacher would see her post and feel shame that she'd so badly underestimated Audrey. She could imagine the chat in the staff room — *Audrey, working in a bookshop? I feel terrible that I didn't encourage her more.*

She allowed herself a little daydream where she won the Nobel Prize for fiction, and gave a big speech thanking her teachers for giving her the motivation to prove them wrong.

Except that they weren't wrong, were they? What was she good at, really?

She was good at washing hair and good at making people laugh. She'd been told she was a good listener. Not exactly the "marketable skills" the careers department were always talking about.

On paper, working in a bookshop looked impressive. It was a shame it was about as thrilling as waiting for nail polish to dry. And she was starting to panic that she might not get a job in a hair salon, after all. So far, they'd all said no to her. She was ticking them off her list one by one and she had more to see this afternoon, but she was starting to lose hope. There was an upmarket salon a few steps away from the bookshop, but Audrey hadn't bothered talking to them. A place like that was never going to employ someone like her.

What if she couldn't get a job? How would she eat?

The door opened, the bell clanged and an elderly man stepped through the door. Something about the way he held himself — straight, spine elongated — made Audrey think that perhaps he'd once been in the military. But that would have been a long time ago. His hair was white and stuck out in uneven tufts at the side of his head. Her fingers itched to reach for scissors. She knew she could improve his look.

"Bonjour." Audrey hoped that if she dazzled him with her smile, he'd be too distracted to ask her a question about the books. Fortunately he didn't seem to want any assistance. He greeted her politely, walked stiffly to a section at the back of the shop and browsed for half an hour.

Audrey watched, curious, as he selected a book from a shelf, flicked through it, then put it back and picked up the one next to it. After half an hour he left, giving her a nod and a smile on his way out.

Totally weird. Still, he hadn't slipped one into his pocket as far as she could see, so what he was doing with those books was none of her business.

If he wanted to flick dust on himself, that was up to him.

Audrey decided that if everyone was as undemanding as the old man, the job might not be so awful. She was a book babysitter, that was all.

Her luck didn't last.

The next three people to walk into the shop all spoke French and grew more and more impatient when Audrey looked at them blankly in response to their questions.

One man became so enraged she was afraid he might burst a blood vessel.

"It's just a book," she muttered, starting to feel stressed and flustered. At least when someone yelled at you in your own language you could defend yourself.

The more he shouted, the stupider she felt.

In the end he stormed out, slamming the door behind him.

194

"And you have a nice day, too!" Audrey yelled at the closed door, before slumping in her chair. She was starting to wonder if a free apartment was worth all this aggravation.

Her next customer was an Englishman in his fifties who clearly didn't believe in shaving or using deodorant.

"What do you have on the French Revolution?"

Audrey checked the chart she'd been given, but couldn't make any sense of it so instead she gestured vaguely. "French history is over there. If it's not on the shelf, we don't have it."

"I'm writing a book."

"Good for you." Audrey glanced around her. It seemed to her that there were already more than enough books out there, but who was she to judge? "Keep at it. You can do anything if you try."

She didn't believe it for a moment. If it was true, then she'd be able to read without getting to the end of the page and discovering she couldn't remember what had happened at the beginning. But she kept that fact to herself. People needed encouragement, not the truth. If her teachers had been more encouraging, maybe she would have done better.

Or if her mother had preferred her to a bottle of cheap wine.

She rubbed her hand over her ribs, trying to ease the constant burn of anxiety and guilt.

Had she done the wrong thing leaving her? What if Ron wasn't up to the job?

She'd longed for freedom and to spread her wings, but she felt as if her wings were locked together by a chain, preventing her from flying.

To stop herself worrying about her mother, she thought about Grace.

Audrey wondered how she was doing after her scary incident. She felt sorry for her, although part of her found it reassuring to know that there were other people out there whose lives were crap, too. Usually she felt as if she was the only one.

If Audrey had booked a fancy trip to Paris and her husband had left her for another woman, she would have emptied their joint account, killed him and then taken the holiday.

Maybe that was why the man had managed to snatch Grace's handbag. She probably hadn't been concentrating. For five minutes Audrey had felt like a hero, and she'd never felt that way before. She was used to rescuing her mother, but no one ever thanked her for that. And no one had ever offered to buy her a meal in a fancy restaurant. If she ate as much as she could, she wouldn't have to spend money on food for a couple of days. She'd be like that python she'd read about once, digesting slowly.

A woman stepped up to the desk. "Do you have anything on Coco?"

Audrey looked at her blankly. "Cocoa? You mean like chocolate?"

"Coco Chanel. The famous couturier. Dress designer."

"Oh, right." Would that be under clothing or famous people? She waved a hand. "Try the middle shelf on the right."

"You're waving to the shelf on the left."

Left. Right. It was all the same to Audrey. "My waving wasn't related to the position of the shelf. It was more general in nature. Be careful on the ladder, it has a mind of its own."

"I'm scared of heights. Could you do it for me?"

Audrey was more scared of books than heights, but she hauled herself out of the chair and clomped her way to the ladder. The titles blurred in front of her eyes. She squinted, trying hard to read them but some of the letters were faded, which didn't help.

She decided old books were even harder to read than new books. The dust made her nose tingle. "No. We don't have anything. Sorry."

She scrambled back down the ladder, sneezed twice and faced her very unsatisfied customer.

The back of her neck prickled with sweat.

At least when people were having their hair done they were usually happy.

It turned out to be the longest morning of her life and she found herself on the receiving end of as many disapproving frowns as she had when she'd been at school. Her greatest skill, being chatty and friendly, wasn't any use to her here. It was hard to be chatty when your entire vocabulary consisted of swear words.

As lunchtime approached, she checked the time on her phone. She was going to spend the afternoon trailing around hair salons again.

The door opened again. The jangle of the bell was starting to drive Audrey insane. The sound of it made her edgy and nervous.

The whole of Paris lay beyond their door. Why people wanted to spend their time in a musty bookshop she had no idea.

She got up, braced for another elderly visitor but this time it was a young man. She guessed him to be in his early twenties.

His hair was dark and a few strands flopped over his forehead. He had the bluest eyes she'd ever seen and the easy confidence of someone who life hadn't yet taken a swipe at. His jeans were faded and snug around his hips and his biceps pushed at the sleeves of his T-shirt.

There was no way someone who looked like him would choose to spend time in a bookshop, so Audrey assumed he was lost. Wherever he was going, she hoped he'd take her with him.

"Can I help you?" It was one of the few phrases she knew in French, but something about the way he was looking at her sent all words flying from her head.

"I'm Etienne."

Audrey stared at him. "You're kidding." She already had a clear image of Etienne in her head and he looked nothing like this. It took her a moment to align expectation with reality.

This guy with the crooked, sexy smile was Etienne?

"I don't generally joke about my own name." His smile was wide and genuine. "You must be Audrey." He spoke perfect English, with just enough of an accent to make Audrey's knees wobble. He reminded her of a slightly edgy film star from one of those foreign movies you had to watch with subtitles. Audrey hated subtitles. She'd barely got to the end of the first word when they vanished from the screen.

"Yeah, I'm Audrey." She stuck out her hand, conscious that it was probably filthy from handling ancient books. Still, if he worked here, then he had to be used to that. "You're not what I was expecting." She was desperate to text Meena. *I met this super cute guy.*

"What were you expecting?"

Bookish and boring.

"Someone different." Great, Audrey. Knock him dead with your verbal repartee. He probably thought she was stupid, except he was still holding her hand and looking at her in a way that made her feel all melty, like ice cream on a hot day. She felt a jolt of electricity. A connection.

"I am early for my shift. I wanted to meet you. Most people who come to this place are decades older than us. That gives us something in common."

"It does." The idea of having something in common with him cheered Audrey.

He finally let go of her hand, swung his backpack from his shoulder and pulled out a laptop. "Working here is great because you have time to study."

"Good to know." *Kill me now.* If there was one thing worse than working in a book-shop, it had to be studying while working in a bookshop.

"I'm hoping to get this essay done this afternoon in the quiet moments."

"You have an essay to do? In the summer holidays?"

"I'm taking extra classes."

Of course he was. Someone who looked like him was bound to have flaws.

Etienne switched on his laptop. "How are you enjoying the bookshop?"

"Love it," Audrey lied. "Working here is my dream."

"Mine, too." He gave her that smile again. "You love to read?"

"Doesn't everyone?" The idea that they might have lots in common died a death. Still, with looks like that did it matter? As long as he didn't want to talk about books, they should be okay. And if he did — well, some girls faked orgasms. She was going to have to fake book interest.

He entered his password and opened a document. "Who are your favorite authors?"

"Oh, you know —" Daunted by the dense lines of French on his screen, Audrey fumbled for an answer. "The usual."

"The usual?"

Audrey had that same frozen feeling that came with exam pressure. Her brain stalled. She couldn't think of a single author. Why hadn't he asked her about movies? That was her idea of relaxation, not slogging through a book.

"Too many to name." She stood up, hoping her tight jeans might distract him. Did that make her shallow? Probably, but Audrey was fine with shallow. She wanted a relationship to be fun. She didn't want drama or intensity. Her life was already full of it.

She walked across the shop to shelve a book. Why, oh, why, did he have to be a book lover? The world obviously hated her. As she pushed it onto the shelf, Etienne frowned.

"It should be alphabetical, within the botany section."

Audrey felt heat flood her cheeks. She didn't know what botany was, and she couldn't spell it. She always got her *b*s and *d*s mixed up.

"It will be fine here." She thrust it into a gap on the shelves and caught his quizzical gaze. "What?"

"Nothing." He brushed his hair away from his face and it immediately fell back in the same place. "So tell me about you. You live in London? With your parents?"

"Yes." It occurred to her that here, in her new life, she was lying as much as she had in her old one. "You?"

"My parents have an apartment in Paris that I use in the summer. They go to their house in the Côte d'Azur."

Audrey had no idea where that was, but she nodded knowledgably. He obviously had parents who didn't reel around drunk most of the time. "Nice."

An apartment in Paris could be good. Convenient. Better than her place, for sure. She couldn't see herself having sex against that iron bed frame upstairs. And then there was the fact that the room was boiling hot.

"This is a summer job for you, or a gap year?"

"Just the summer at the moment, but I might stay on longer." It depended what happened with her mum and Ron. She still hadn't adjusted to not having to check up on her every moment. She checked her phone every hour for messages, but so far there had been nothing. Audrey wasn't sure if that was a good thing or a bad thing.

"You are going to university?"

Her most hated question.

"I'm not going to university yet. I want to

live life a little first."

She was putting studying behind her forever.

Etienne picked up the small stack of books on the desk that Audrey hadn't touched and started shelving them.

At least now she wouldn't have to put them in all the wrong places. "Thanks."

"No problem. So, are you going to be learning French while you're here? That's what most people do. They work here in the mornings, go to classes in the afternoon and evenings. That is why you are in France, no? For the language?"

"Yes. And also for the culture. I love art." It wasn't really a lie, was it? The truth was she didn't know anything about art. Maybe she *would* love it.

"You have visited the Louvre?"

"Not yet."

"If you like, I could show you round." He colored slightly, saying, "But no pressure."

She imagined the two of them strolling together along cobbled streets. Maybe they'd hold hands. Eventually, perhaps, they'd go back to his place. "Sure. If you have time." She was careful not to look too enthusiastic.

"Anything in particular you want to see?"

"I haven't been here before, so anything is great."

"We ought to pick just a couple of things. The Louvre is big, and you can have too much of a good thing." He flashed her a smile, and she smiled back.

He was gorgeous, and he gained plus points for not wanting to grow old in a museum.

"I'm not going to have a lot of free time. I'm looking for another job."

"Waitressing?"

Clearly he'd never seen Audrey trying to read a menu. "I'm a hairdresser." Technically she wasn't *actually* a hairdresser, but she might as well give herself a promotion as no one else was going to do it.

He looked bemused. "If you're holding down two jobs, how are you going to learn French?"

"Evenings?"

"I could help you with that, too, if you like."

She imagined the two of them sprawled across her bed in her attic room. He'd be trying to improve her pronunciation and his mouth would drift toward hers —

Unfortunately, for that scenario to become reality she'd actually have to learn French and that was never going to happen.

"Let's see how it goes, but thanks." She stood up. "As you're here now, I presume I can go?"

"Of course. I will see you tomorrow. I look forward to it." He gave her a long look that made her knees quiver.

"Me, too."

Pathetic. She could at least have thought of something funny to say. All she had going for her was her sense of humor and that seemed to have deserted her.

She ran up the stairs to her room and spent five minutes on her hair and makeup. The first thing people did when they walked into a salon was look at the hair of the people who worked there so she needed to make a good first impression. She needed a job, and she needed it fast.

She knew she was good with hair. To her it was an art form, although not the sort of art they displayed in the Louvre.

She picked up a hairbrush and some product, and then spritzed, sprayed and twisted until she achieved a look she was satisfied with. Then she rummaged through her clothes. In the end she grabbed an oversize T-shirt she'd stolen from Ron. She belted it around the middle and stared at herself in the mirror.

It worked, even if she did look a little like

a Roman centurion.

She locked the door and headed downstairs into the sunshine.

She walked past the posh salon and paused.

Oh, hell, why not? They could only tell her to get lost.

She pushed open the door, braced for rejection.

The owner's name was Sylvie and she spoke reasonable English. Instead of an interview, she asked Audrey to wash her hair.

For once, Audrey was able to demonstrate her skills. She'd smoothed, stroked, massaged and rinsed and tried not to think about the salon at home and what everyone was doing there.

Sylvie hired her on the spot.

Audrey was stunned. It was too good to be true. "But — I can't chat in French." She felt compelled to point that out in case the woman hadn't understood her deficiencies in that area.

Sylvie shrugged. "Sometimes they prefer silence. A head massage is a good time to be quiet with your thoughts, no? More important, you have gentle hands and you pay attention."

Audrey couldn't believe it. She'd got the

job. *She'd got the job!* She was so pathetically grateful and relieved that she wanted to hug Sylvie and dance around the sleek, elegant salon, but she managed to contain herself and simply muttered her thanks in both languages.

Something had gone her way at last.

Having signed some forms and firmed up details, she left the salon and punched the air.

When would Sylvie pay her? Did she have enough money to stretch that long?

She was in the mood for celebrating and headed to Grace's hotel.

Grace had written down details of her suite, so Audrey slipped on a pair of oversize sunglasses, hoisted her bag over her shoulder and strode across the marble lobby as if she knew where she was going and had every right to be there.

The suites were on the top floor of the hotel, identifiable by the names outside each door.

She was squinting at a set of letters when a door opened along the corridor and Grace appeared.

"There you are! I was on the balcony and saw you arrive."

Hiding her relief, Audrey loped along the corridor and into the suite.

The first thing she noticed was how tidy it was. She thought about her own apartment. All the outfits she'd tried on were still strewn over the bed. She'd have to clear them up before she went to sleep. She knew for a fact she'd left two pairs of shoes on the floor, and she hadn't washed up her breakfast bowl.

Her apartment looked well and truly lived in. Trashed, even. This place looked as if no one had ever stayed here.

Grace closed the door. She was wearing a tailored dress and looked as if she was about to go for a job interview. "I'm pleased you came. I wasn't sure you would."

If she'd understood the state of Audrey's finances, she wouldn't have been in any doubt.

How much was it okay to eat without looking rude?

She wondered if she could drop a couple of bread rolls into her bag unnoticed.

"This place is like a palace." Audrey gazed up at the ornate ceiling. "Not sure I'd want to do it in the bed with all those babies staring down at me."

"They're cherubs."

"Whatever. It's unnerving."

Grace smiled. "Are you hungry? We should probably go ahead and order. It might take a while for them to bring it if they're busy in the kitchen."

"Sure." What Audrey fancied was a juicy burger with everything on top but she was pretty sure a place like this wouldn't do burgers. They probably only served fancy food where you were given a mouthful of something and expected to drool over how beautiful it was. "How is your ankle?"

"I've rested it today, so not too bad. It would have been a whole lot worse if it hadn't been for you." Grace held out a menu. "Take a look and tell me what you'd like to eat."

Audrey recoiled as if someone had handed her a live cobra. "I can't read French. You choose."

"This menu is in English, so you'll be fine."

Audrey took the menu and stared at the page in her hand.

The words swam, jumbled in front of her eyes.

The one time in her life she could pick anything from the menu, and she couldn't even see her options. The more her stress levels rose, the more elusive the words, and in that moment she realized that her nightmare hadn't ended with school. She hadn't left it behind. It was going to come along with her for the rest of her life. Every time she met a guy she liked. Every time someone handed her a menu. Anytime someone asked if she'd read a certain book —

She thought about Etienne. *What's your favorite book?*

No one was going to want to be with someone as stupid as her.

Audrey blinked. She wasn't going to cry. She never cried in public.

Just take a guess, Audrey.

"I'll have the steak." There was bound to be steak on the menu. This was France. "And chips. Fries. Whatever they call them here."

Grace glanced at the menu over her shoulder. "Which steak? Which sauce?"

Surely steak was steak.

Audrey thrust the menu back at Grace. "Whatever. You choose. Thanks."

"What about a starter?"

"I'll have whatever you're having."

"I'm having escargots. Snails."

"Snails?" Audrey felt her stomach roll. "That's gross. Who eats snails?"

"They're a delicacy. I know it sounds strange, but they really are good. I'll order, and you can try one."

Over her dead body. And if she ate a snail she would definitely end up as a dead body.

"Soup will be great." Thank goodness she hadn't picked something randomly from the menu. Being confronted by a plate of snails would have been a low point even for her, and she'd had her fair share.

"Take a look at the drinks menu." Grace pushed it across to her, and Audrey started to wish she'd never come.

"I'm pretty thirsty. I'll have anything fizzy."

"In that case I can get you something from the mini bar."

She expected Grace to hand her a sugary drink of some sort, but instead she mixed juice with sparkling water, added crushed ice and a few slices of fresh orange and handed it to Audrey.

"I always find sparkling water refreshing in this hot weather, and the hotel leave slices of fresh fruit. Try that."

Audrey poked at the orange slices. "I don't eat fruit." She saw the shock in Grace's eyes.

"You don't like fruit?"

Audrey shrugged. "It's more that I can't be bothered."

"What about vegetables?"

"I eat tomato if it's on a pizza. And peas. I like peas."

"Right, well —" Grace recovered slightly. "Try the drink. The orange sweetens it,

212

that's all."

Audrey sipped. "It tastes pretty good. What about you? This is France. Aren't you supposed to be drinking a full-bodied red wine or something?"

Grace prepared herself the same drink as Audrey. "I'm not much of a drinker."

That was one of the great things about being an adult — you didn't have to pretend to do things just to be cool. Anytime Audrey was at a party, she had to find a way to pretend she was drinking without actually drinking. To admit that she didn't drink alcohol would have been like painting a target on herself.

"Chocolate," Audrey said. "I'm addicted to chocolate. How about you?"

"I'm not addicted to anything." Grace turned away and Audrey was left with that same uneasy feeling she always had with her mother.

She was never quite sure what she'd said to cause offense, but she'd said *some*thing. Her mother changed mood with the wind. Grace was obviously the same.

Instantly on guard, she put her glass down. "Can I use your bathroom?"

"Of course. Door on the left."

Left.

Audrey's heart beat faster. Left.

213

She made a guess, walked confidently to the nearest door and found herself in the dressing room.

Fuck. Fuck, fuck, fuckity fuck.

She turned, burning up with humiliation and saw Grace frowning.

"Audrey —"

"Yeah, yeah, I'm an idiot, I know. I don't listen properly. I've had a long day, I'm tired, I'm not thinking straight —"

"It's this one." Grace stood up and walked to a different door.

"Thanks. I knew that." Audrey pushed past her. This wasn't a treat, it was torture.

She locked the door and stared in the mirror, willing herself to get back under control.

She had to get out of here. She'd say she felt sick.

And she was never, ever eating with some stranger she'd never met before, even if they seemed kind on the surface. Her mother was kind occasionally, but it was like petting a dog. You never knew when it might bite.

Taking a deep breath, she left the bathroom. "Actually, I'm not feeling too good, so I thought I'd take off."

"Oh!" Grace looked startled. "Why? We haven't eaten yet."

"Look — I —" Audrey glanced around

desperately, wishing she'd never come. Even for a free meal, this wasn't worth it. "This place isn't me, okay?"

Grace gave a faint smile. "It isn't me, either. Why do you think I invited you here tonight? I couldn't face eating in that stuffy restaurant on my own again. Please stay, Audrey. It's a lovely sunny evening. It will be fun. I was thinking that we could people watch from the balcony. How do you like your steak?"

Audrey stood frozen, torn between wanting to get the hell out of here and consume a free steak. The hunger pains won. "Cooked?"

Grace walked to the phone. She spoke in rapid and fluent French that left Audrey feeling more inadequate than ever and then joined her on the balcony.

The view was incredible.

Audrey fished around for something to say. "So how long are you staying here?"

"I booked a month, but I'm not sure I'm going to make it that long." Grace sat down.

Everything about her was tidy, Audrey thought. Her dress was ironed and perfect, and she was wearing tights. *Who wore tights in summer?*

"This place would be, like, most people's dream."

"I think with the right person, it might be." Grace stared across the flower-festooned balcony toward the Eiffel Tower.

You didn't need to be a genius to work out she was thinking about her husband.

Why did anyone bother with love when it was so complicated?

"So your husband left and you were stuck with this holiday. You didn't have anyone else you could bring?" Audrey sipped her water. "Do you have kids?"

"I have a daughter the same age as you. She's traveling with a friend this summer. I miss her terribly, but don't tell her I said that. I expect your mother feels the same way about you."

Audrey knew for a fact her mother wouldn't be missing her at all. She hadn't been in touch with Audrey, except to reply to a text.

Fortunately she'd had an email from Ron earlier, telling her not to worry about her mother.

She wasn't sure it was good news that he seemed to realize there was something to worry about.

"You should probably immediately take a French lover. The hottest guy you can find."

"And what? Post his picture all over social media?"

Audrey shrugged. "Yeah, go for it. Lip-lock by the river Seine at sunset, eye gazing, bubbles rising in champagne — that kind of thing. Hashtag *stuff you.*"

Grace gave a tentative smile. "That's not the kind of person I am." She sat back in her chair. "I envy you working in the book-shop. Mimi — my grandmother — has talked a lot about it over the years. Are you hoping to study English when you get to college?"

"I'm not going to college. I'm going to get a job." Why did it make her feel embarrassed to admit that? What was so good about run-ning up a ton of student debt? She glanced at Grace, expecting judgment. "I'm pretty good with hair. I thought I might do extra training. Get to be really good, you know?" She waited for Grace to make a dismissive comment about hairdressing as a career choice, but she didn't.

"Your hair is beautiful," she said, "so I can already see how good you'd be at that. And you are such a great listener. You'd be warm and kind, not scary like some hair-dressers."

There was a knock on the door and their food arrived.

Audrey resisted the temptation to snatch it out of their hands.

They unloaded the food onto the table and then raised the silver domes with a dramatic flourish that seemed deserving of a round of applause.

Audrey struggled to keep her eyes from rolling, but then she caught Grace's eye and saw she was laughing. Relieved, Audrey allowed herself to smile, too.

When they were on their own again, Grace pushed a large bowl of fries toward her. "I ordered two large bowls. If you're anything like my daughter, Sophie, you'll eat them both."

"I can't believe anyone could find a hairdresser scary. I mean, this place is scary. Serious-looking waiters, terrifying menus, all that shiny gold everywhere — What's that?" Audrey pointed to something red in a small bowl. "It's not snail's blood or anything?"

"It's ketchup."

"No kidding." Audrey poked it with her knife to check. "I've only ever had ketchup from a bottle."

"Me, too. I wonder if they employ someone specifically to decant ketchup into tiny bowls?"

Audrey decided that Grace might look stuffy, but she didn't act stuffy. She dipped a fry in the ketchup, forcing herself to pause before devouring the steak. "How can a hairdresser be scary?"

"It isn't the individual that's scary, but the power they wield."

"Power?"

"Yes, power. They have the power to make you look awful. A cut too short, a color too bright —" Grace had ordered fish, and she filleted it neatly, slicing down the back and carefully removing the bone. It came out whole, like something out of a cartoon.

Audrey stared, impressed. "I want to learn to do that."

"Bone a fish? It's not hard."

Audrey found a lot of things hard that other people didn't. The one thing she was confident talking about was hair. "If a color is too bright, you just need to ask them to put a toner on it, that's all. If the cut is too short —" she shrugged "— that's hard. I suppose you could have extensions, but that's a nuisance. Better to make sure you want to go short before you do it." She narrowed her eyes and studied Grace. "You'd look great with short hair. You have good bones. It would emphasize the shape of your face and make your eyes stand out. In a good way," she said as she tucked into her steak, "not in a bulbous eyes insect way."

"That's a relief. Bulbous insect isn't the

best look." Grace took a small mouthful of fish. "I've always been too scared to have it cut."

Audrey chewed. She'd never tasted anything like the steak. "You've never had it short?"

"I'm too much of a coward."

"I could show you what it would look like. All I'd need is some pins and hairspray." Audrey cut another piece off her steak. "This is delicious. And the ketchup is the same as home. I bet it actually did come from a bottle. Is this your first trip to Paris?"

"Second. Last time I visited, I was your age."

"No kidding." Audrey realized she'd consumed an entire bowl of fries. Grace hadn't eaten a single one. "Who did you stay with?"

"A family. They had a daughter my age, and a son a few years older. He was a talented pianist."

"So this son —" Audrey shoveled food into her mouth "— where is he now?"

"I don't know. I haven't thought about him for years."

Audrey saw the flush spread across her cheeks and grinned. "But you're thinking about him now. Did the two of you have a thing?"

"No, we didn't have a 'thing.' "

They'd had a thing.

Audrey wondered if Grace had taken her tights off.

"But you liked him. And he liked you."

"It was complicated." Grace pushed the other bowl of fries toward her. "Finish these, too, or I'll be tempted."

Audrey didn't need encouragement. She was happy to consume anything put in front of her.

"They're delicious."

"Were you busy today? How was the bookshop?"

Your average nightmare.

She almost told the truth, but she didn't trust Grace. She didn't trust anyone.

"It was great, thanks."

"Good." Grace stood up. "I'll ask them to clear the table, and we can have dessert."

The sun was setting over Paris, red streaks fingering their way across a darkening sky.

Audrey wondered what Etienne was doing. Probably having wild French sex with some bookish person.

Afterward, instead of lighting a cigarette, they probably opened a book and read together.

A team of uniformed staff appeared in the suite and cleared the table.

A man handed Audrey another menu.

"What's this?"

"For dessert, mademoiselle." He hovered, waiting for her to choose and Audrey felt her palms start to sweat.

She was about to say that she didn't want anything, when Grace turned to the waiter.

"We'll call down when we've chosen." Her tone was cool. "Thank you." She walked the man to the door of the suite and closed it firmly behind him.

Audrey stared hard at the menu, feeling as if someone was shining a big spotlight on her.

She felt Grace's hand on her shoulder.

"Is it dyslexia?"

"What? What are you talking about?" Audrey felt her face burn and slumped slightly in her chair. "How do you know that?"

"One of my students with dyslexia struggles with left and right. You remind me a little of her although no two people struggle in exactly the same way, of course. I've worked with lots of children and young adults who have dyslexia. It's very common."

Feeling exposed and vulnerable, Audrey put the menu down. "It doesn't bother me much."

Yeah, right.

Grace picked up the menu. "Tell me your favorite dessert and I'll order."

Audrey felt the pressure in her stomach ease. "Anything chocolate."

"And I love *Île Flottante*. Literally that means floating islands. It's meringues on crème anglaise. It's much better than it sounds."

"It sounds gross."

"I'm sure it will be delicious. I'll order that and a chocolate tart."

Audrey shrugged. No way was she eating a snail, but she could probably force down a floating island, particularly if it was followed by chocolate.

In the end the desserts were delicious, and she wolfed down both.

Grace ate a tiny portion of each. "Are you planning on going to French classes?"

"No." Audrey scraped her plate clean. Could she lick it? No. That was probably going too far. "I'll look up anything I need."

"I can help, if you'd like me to. I can teach you the basics. I could help you with reading, too."

Audrey put the spoon down. Who was this woman? First a free meal, and now this. Why on earth would she offer to help a stranger? "What's in it for you?"

Grace blushed. "I like helping."

There had to be a catch. Even her teachers hadn't wanted to help her and they'd been *paid.*

People didn't do that, did they? They didn't help for no reason.

It felt weird to Audrey, and suddenly all she wanted was to get out of there. "No thanks. I'm good." She stood up. "I guess I don't have to wash up, so I'll go now and maybe I'll see you around."

"Audrey —"

"The food was great, thanks. And I'm glad your ankle is better." Audrey shot toward the door before Grace could intercept her.

French lessons? She'd rather eat a snail.

And why would Grace offer to help someone she didn't even know? Audrey had no idea, but there had to be a reason and she didn't intend to hang around long enough to find out.

GRACE

"Table for one, please." Grace hovered at the entrance to the hotel restaurant, trying to look as if a table for one was her choice. She'd been here for four days and it still felt strange. Maybe she should find a café for breakfast instead.

Before this holiday, when had she last eaten alone?

The answer was never. There was always someone with her. David. Sophie. Mimi. Monica. Her life was filled with a small circle of people she loved and trusted. And that wasn't an accident. She'd chosen a life that was safe. Everything in her life was planned and scheduled, from her teaching to her socializing. She planned a week's worth of meals and laid her clothes out the night before. Chaos wasn't allowed to peep through the crack in the door.

Here she was, faced with a whole month of empty days, and she had no idea what to do with the time. It was like swimming every day in a single roped-off lane of the local swimming pool, and then suddenly finding yourself alone in open water.

Fortunately, she had a life belt. In her bag was a guidebook of Paris that would enable her plan how she was going to spend her time.

As the waiter led her to a small table by the window, Grace smiled at the people at the table nearest to hers. They didn't smile back.

Did she look desperate?

Probably. She might have invited Audrey to join her for another meal, but she'd scared her away with her offer to teach her French and help her to read. And she was furious with herself. Why was it that she always had to step in and fix everything?

It was an infuriating habit, and Audrey clearly thought so, too.

Yet another person she'd driven away.

The list was growing.

Feeling depressed, she took the menu from the waiter.

"Thank you."

"And will Monsieur Porter be joining you today?"

"Not today." And not any day soon. Monsieur Porter was eating breakfast with another woman, probably while naked.

She ordered coffee, placed the menu on the table and pulled the guidebook out of her bag without enthusiasm. What should she do today? Normally at this point she and David would be haggling. Her love was art galleries, and his was food so whenever they traveled they compromised.

Today there was no need for compromise. She could do whatever she pleased.

But what was that? There had never been a time when she hadn't had to take someone else's feelings into account. She wasn't sure she even knew what she wanted.

Maybe she'd start with the Louvre. She'd ask the concierge to make her a lunch reservation somewhere nearby. And perhaps they'd be able to book her tickets to a concert.

She scribbled on her notepad, compiling a plan for the next few days with the aid of the guidebook. She'd filled in four days when it occurred to her that she was doing it again. Organizing everything.

Last time she'd been in Paris, there had been no plan.

She and Philippe had drifted from hour to hour, as absorbed by each other as they had been by Paris.

It had surprised her to discover she was

capable of spontaneity. It was Philippe who had dragged out that side of her.

She put her pen down, ripped the page out of the notebook and scrunched it into a ball.

Today there was not going to be a plan. And not tomorrow, either.

It was time to find that side of herself again.

Her heart beat a little faster. She'd eat lunch where and when she fancied it. She'd stay in the Louvre as long as she wanted to. Or maybe not go at all.

The waiter returned with her coffee, and Grace ordered from the menu.

"Scrambled eggs and coffee, please."

He bowed his head. Clearly, he was wondering what sort of anniversary celebration it was when the wife didn't know when her husband was going to show up.

She closed the guidebook and turned to look out of the window.

The sun beamed down, bathing the streets in sunlight, as if determined to show Paris at its very best. Grace watched through the window as people strolled down the wide boulevards.

What was David doing now? Did he ever think of her? Did he ever feel regret?

She was jolted from her thoughts by a

commotion at the far end of the restaurant and the sound of a high, shrill voice.

"What do you mean you have a dress code? It's breakfast, for God's sake. What do you expect me to wear? Bloody silk pajamas?"

The voice was familiar, and Grace peered across the restaurant and saw Audrey glaring fiercely at the uniformed waiter standing in her path.

Her hands were on her hips. "I'm here to see a friend, okay?"

Grace's heart lifted. As the days had passed and she hadn't heard from Audrey she'd assumed she'd scared her off, but maybe that wasn't the case.

She stood up and hurried across the restaurant. "Audrey!" She gave the waiter a smile and switched to French. "She's with me."

The man didn't return the smile. "We have a dress code in the restaurant, madame. I'm sure you understand."

"I do understand." She had her own codes and rules and she rarely diverted from them. She was starting to realize how irritating that might have been for David. "On this one occasion, I'm sure you'll be willing to overlook it."

The waiter eyed Audrey's ripped jeans. "I

don't think —"

"If you could lay another place at my table and bring a menu, that would be appreciated." Without giving him the opportunity to protest, she shepherded Audrey back to her table.

Audrey slumped into the chair opposite Grace. "Okay, that was pretty cool. I have no idea what you said, of course, but you, like, *shriveled* him with your eyes. He was going to throw me out. I'm not polished enough for this place. They don't approve of me."

Grace heard the wobble in her voice.

"It's a hotel. We don't need their approval. I'm paying a fortune for the privilege of staying here, so the least they can do is let me choose my own dining companion."

Audrey chewed her fingernail. "You're probably wondering why I'm here."

Grace knew a teenager in crisis when she saw one, but that didn't explain why Audrey had come to find her at the hotel. Why not call her own mother?

Maybe she felt awkward admitting that her Paris dream wasn't going well.

She studied Audrey's face and saw the blotched pallor that suggested a fit of crying. She reminded Grace of a flower that had been drenched in a storm and lost all its petals. "Did something happen?"

Audrey finished mauling one nail and started on another. "She fired me."

"Who?"

"Elodie. She owns the bookstore." Audrey sniffed and wiped her nose on the back of her hand. "A woman came in this morning and asked me something in French, she wouldn't even speak slowly, and I had *no idea* what she was saying and then Elodie arrived in the middle of it and this woman complained about me. Not that I understood the words, but there was no misinterpreting the tone. Turns out I'm fluent in angry voice. After she went, Elodie told me I can't stay. She wants a French speaker, or at least someone who is willing to learn French. She's given me a week to find somewhere else to live. And I have a job at the hairdresser now, but that doesn't pay enough to cover rent and food. So I'm totally stuffed." There was a hiccup in her voice, and Grace reached into her bag for a tissue.

"Here —" She handed it across the table.

She badly wanted to fix this but last time she'd offered help, Audrey had fled. This time she was *not* going to push her help on anyone.

"Why don't you eat something?" She

231

gestured to the waiter who approached hesitantly, sending a glance toward his boss.

"Madame?"

Grace ignored both the menu and his disapproving expression and thought about what Sophie liked when she was miserable. "We'd like a large pot of hot chocolate, please. Also, a plate of toasted English muffins, scrambled eggs and crispy bacon." She froze and glanced at Audrey. "You'd probably like to order for yourself."

Audrey shook her head. "I like what you ordered."

"When did you last eat a piece of fruit?"

Audrey slumped in her chair and lifted one shoulder. "That drink you gave me the other night."

"We'll also have a fresh fruit platter." It felt so good to be able to care for someone. To be needed, even if this was only a very small thing.

The waiter retreated, and Grace turned her attention back to Audrey.

It almost killed her to wait, but she waited.

Audrey scrubbed at her cheeks with her palm. "So I was wondering — I mean, you speak French, so I thought maybe — well, you could teach me a few phrases. Just say them into my phone and I'll memorize them. If you have time. And you probably don't, and that's fine. I shouldn't even have come." She half rose, and Grace felt a flash of sympathy.

"I'd be happy to teach you some phrases. As few or as many as you like."

Audrey sat down slowly. "Thanks. Then I can look for a new job."

"Maybe if you explained to Elodie that you're learning basic French, she might let you stay."

"She won't."

Grace sat back as the waiter arrived with the hot chocolate. She waited while he poured a cup for Audrey.

Audrey picked up the cup and sipped. Her hand shook a little. "This tastes good."

"It's Sophie's favorite whenever she has had a bad day and needs a little comfort."

Audrey watched her over the rim of the cup. "I was rude the other night. I don't get why you'd do this, that's all."

That was easy to explain, but did she want to?

Exposing your weaknesses didn't come easily, particularly to someone you didn't know. But if she wanted Audrey to trust her, didn't she have to trust Audrey?

"My daughter is eighteen and leaving home, my husband no longer wants my company — I feel a little useless." It was easier to say than she would have expected. "A lot useless, if I'm honest. When you know me better, you'll discover I have a tendency to organize everything and everyone. I don't blame you for being a little freaked-out. Sometimes I'm like a Labrador dog. I mean well, but I'm clumsy."

Audrey gave a cautious smile. "I have a Labrador back home. His name is Hardy, and he's exactly like that. He knocks everything with his wagging tail."

"Do you have a picture?"

"Yeah, somewhere." Audrey picked up her phone and scrolled through photos until she found one of a dog. She showed it to Grace.

"He's adorable. No wonder you love him."

"I miss him a lot."

The waiter delivered their food. Plates of soft fluffy scrambled eggs and crispy bacon. Muffins toasted to a golden brown. Grace pushed the plates toward Audrey.

"Help yourself."

Audrey speared a strand of bacon and glanced at the guidebook by Grace's plate. "You were about to spend the day exploring Paris. You don't need me hanging around."

Grace heard the edge in her voice and sensed that she was being tested. "One of the advantages of being alone is that I can be flexible about what I do. There will be plenty of time to explore Paris."

"Just to warn you, teaching me wouldn't be fun or rewarding. I'm useless. If you believe the teachers at school, my life is basically over."

Grace thought about Sophie. She knew enough about teenagers to know that living with them was like riding a roller coaster. One minute they were up, and then they were down. All you could do was keep yourself strapped in and go along for the ride. "You've had a bad morning. It's natural to feel low when things aren't going right."

Audrey reached for a muffin, and Grace noticed that her fingernails were bitten to nothing.

At eighteen she'd had no fingernails, either. She'd wanted to help her mother but hadn't been able to.

"Would you like me to come to the bookstore with you? Maybe I could translate so that you can talk to Elodie."

Audrey gave a half smile, but it lacked the suspicion of her earlier offerings. "What are you, my fairy godmother?"

"Let's settle for friend. I want to help, that's all."

"Okay." Audrey devoured the eggs and bacon and then started on the muffins.

235

"What if you teach me something and I just don't get it?"

Grace saw the insecurity behind the flippancy. She'd encountered it many times. Students who struggled but were afraid to admit it. It was particularly difficult in the teenage years when no one wanted to be different and everyone was trying to find their place in the world. "Then I'll try another way. There isn't just one way to teach something. We can focus on learning the things you'd find useful."

"Okay, but I can tell you now that the bookstore idea is a waste of time. Elodie is a dragon."

"Why don't we talk to her anyway? I want to ask her about the history of the bookshop and see if there is anyone who might remember my grandmother." Grace poured more hot chocolate into Audrey's cup.

Audrey fiddled with her fork. "She's mad about something else, too."

"What else?"

Audrey's cheeks were pink. "She thinks I stole money."

Grace remembered the money she'd seen Audrey push into the pocket of her jeans. "Did you?"

"No." Audrey caught her eye. "Well, kind of, but not really. I was borrowing it, that's

236

all. I've got a job now, but I've only worked there for a couple of afternoons and they don't pay me until I've been there for a few weeks so it's been tough." She poked at the remains of the egg on her plate. "I tried to explain. I had money saved, but then — well, something happened, and now I've got nothing spare to fall back on. But soon I will. I'm good at washing hair so the tips should be good. I tried to tell her I was going to pay her back, but she didn't want to hear it."

Grace opened her mouth to ask what had happened to the money, but Audrey's face was so pale she decided not to. She stood up. "Are you done eating? Let's go upstairs so that you can freshen up, and then we'll go together."

Audrey didn't move. "What if she has me arrested?"

"She won't."

"You'd better be right. Otherwise you'll be visiting me in prison."

They walked up to the suite, and Grace opened the door. There was something about this hotel room that depressed her. Maybe it was because David was missing.

The moment she saw the place, she started to laugh. "I don't believe it."

Audrey peered over her shoulder. "What?"

"I was trying not to be so organized and tidy. I left a few things strewn around the place, even though it almost killed me to do it. And they've tidied it away. Again. They keep doing it. Every time I drop something, they clear it up. I left shoes on the floor and a shirt on the bed."

Audrey looked bemused. "You want to be untidy?"

"Not untidy exactly. Just less fixated on controlling everything about me."

"I don't get you, Grace."

"You're not alone," Grace said sadly. She waved her hand in the direction of the bathroom. "Make yourself at home. Take a shower if you like. There are plenty of towels."

"Want me to drop them in a wet heap on the floor when I'm done?" Audrey nudged her. "See? Maybe I do get you."

Grace laughed. "Maybe you do. Go ahead and drop the towels wherever you like."

"I will. And if you need help learning to be messy, I can probably help. Come and see my place and you'll see what messy really is."

While Audrey vanished to the bathroom, Grace packed her bag for the day.

She pushed the phone into her bag, along with cash and other items she thought she might need. Her passport was safely locked in the hotel safe.

She could hear the sound of the shower, so she messaged Sophie and checked her emails.

There was an email from Mimi, including two photographs of the garden.

Grace felt a pang of homesickness and then remembered that the home she'd loved didn't really exist anymore.

Audrey emerged from the bathroom, her face scrubbed of makeup and her hair damp. "I almost drowned in your shower. There are like forty different jets hosing you down at the same time."

"You look great," Grace said. "Let's go."

They left the hotel together and walked across the river in the sunshine.

As Grace walked into the bookshop, Audrey hung back. Grace had a feeling she was ready to run.

A woman, presumably Elodie, sat behind the desk talking to a young man.

"No way," Audrey muttered. "We're not doing this. That's Etienne. I don't need him to witness my humiliation."

"We're doing this." Grace caught her hand and tugged her toward the door.

Elodie glanced up as the bell rang. Her welcoming smile lasted until she noticed

Audrey hovering behind Grace.

"I'm Grace." Grace stuck out her hand and switched to French. She explained that she would be giving Audrey French lessons, and asked if Elodie might consider giving her a second chance.

While she was talking, she noticed Etienne smiling at Audrey. It seemed likely that Audrey smiled back because he became suddenly flustered and dropped the books he was holding, earning himself an impatient look from Elodie.

Elodie either hadn't noticed the interaction between them or she wasn't interested. "She stole from me."

Grace explained about the cash flow issues. "What she should have done was to discuss it with you, and I'm sure you could have arranged to advance her a little money, but she didn't want to do that. It might have been a language issue, but whatever it was I guarantee she won't do it again." Was she crazy making a guarantee like that? It wasn't as if she knew Audrey well, but what she did know was that without Audrey she would very likely be without a passport and most of her money. And she liked the girl. Despite David, she refused to believe that her instinct about people had totally deserted her. "I'll take personal responsibility."

"I'm not sure."

To her surprise, Etienne stepped in, talking in rapid French. "Can you remember when you were a student? It is hard at the beginning when you have no money and you're not paid until after you've worked. She has a job at the salon. I saw her in there yesterday."

"If she had money issues, she should have asked for a loan."

Etienne frowned. "That isn't so easy to do. There is pride for a start."

"So it is better to steal?"

"She borrowed it," Etienne said emphatically, and Grace was relieved to have that extra voice of support.

"Some translation would be good here," Audrey muttered, but Grace sensed that Elodie was wavering and made a final plea.

"She is eighteen. Didn't you ever do anything you regretted when you were eighteen?"

Elodie met her gaze and there was a flicker of something in her eyes. She gave a reluctant smile. "Perhaps, but overlooking the money incident doesn't change the fact that she can't communicate with any of the customers. Even if she has French lessons, I

241

can't leave her in the shop on her own."

Grace thought quickly. "If I do it with her, she won't be on her own."

"I can't afford to pay two people."

"I would be a volunteer." She had to be mad, surely? Who chose to work on their vacation? On the other hand, this was the strangest vacation she'd ever been on and it might be good to do something she would never normally do. "I can help Audrey when there are customers, and when there are no customers I will teach her French."

Elodie looked curious. "How do you know each other?"

Grace told Elodie everything, and it was obvious that the other woman was surprised by the story. Etienne was, too.

He grinned at Audrey. "You did that? *Incroyable.*"

Elodie seemed less enamored. She gave Audrey a long, assessing look. "We will try it again."

Grace felt a rush of satisfaction and turned to Audrey, finally ready to translate. "It's all fine. We will both be here in the mornings, and I am going to teach you French."

Audrey looked uncomfortable. "You can't spend your mornings here. You're on holiday. You want to explore Paris."

That was what she'd planned to do with David, but Grace didn't want to do the things she would have done with him.

"Working in a bookshop has always been a dream of mine."

Audrey muttered something about some people having weird dreams. "But thanks. I mean, really. Thanks." She looked at Elodie. "Sorry about the money."

Elodie tightened her lips. "We will forget it and make a fresh start, no?"

She could have been describing Grace's life. She was starting fresh, too.

"I'll begin right away." Grace put her bag behind the desk. "I'm going to spend some time exploring the shop, so I have a feel for where things are shelved."

It felt good to have a purpose, and there was no doubt that the bookstore was charming.

"Our older books are in the rooms toward the back. Fiction on the left, nonfiction on the right." Elodie stood up and smoothed her skirt over her legs. "Newer volumes are at the front. We have some first editions locked in the cabinet. They are valuable, so we never let anyone browse without supervision."

Grace strolled through the small rooms, examining the shelves that were at eye level and lower. They were carefully labeled, with each book in alphabetical order.

She tried to picture her flamboyant grandmother spending hours here, and failed. It just didn't seem like a place Mimi would fall in love with. It made no sense to her. What was she missing?

"Does the name Mimi Laroche mean anything to you, Elodie?"

The woman shook her head. "Should it?"

It had been too much to hope for. "My grandmother was born in Paris. She spent a great deal of time in this bookstore, particularly after the war."

"In that case she would have met my grandmother, Paulette. She was still coming here and spending half a day with the books until the week before she died. That was five years ago." Elodie gestured to an old photograph on the wall. "This was taken in 1960."

Grace studied it and pulled out her phone. "Could I take a photograph of it? I'd like to send it to Mimi."

"Of course. And if she has any stories to share, I'd love to hear them. Is she still a keen reader?"

That was the strange thing about this. Grace had never seen her grandmother pick up a book. "Her eyesight isn't as good as it

244

once was."

"My grandmother had the same problem. Fortunately she didn't lose her hearing, so she fell in love with audiobooks." Elodie reached for her bag. "You are sure you don't mind staying here this morning? I would love to talk a little more, but I'm trying to rent the apartment upstairs and it is proving more challenging than usual. I have a lovely couple who want to take it from the end of August, but I can't afford to let it stay empty until then. I am going to talk to a few rental agencies. If you have any questions you can always call me."

"We will be fine." An idea blossomed in Grace's head, wild and totally unlike her. Could she really do something so unplanned? So impulsive? "Your apartment — I don't suppose you'd like to rent it to me, would you?"

Elodie looked surprised. "You're looking for an apartment?"

She hadn't been, but now the idea had come alive in her brain, she realized how much she wanted to do it. So far she'd been following a path she'd planned to take with David. She felt his absence everywhere. If she was ever going to move on, she had to find a way to deal with that. She was no longer half of Grace-and-David. She was

245

100 percent Grace.

Mimi would be proud.

"I'm staying in a hotel right now, and — well, it isn't quite the way I planned it." Grace didn't elaborate. "I'd prefer the freedom of an apartment, and I can't think of anything more perfect than living above the bookshop."

Elodie put her bag back down on the desk. "You are able to cancel your hotel?"

She thought about the terms of her reservation. It was possible they'd charge her for tonight, but that would be all. "Yes. When would the apartment be ready?"

"It's ready now. I was preparing for a short let, so the bed is already made up with clean linen, and there are fresh towels in the bathroom."

"Perfect. I'll move in this afternoon."

Elodie seemed surprised. "You should perhaps see it first? The apartment is probably nothing like your hotel."

Thank goodness.

Grace thought of the staff, constantly asking when David would be joining her. "It will be exactly what I need."

She joined Elodie on a quick tour of the apartment. It was charming, with high ceilings and tall windows overlooking the street.

Elodie flung open a window. "Whoever

246

lives here has to care for the plants on the balcony."

There was a balcony?

Grace followed Elodie into the small kitchen and it turned out that there was indeed a balcony. A jungle of plants crowded around a small table with intricate ironwork. She imagined herself drinking her morning coffee out there, or sipping a cool drink in the evening.

"It's perfect." Grace pulled out her phone. "I'm going to contact the hotel now and cancel my reservation. I'll also ask them to pack up my things." And it would be the last time the hotel staff folded one of her shirts.

After she'd made the call, they dealt with the finances and Elodie handed over the keys.

Grace felt a little dizzy. A couple of hours ago she'd been contemplating how to spend her time in Paris. Now she had an apartment and was volunteering in a bookshop.

She could come and go as she pleased.

Audrey was hovering. "So — er — you're living here now?"

"Yes, and I have you to thank for it. I never would have thought of renting an apartment if it hadn't been for you."

"Er — you're welcome? Although I don't

think I had much to do with it."

"You had everything to do with it. And now we are going to do something about your French so that you can always handle the basics. We'll start with greetings, so you can dazzle people with the warmth of your customer service the moment they walk through the door."

Elodie finally smiled at Audrey. "I wait to be dazzled." She gave Audrey's shoulder a squeeze, perhaps more relaxed since she'd witnessed Grace's affection for the teenager. "We will try this again, no?"

As the door closed behind her, Audrey stood with her arms folded, a wary look on her face. "So now what? I suppose you want me to get paper and pens or something."

"No paper. No pens. No writing or reading, at least not to begin with."

"I thought you were going to give me a French lesson."

"I am. But that isn't going to involve writing, reading or any of the other things you find hard. We're tackling this a different way."

Audrey's eyes narrowed. "What way?"

"Are you always so suspicious?"

"Yeah, it's called being street-smart."

Grace wondered what her life had been like that she constantly felt she had to watch her back. "We're going to have a conversation. And don't tell me you're not going to be able to do that, because I haven't noticed you holding back when it comes to talking. For the rest of the morning, we are only going to talk in French."

"In that case it's going to be a quiet morning."

Grace had a feeling Audrey was going to surprise herself. "First you're going to learn to greet someone and ask how they are."

"What if I don't care how they are?"

Grace laughed. She'd laughed more since she'd met Audrey than she had in the entire six months previously. "You're going to pretend."

"What if they answer me and I don't understand?"

"We'll get to that. I'm going to speak and you're going to repeat what I say."

Normally before a lesson she made a detailed plan, but nothing in her life was the way it used to be. Later she'd think about techniques she could use to help Audrey, but for now the best thing seemed to be to just get started.

AUDREY

"Oh, my God, the view is *insane,* although I don't see what any of this has to do with learning French."

It was five days since she'd almost lost her job, and she and Grace were at the top of the Eiffel Tower.

Grace took a photograph. "You bought the tickets in French."

"True. I'd forgotten about that. And mine cost less because I'm *jeune.*" It was weird, Audrey thought. With Grace, she learned without even realizing she was learning.

She peered down. The whole of Paris lay at her feet. "If you're sick, how long do you think it takes to hit the ground?"

"Audrey!"

Audrey grinned. "Just seeing if I could shock you."

"I'm easily shocked."

It was true, and Audrey had decided that shocking Grace might be her new favorite pastime. She never would have thought she could have enjoyed learning a language, but Grace made it fun.

"Can you come up here at night?"

"Yes. It's beautiful."

"You've done that?" Audrey glanced at her and saw a faraway look in Grace's eyes. "Did you kiss him here?"

"That is none of your business."

"That means you did."

Grace stepped back. "Time to go down."

"Where next?"

"We are taking an open-top bus tour of Paris."

"They can't afford a roof? Just kidding." She hesitated, and then slid her arm into Grace's. "We have the same thing in London."

"I'm going to point out a few things and teach you the words in French."

"There's always a downside." Audrey moaned that Grace made her learn words constantly, but deep down she was quite enjoying it. Apart from that one little moment in the hotel, Grace was always consistent, which made a pleasant change.

Grace was kind and patient, and she made learning easier than usual.

There was no sweating over books, and no smudging of ink while she tried to form letters. Instead, Grace took a practical approach. She taught Audrey greetings, and made her repeat them over and over again and whenever a customer entered a shop. *Bonjour, ça va? Comment allez-vous?* When someone responded with words Audrey didn't understand, Grace translated. Then she recorded all the new words using Audrey's phone and encouraged her to listen to them and repeat them aloud before the next day.

Grace used unorthodox methods to help her remember the words. She put stickers on items in Audrey's apartment. *Bed=le lit. Chair=la chaise.* Audrey had fun switching them around and pretending she'd mixed up the words even when she hadn't.

The most laughs came when Grace acted out a word and made Audrey guess what it was.

"Er — I don't know." She'd watched as Grace had mimed a weird pecking motion. "Whatever happens, *never* do that in public."

Grace had tried again, and Audrey had burst out laughing. "Are you a camel? No, you haven't taught me the word for camel." Audrey thought about the words they'd learned. "Er — you're a chicken?"

"En francais!" Grace insisted, and Audrey

252

shrugged.

"I don't know. You need to buy me a chicken and stick a label on it to remind me."

"You do know. Here's a clue —" Grace started doing an imitation of breaststroke and Audrey grinned.

"It's a swimming chicken? Oh, wait, I get it — pool — *poulet.*"

"Yes! Well done."

They were both laughing. Audrey knew the sight of Grace pretending to be a chicken wasn't something she was going to forget in a hurry.

"I think you should teach me the word for *cow.*"

"Is that a word you'd find useful?"

"No, but I want to see you acting out a farmyard."

In between the laughter, she learned. Grace was so excited by her progress that she started to think that maybe she wasn't such a hopeless case.

A few days later, Grace stuck a gold star on Audrey's T-shirt. "Congratulations. You've learned a hundred words."

Audrey looked at the star. "What? Am I six years old?" It was like one of the ones they gave you in kindergarten, except she'd never been given one. She'd never been given a sticker in her life. She decided to keep it on, and told herself it was because she didn't want to offend Grace. "This is the kind of thing they give you as a reward for not biting the dentist."

"Do you know the French word for dentist?"

"No, and I'm not going to need it. You couldn't drag me to a dentist so don't waste your time teaching me that."

"One hundred words, Audrey! You've learned a hundred words."

"Great! Only another nine million left to learn."

"This is a marathon, not a sprint. You're doing great! And your pronunciation is perfect."

"I've always been a good mimic. I bet I can copy your voice." She gave a perfect imitation of Grace and had the satisfaction of seeing her laugh.

Even after a few days she felt much more confident when the door opened, the bell rang and a customer walked into the shop.

They had a routine now. Audrey would greet them and Grace would subtly take over the conversation so that the person didn't even realize Audrey had stopped contributing.

Audrey had started working in the hair

salon down the street in the afternoons, but when she emerged Grace was always waiting for her, ready to teach her something new. She was so easy to be with, and spending time together felt like a natural thing.

As well as the bus, they used the Métro system, which as far as Audrey could tell was no different from the London Underground.

Grace insisted on paying for everything, which made Audrey feel uncomfortable, but she promised herself that as soon as she'd saved up some tips from her hairdressing, she'd pay her back. Or maybe she'd buy her a gift. Apart from food and tickets to things, Grace never seemed to spend money on herself.

They'd eaten dinner twice, and each time Grace had insisted that Audrey order in French.

The first time, Audrey had almost walked away. "I'll mess it up." She'd shrunk in her chair as the waiter approached. "I'll order octopus by accident."

"Do you know the word for octopus?"

"No."

"Then how can you possibly order it by accident? What do you want to eat?"

"Chicken and fries."

"And you know the words for those because we learned them yesterday." Grace had been cheerfully persistent. "If you don't do it, I'll stand up and do my chicken impression."

"You wouldn't." Audrey got ready to dive under the table.

"If you can talk about bodily functions at the top of the Eiffel Tower, I can do my chicken impression. Order. Have confidence. What's the worst that can happen?"

"Apart from ordering octopus? The list is endless." But under Grace's watchful eye she'd stumbled over the words, ordered herself chicken with a side of fries, and been both surprised and delighted when the food that arrived was exactly what she'd ordered.

"Well, hey — nothing with eight legs." Feeling ridiculously proud of herself, she poked at the chicken with her fork and saw Grace smile.

That had been the night before and now they were in a different restaurant, this time close to the river.

Having had success the night before, Audrey ordered the same thing again. She loved this bistro, with its tablecloths and waiters in aprons. "So you prefer the apartment to the hotel?"

"Definitely. It's charming." Grace had ordered a salad, although it was more elaborate than any salad Audrey had seen before.

Audrey emptied the bowl of fries onto her plate alongside the chicken and heaped salt over them. She saw Grace wince. "What?"

"That's a lot of salt. And you ate the same thing last night, too."

"I know. Delicious. Or *délicieux,* as you'd probably make me say."

"Would you like a little of my salad?"

"No thanks. It's too green."

"Green is good for you."

"Not everything green is good for you. Caterpillars are green, although you're probably about to tell me that the French eat them." Audrey tucked into her food. "So today in the salon I learned five new words, and tomorrow I have a date so I need you to teach me a few very specific words for that."

"You have a date? That's exciting. Who with?"

"It's private, Grace. I don't ask you about your sex life."

"I don't have a sex life. I'm a sad, soon-to-be divorcée, remember? But I hope you have fun on your date. Not that you want my opinion, but I think Etienne is pretty cute."

Audrey put her fork down. "How do you

know it's Etienne?"

"I *hope* it's Etienne." She caught Audrey's eye. "I've seen the way you look at him. And the way he looks at you. When you're both in the bookshop at the same time it's like a lab experiment."

"He looks at me?"

"You know he does. And then there is the fact that he jumped to your defense when Elodie wanted to fire you."

"She *did* fire me." Audrey fiddled with her fork. "He defended me? What did he say? You never did tell me."

"He reminded her what it was like to be a student and short of money. I was impressed that he was willing to risk his own relationship with Elodie to support you."

"Yeah, I'm impressed, too." She wondered how far Etienne would have gone. "So if I killed someone do you think he'd hide the body?"

"Let's not put that to the test," Grace said. "Where are you going on your date? Dinner? Dancing?"

Audrey acknowledged the generation gap with a grin. "You mean like tango and stuff? I don't think so." Although a naked tango had come to mind more than once during the week. Grace was right that she and Etienne had exchanged a few long, lingering glances. She was fairly sure he was interested, and she was definitely interested. She'd never felt this way before. Grace had caught her grinning at nothing a couple of times, and that had been embarrassing although also nice in a way. Grace noticed things.

She wondered what Etienne had planned for their date. Would they grab a drink and then go back to Etienne's place for crazy sex? And what about alcohol? She didn't drink, but she didn't want Etienne to think she wasn't cool.

She felt a ripple of nerves. Her sex life so far involved a few deeply unsatisfying encounters on top of a pile of coats at house parties. Deep down she was terrified there might be something wrong with her. What if her messed-up childhood had messed up other parts of her? She could never let go and relax. She was so bad at it she ended up thinking about something else or worrying. Anxiety about her mother had been a permanent burn in her insides. "I guess we might go to a club. Or maybe back to his place."

On the other hand if the sex was terrible, that might be awkward.

Still, the idea that she could finally do whatever she wanted without having to

259

think about her mother or anyone else left her feeling breathless. This was the type of freedom she'd been longing for. She had an apartment. A job. An almost boyfriend. She was in Paris.

What could possibly go wrong?

"He has his own place?"

"It's his parents' place, but they go to the south of France in the summer."

"Wait —" Grace put her fork down. "So they won't be there?"

"No, and that's good. I've known him, like, five minutes. We're not exactly at the 'meet the parents' stage." If she didn't meet anyone else's parents, then they wouldn't expect to meet hers.

"Well, he seems like a lovely guy. I'm sure he'll bring you home after, but if he doesn't you can always call me and I'll meet you."

Audrey was thrown. No one had ever offered to meet her before. She imagined Grace being mugged on her way to save Audrey from the best sex of her life.

"You're doing that because I remind you of your daughter?"

Grace frowned. "No. I'm doing it because you're a friend. Take my number." She scribbled it on a paper napkin. "If something happens, call me. It doesn't matter what time it is."

Audrey put the number in her phone. Not that she was going to use it, but if it made Grace happy —

"It's a date. I hope something does happen."

"I mean something bad. You're a young girl and Paris is a big city."

"Do you worry this much about your daughter?"

"More." Grace picked up her fork again. "It's the curse of motherhood."

Audrey was pretty sure her mother didn't suffer from the same curse. She felt a pang. "Your daughter is lucky to have you. If you want to help me, you can teach me a few very specific French words. Just the essentials. The kind of stuff a girl might need on a date."

"You mean small talk? The weather, and 'that was a fun evening,' that kind of thing?"

"No. I mean the French word for *condom*. That kind of thing." She looked up as Grace choked on her salad. "What? You don't know the word for condom?"

"I do, but —" Grace breathed. "You don't know him, honey."

"Hopefully after tonight, I will. I mean, sex is a great way to get to know someone, right?"

"I — Maybe you should see each other a

few times first. What if you don't get along that well? What if you discover the two of you don't want the same thing?"

"I want to have fun. That's it. But I want to have safe fun, which is why I need the word for condom. I take precautions. That's a good thing." She felt suddenly defensive. She wasn't usually so open with people. "Forget it."

"I said the wrong thing. I'm sorry." Grace picked up her drink. "I'm worried about you, that's all. I don't want to see you hurt. But maybe I'm just a little jaded about love. You shouldn't listen to me."

Audrey softened. "You don't have to worry about me. I've been looking after myself for a long time. I'm pretty independent."

"I expect your mother is worried sick about you."

Audrey thought about all the times she'd walked to school on her own, talked to the teachers alone, fed herself and taken care of her drunk mother.

She licked the salt from her lips. "Yeah. Probably can't get me out of her mind."

"Well, you have my number so you can call me if you get into trouble."

Audrey had never called anyone in her life. She'd never had anyone she *could* call.

There was Meena, of course, but Audrey was usually the one protecting her, not the other way around. She looked at Grace, and saw the kindness there. For a moment Audrey was tempted to tell her the truth about her life, but something held her back. Once the truth was out there, you couldn't pull it back, and Audrey had never told anyone before. She didn't want to say something she'd regret.

"Sure," she said. "I'll call if I'm in trouble."

"Good. In that case I won't worry about you. But take a cab home. And don't use your phone in the street."

"You're teaching me street smarts? I'm not the one who got mugged and lost my purse."

Grace looked embarrassed. "Point taken. Sorry."

"Don't be sorry. You're a good person, Grace. If you ask me, your husband is batshit crazy for leaving you." What the hell was that about? Grace was kind and loyal and everything a mother was supposed to be if you believed what you saw on TV. She was the type who would pick you up and hug you when you fell, make you nutritious meals and listen to your woes. "So is your daughter messed-up about your divorce?"

"We're not actually divorced yet, but yes, she's pretty upset. She's close to her dad. Are you close to your dad?"

"Sure." Audrey kept her face deadpan. "We're inseparable."

"What does he do?"

"Oh, you know —" *screws women and then leaves them pregnant* "— this and that. How about your bat-shit crazy husband? What does he do?"

"He's a newspaper editor. He's worked for the same company his whole career."

"So that's why, then." Audrey finished her drink.

"That's why?"

"Why he had an affair. He'd let his life get boring. Why are you frowning?"

"Because you put the responsibility squarely on him."

"Who else?" Audrey shrugged. "Whatever happened to adventure? Traveling? You never wanted to do any of that stuff?"

"I wanted stability." Grace paused. "I had a slightly chaotic upbringing. I wanted Sophie to have a stable childhood. It's the reason I became a teacher, because it was a job that matched her hours and gave me the time off I needed."

"I get that." She'd wanted stability, too, but now she wasn't even sure she'd recognize it if she saw it. "I bet you're a great mum. You're the kind of mum who would book a mother-daughter spa day on her birthday. If she was struggling at school, you'd get her a fucking tutor."

Grace's brows rose. "If you're going to swear, could you at least do it in a quieter voice? The people at the table next to us are frowning."

"Well, they should be minding their own business, not listening to us."

"They can't help hearing — your voice carries."

"You don't ever swear?"

"I try to find other ways to express myself."

Audrey grinned. "So when you trap your finger in the door or drop a bottle of red wine on a white carpet, what do you say?"

"I try not to lose control, but if it's something really frustrating I might say darn."

"Darn? *Darn?*" Audrey snorted with laughter. "What about when you've had a drink? Do you swear then?"

"I don't drink."

Audrey stopped laughing. "What, never?"

"No."

"So you don't swear, you don't drink, you don't smoke, I'm assuming you don't do

265

drugs, so what do you do when you want a wild night out?"

"David and I usually went to dinner. Or sometimes we barbecued with friends. I don't suppose it really counts as wild, but —" Grace pushed her plate away. "My life must sound very boring to you. Talking about it now, it sounds boring to me, too. But I'm a lot older than you, of course."

"What does age have to do with it? Age doesn't stop you having fun."

"You sound exactly like Mimi."

"She's your grandmother, right? And does she say darn when she traps her finger in a door?"

"No. Her language is much more colorful. But she often says it in French."

"So you go to dinner and you barbecue. No offense, but you're not blowing me away here, Grace."

"You're right. Maybe David wasn't crazy. Our lives had become too predictable. Apart from the vacations I booked for our anniversary every year, we didn't do much that was different. That was probably my fault." She looked troubled, as if she was realizing something for the first time.

Audrey leaned forward. She didn't know much about relationships, but she knew a lot about handling people who were upset.

266

"There were two of you. How is it your fault?"

"I'm quite rigid in my approach to life. I'm a little inflexible." Grace said it softly, and Audrey looked at her in disbelief.

"Are you kidding? You hang off the Eiffel Tower when you're teaching me French. You act out words. Believe me, you are the most flexible, least boring teacher I've ever had."

"Teaching is different. It's about responding to what the person needs. Another student might do better with books and more conventional study, but I didn't think that would hold your attention."

"Exactly. See? Flexible. If you can do it in one part of your life, you can do it in others." Audrey tapped her fingers on the table. "Maybe it's your view of yourself that's inflexible. You're not seeing what I'm seeing."

"I like order."

"Yeah? Well, order is good. Order is what gets you to work on time, dressed in the right clothes." *And preferably sober.* "Don't knock it."

"I need to stop trying to fix things the whole time. I do everything myself, instead of delegating. And I need to work on being more . . . spontaneous, at least some of the time."

Audrey decided it was time to lighten the mood a little. "We'll schedule it in. Being spontaneous."

Grace smiled. "Schedule being spontaneous? That sounds like an oxymoron."

"I wouldn't know, but we should dance down the Champs-Élysées. Strip off our clothes and swim in the Seine. Although that would be insane. Get it?" She laughed at her own joke. "In-Seine."

"I get it." Grace laughed, too. "I'm not going to strip off and swim in the Seine."

Privately, Audrey thought Grace could do with stripping off at least a few layers. She was all buttoned-up shirts and long pants that showed no flesh. "Whatever — it's time to start thinking about yourself. Putting yourself first. When did you last do something just for you?"

"I'm here, in Paris."

"But you came because if you hadn't, then your daughter wouldn't have done her whole summer traveling thing. You check your phone all the time in case she needs you, and now you'll also be checking your phone in case I need you, which I won't, by the way. You call your grandmother — you agreed to work in the bookshop and teach me to help me out. It seems to me you do a lot of thinking about other people, but not a lot about yourself."

"I'm fine." She looked so anxious that Audrey felt bad for her.

"Hey, if you're going to make me do new stuff that is scary, then you have to do it, too."

"That's different."

"It's not. I'm building a new life here, and you should be, too. Otherwise you'll go back home to the same shit — sorry, I mean the same situation — you had before and nothing will have changed. This is your chance to do something for you." She pushed her plate away. "I'm guessing you don't like nightclubs, but there must be other ways to meet people. Museum evenings or something. Art appreciation." What would someone like Grace like? "When you were in Paris the first time, did you meet any guys? Oh, wait — you met the older brother." She couldn't imagine Grace as a teenager. Had she ever worn short skirts and done the walk of shame? It was only because she happened to glance up at that moment that she saw Grace's cheeks turn pink. "What was his name?"

"I don't know what you —"

"Grace!"

Grace sighed. "His name was Philippe."

For a moment, she caught a glimpse of

another Grace. A less perfect, less tightly held together Grace. "What's he doing now?"

"We haven't been in touch since I was last in Paris, which was before you were even born."

"You've never looked him up?"

"No. I tried to forget about him."

"Mmm, well, we should check him out. He might be single." Audrey pulled her phone out. "What's his second name?"

"It doesn't matter if he's single. I'm married."

Audrey wondered if she should point out the obvious. Grace might consider herself married, but David clearly didn't.

Who the hell would leave someone as kind and loyal as Grace? If she ever met David, she might just punch the guy. She decided she had to be cruel to be kind. "No offense, Grace, but you're not looking that married from where I'm sitting. It takes more than a ring and a piece of paper. It takes the man to be present. He isn't present, and *that* is his biggest flaw."

"Good point. Brutal, but good." Grace sniffed. "You have a very clear way of seeing things."

With everything she'd seen and heard in the salon, she probably had more experience than the average marriage counselor.

Also, she'd seen her mother work her way through a few different men. They all had one thing in common. They didn't stick. Audrey felt a moment of panic. David and Grace had split up after twenty-five years, so obviously there was no safe point. Was she ever going to be able to relax? What if Ron didn't stick? What if right now her mother was driving him crazy? Audrey still checked her phone for messages every hour and she couldn't shake the nerves and unease that seemed to have taken up permanent residence in her stomach. And then there was the guilt, too. The feeling that she'd abandoned her mother.

Anxiety started to swirl inside her and she decided it was time to change the subject for both their sakes. "What's his second name? Philippe? I'm going to find him on social media."

"You are not."

"Oh, come *on*. What's the harm?"

Grace gestured for the bill, and Audrey wondered why she was so resistant. It was obvious her husband wasn't coming back, so the sooner she moved on the better.

This Philippe guy sounded like a good place to start.

"Let's see what he's doing. You don't have

to get in touch."

Grace paid the bill and stood up. "Let's go."

Audrey wondered what exactly had happened between Grace and Philippe. "Where are we going?"

"To the market. We're going to learn vocabulary for fruit and vegetables."

"Why? I hate fruit and vegetables," Audrey grumbled. "Why can't we learn the French for junk food? Hamburger, fries, extra deep-fried crap."

"Don't say crap."

"Well, extra deep-fried darn doesn't make any sense at all." She was encouraged to see Grace smile. "Why won't you teach me to ask for junk food? I thought you were my friend."

"I am your friend, which is why I'm not going to give you the words that will help you abuse your body."

"Does that mean you won't teach me the word for condom?"

"No. I'm going to teach you that one. In fact, we're going one better — we're going to a pharmacy and you're going to ask for them yourself."

Audrey shrank. "Over my dead body."

"If you carry on eating all that salt and junk food and no fruit and veg, it will be over your dead body."

"Do you nag your own daughter this much?"

"Much more."

"Well, shit — I mean darn, no wonder she went traveling." But Audrey slid her arm into Grace's. "Okay, we'll go to the pharmacy but while we're there we're going to buy you condoms, too."

Grace made a sound that was somewhere between a gasp and a laugh. "I have no need for condoms."

"You will if I have anything to do with it."

"You don't have anything to do with it."

Audrey gave a smug smile. "We'll see about that."

GRACE

Grace put the bunch of flowers she'd bought into a vase and set them on the table by the open window. As promised, she'd already watered the pots on the little balcony. It was an oasis of greenery, suspended above the Paris street below. Herbs grew in scented profusion, nestled in sunbaked terra-cotta pots, next to the vermillion splash of geranium and the tumble of lobelia.

It was late evening and she left the French doors open, appreciating the whisper of cool air that flowed through the apartment. Across the street she could hear the sounds of someone practicing the clarinet, the tap and thump of pointe shoes from the ballet school next door and, more distantly, the hum and buzz of Paris.

Even though it had only been a few days, already the apartment felt like home. With its high ceilings and calm decor, there was a peace to it that Grace found infinitely more soothing than the opulence of the hotel. Best, of course, was the fact that no one inquired about David. It had been like trying to walk on a broken limb, impossible to forget the injury.

Here, in this new private world where she was the only inhabitant, her old life receded.

She'd spent the afternoon exploring a new gallery, then returned, hot and sticky, her feet protesting, to the sanctuary of the apartment. She'd taken a cool shower using some of the luxurious toiletries she'd brought from her hotel room, and changed into a dress. She'd pinned her still-damp hair away from her neck.

Because she had no intention of leaving the apartment, she didn't bother with makeup.

From above her she could hear the sound of footsteps and the creak of floorboards. Audrey was getting ready to go out.

Tonight was her date with Etienne.

Anxiety flashed through her. Not because Audrey reminded her of Sophie, but because Audrey reminded her of herself.

She'd been exactly Audrey's age when she'd first arrived in Paris. Granted, she hadn't had Audrey's street smarts, but she'd had the same almost giddy excitement at finally being away from home. It had felt like an escape. Freedom, finally.

And that feeling of freedom could lead to problems. It was like letting a puppy off the leash for the first time. Why was it that she had more concern for Audrey than she had for Sophie?

Probably because Sophie had inherited almost all David's traits. She was sensible, practical and reliable.

On the surface Grace was all those things, too. She was the only one who knew that underneath she was someone quite different. She'd buried that part of herself but somehow being with Audrey had uncovered it.

She walked to the little kitchen and unwrapped the cheese she'd bought earlier.

With no one to feed but herself, she hadn't seen the point in spending hours fussing in the kitchen so she'd bought a selection of good French cheese, a baguette with a perfect golden crust, some grapes, a ripe pear and a bottle of good red wine.

Wine.

She didn't drink, but tonight she was drinking.

Something else she wouldn't have done had she been with David.

It was the ultimate departure from her old life.

She added cheese to her plate and broke a chunk off the baguette. Then she poured half a glass of wine and took it back to the little bistro table that lay in a pool of lazy, hazy sunshine.

There was a clatter from upstairs, followed by the muted sound of swearing.

Grace glanced up toward the open window and wondered if she should check on her.

No, Audrey wasn't her responsibility. She didn't want to be overbearing.

She sliced into the cheese and spread a little on the bread. It tasted like heaven.

The moment she took her first sip of wine, she remembered.

They'd taken a picnic to the river. Philippe had spread out a blanket and unloaded a feast from a bag. Local sausage, fresh figs, bread still warm from the bakery. He was the one who had pressed a glass of wine into her hand, even though she told him she didn't drink. Up until that point she hadn't touched a drop.

"This isn't drinking," he'd said, lifting his glass to hers. "It's living. You need to live, Grace. Not just a little, but a lot."

She hadn't disagreed.

Food, she'd discovered, tasted different in France, and Philippe was the one who had

277

introduced her to all the different flavors. The first time he kissed her, she wasn't sure if the turmoil inside her was from the wine or his kiss.

He'd invited her to live a life that was far from the one she was used to.

For a short time, she'd lost herself in the world he'd created.

With Philippe she'd discovered the secret Paris. Not the sites that attracted the crowds, like the Louvre and the Eiffel Tower, but those hidden gems that the locals talked about in whispers and rarely mentioned in guidebooks. They'd strolled hand in hand along the riverbank, enjoyed long leisurely breakfasts in arty cafés, lain together in dappled sunshine on lawns that sloped down to the river. They'd explored crooked streets and little-known art galleries.

It was as if a curtain had been lifted, revealing an alternate life. She'd seen possibilities, and a world she wanted so badly it was like the most painful type of hunger.

Now, years later and with one swallow of red wine, that feeling was back.

She took another sip of wine, and finished the cheese. If Paris had a taste, it was this. The fruity tang of red wine and the smooth creamy texture of good goat's cheese eaten at room temperature while the last of the sunlight spilled through the open doors.

She'd been determined not to think about Philippe, but now she could think of nothing else. The past swirled into her mind, cascading past all the barriers she'd built.

She stared at her laptop.

The tap of a few keys and she'd have the answer. She'd told Audrey that he probably wouldn't be on social media, but she knew he would. The platform had been invented for people like him. His life had been crowded with people. Friends from school, friends from college. Friends of his parents, of his sister. Friends he'd met through his love of music. He was a talented pianist and had played for Grace a few times. He moved easily through life, meeting each day with a confidence and expectation that Grace envied.

No wonder she'd fallen for him. She'd been lost and a little desperate. He'd been the equivalent of a bright light in a tunnel.

Had he ever wondered about her?

Was she simply the girl he'd waited for that night on the bridge?

A knock on the door shattered her thoughts, and she stood up quickly. She locked it all away — the past, her thoughts,

279

Philippe — and walked across the living room.

Audrey tumbled through the door, a blur of color, perfume and exuberant youth. She wore green, a short dress that fell in a careless sweep from spindle-thin straps to midthigh. It was a dress you wore when you were young, brave and in perfect shape. "What do you think? I found it in the market on my way home from work, and I asked for it in French. Are you impressed?" She spun and the dress lifted and twirled with her.

"I am impressed." It was easy to imagine Audrey summoning up those words, eyes fierce, determination lighting up her features. "Your hair looks fantastic."

"They were quiet in the salon this afternoon, so they did it for me." Her hair was always pretty, but tonight it drifted over her shoulders in twirling spirals, a sunset blaze, flame red against the pale bare skin of her shoulders. She smiled, lips glossed, drunk on anticipation and possibilities. Eyeliner and mascara made her eyes look huge. She looked gorgeous, and Grace felt a flash of anxiety.

No. She wasn't going to tell her to be careful. She wasn't Audrey's mother.

And she knew her reaction came from her

own need to control everything around her rather than any real need for caution. She'd met Etienne. He seemed like a good guy. Young, of course, but young didn't have to mean careless or reckless. Watching them together reminded her of how it felt to be eighteen and in love for the first time.

Of course, she hadn't been streetwise. Audrey was definitely streetwise.

Grace tried not to think about the glimpses of vulnerability.

"Is he picking you up here? Do you have everything you need? Money? Your phone? Is it charged?" *Shut up, Grace.*

"I have everything. And he isn't picking me up. I'm meeting him in a bar."

Which bar? What time? What will you do if he doesn't arrive? Do you have money? Don't drink too much.

She buried the worries under a smile. "Have fun. If you need anything, call."

Audrey glanced around Grace's apartment. "What are you doing this evening?"

"I'm going to read my book, water my plants, message Sophie and call my grandmother."

"You really do live life on the edge, Grace. Be careful you don't break your ankle or fall off the balcony while you're watering." Audrey punched her lightly on the arm. "If

281

you get into trouble, call me."

"Very funny."

"You should look up that guy."

Grace hoped her flush didn't give her away. "Do you ever give up?"

"Nope. Do it. Just a peep. A tiny, sneaky little look. He'll never know."

Grace rolled her eyes. Whatever Audrey might lack in reading skills, she made up for in dogged determination.

She glanced at the clock, surprised by how late it was. She'd intended to call Mimi earlier but she'd lost an hour at least, sitting in a pool of sunshine sipping wine and thinking about the past.

Years had blurred the edges of her memory, softened the pictures, created questions and alternate scenarios.

What if, what if —

Audrey departed, leaving the scent of lemon and verbena hovering in Grace's apartment. There was the sound of heels clattering on stairs, the squeak of door hinges that no one remembered to oil and then a firm slam.

Grace sat down again and opened the laptop. In a moment she would Skype Mimi, but first —

Her fingers hovered over the keys.

Was she really going to do this?

282

Was she going to look?

All pretense at control seemed to have left her, and she took another sip of wine and typed in his name.

As she'd expected, he wasn't hard to find. It took less than a minute for her to locate his photo and discover that he was now a celebrated pianist. There was a glossy website, complete with a list of concert dates, a biography, a list of recordings.

She clicked on his photograph, not one of those staged corporate poses with a fixed toothpaste smile, but snapped in mid-concert with his hands on the piano keys and a look of concentration on his face.

Music was his main passion, but there were many others. Food. Wine. Literature. Philippe was a man who grabbed life with both hands and squeezed until there was nothing left he could drag from it.

She went to his Facebook page, searching for a more personal story. His page was private, so all she could access were the few photographs he'd posted on his profile.

Philippe, bare chested, hat pulled low over his eyes, standing on an endless curve of sand.

Philippe, playing at the Carnegie Hall in New York, and at the Wigmore Hall in London.

Was there a wife? Had he married?

She flipped back to her own profile, trying to see it through the eyes of someone who didn't know her. The photograph was one Mimi had taken at a backyard barbecue that David held every year for the neighbors. Her hair was neat, her makeup securely in place. Her smile was fixed. Controlled. What had she been thinking when that photo was taken?

She didn't look like a woman who had once drunk too much red wine and kissed a Frenchman on a riverbank.

She returned to Philippe's page. It would be simple to send him a friend request. What would his response be?

Better late than never.

Or maybe he'd ignore her.

Her finger hovered and then she flipped her laptop closed and picked up her book instead, closing her hands over it to make it harder to do the one thing she knew she probably shouldn't do.

Beyond the windows, the sky was darkening, streaks of red giving way to midnight blue.

She wondered what Audrey was doing.

She checked her phone, but there were no messages, just an email from Sophie with few photos uploaded from Rome. The

Colosseum. The Trevi Fountain.

Having a brilliant time, Mom. How is Paris?

She emailed back, Paris is great.
For once it didn't feel like a lie. Since
moving into the apartment, she was beginning to enjoy herself. It was as if she'd left a
part of her life behind at the hotel.

Yawning, she stood up and took her plate
and empty glass into the kitchen.

She'd call Mimi and then have an early
night.

She brewed coffee on top of the stove, the
way Philippe had taught her and carried it
back to the table. The scent of it was enough
to make her contemplate moving to Paris
permanently. This was coffee the way it was
supposed to taste.

Normally when she rang, Mimi answered
immediately, but tonight there was a delay
and when her grandmother finally answered
she looked flustered.

"Grace! How are you?"

"How are *you*?" Grace adjusted the tilt of
the screen. "Are you out of breath? Don't
tell me — you were having wild sex with a
former Russian spy you met when you were
a dancer." She heard a noise in the background. "Is someone there with you?"

"John, the gardener, came over with fresh peaches, but he was just leaving. Tell me about you. Are you lazing around in pampered luxury?"

"Better." Grace curled her legs under her on the sofa and settled in. It was good to have something positive to chat about at last. Over the past few months it felt as if all she'd done was cry and complain. "I'm staying in an apartment and living like a Parisian. Are you impressed?" It was a superfluous question. Her grandmother would be thrilled that Grace had found the energy to be proactive.

"An apartment? Grace!" Mimi's face brightened. "What happened to the hotel?"

"I found a French lover and the hotel complained about the noise. They weren't wild about us swinging from the chandelier, either. Apparently it was antique."

Mimi's laugh was higher than usual. Her eyes flitted beyond the screen.

Grace froze in mortification. Was John still standing there? If he was, then she'd never be able to face anyone at Rushing River Senior Living again. She'd have to give her French classes with a bag over her head. "Mimi? Are you on your own?"

"Yes. I am a little distracted, that's all. Your call was a surprise."

Her grandmother loved surprises.

"I wanted to talk to you."

"Tell me about the apartment. Does this mean you're thinking of staying longer in Paris?"

The Mimi Grace knew would have asked about the French lover.

Or maybe her grandmother knew she was joking.

"I can't stay longer because of Sophie." But once Sophie left home, she could do anything. A few months ago that thought would have terrified her, but now? She explored her feelings gingerly, like someone staggering to their feet after a bad fall, and realized that the breathless panic that had gripped her since that awful Valentine's Day dinner had left her. She no longer felt scared. Sad, yes, but fearful of the future? No. Maybe it was the wine. Or maybe it was simply that she'd removed herself from her old life. This new life she was living had never included David. Here, the loss was more of an ache than a stab. She could feel her strength returning. "It's a short-term rental. I'll email you the address. I think you'll approve. I'm living above your bookshop." Why wasn't her grandmother looking at her? "Mimi?"

"Yes?" Mimi's eyes slid back to the screen.

"Tell me about it."

Grace tried to read her grandmother's expression, but the signal wasn't brilliant and the image was a little blurred. "Is something wrong?"

"What could be wrong? I live in paradise. Now tell me about the bookstore. Is the door still blue? Does it still have a bell that clangs like a ship about to sink?"

"It does. I don't think it has changed in the last hundred years. We're probably wading through the same dust you did. It's owned by a woman called Elodie. She mentioned her grandmother, Paulette. Did you ever meet Paulette?"

"I'm not sure —" Mimi looked vague. "Maybe. Or maybe not. The past is hazy."

Grace knew for a fact that her grandmother's memory was perfect. If the past was hazy, then it was because there were things she didn't want to share.

It was frustrating. She really wanted to know more about Mimi's link to the bookstore.

"I love that it has so many different rooms. It feels almost like a maze. What did you love most about it?"

"The atmosphere."

At least her grandmother wasn't pretending it was the books.

Grace still struggled to imagine her free-spirited, wild grandmother spending time in the bookstore. It would be like trapping a bird in a cage.

"I've made a new friend. Her name is Audrey, and she's Sophie's age. You'd love her. She reminds me a little of you. She works in the bookstore."

"That's good. I do love to be around young people, although these days everyone is a young person to me."

Grace took a deep breath. "I did something this evening." If anyone could give her advice, it was her grandmother. "Something that isn't like me. I tracked down Philippe. He's a concert pianist. He performs all over the world. I'm thinking of sending him a friend request. What do you think?"

"I think it sounds like an excellent plan."

"It's not a *plan* exactly. These days I don't have much of a plan. I wake up and see what I feel like doing, but I did wonder —" She bit her lip. "You do remember me mentioning Philippe?"

Mimi beamed at her. "Of course! He was your first love. Handsome, charming, smart — and an *amazing* lover."

Grace almost fell off her chair. "Er —"

"All Parisian men are amazing lovers. They treat women the way they treat food

289

— as something to savor and enjoy. In Paris, love is not something to rush. You should definitely contact him. I always thought you might go back one day and marry him."

"I married David."

"Yes. Shame. Still, we all make decisions we regret sometimes."

Mimi *adored* David. Since when had she thought the marriage was a mistake? And why was she suddenly so determined to push Grace toward someone else?

She opened her mouth to say she didn't regret marrying David, but Mimi was talking again.

"Call him, Grace! Get in touch."

"You always say we can't return to the past."

"That depends on what's in the past. In this case, you should. You have to live life. After all, it's nothing more than David has done. Contact Philippe."

"He might be married."

"*Bah,* so what? In Paris, no one cares about such things."

"I care, but if he isn't married, then maybe it would be fun to meet up. Drinks, or dinner."

"Dinner. Romance. Sex. Paris was made for this, no? You have no idea how happy I am that you're not sitting there pining over David."

"Well, actually —"

"Good sex cures everything, I always think." Mimi straightened. "My yoga class is in ten minutes so I should go. Call me again soon."

Grace was so taken aback by the whole conversation she didn't ask why her grandmother was cutting the conversation short.

"Take care now." Baffled, she closed the screen, and Mimi's face disappeared.

Grace stared into space.

There was something wrong with her grandmother.

MIMI

Mimi closed her laptop and studied the man hovering in the doorway. "You were supposed to leave!"

"I was going to, but then I heard her voice." David walked back into the room and sat down on the sofa. "I didn't expect her to sound so — so —"

"So what? So happy? You want her to be miserable, is that it?"

"No!" He ran his hand over the back of his neck. "You know that isn't it."

"All I know is that you broke my granddaughter's heart, and now suddenly you're knocking on my door."

He'd avoided her, presumably too ashamed of his behavior to face her. But today he was here, which meant something must have changed.

"I've known you forever, Mimi. I know Grace is out of the country and I wanted to check on you."

Was she stupid to believe him? Maybe she should have shown him the door, but he was like a son to her and she found it impossible to cut him out of her life.

David was a good guy who had done a bad thing, or at least a foolish thing.

"I'm fine. Never better." She decided to test her theory. "How are you? Where's Lissa this afternoon?"

"She's gone to the mall with her friends. Shopping."

"I'm sure it's good for her to hang out with people her own age."

David winced. "That's harsh, Mimi."

Was it? She felt a flicker of guilt and then remembered what he'd done to her grand-daughter. To her Grace.

"Do you expect me to protect your feelings?"

"No. I don't expect that." He looked stressed. Tired. Like a man who hadn't slept a full night in months.

Too much sex, Mimi thought savagely. Or maybe not. Maybe it was something more.

Was it possible that things with Lissa and David weren't as rosy as they had been?

"Would you like coffee?"

"Yes. I'll make it." He moved to the kitchen, as comfortable in her home as he was in his own. Before he and Grace had separated he'd visited Mimi at least once a week on his way home from work. He'd entertain her with ridiculous stories and make her laugh. She'd missed that.

She'd missed him.

It had been six months since he'd left Grace, and she saw the changes. His hair was shorter. The shirt he was wearing fitted him closely. He'd obviously been using the gym. She imagined Lissa dragging him to the store and trying to dress him like a man who wasn't old enough to be her father.

"Who is Philippe?" There was a roughness to his voice. "She's never mentioned a Philippe."

"No? Well, he was in the past, of course. Before the two of you got together."

Mimi felt her heart pound. She'd never been good with relationships, not her own or other people's. "She met a lot of people when she was in Paris. That was the purpose of her trip. To improve her language skills." And to escape. Mimi had pushed her, *go, go, get away from this life and see how bright the world is beyond this dark place.*

Had she done it for herself? To lessen her guilt?

Did it even matter?

In the end, it hadn't been enough. Grace had come home. And she'd stayed.

David made coffee in a French press, the way she liked it. He carried it to the low table by the sofa, along with two porcelain cups that she'd brought with her from Paris and which had survived the years. A breeze wafted in through the open doors, and Mimi sat in her favorite chair, which gave her the best view of her garden.

"He's a pianist? Grace listens to Mozart piano sonatas when she cooks."

"Does she?" Mimi tried to look vague.

"Was she in love with him? Why has she never talked about him?"

"She married you, David." Mimi pressed the plunger gently and poured the coffee. For a moment her small apartment smelled like a Paris café. "You were her choice." She drove the knife home and saw a flush spread across his cheekbones.

"I'm worried that she's vulnerable right now."

"Oh?" Mimi sipped her coffee. "Did she sound vulnerable?"

"No." He ran his hand across his jaw. "She sounded — together. Excited. And what did she mean about not having a plan? Grace always has a plan. She didn't sound like herself."

Mimi thought about the image on the screen. Grace hadn't looked much like herself, either. She'd been wearing a loose, flowing dress. There had been an empty glass next to a bottle of wine.

If David had seen what she'd seen, he'd be asking more questions than he already was.

She was asking a few of her own.

"I'm sure it makes you happy to know she is moving on and rebuilding her life, also." She noticed that he didn't look happy. He hadn't touched his coffee. "You don't need to worry about Philippe hurting her while she's vulnerable. You can relax. I know he would be very careful with Grace."

David didn't look relaxed. He looked as if he wanted to put his fist through something.

He opened his mouth to say something, but at that moment his phone rang.

He checked the number and pulled a face, embarrassed. "It's Lissa —"

"Take it," Mimi said sweetly. "The poor little thing might be lost in the mall."

He gave her a look and turned away. "Hi, Liss. What's the problem?"

Mimi tilted her head and listened shamelessly. Well, what was she supposed to do? He was having the conversation right here in her home. She couldn't be expected to leave, could she?

"Yes. If you like it, buy it." David lowered

his voice. "I'll give you the money when you get home."

Reduced to paying to keep the girl happy, Mimi thought, brushing imaginary dust from her skirt. So tacky.

"When? This Saturday? What sort of party? Who exactly is going?" His shoulders slumped. "I know . . . I know you find it boring being in the apartment . . . Yes, I know you miss your friends . . . Of course we'll go if that's what you want."

There was a bit more placating. A bit more cajoling. And then he finally hung up. He gave Mimi a sheepish look.

"Sorry about that."

"Don't apologize! It's a full-time job being a sugar daddy."

He gave a laugh that sounded more tired than amused. "You never give up, do you? It's not about the money, you know. The truth is, she's given up a lot for me and I suppose I feel I need to compensate."

Mimi couldn't see a single thing that Lissa had given up. But she could see what she'd gained. An attractive, decent man. Something that had always been missing from her life since her no good father walked out.

David, on the other hand, had given up a great deal.

He'd given up her Grace.

Upset, frustrated, she dug the knife in. "It must be fun to return to your teenage partying days. It makes Grace's moonlight dinner in Paris seem quite ordinary."

David paused. "Do you really think Grace will —" He paused. "When you talk to her again, will you tell her I said hello? On second thought, never mind. Forget it. Don't tell her anything."

"I doubt I'll speak to her again for a while. She's having far too much fun in Paris to bother with me."

Was she meddling?

So what if she was?

Mimi stood up and poured herself a glass of water. Her hand shook a little. She felt old. Tired.

She heard the sound of a chair scraping and then footsteps.

"Is the lock on your back door still sticking?"

"Don't think you can get around me by fixing my home. Do you really think I care about a door?"

She was sick of the door.

"I have my toolbox in the car. I can easily fix it."

She should tell him to go away, but having to tug at the door every day was driving her crazy. She'd actually kicked it that morning, and been relieved no one was around to witness her childish reaction. "Do what you want to do."

She heard the sound of the front door opening and watched as he strode down the path to his car.

Her shoulders slumped. She'd missed this. She'd missed his visits, his conversation and his kindness.

She felt torn. Was it disloyal to let him fix things around her home? There was the wardrobe door, too, that creaked whenever she opened it.

But she was angry with him. So angry.

And then he was back, shirtsleeves pushed back revealing those strong arms. Strong. Capable. Liar.

She straightened. "This doesn't mean I forgive you."

"I know." He flipped open his box and pulled out a tool. She had no idea what it was. She was good at breaking things, and hopeless at fixing them.

She watched him as he worked.

He removed the new lock from its packaging and fitted it carefully. "She's going to make contact with this Philippe, isn't she?"

"Do you understand the meaning of the word *hypocrisy,* David?"

"I'm worried about her, that's all."

"You lost the right to worry about her six months ago." Why was she being so harsh? Perhaps it was because she'd also made bad choices. She'd also done things she wasn't proud of.

He checked the handle. Opened and closed the door a few times, then closed the toolbox. "I don't know what happened, Mimi. I don't know exactly where or when it went wrong. It's been a long time since I felt Grace needed me."

"You of all people should have known how much Grace needed you."

"How? When? She organized everything. Planned everything."

"Of course. Above all else, Grace hates chaos."

"And I lost sight of that in the middle of everything." He sighed. "I went to the bakery to buy bread this morning. Clemmie gave me a stale loaf."

Good for Clemmie.

"Clemmie is very fond of Grace."

David paced to the window of Mimi's small apartment and stared down toward the river.

"This place is beautiful in the summer."

"Shouldn't you be going? You can't leave a child lost in a mall. It wouldn't be right."

He gave a weary laugh. "You're right. I

300

should go." He walked across to her and kissed her on the cheek. "I'll see you soon, Mimi."

"Don't worry about me. You'll be too busy partying and trying to keep up with whatever it is teenagers like to do these days."

He ignored that. "Will you tell Grace you saw me?"

"No. Why would I? You're her past and what she needs to do now is focus on her future."

"What if she gets involved with him?"

"I hope she does. She deserves to be as happy as you are." She couldn't remember seeing a man more miserable. "And now you know she is rebuilding her life and seeing other men, you can stop feeling guilty and enjoy your new life."

He didn't look as if he was enjoying his life. He looked traumatized. He fumbled his way to the door. "I'll — Goodbye, Mimi."

"Goodbye."

As the door shut behind him, she closed her eyes.

So now she had a decision to make.

Should she tell Grace he was here?

Or should she keep that information to herself?

AUDREY

Audrey rolled over in bed and discovered she was alone. The rumpled sheets and the dip in the pillow next to her told her she hadn't imagined the night before.

She sat up, bleary-eyed. There was her dress on the floor. Her shoes by the door. Her clothes, signposting the events of the previous evening.

In the end they'd gone to a bar. He'd ordered a fashionable brand of beer and insisted she try one, too. The music had been so loud they'd had to sit nose to nose in order to have a conversation, although to be fair they'd done more kissing than talking. They'd been so wrapped up each other, he hadn't noticed that she hadn't touched her drink.

Etienne had known a lot of people. They'd drifted past, speaking rapid French, but Etienne had always replied in English so that Audrey was included.

She rolled onto her back and stared up at the ceiling. She liked him. *She liked him.*

And there was nothing wrong with her.

Remembering, she smiled.

There was the sound of a door opening and then he shouldered his way into the room carrying a tray. He paused in the doorway and grinned. "You're still here."

"Why wouldn't I be?"

He gave a shrug that was as cute as it was awkward. "Morning after. Things look different in daylight, no?"

If anything, he looked even better than he had the night before.

She wished she had sprinted to the bathroom and at least brushed her hair. "I had fun last night."

"Me, too. I don't know what you like for breakfast, so I made a selection." His chest was bare, but he'd pulled on a pair of shorts. They rode low over his hips and she felt her mouth dry.

They hadn't said much to each other the night before, but what if he suddenly wanted to talk? What if he picked a topic she knew nothing about? She didn't want to look stupid. She felt more self-conscious about conversation than she did about sex.

She sat up in bed, holding the sheet across her breasts.

303

"Your apartment is like a hotel."

"My parents' apartment." He put the tray on the bed. The smell of freshly brewed coffee mingled with warm croissant. His hair flopped over his forehead and his jaw was dark with morning shadow.

He was so unbearably cute her stomach clenched.

"So they're like mega successful, I'm guessing." She reached for a croissant. "Should I use a plate? I don't want to get crumbs everywhere."

"If you do, I'll lick them off you." He leaned forward and kissed the corner of her mouth. "You're incredible. Your hair looks as if it's on fire."

No one had ever told her she was incredible before.

The way he looked at her made her *feel* incredible.

The croissant was the best thing she'd ever tasted. Buttery, flaky and still warm. "Where did you buy this?"

"At the bakery next door." He slid off his shorts and joined her in bed, making a grab for the coffee before it spilled everywhere. "Are you tired? We didn't get a lot of sleep."

"I feel great. Are your mum and dad away all summer?"

"They get out of Paris and go to the

304

beach." He was casual about it. "My dad's an investor, so he works from home."

She had no idea what that was, but it obviously paid well if this apartment was anything to go by. "That sounds good."

"How about your parents? What do they do?"

His family was obviously normal. If she told him the truth about hers, he would stop thinking she was incredible.

"My mum is an office manager. She works for a bunch of lawyers. She's just married again." It was a part truth. Her life was full of part truths. Hiding a chunk of your life led to a type of isolation that was hard to describe. The fact that no one really knew her created a particularly acute brand of loneliness.

"You have a stepdad? Does he beat you?"

The thought of Ron beating anyone made her smile. "No. He's pretty cool, in fact. I bet your parents have been married forever."

"Yes, but that's enough boring talk about parents." He pulled the coffee mug out of her hand and put it on the bedside table. "I don't want to think about my parents just before I do all the things I'm planning to do to you."

"I was drinking that!" She squealed with laughter as he tumbled her back on the bed.

"What's the time?"

"I don't know. I'm a lazy student, remember? I never look at the time in the mornings."

"But I'm supposed to be working." This close she could see the pinpricks of dark stubble on his jaw and the sleepiness of his eyes as he smiled into hers. She felt the weight of him, pressing down on her, the roughness of his thigh against hers. Her heart kicked against her chest and desire almost punched the breath from her body.

She'd never done this before. Never laughed during sex. Never woken up in someone else's bed feeling as if she belonged there. Sex had always been its own thing for her. Never part of something else. She'd never been held. Never nestled and nuzzled. It felt good.

He lowered his head to hers, and his kiss was so gentle she wanted to cry. He didn't make it all about him. He took time to find out the stuff she liked, too. It wasn't just about passion; it was about feeling.

He murmured something in French, coaxed her mouth open with his and deepened the kiss. It made her dizzy, the taste of him, the erotic slide of his tongue against hers.

His hands were sure and skilled, so different from the inept fumbling she'd experienced before. Etienne didn't rush. He didn't want to just "do it" and then get the hell out so that he could boast to his friends.

"I like you." He kissed her jaw and her neck. "I like you a lot."

It made her feel special to hear him say it. She ignored the fact that he didn't know her. Did anyone ever know anyone? She knew for a fact there was a ton of stuff Ron didn't know about her mum.

"I like you, too." It felt a little weird to say it aloud. What did it mean exactly? Like wasn't love. It was way too soon for love.

But like was nice. It felt special.

He shifted above her. "Am I too heavy?"

"No." She liked it. She like feeling him. He was a hard, muscular barrier between herself and life.

Afterward, she fell asleep again and woke disorientated and panicking.

Sun spilled through the window so she knew it was late. "Shit. I didn't mean to fall asleep. What time is it?" She reached for her phone and swore again. "I'm late. I'm totally stuffed. *Fuck* — I mean darn."

"Darn?" Etienne yawned. " 'Shit' I know, and also 'fuck,' but what is this darn?"

"Darn. You know — oh, never mind." She scrambled out of bed, grabbing her clothes.

Etienne levered himself up on his elbows, watching her from the bed with sleepy eyes. "You can use my shower if you like."

"No time. I'm already late. I'm going to lose my job. If I lose my job, I lose my apartment." How could she have been so stupid?

"You could move in here, with me."

"Don't let's get ahead of ourselves." She dragged on her dress. She'd felt pretty in it the night before. Now it felt wrinkled and wrong. Her heels were too high to suffer a walk over the cobbled streets. How could she have lost track of the time? How long would it take her to get back to the book-shop from here? She didn't even know exactly where she was.

She didn't have time to look in the mirror but she knew most of her makeup had settled under her eyes.

She found her purse and glanced back toward him. "Thanks." Was that the wrong thing to say? She had no idea.

He grinned that sexy, lopsided smile that she found impossible to resist. "One of my friends is having a party tomorrow night. Come with me?"

She paused with her hand on the door. A party in someone's house was different from a drink in a bar. But Etienne was nice, and the friends she'd met the night before had seemed nice, too.

"Sure," she said. "What time?"

"I'll pick you up at eight."

Audrey blew her budget and took a cab back to the bookshop, fidgeting in the back seat the whole way.

She saw the driver glance at her in his rear-view mirror and read disapproval in his expression.

When he pulled up outside the bookshop she shoved a few notes at him and raced inside.

Please, please don't let Elodie be there.

There was no sign of Elodie. Just Grace, talking to the white-haired old man who was fast becoming Audrey's favorite customer. His name was Toni, and he arrived at the bookshop at the same time every day, chose a shelf and flicked through every book one by one. Audrey still hadn't figured out what he was doing. Surely no one could read a book that fast?

Right now, he had his hand on Grace's shoulder in a soothing way. He seemed to be reassuring her about something.

"Hi, Toni." Audrey beamed at him, trying to look as if it was normal to show up wearing last night's crumpled dress and high heels. "How are you doing?"

"I'm well, thank you." He let his hand

drop and smiled at Grace, as if he'd been proved right about something.

Grace sat down hard on the chair. "Are you okay?"

"Yes. Why wouldn't I be?" She saw Grace scan her dress and wished she'd stopped to buy a new outfit on her way home.

Usually Grace smiled a lot, but today her mouth was set in a tight line.

Crap.

Normally Audrey didn't give a damn what people thought of her, but for some reason she really didn't want Grace to think badly of her. "I'm sorry I'm late —"

"Go and take a shower and change. I'll hold the fort." Grace stood up and picked up a stack of postcards from the desk. "Let's carry on going through these, Toni. This one must have been taken from across the street, don't you think?"

Toni took it from her and peered at it. "Yes. There used to be a café right there."

Audrey hesitated. She wanted to redeem herself, but didn't know what to say. The best thing she could do was get out of last night's clothes. She shot upstairs to her apartment, showered in two minutes flat and pulled on jeans and a clean T-shirt. If she took the time to dry her hair, would Elodie appear and notice she was missing?

Knowing her luck, probably.

She scooped it into a knot and secured it at the back of her head, flung open the window to let in some air and clattered back downstairs.

She pushed open the door and froze.

Elodie was standing there.

Her stomach lurched.

Goodbye, apartment. Probably goodbye Paris, too, because she couldn't afford anything else on what she earned at the salon. Goodbye, Etienne.

That part bothered her more than anything.

Audrey braced herself to be fired and publicly humiliated, but instead of exploding as she had the time before, Elodie beamed at her.

"Thank you!" She reached out her hands to Audrey. "Grace was telling me that you have spent half the morning clearing out the boxes of books in the back. They've been there forever. I never seem to have time to sort them. No wonder you were covered in dust and needed a shower. I'm so grateful."

Grace stood stiffly. "I was telling Elodie how you sorted them into fiction and non-fiction, and then into categories. We're going to shelve them together later."

311

Audrey stared at her.

Grace had lied for her? *Grace?*

Was she even capable of telling a lie?

It must have half killed her, but she'd done it for Audrey.

"Yeah, those books were — pretty dirty."

Elodie waved her hand. "It is a job I have been meaning to do for at least two years, so I'm pleased that finally you have made a start. Thank you, Audrey."

Audrey felt color flood into her cheeks. She felt like a total fraud, probably because she *was* a fraud. She was *never* going to be late again. "You're welcome." She waited until Elodie bustled out of the shop, and turned to Grace.

"Thanks. You didn't have to do that."

"I didn't want you to lose your job."

"Yeah, well, thanks again. I put you in a difficult position. I know you're not exactly the lying type, so I don't blame you for being mad at me."

She should be used to it by now. Her mum often yelled. She made her teachers frustrated.

"I'm not mad because I had to lie for you, I'm mad because you worried me half to death. Audrey, you didn't come home last night." Grace's voice rose. "Do you have any idea how it felt to knock on your door

312

this morning and get no answer? I called your cell phone, and it was switched off. I pictured you lying in a gutter somewhere and I had no idea where to even look for you. I was trying to figure out how I could ask Elodie for Etienne's number when you walked in. Toni was the one who persuaded me to wait." She sat down hard on the chair and breathed. "Sorry. I'm sorry. I didn't mean to yell, but I was so scared."

Audrey opened her mouth and closed it again.

"You're mad because — you were *worried* about me?"

"Of course! What else?"

"I assumed you were mad because I was late and you had to tell a lie for me."

"I was so relieved to see you safe and, well, I would have told a million lies for you." Grace rubbed her hands over her face. "You're probably thinking I overreacted, and maybe I did. It's part of being a mother, I think. You always imagine the worst."

Audrey felt her eyes sting. It hadn't occurred to her that Grace might be worried. "I was fine. We hooked up and I stayed the night at his place. And overslept." It was probably better not to mention the morning sex. "His apartment was farther away than I thought so it took longer than planned. I promise it won't ever happen again."

Grace twisted the ring on her finger. "I should be the one apologizing to you. You're an adult. Your mother is probably back home fighting the urge to call you every five minutes, and here I am acting like a mother hen and stepping in when I shouldn't."

No one had ever mothered Audrey, least of all her own mother.

"I — I'm glad you care." There was a lump lodged in her throat. Grace had to be the kindest person she'd ever met. "How was your evening? Did you contact Philippe?"

"I did not." But there was a glimmer of a smile there.

"Why not? Send him a friend request. No arguments."

"You can't interfere with my love life."

"Why not? You interfere with mine." Audrey folded her arms. "I'll make you a deal. I'll text you and let you know I'm safe next time I go out, providing you send that friend request."

"You're very manipulative."

"Thanks."

"It wasn't a compliment."

"Life's tough, Grace. How have you even survived this far? You're like this —" she waved her hands "— perfect person. You don't swear, you don't drink —"

"I had a glass of red wine last night."

Audrey pressed her hand to her chest. "I'm *shocked.* Go you. Tonight, a glass of wine. Tomorrow, kissing a hot guy under the lights of the Eiffel Tower."

"You have a wild imagination."

"Send that friend request."

Grace sighed and pulled out her phone. "If this goes badly, I'm coming for you."

"Do it." She watched as Grace finally sent the friend request. "Yay! Doesn't that feel great?"

"It feels terrifying."

"It's a whole new beginning."

"Or maybe the biggest mistake of my life." Grace pulled a piece of paper out of her bag. "This is for you."

"What is it?"

"It's a list of audiobooks I think you might like. I chose them because I think you might like the story, but also because the narrator is good. If you have to listen to someone's voice for a long time, it has to be one that you like."

"Yeah, I get that. I mean, Etienne has this really sexy voice." She gave Grace a sideways look. "Sorry. TMI. I swear I was careful."

"Did I ask?"

"Yeah, just not with your mouth. It was

315

right there in your eyes." Audrey read through the list slowly. "You have nice writing. Easier to read than most people's."

"They'll let you download a couple of books free to try it so you don't have to spend any money to begin with."

"Cool. I like free things." She dropped the paper into her bag. "Thanks."

"Do you have something in your fridge to eat tonight? Would you like to eat with me? You could come down around six if you like."

"Yeah, sure." She was surprised by how much she enjoyed spending time with Grace. She was calming. Reassuring. It was like swimming in a deep pool, knowing there was a life belt within reach.

She was also a good cook, despite her obsession with fruit and vegetables.

"Good. I'll make us dinner. And we can learn vocabulary for asking directions."

Audrey started to rethink dinner. "Even if I learn the words for left and right, I still won't know which way to go. I'm crap at directions. Always have been."

"I had an idea about that." Grace dug into her bag again. "I bought you this. I hope you like it." She handed over a small blue box, and Audrey stared at it, mystified.

"What is it?"

"Open it and see."

She flipped it open and felt her throat thicken. The silver ring looked like lace. "It's pretty. I can't believe you bought me this."

"Wear it on your right hand. Ring. Right hand. Turn right. That way you won't forget and get lost."

The thickening in her throat grew worse. No one had ever given her something so pretty before. Even her mum didn't buy her jewelry. "I don't know what to say."

"Try something in French."

Audrey laughed and the weird feeling in her throat passed. *Merci beaucoup.*

The ring was pretty, but what really touched her was the thought behind it. Grace had been thinking about her. Figuring out ways she could help.

No one had tried to find ways to make things easier for her before. And no one had ever bought her anything as pretty as this ring.

To show her gratitude, she went into the back room to carry on with the work Grace had started. Immediately, she started sneezing. She opened her mouth to swear and closed it again. Grace hated swearing, didn't she? "This place is one big dust mite. What are these boxes anyway?"

The boxes were stacked high, most of

them unopened.

"People bring them in. Donate them. Sometimes they're clearing out, but sometimes a person has died." Grace gestured to the pile she'd already sorted. "I'm going to shelve these. Take your time. If you can just sort into fiction and nonfiction, I will do the rest. And if any of them are confusing and not obvious, make a separate pile."

"Are any of them valuable?"

"Unlikely, but Elodie will check before we shelve them."

Audrey spent the rest of the morning wrestling with old books and dust, and thinking about Etienne. When she heard the bell clang at lunchtime her heart quickened but she stayed in the back room. How was she supposed to react? She'd never been the type to fall heavily for boys like some of her friends, but she did like Etienne. She liked him a lot. But did she want him to know that?

Deciding to play it cool, she pushed her hair out of her eyes and stood up.

She could hear him talking to Grace. They were laughing together.

She strolled out of the back room into the cool shade of the shop. "Hi, there."

"Hi." He gave a smile that was just for her. It was a smile that acknowledged a memory, but also made a promise. *Tomorrow. Already thinking about it.*

Her heart skipped and danced, her hopes held in check by her brain. She was lonely, wasn't she? People did stupid things when they were lonely. They made decisions they regretted later. "I was sorting through books, but as you're here now I'll get going. They're busy in the salon today." For some reason that look he gave her made her feel weightless and giddy. She floated through the afternoon, washing hair and massaging scalps. This came naturally to her. It was as if her fingers knew how to do this without any help from her. Maybe she could find a salon to train her. Some of them did that, didn't they? She could learn how to cut. Work her way up. Maybe even one day own her own salon. She knew she'd be good at it.

It was later, much later, when she finally knocked on the door of Grace's apartment.

The moment Grace opened the door, Audrey knew something was wrong.

Grace had showered and changed, and her shirt buttons were done up unevenly.

Knowing Grace, that had to be a sign that the world was falling apart.

Audrey stepped inside. "What happened?" There were delicious smells coming from the kitchen, so that was one thing.

"He replied!"

"From your panicked look I'm assuming you mean Philippe? And?"

"He accepted my friend request and immediately messaged me to invite me to dinner tomorrow night."

"That's great!"

"It is not great." Grace paced the length of her apartment, curling and uncurling her fingers. "Why did I send that friend request?"

"Because I encouraged you, but I refuse to apologize. I was saving you from yourself. Calm down. It's dinner, that's all. Where are you going?"

"Nowhere! *Obviously* I can't go."

"You have to eat a meal. He has to eat a meal. You'll eat the meal together. No biggie."

"We both know it's a lot more complicated than that."

"Do we?" Audrey sat down on the sofa and studied the plate of nibbles. "Are these for eating? My brain works better when it's fed."

"Help yourself."

"Thanks." She selected what looked like a tiny square of French bread topped with something that smelled delicious. "Tell me why it's complicated."

"For a start because I've been with the same man for twenty-five years. I know nothing about dating."

"No problem. I might not know anything about French verbs, but I know all there is to know about sexy lingerie. This is delicious by the way —" Audrey caught the crumbs in her palm. "I never thought I liked olives until I came to France."

"My lingerie isn't an issue. If I go, and I still haven't decided, I won't be taking my clothes off."

"Why not?"

"It's dinner. Catching up with a friend."

"Not dinner and sex?"

"Definitely not dinner and sex."

"So why are you so stressed-out?"

"I don't know. Maybe because I was eighteen when I saw him last." Grace smoothed her beige dress over her thighs. "That's a long time ago."

So it was a confidence thing.

Audrey chewed. It was weird. Grace had to be at least . . . er . . . how old? She was completely crap at guessing ages.

She trod carefully. "How many years since you saw him?"

"Are you asking my age? It's not something I hide. I'm forty-seven."

Forty-seven?

Audrey had guessed her to be at least fifty. Forty was old, too, of course, but not as old as fifty.

"Okay, so I'm going to say it the way it is and you're not to get mad at me." Audrey helped herself to another delicious morsel from the plate next to her. "You're only forty-seven, but you dress like —" she waved a hand "— the way you do. What is that about?"

"I'm dressing my age."

"No. You're dressing like a grandmother. We have to fix that."

"We're not fixing anything. This is the style I like."

Audrey took another bite of food. She didn't want to hurt Grace's feelings, but still — sometimes you had to be cruel to be kind, didn't you? "All I'm saying is that I think we could make a few small changes. I mean, the tights have got to go, obviously. Who the hell wears tights in the summer?"

"I do."

"Not anymore you don't. Take them off."

Grace pressed her hands to her thighs, as if she was afraid Audrey might physically remove them. "I like them."

"No one 'likes' tights, Grace. They're an abomination. Need me to learn how to say that in French?"

"I do not. And I disagree. Women of a certain age shouldn't be showing their legs."

"Maybe not if you've got veins and things, but you haven't." Audrey studied Grace's legs. "All you need is a little fake tan and you're away."

"I'm not turning my legs orange."

Audrey sighed. "They won't be orange. And if you want me to learn a ton of new French words, then you are going to have to lose those tights. That's the deal."

"The new words are for you. To help you."

"And the new way of dressing is for you. To help you. We need to brighten up your look a little. You wear a lot of beige and black. I mean, you look great, don't get me wrong, but it makes you look older than you are."

"Beige and black are classic, safe choices."

"If you work in a funeral home maybe. We need to make sure that when you meet Philippe for dinner, you wow him."

"I'm not meeting him for dinner."

"Yeah, you are." Audrey stood up. Where should she start? "I think you're wearing your clothes a size bigger than you should."

"Tight clothes don't look good on a woman my age."

Audrey thought about her mother. Spilling flesh. Tight waistbands. "You're right. But there's a difference between clothes that are tight and clothes that fit well." She paced around Grace, looking at her from every angle. "Lift your dress up."

"Excuse me?"

Audrey reached out and hoisted it up herself. "Why do you always wear dresses that end midcalf?"

"I hate my knees."

"Is that why you wear tights? Your knees look fine to me, but we can get something that ends below the knee if it makes you more comfortable."

"You want to help choose my clothes?"

"Not help. I don't need help. I'm choosing them. I'm also doing your hair and makeup." Audrey pulled the clip out of Grace's hair. It tumbled loose over her shoulders. Her fingers ached to pick up scissors. "You look good. You're the kind of person who never leaves the house without sunscreen and a hat, so your skin is great. You don't have any gray in your hair. How long have you been wearing your hair like this?"

"Thirty years."

"You've had the same hairstyle for thirty years? Well sh— I mean, darn." Audrey helped herself to a cherry from the bowl on

324

the table. If she stuffed her mouth with cherries, there would be no risk of her saying all the things she wanted to say. "Time for a makeover." She spat the cherry stone into her palm and was about to put it down on a book Grace was reading when she caught her eye.

"The garbage can is in the kitchen, Audrey."

"Good. I knew that. Thanks." She strolled into the kitchen, threw the stone in the bin and walked back into the living room. "I'm almost house-trained. Are you impressed? Now sit down and don't move." She pulled out one of the dining room chairs. "I'm nipping upstairs to fetch a few things, but I'll be back in a minute."

She sprinted to her apartment, grabbed what she needed and returned to find Grace still standing in the same place.

"What exactly are you planning?"

"Changing things a bit, that's all."

"I hate change."

"You're not going to hate this change." Audrey gestured to the chair. "I'm going to show you some colors and styles. If you don't like it, I won't be offended."

"You're not going to cut it?" Grace grasped her hair protectively. With her hair loose and her buttons uneven, she seemed vulnerable.

"Not yet. But I am going to show you what it would look like shorter." She opened the case Meena had bought her for her birthday, and pulled out hair grips. "Close your eyes."

"I want to see what you're doing."

"Do I tell you how to teach French? Have a little faith. I'm good at this, I promise." Audrey combed through Grace's hair, studying the color and texture. "You have nice hair. It's in good condition. That's going to help."

"I condition it regularly."

Of course she did. Grace would never do anything so reckless as to leave her hair to fend for itself.

Audrey moved in front of her, twisting Grace's hair away from her face, lowering it a little, looking at different lengths. "I want to try something." Holding the pins between her teeth, she combed, tucked and pinned until she'd produced a style that mimicked short hair. "It would look better than this if it was cut, obviously."

"Are you going to let me look?"

"Not yet. Where's your makeup case?"

"In the bathroom."

"Don't move." Audrey was back in a flash, makeup case in her hand. "You have expensive makeup."

"David gives it to me for Christmas and birthdays."

"He buys your makeup?"

"No. I buy it."

"Oh, right. I get it. You buy it, and he wraps it."

"I usually wrap it, too."

"Shit, Grace — I mean double darn —" Audrey selected a tinted moisturizer. "Do you hand it to yourself and wish yourself happy birthday, too? How about sex? Do you do that yourself or does he help out?"

"I'm not dignifying that with a response."

"Is he the only guy you've ever slept with?"

"You can't ask me questions like that."

"I just did. So was David the only one?"

Grace hesitated. "No."

Audrey grinned and nudged her. "You minx, you. Who else? No, don't tell me. It's Philippe, isn't it? That's why you're nervous about seeing him. You cared about him. So who else?"

"No one else."

"That's it? Two men? Crap, Grace, you're practically a virgin." Audrey swept a tiny sponge across Grace's cheeks. "Why do you buy your own gifts?"

"Birthdays and Christmases were unpredictable when I was growing up. It's impor-

tant to me to know I'm going to like what I
open so I generally choose it myself."

So she wasn't the only one whose childhood had been unpredictable.

What exactly had happened to Grace?

She kept her response neutral. If Grace
wanted to talk about it, she'd talk about it.
"That sucks, Grace."

"I know it sucks. A lot of things in life
suck."

"Tell me about it." She deftly applied
highlighter and blusher. "You have good
bones."

"Did your mother teach you to apply
makeup?"

"Kind of." Did learning to cover the
outward signs of a night of drinking count?
"Your lipsticks are all too dark." Audrey
removed them one by one, twisted them up,
checked the color and rejected them. "You
need something paler. Nude, with maybe a
hint of pink. And gloss. It's summer. But
don't worry. We can fix that later." She
stood back. "Go and look in the mirror."

Grace stood up and walked to the bedroom.

Audrey heard her gasp.

Good gasp? Horrified gasp? *What-have-
you-done gasp?*

"Oh, Audrey —" Grace appeared in the

328

doorway, her eyes shining. "I love it. You are *so* clever."

No one had ever told her she was clever before. Audrey felt a couple of inches taller. "I'm glad you like it."

"Can you do this again tomorrow night?"

"I thought you weren't going to dinner?"

Grace lifted her hand to her hair. "I might have changed my mind about that."

"It wouldn't stay like that. The pins would fall out."

Grace hesitated and then lifted her chin. "So cut it."

Audrey was surprised. "Seriously?"

"As you say, it's time for a change."

Was this a good moment to confess that she didn't actually cut hair? No. If she did that, Grace would lose her nerve. And she was sure she could do it. She'd done her own a million times. And she'd done Meena's. "Are you up for just a few golden highlights, too? Not many. Just a couple to add a little definition and frame your face. It will look great, I promise."

"Don't I have to go to a salon for that?"

"I have what I need. My old boss gave it to me so that I could do my mum's colors."

"In that case, go for it. Whatever you think. I'm in your hands."

It took Audrey an hour to do the highlights

and another hour to wash and cut Grace's hair using the scissors that had been a leaving gift from her friends in the salon in London.

As chunks of hair fell to the floor, she felt a flicker of nerves.

What if Grace hated it?

Still, it was too late now. She could hardly stick it back on.

She combed the hair carefully, checking the cut. She'd left the sides a little longer and she curved them under as she dried the hair so that the hair framed Grace's face.

"There." She switched off the drier. "You're done." Her palms were a little sweaty. The change was more dramatic than she'd anticipated. What if Grace hated it?

"Can I look?" Grace removed the towel from her shoulders and walked to the bedroom.

Audrey closed her eyes and crossed her fingers.

There was silence. More silence. And then she heard a sound.

"Grace?" Was she crying? Shit. Shitty shit. Panicking, Audrey dragged herself to the doorway of the bedroom.

Grace was standing in front of the mirror, tears pouring down her face.

Audrey's stomach clenched. "I'm sorry. I

thought — I'll fix it. I'll do something — I —"

"Don't do anything. I love it." Grace wiped her cheeks and turned to look at Audrey. "I love *me.* For the first time in months. Maybe longer. You have no idea." She sank onto the bed and sobbed. Not delicate tears, but great gulping sobs. "When he left, he didn't just take his clothes from the closet, he took all my confidence. Every last scrap. She was so *young,* and it was all so brutal, and every time I looked in the mirror all I saw were the reasons he left, so I stopped looking."

Audrey stood frozen. She was used to her mother crying. But Grace crying? That was a whole different thing. It made Audrey want to cry, too. There was a huge, massive lump in her throat. She put her hand on Grace's shoulder. "I think you're beautiful. Inside and out. That's the truth. You're the best person I've ever met, Grace."

Grace stood up and hugged her tightly. "I've been trying so hard to move on. To not be me. To be different."

"You don't need to be different." Audrey had never been held so tightly in her life. "You're great the way you are."

"No. The real me is boring and does everything the same because it's safe. My hair has been the same all those years because I'm too afraid to change it. But what you've done is amazing, and it makes me realize that change can be good. I need to do more of it. I need to give my whole life a haircut."

Audrey felt the sting and spill of tears. Shit. If she ever met Grace's husband, she'd floor him. "You're smudging your makeup. Worse, you're smudging mine." She sniffed. "We're going to have to start again, you know that?"

Grace made a gurgling sound that was close to a laugh. Then she pulled away and walked back to the mirror. She moved her head experimentally. Her hair swung with each movement, smooth and silky.

"How many times have you done this cut before?"

And now they'd reached the awkward part.

Audrey stood on one leg and then the other. "That might have been the first time."

"You don't normally cut hair short?"

"I don't normally cut hair at all." Mmm. *Probably should have lied about that, Audrey.*

Grace frowned. "But you said you worked as a hairdresser."

"I said I worked in a hairdressing salon. I wash the hair. Do treatments. Toners. Head

332

massages. That kind of thing."

"So this is the first time you've actually cut hair?"

"Yeah." She waited for Grace to freak.

But she didn't freak. "In that case I think we both know what career direction you should be taking. You have real talent, Audrey. Tomorrow we are going to your salon together so that we can show them what you've done."

"I can't cut hair here in France. I don't speak French."

"Hair is a universal language." Grace swung her head from side to side again. "So what should I wear on my date?"

Audrey finally relaxed. "You really are going?"

"Too right I'm going." Grace turned to look at her and there was an expression on her face that Audrey hadn't seen before. "I need to show off my new hair."

GRACE

Grace turned her head from side to side, admiring her hair in the mirror.

She felt excited but also nervous, which was crazy, of course. What did she have to be nervous about?

She was having dinner with an old friend, that was all.

Except, Philippe had been more than that, hadn't he?

First love.

When she'd left Paris without even having a chance to say goodbye, she'd cried the whole way home on the flight. She cried for the life she was leaving and the life she was returning to. The crew had kept her plied with tissues.

She'd stepped off the plane into the chaos and conflict of her life. It was like plunging into freezing water after swimming in a tropical ocean. Suddenly she was negotiating a world filled with jagged edges instead of smooth curves. The only solid thing had been David. It had been like grabbing a tree, knowing that it wouldn't move as the floodwaters of life rushed over her.

David had put her back together, piece by piece.

Eventually he'd replaced the piece that had belonged to Philippe. It was as if he had never existed.

"Grace?" There was a hammering on the bedroom door and Audrey's voice. "What are you doing in there? You'd better not be messing with your hair! Are you ready?"

"Yes." She took a last look at her reflection.

She didn't see David's wife. She saw herself.

Maybe beauty wasn't what you saw in the mirror. It was what you felt inside.

The woman in the mirror didn't have a plan. She didn't ever glance at a list. She went where the impulse took her.

She opened the door and Audrey whistled.

"That outfit is perfect. Stunning. And those gold sandals are right on trend."

The strappy gold sandals had been just one of many outrageous purchases.

Grace had been afraid Audrey would want her to buy clothes designed for a woman half her age, but that hadn't happened.

They'd found a small boutique and the first thing Audrey had picked out was a beautiful dress in Mediterranean blue. The top was fitted and left Grace's arms bare, and the skirt flowed from the waist in tiny pleats. Audrey had also talked her into buying a pair of gold strappy sandals and a sun hat with a wide brim and a ribbon. While Grace had been trying everything on, Audrey picked out a couple of tops, a pair of well-cut jeans and a white floral skirt that fell just below the knee. It was bright and summery, but still sophisticated.

"You should be a stylist." Grace did a twirl in the blue dress, loving the way it felt and looked. Was that really her in the mirror? She'd had no idea that clothes could make her feel this good. Some of her friends bought new outfits every week, but Grace had invested in a capsule wardrobe that could be easily adapted for every occasion in her life.

This was the first time she'd had to dress for dinner with an ex-lover and nothing in her wardrobe covered that.

How could a dress give you confidence? She didn't know, but this one did.

"What do you think?"

Audrey folded her arms. "What do *you* think?"

336

"I love it!"

"Good. So do I. Now try these —" Audrey thrust another couple of dresses at her, and Grace took them, ignoring the part of her that said she didn't need a whole new wardrobe.

If the clothes didn't fit her life, then she'd change her life.

She spent more in that one shopping spree than she had in her entire life and she had no regrets.

Now she tucked her purse under her arm and studied Audrey. "You look good, too."

"I didn't know what to wear." Audrey glanced down at her jeans and shimmery top. "It's a party at the house of one of his friends. My bottom half could be underdressed, and my top half could be overdressed but I figure at least one half of me is going to fit right in."

"What type of party is it?"

"The sort where people get drunk, dance, throw up in the bathroom and sometimes have sex. Not all at the same time. In other words, the usual type. No fancy dress thankfully. My friend Meena and I once went as cats to a party and the mask made me itch. It was fun having a tail, though. And now you're looking anxious. You don't have to worry about me, Grace."

"Where is the party?"

"I don't know. I'm not the one with the sense of direction, as you know. Etienne is picking me up, so luckily for me it's not my problem."

"Do you know the friend who owns the house?"

"Duh, no? What do you want? References?" Audrey gave her a look, and Grace felt like an idiot.

"Sorry. You're right. I should be worrying about myself, not you."

Audrey patted her on the shoulder. "Don't stay out too late. If you get in trouble call me. Do you have a condom in your bag?"

"I'm not going to need a condom."

"You never know." Audrey smoothed a strand of Grace's hair. "I'm loving this look. Was it easy to do this morning?"

"Yes. I wish I'd had it cut years ago." Lately it had felt as if life had been happening to her. She'd had no control. She'd had no choice about what happened with David. But now she'd made a few small choices of her own — apartment, haircut, dinner with Philippe — and it felt good.

"Only one thing missing." Audrey handed her a little bag, and Grace opened it.

"You bought me lipstick?"

Audrey took it from her and twisted it so

338

that Grace could see the color. "Try it."

The color was little more than a subtle sheen, but it was perfect. "Thank you. That's incredibly kind. But you must let me pay."

"No way." Audrey's cheeks were pink. "I had good tips this week and you're always treating me. So where are you meeting him?"

"At a café near the river. He's booked a table outside, which I guess will make it easier for me to run if the whole evening is a disaster." Her phone rang and she grabbed it. "It's Sophie. I should get this."

"I'll see you later. Or maybe tomorrow. I promise not to be late." She vanished, and Grace stared after her for a second before she took the call from her daughter.

"Sophie! How are you, honey?"

"Great! Mom, you won't believe the stuff we've been doing in Rome. It's so cool . . ." She chattered away, bright and excited while Grace listened. She was relieved Sophie was having such a good time.

When had Audrey last spoken to her mother? Grace tried to remember a time when she'd seen her on the phone.

"How are you, Mom? How are you feeling?"

"I'm feeling great." She'd said those words

numerous times since David had left her, but tonight was the first time she'd meant them.

"What are you doing tonight?"

"I'm intending to enjoy Paris. Have dinner and maybe a stroll along the river." And she wasn't going to feel guilty. It had been David who had made the decision to end their marriage, not her.

She was picking up the pieces of her life, that was all.

She was in Paris, wearing a dress she loved, and she had a date in a pavement café.

Wedging the phone between her cheek and her shoulder, she twisted her wedding ring on her finger.

She remembered the day David had slid it onto her finger. She'd been nervous that he'd lose it, or forget it, that the wedding would never happen.

She'd been a mess. Still grieving her parents. Confused and guilty. Always guilty. Always thinking about other people.

Sophie was still talking. "I should go, Mom. Chrissie has found this amazing club."

Another club? Sophie used to be all about museums and art galleries, but lately all she seemed to talk about was parties and the people they'd met.

Grace opened her mouth to tell her daughter to be careful, but then imagined Audrey rolling her eyes and making strangling sounds. She still wasn't comfortable not knowing the details of her daughter's life. When they were young you controlled almost everything about their world. You arranged the playdates and the trips to the movies. You never had to worry about where they were or who they were with. Letting go of the reins wasn't easy. "Have fun. Talk to you soon." Proud of herself for not interrogating Sophie on exactly where she was going, she ended the call.

She tugged off her wedding ring and left it on the table.

Without looking back, she locked her apartment.

The restaurant was only a short distance from the bookshop so she chose to walk.

Summer had descended on Paris, bringing with it sunshine and throngs of tourists. They crowded along the streets, sprawled by the river, watched pavement artists at work, took photographs constantly. The heat was oppressive, the air still with not a breath of wind.

Grateful for the sun hat, Grace leaned on the bridge for a moment and watched the sunlight play over the surface of the water. The river Seine wound lazily through Paris, the buildings that clustered along its banks mirrored in its glassy surface.

She'd been dreading traveling alone, but now she was glad she had. It had been exactly the right thing to do.

She had no idea how the evening would end, or what tomorrow would look like, but for once she didn't feel as if she needed to know. That in itself was progress.

She heard the sound of music and laughter and saw a river cruiser drifting beneath the bridge. When she'd been in Paris the first time she'd thought it looked like fun, but Philippe had dismissed it as something for tourists.

The restaurant he'd chosen for tonight was tucked away in a paved courtyard and by the time she arrived it was already crowded with not a spare table to be found inside or out.

She felt a flicker of nerves. Would Philippe be angry with her for the way she'd ended their relationship?

Not that angry, surely, or he wouldn't have agreed to meet. Unless he just wanted a chance to tell her what he thought of her.

She saw him right away, seated at a small table, shaded by a vine. He was reading.

Not his phone like everyone around him, but a book. He sat with his head bent, engrossed, lost in the words. He gave his whole self to everything he did. There were no half measures where Philippe was concerned. His inky black hair showed not a fleck of gray. His skin was bronzed from the sun. His clothes were casual, yet effortlessly stylish.

It had been years since she'd last seen him but seeing him lost in a book made it seem like yesterday.

Philippe had always had a book under his arm, the pages marked, corners turned in. They'd argued about whether it was right to defile books. He'd believed that a book should live a life, show signs of age and use. Battered was good because it meant someone had read and read. Best of all were notes, above the text and in the margins. He'd added passages, lines, words —

She'd lain next to him on the grass, watching as he scribbled.

Are you rewriting Shakespeare?

He'd grinned. *Just the parts he got wrong.*

The memory was so vivid that she caught her breath and he glanced up even though he couldn't possibly have heard her.

His gaze held hers and for a moment there was a throb of tension in the air. Then he put the book down and uncoiled himself.

He was taller than David. Not as broad. More athletic. *Stop it, Grace. Stop making comparisons.*

David had pushed her out of his life, and it was time she pushed him out of her head.

She was pondering whether to shake hands or kiss him when Philippe pulled her in for a tight hug, removing the burden of decision-making.

It made her think of those first heady days when they'd gone everywhere together.

She'd been staying with his family and the plan had been for her to spend time with his sister, but she'd broken her leg and so the job of entertaining their American guest had fallen to Philippe. She'd heard raised voices one evening, as he'd protested.

She's my sister's friend. What am I supposed to do with her?

In the end they'd found plenty to do. The connection had surprised both of them.

And here they were, face-to-face again. Something she'd never thought would happen.

It felt like a first date.

He cupped her face in his hands, kept his eyes on hers in a way that made her insides squirm. "I spent months planning what I would say to you if I ever saw you again."

344

Grace swallowed. Guilt swamped her. "Are you going to yell at me?"

"I'm not the yelling type, particularly over something that happened almost thirty years ago." He smiled and ran his thumb along her jaw. "It's good to see you, Grace."

He spoke in French. He'd always insisted on it. *You're here to learn. How will you learn if we speak English?*

"Thirty years is a long time."

"You haven't changed at all. You're still beautiful." He used charm like a blowtorch, melting resistance.

It made her smile, but there was also a feeling of relief that he didn't seem to hold any grudges for the way she'd ended things.

"You're still a charmer."

"And much good that did me." He pulled out the chair for her. "I hope you're hungry because the food here is the best in Paris."

"Your opinion?"

"Perhaps." He flashed her a smile. "But when it comes to food, my opinion is the only one that counts."

Grace picked up the menu but he reached out and touched her arm.

"Can I order? I'm not being sexist and controlling. It's more that I want you to taste the best things on the menu. This place is an experience you shouldn't miss."

The fact that she nodded was a sign of how far she'd come. She put her menu down. "Go ahead."

He turned to the waiter who was hovering and ordered multiple dishes, with detailed instructions of how they should be served.

She listened, fascinated. "Did you ever think of being a chef?"

"No, but I do love to cook." When their wine arrived, he tapped his glass lightly against hers. "To old friends."

"Old friends."

"So —" He put his glass down. "I will start the conversation with a question."

"Go on."

"Why wait almost thirty years to get in touch? I can't figure it out. When you left, I waited to hear from you. I waited six months, then a year, and after eighteen months I forced myself to accept I was never going to hear from you again."

How could she explain that she'd known the only way to move on was to make a clean break? "Things were difficult when I went home. My parents were killed."

"I'm sorry." His voice softened. "Why didn't you tell me?"

"I was a mess. It was — complicated." She didn't want to talk about the details. She didn't want to taint the evening with that part of her life.

Instead, she told him how her life had changed, about Mimi and also about David.

Philippe was a good listener, paying attention to not just what she said but what she didn't say.

"He was there for you. Your rock. I can see why you would have forgotten me."

She hadn't forgotten him. Instead, she'd managed to lock him securely in a compartment in her brain that she never opened.

"I'd known him forever, but we didn't start a relationship until that summer I returned from Paris."

"You'd lost your parents. You needed someone familiar to lean on."

He was implying that she'd been vulnerable and it was true, she'd been vulnerable, but that wasn't why she'd fallen in love with David.

"We got married. We have a daughter. Sophie."

"And is Sophie here in Paris with you?"

"No. She's eighteen years old. Traveling with a friend."

"And David?" He asked the question casually but she sensed an undercurrent that she couldn't quite interpret.

"We're separated. He left me a few months ago."

"Then he's a fool." His gaze met hers. "And that answers my question about why you chose this moment to get in touch."

"You make it sound terrible! I was in Paris anyway, and this is my first visit since I was here at eighteen, and —"

"Stop." He reached out and took her hand. "I'm glad you got in touch, Grace. Tell me what you've been doing since you arrived in Paris."

She told him the whole story, and if he thought it strange that she'd checked out of a five-star hotel in favor of a small apartment, he didn't comment.

"I know the bookshop. It's charming."

Talking about the bookshop made Grace think of Audrey. She wondered how the party was going.

Their food arrived at their table, along with the scent of herbs and garlic. Char-grilled chicken, a salad tossed in walnut oil, a delicate potato dish.

She thought back to that night in Bistro Claude. It had been a shadow of the real thing.

She and Philippe ate, and while they ate they talked. The conversation flowed as easily as the wine, but there was an edge to it.

An unfamiliarity.

"I looked at your website." Grace helped herself to more salad. "You have a manic schedule."

"I do." He served her some chicken. "Try this. They marinade it in herbs and lemon juice and it's deliciously tender."

She sliced into the chicken. "I was lucky you happened to be in Paris."

"I'm here for two weeks, then on to Budapest, Prague and Vienna."

"Don't you miss home?"

"Home, for me, is a concert hall. What do you think of the chicken?"

"It's delicious. After I left — did you find someone else? Tell me you fell in love."

"I did, although not with a woman." He must have seen her surprise because he laughed. "Not with a man, either. I fell in love with music. The piano. The life of a musician."

She swallowed. "You're saying you didn't love anyone after me?" That wasn't what she wanted to hear. She wanted to hear that he'd married the love of his life and had two adorable children.

"There are women, of course, but no one special." He gave a half smile and raised his glass. "Once you've had the real thing, everything else seems fake."

349

Her heart ached. "I'm sorry —"

"Don't be." He put his glass down. "You did me a favor. It's because of you I have the life I have now."

"What about family? Kids? A job shouldn't be everything."

"Music isn't a job to me."

She felt sick. "So you're saying that I broke your heart and you never dared try love again? That's terrible. I feel terrible."

"Don't." His voice was soft. "You did me a favor, Grace. I was heartbroken, it's true, but because of that I focused on my music. All the things I had enjoyed before, partying, dating, drinking, none of them could hold my interest. But the piano did. I played seven, eight hours a day, trying to fill the emptiness."

"You always were talented."

"Talent without hard work is like icing without cake. You need both. Because of you, I went from being a mediocre pianist to a good one." His eyes gleamed. "You are partly responsible for this life I have, so dinner is on me."

How could he joke about it? "You're saying I made you miserable so you practiced for hours. How is that supposed to make me feel good?"

"It was more than hours of practice." He

leaned back. "Before you, my playing was missing something. Not technique, but passion. I was young. I had great teachers, and they all said the same thing — that my playing was technically brilliant but lacked emotional depth. Loving and losing did more for my playing than any master class."

Grace managed a smile. "I charge by the hour for heartbreaking."

He reached for his glass. "Don't feel guilty, Grace. It is all part of life. Each experience teaches us something different and moves us to a different place. Nothing is wasted."

Was that true?

"I saw the reviews of your last concert. 'Good pianist' wasn't mentioned. I saw 'electrifying,' 'exciting' and 'one of the most talented musicians of the decade.' "

"Come to a concert and you can judge for yourself."

"Seriously?"

"Why not?" He passed her a basket of bread. "Try this."

"I don't eat bread."

"This isn't ordinary bread. It's infused with rosemary and sea salt. Try it."

She tried it and almost moaned with pleasure.

He was a man of many passions, and food

was one of them. She liked that about him. He was the one who had taught her that food should never be about quantity and always about quality. A perfect ripe brie, a juicy steak. A glass of full-bodied red wine. He'd opened the door to a life she'd never seen before. Growing up, food had been another source of chaos in her household, never pleasure.

As they ate, she felt herself slide back in time.

Philippe was demonstrative, expressive and passionate. The time she'd spent with him had been a shocking contrast to the emotional poverty of her upbringing. At home, no one had wanted to know how she felt. No one cared. No one talked enthusiastically about books, art or music. No one said *you have to read this* or *listen to this because it's sublime* or *try this because you will never taste anything more exquisite.*

Philippe had done all those things. He'd swamped her with experiences and drowned her senses. He'd wanted to know everything that was going on in her mind and it was so alien that to begin with she hadn't been able to find the words, and when she had she'd stammered them out and waited for him to tell her she was wrong. That what she was feeling wasn't valid. But he never had. He hadn't cared that she knew little about music. He'd been interested in whether she enjoyed it, whether the music stirred her in some way.

Even when she'd been anxious, worried about what was happening at home, he'd made her laugh. *That's tomorrow. Let's enjoy today. Taste this, listen to this . . .*

She picked up her glass and took a sip. "It's delicious."

"It's from a vineyard near my uncle's house in Bordeaux. The climate is perfect for the grape." He talked about the vineyard, and the few weeks he'd spent there in the spring after a long concert tour. And all the time he was watching her, studying her with those blue eyes and that gaze that saw everything.

She was eighteen again and standing on the edge of something new and overwhelmingly exciting.

She told him about a holiday she'd taken to the Californian wine country, and they talked about climate and grapes. She told him about the cookery classes she'd taken and they shared a laugh over her first attempts to make macarons.

"They looked like spaceships. And I made such a mess!"

"Still, I'm impressed." He took a sip of

his wine. "I have only ever bought dessert."

"About this concert —"

"I'm playing Mozart."

"Could I bring a friend? Her name is Audrey," she added it hastily, in case he thought she was planning on bringing a man. "I met her here, in Paris."

"I will arrange four tickets. Bring anyone you like. Give me your address and I'll send a car for you. And afterward I will take you for dinner. But promise me one thing —"

"What?"

"That you'll wear that dress."

He was looking at her the way men looked at attractive women, so openly interested that she felt flustered. She could feel the undercurrents, the sexual tension.

It was something she wouldn't have imagined six months before, but now? Her life had changed. Everything was different.

"I'll wear this dress."

She saw the woman at the next table looking at them. Maybe she recognized Philippe. How must they look? Like two people on a date. Enjoying each other's company. Everything about the scene suggested romance. The flicker of candles, the faint hum of music in the background. The way he occasionally reached across and touched her hand. The way he focused on her, his blue eyes fixed intently on hers.

"Remember the night I took you around Paris on the motorcycle?"

"How could I forget? It was raining, and I was terrified. You were unpredictable, unreliable, ridiculously reckless — I still have nightmares about it. Also about climbing over the wall of the palace — we could both have been arrested."

"You were so cautious and careful." He took a mouthful of wine, his gaze fixed on hers. "Are you still like that, Grace?"

"Invite me on the back of your motorcycle and I'll tell you."

He laughed. "I sold my motorcycle a long time ago. These days I prefer to travel in comfort. But the fact that you're asking tells me you *have* changed."

"No one can reach the age of forty-seven and not change."

"Life sculpts you into a certain shape, that's true, but it's almost always better. Just as some wines are better when they have had time to mature. This is probably the reason older women are invariably more interesting than younger ones."

David hadn't thought so. He'd chosen the younger one.

"Some people find youth attractive."

"Those with an unsophisticated palate.

355

There is nothing more attractive than a confident, older woman." There was an intimacy to his gaze that made her deliciously aware of her body. She felt the tingling of her skin, the stirring low in her belly and the rapid thud of her heart.

After so many years with David, it came as a shock to realize she could be so intensely attracted to another man.

"You like my dress."

"I like what's *in* the dress. Age brings a level of freedom, doesn't it?" His gaze dropped to her mouth. "You can take more chances. You have less to lose."

She had nothing to lose.

Her whole body felt charged and on edge, as if she'd been plugged into a power source. She had to be careful. David's brutal rejection had left her feeling needy, and Audrey's makeover had left her feeling reckless. It was a risky combination.

Between her and Philippe there was a shimmer of tension. An awareness that she felt as an ache in her throat and stomach.

They talked until the waiters had cleared the table, until the sun had set and most of the other diners had left.

It was only when she felt a chill on her arms that she realized it was late.

"I should probably go."

"Why? Is there a curfew?"

"No."

"Then why rush?"

"Habit, I guess. Do you live near here?"

"Close. My apartment is ten minutes away. Join me for coffee." He said it casually, but there was nothing casual about the look in his eyes.

And she knew he wasn't offering her coffee.

"I'd like that." It hadn't been part of the plan, but she no longer really had a plan. She'd always been frightened to let life just happen. She'd seen spontaneity as being about lack of control, but now she realized it didn't have to be that at all. She was still in control. Still making the decisions. She'd thought it was important to know everything that was going to happen, but she'd never appreciated the fun of not knowing.

His eyes darkened, and she finally acknowledged that this had never just been about dinner. The moment she'd sent that friend request, she'd known they might end up here.

Deep down she'd been asking a question she'd never asked herself before. What would have happened between her and Philippe if she hadn't left?

In a way, Philippe represented the life she

357

hadn't chosen.

He stood up and insisted on paying the bill even though she argued.

He pressed the tips of his fingers over her mouth to silence her. "You can pay next time."

Grace agreed, surprised how badly she wanted there to be a next time.

As they walked from the restaurant, he looped his arm around her shoulders. She leaned into him and slid her arm around his waist. It was as if her body had suddenly woken up from a long sleep.

"This is it." He paused outside a tall, elegant building. "I live on the top floor. I keep everyone awake with my piano playing."

She couldn't think of anything she'd like more than to be woken by the sound of the piano, especially if he was the one playing it.

The tension was almost unbearable. She glanced at him, wondering if he felt the same way and he drew her against him.

"Grace." He murmured her name against her hair, holding her tightly. "Grace, Grace." His body was lean and hard and desire rushed through her. She hadn't been hugged by a man for — how long? Too long. She'd been starved of affection. His attention broke her emotional fast. It was like a flash flood soaking a parched riverbed.

She breathed him in, clung. For the past six months she'd been numb. She hadn't felt anything much except pain and panic. And now she was feeling everything.

Was it because she was needy and desperate, or because she and Philippe had always had an intense connection?

She rested her cheek against his and then he turned his head and took her mouth with his.

Right there on the street under the soft spill of light from the windows, he kissed her, and she drowned in it, submerged by sensation, rocked by raw passion.

She slid her arms around his neck and he gave a ragged groan and deepened the kiss, caging her head in his hands as he plundered her mouth. His kiss was skilled, sensual and shockingly explicit. The passion of it, as if he was determined to drink every drop of pleasure.

When he finally lifted his head, she was dizzy and disorientated.

Her phone pinged, shattering the moment.

"Leave it." His voice was unsteady and he found his keys and unlocked the door. "Whoever it is can wait." He looked into

359

her eyes then, and she was so giddy by what she saw in his that she almost did ignore the phone but her maternal instinct was too powerfully developed to be overridden that easily.

"It might be important."

She dug around in her purse and found her phone. She read the message and felt her heart race. Desire was replaced by anxiety. "I have to go. I'm so sorry." A moment before she'd been able to think of nothing but having sex in his apartment. Now she could think of nothing except how quickly she could get a cab.

Philippe leaned against the doorway, studying her from beneath those lush, dark lashes. "Leaving me again, Grace?"

She felt a flash of frustration that life could be so unfair, but the feeling was immediately eclipsed by anxiety.

"It's Audrey," she said. "My friend. The girl I told you about, who works in the bookshop with me. She's in trouble."

Audrey

The evening had started well.

For the whole of her last year at home, she'd dreamed of this. Of having the freedom to come and go as she pleased. To date. To laugh. To dance. To not feel responsibility for anyone but herself. To not have to watch what she said and pretend because people here didn't know her.

To be young.

For the most part she'd stopped living a lie and started living the truth.

And here she was at a party in Paris. Not some nameless nightclub, but a real party in a real house with real French people.

They'd traveled by cab, she and Etienne pressed close together in the back seat. He'd flung his arm around her and the slow stroke of his fingers on her bare arm had felt good.

He chatted about his friends, his sisters, about Paris.

He'd stopped talking about books, which was a relief.

When he kissed her, she kissed him back and when they finally pulled away from each other, the taxi had come to a stop outside a tall house in a narrow road.

She could hear the sound of pounding rock music and the shriek of laughter coming through the open windows. The air smelled sweet, although she had no idea what the scent was. Roses and honeysuckle, maybe. It was the kind of thing Grace would have known.

Audrey felt grown-up and sophisticated. She wanted to message Meena but didn't want to look uncool. There'd be time for that later.

The door opened, and they were drawn inside into the crush of people. Too many people for the size of the house. They were squeezed together, temperatures rising in the unforgiving summer heat.

Audrey had wondered if her outfit might be too casual, but people were wearing everything. And nothing. She saw a girl, breasts bare, racing up the stairs with a man chasing after her.

No one but her seemed to notice.

The air was flavored with perfume, cigarette smoke and another smell that she recognized. Weed. Was that legal in Paris? What if they were all busted?

Etienne elbowed his way through the crowd, laughing and chatting as he went. He seemed to know almost everyone there, and Audrey saw girls smile at him. Several of them sidled up and kissed him on both cheeks. Audrey hovered by his side, trying to look cool and totally at home, but she understood none of the words that flew past her. Everything felt alien, from the language to the behavior. The French were so open and demonstrative, always kissing and hugging.

Etienne slid his arm around her and pulled her closer to protect her from the crush. "Drink?"

She nodded, thirsty. What she wanted was a soda or something.

He didn't let her go. Instead, he kissed his way down her jaw to the corner of her mouth.

Audrey felt her stomach swoop. He was so gentle and he kissed like a god. She really liked him, and now she wished they'd just gone back to his place and not bothered with the party.

A man appeared, loose limbed, eyes glittering. He looked edgy and a little dangerous. Drunk or high? Audrey wasn't sure.

He and Etienne talked and laughed for a minute and then Etienne introduced her.

"Mmm." Marc leaned and kissed her on both cheeks. "You're English? Welcome. You don't have a drink? What can I get you?" He was standing a little too close for comfort and she pulled back.

"Soda would be great, thanks."

Marc looked amused. "Soda?" He glanced at Etienne. "You are dating a schoolgirl, no? Do you have to have her home by nine?"

Audrey was flooded with embarrassment.

"I'm thirsty, that's all. I'll have a vodka, too," she said quickly. "Vodka and tonic." It didn't mean she had to drink it. She'd find a way to spill it or leave it on the side. No way was she admitting she didn't drink. She'd be a social pariah and she'd humiliate Etienne in front of his friends.

Marc stroked his finger down her cheek. "You have the cutest accent. When you are tired of Etienne, call me."

She clenched her hands into fists by her side to stop herself from punching him.

Etienne said something to him that Audrey didn't understand, and Marc gave a wolfish grin.

"I'll fetch your drinks." He spun on his heel and disappeared into the crowd, laughing, exchanging a few words as he walked.

"Ignore him." Etienne pulled her against him. "You're so pretty, everyone wants to know who you are. Shall we dance?"

"Yeah." At least then she could forget she was the only one who couldn't speak more than one language. Still, did that matter? The music was too loud for conversation anyway. A party was a party, wherever you were in the world. Everywhere she looked people were laughing, drinking, kissing.

A lot of the people seemed older than her, though. Late twenties?

He kept a tight hold on her hand, and they squeezed and wriggled their way through the crush of people to the room where everyone was dancing.

Audrey lost herself in the rhythm of the music. When she danced, all her problems were pushed to the edge of her consciousness. She raised her arms above her head and moved to the heavy, pounding beat.

Etienne was a good dancer, too, his movements fluid and sexy.

She danced until she felt someone touch her arm and there was Marc, holding out a drink.

"Thanks." She took it gratefully, took several gulps and almost choked.

It was neat vodka. Her eyes watered. She assumed he'd forgotten both the tonic and her request for soda, but then she saw the gleam in his eyes and knew he hadn't forgotten.

He was waiting to see what she'd do.

Audrey took another massive gulp of her drink, and almost choked. It was disgusting. It tasted like lighter fuel. Her eyes watered. How did her mother do it? How did anyone do it?

Unused to drinking, she felt the effects almost immediately. Warmth spread through her limbs and her head spun a little, but she managed to give Marc a cool look.

"Delicious. Thanks."

Marc laughed. "I'll fetch you another."

She wanted to tell him not to bother, but Etienne waved him away.

The alcohol made everything seem lighter and brighter.

"Is there any food?"

"No. Just drink." Etienne seemed amused by the question and she didn't want to look like a killjoy, so she laughed, too, even though she was cursing herself for not eating something substantial before she left her apartment.

It wasn't as if she didn't have experience in handling alcohol. She was always trying to force her mother to eat to dilute the effects.

Etienne lifted her hair, kissed the side of her neck and said something to her in French.

She closed her eyes. "I have no idea what you're saying, but whatever it is it sounds good." Someone shoved past them, slamming them closer together.

Etienne pulled her closer, shielding her. "I'm telling you you're beautiful."

As the crowd thickened, they were squashed together against the wall. "I only have your word for that." She slid her arms around him. "You could be saying anything. You could be saying 'your bum looks big in those jeans,' but I'd never know."

He cupped her face in his hands. "You look incredible in those jeans."

His mouth touched hers and everything around her faded. There was only the throb of her pulse, the slide of his tongue and the stroke of his hands.

When he finally lifted his head, she felt dizzy.

The summer heat pumped through the open windows and she felt the prickle of sweat on her skin. Her mouth was dry, and she felt thirstier than she ever had in her life.

Marc appeared with more drinks.

He raised his eyebrow when he saw her

still holding her glass. "Drink up!"

She drank and for some reason it didn't taste so bad this time. At least it was fluid.

Marc exchanged her empty glass for a full one.

Audrey took it. It wasn't what she'd asked for, but what the hell? Drinking for one night wasn't going to hurt, was it?

She wondered what Grace was doing and whether her dinner was going well.

Then she thought about her mother, but that ruined her happy mood so she stopped wondering.

She'd call tomorrow, and if she didn't get an answer she'd call Ron. Technically, he was her stepdad now. She was allowed to call him.

She drank and danced and then she and Etienne moved to the back of the room where it wasn't so crowded. The doors were open into a little courtyard garden. Fairy lights were strung around plants and pots.

"It's like a scene from *A Midsummer Night's Dream,* don't you think?" Etienne took a mouthful of beer.

Audrey had never seen *A Midsummer Night's Dream* and hadn't read it, either, but for once it didn't seem to matter. Her brain was probably numbed by vodka. Every time she tried to sip slowly, Marc appeared by her side and topped up her drink.

"It's a pretty garden."

"You want to take a walk?"

No, she didn't want to walk. Her head was swimming and her feet hurt. She was beginning to wish she hadn't chosen vanity over comfort. They made her legs look long, but after an hour of dancing her feet felt as if they'd been chewed by a great white shark.

On the other hand the garden was small and maybe fresh air would be good. "Sure. But I'm pretty thirsty after all that dancing. Is there any water? I keep asking Marc, and he just brings me more vodka."

"Marc is a dick," he said it affably, as if he was used to his friend. "I'll find you some. Wait here." He disappeared, and she stood awkwardly, trying to look as if she was perfectly comfortable standing alone in a house full of people who spoke a language she didn't understand.

She thought that when she left London she'd be leaving pressures and insecurities behind, but it seemed they followed you. *Did she look okay? Was she saying the right things? Did people think she was stupid for not being able to speak fluent French?*

She felt decidedly weird, as if her brain was slowly rotating. Probably all that vodka. She should have found a way of spilling it,

369

but if she'd done that Marc would just have fetched her another one.

Where was Etienne? What was taking him so long?

She turned her head to look and someone bumped into her hard. She dropped her bag and the contents scattered across the floor.

Crap. Audrey bent to retrieve it, gathering up tubes of lip gloss, old receipts and some cash. Leaning down made her feel even worse.

She was suddenly flooded with nausea.

Marc appeared with another drink but this time she didn't take it.

"I need to use the bathroom." She shouted it above the music and he waved his hand toward the stairs.

"On the right."

Right. Left. Audrey checked her hand for the ring Grace had given her and noticed that her hands appeared to be shaking.

Why did she feel this bad? She hadn't drunk that much, had she? Her mother drank bottles of the stuff and was never sick. It must be something else.

She stumbled up the stairs, clutching the rail for support, elbowing her way through people, muttering *excusez moi*. The door to the bathroom was locked. It kept moving in her field of vision. She rattled the handle, feeling worse by the minute.

Had they put something in her drink? She thought back. Everyone knew you were supposed to watch your drink in nightclubs and places like that, but this was a private party. Would Marc have dropped something in her drink?

A couple wandered past her and she looked at them through blurred vision. "Have you seen Etienne?"

They shook their heads and disappeared down the stairs.

Finally, the bathroom door opened and a couple staggered out, looking disheveled.

Audrey staggered into the bathroom, banging her arm hard on the door. The pain made her eyes water. Since when had she been so uncoordinated? With a huge effort, she managed to bolt the door before she sank to the floor.

Maybe if she just lay down for a minute her head would steady. But it didn't steady. Instead, it got worse. She felt giddy and suddenly she was drenched in sweat. Nausea rose like floodwaters and she just made it to the toilet before she was violently sick.

She heaved miserably again and again, until there was nothing left in her stomach and then lay on the bathroom floor, wondering if this was what it felt like to die. Her

371

head felt as if it was being crushed, and even the smallest movement hurt.

If she collapsed in here, who would know?

Who would care?

Grace.

Grace had asked her where she was going, and she hadn't even been able to tell her.

Trying to move as little as possible, she fumbled for her phone and sent a message to Grace. She would probably be too busy having a reunion with her musician friend to check her phone, but at least when she finally did she'd know how to find Audrey's body.

She lay still, her head on a bath towel, ignoring the people hammering on the door wanting to come in.

Why hadn't she said no to the drink?

She was exactly like her mother.

The next thing she knew there was more hammering and this time she couldn't ignore it because the door burst open and there was Grace, holding the kitchen knife she'd used to lever open the lock.

Audrey had never seen such naked anxiety on anyone's face before.

"Hi, Grace. I don't feel well." The words ran together with no punctuation.

"Oh, honey —" Grace dropped to her knees beside her.

Audrey felt her hand, cool and steady, on her brow. "Drank too much. Sorry —"

"Hush. Don't talk. You're safe now. I'm going to get you home."

Audrey was dimly aware that she didn't really have a home, but the word sounded so good she didn't argue. Home sounded like a place where you were safe and loved.

Grace soaked the corner of the towel in cold water and wiped Audrey's face and neck. "Can you stand?"

"Etienne —" she mumbled. "Gone." She couldn't hold on to her thoughts long enough to form a complete sentence. Words came and went like flashing images. She felt as if a rock band was performing inside her skull.

"Don't worry about him now. We'll figure it all out later. Can you stand?"

Audrey didn't think she could, but with Grace coaxing and hauling her she managed to stagger to her feet. It turned out that moving wasn't a good thing. "I'm going to be sick again." She made it to the toilet and retched miserably. Her stomach burned. Her throat stung. She hated being sick.

And then Grace was there, smoothing back her hair, stroking her back and murmuring words of comfort.

No one had ever held Audrey when she was sick before. Somehow it made the whole thing not quite so bad. She sank onto the floor of the bathroom again and closed her eyes.

"Can't walk." She knew she was slurring her words. "Leave me."

"I'm not leaving you." Grace opened the bathroom door, and Audrey heard her voice, cool and commanding.

The next moment two guys had slunk into the bathroom and helped Audrey up.

Together they carried her downstairs and outside into the street where a cab was waiting.

Audrey discovered that drink numbed humiliation.

She still didn't know where Etienne was, but it was probably safe to assume he'd done a runner, and who could blame him? She'd do a runner too if she was capable of putting one leg in front of the other.

She slumped in the back of the taxi, only half listening as Grace gave instructions.

"How did you know where I was?"

"Your location was on your text."

Audrey kept her eyes closed. "So now you're a tech wizard."

"I am. Stop talking. We'll soon be home."

"Grace?"

"Yes?"

"Are you mad at me?"

"Never. I might be mad at Etienne, though."

"Washn't his fault." Slurring, Audrey flopped against her shoulder. "Don't leave me."

"I'm not going to leave you, honey. I'm right here."

The journey was a blur, but somehow they arrived home, and Grace helped Audrey up the stairs. She groped the wall for support.

"Not my apartment." She was struggling to walk in a straight line. There was no way she'd make it up the final flight of stairs to her room. The way she felt, she'd happily sleep in the stairwell.

"You're spending tonight in mine, so I can keep an eye on you. I'm going to make you a strong coffee, and you're going to take a shower and drink lots of water."

"Need to lie down."

"Shower first." Grace coaxed her into the bathroom, and Audrey clutched the wall for support as Grace tugged off her clothes.

"I'll drown."

"You're not going to drown." Grace turned on the jets and nudged Audrey into the spray.

Icy jets of water sprayed her, and she

gasped, her head clearing a little.

Then Grace was wrapping her in a large, soft towel and guiding her to the sofa.

"Sit there for a moment."

Audrey sat, shivering like Hardy after a bath.

She felt sicker than she ever had in her life before.

But Grace was there, encouraging her to drink a large glass of water and then a small cup of black coffee that was so strong Audrey almost choked again.

"Shorry. Didn't mean to drink."

"Don't think about it now." Grace took the cup from her and put a couple of pillows on the sofa. "Can you lie down or does your head spin?"

Audrey tried it, and decided it was bearable. She closed her eyes and a moment later she was enveloped by softness as Grace wrapped her in a blanket.

"Grace?"

"Yes, honey."

"I know you wear tights in the middle of summer and dress like a granny, but you're very kind."

That was the last thing she remembered.

When she woke, fingers of sunlight were poking through the shutters. Grace was sitting across from her. She looked pale and hollow-eyed.

Audrey groaned and lifted her head. "What time is it?"

"Ten o'clock."

"Ten!" Audrey tried to sit up but her head exploded and she lay down again. "I'm late for work again. Elodie will fire me."

"It's Sunday. We don't open until twelve."

"Oh." She closed her eyes, but that made the spinning worse so she opened them again. "I remember you giving me water in the night. Have you been there the whole time?"

"I thought you might need me. How are you feeling?"

"As if my head is being crushed by a heavy object." She eased herself upright, trying to minimize movement. "I remember every-thing. I remember Marc and the vodka. I remember being in the bathroom of that place, and you holding a kitchen knife."

"Marc?"

Audrey groaned and pushed her hair back from her face. "It was his party. He kept pushing drink on me."

And it turned out she was *exactly* like her mother. How many times had her mother slept on the sofa because she couldn't quite make it up to the bedroom?

She pushed her hair back from her face

377

again. Her hands shook. Emotion swelled inside her like a tide and she couldn't hold it back.

"I'm sorry." She gulped out the word, tears pouring down her face. "I'm so sorry for everything. For being drunk. For texting you. For making you so worried you stayed awake all night. All of it."

"It's not a big deal, honey. Forget it."

"I c-can't." She hiccuped. "You probably won't believe me, but I've never been drunk before. I don't drink. Last night I drank because everyone else was and I didn't want to be different. Marc looked at me as if I was a child or something and I thought Etienne might be embarrassed to be with me, so I said yes and I never say yes."

"It's called peer pressure, Audrey. It happens."

"Not to me. You don't understand. I was out of control. The thing I never wanted to happen to me, happened to me. And I was so sure it never would. I'm just like her." Just like her mother. She'd lain on the bathroom floor just like her mother. She'd thrown up. Panic drenched her. Her mother must have started this way. One drink and then another. It was something that had always scared her, that one day it might happen to her, too. She didn't want that. She didn't want to be that person.

She wiped her cheeks with the heel of her hand, but the tears kept coming and with it the sobs and then Grace was holding her. Rocking her.

"You're upset because you didn't sleep and you have a terrible headache. You shouldn't think about this now."

"You don't understand." Audrey sobbed on Grace. Why didn't she have a mother like Grace? Why? "You don't know what it's like at home. No one does."

"There, honey." Grace smoothed her hair away from her face. "Do you want to tell me how it is?"

Audrey sniffed. She couldn't possibly share all the things that were in her head. They were too awful. "I've never talked about it."

Grace squeezed her shoulder. "You don't have to tell me anything you don't want to, but if you want to talk, then I'm here."

Audrey took a deep breath. "My mum drinks." There. She'd said it. Finally. She felt as if someone had lifted the heavy weight that had been crushing her forever. And those three words opened the flood-gates for many more. "She drinks a lot. I don't even know how she holds down a job, because most of the time she's drunk but

379

she can cover it up. She's like this amazing party animal. Everyone thinks she is so much fun, but they don't see how she is the rest of the time. I never know where I am with her. One minute she's hugging me and telling me she loves me, and the next she's yelling. And when I suggest maybe she talks to someone, or has a night without drinking, she tells me that there's nothing wrong and I'm the one with the problem." She glanced up, expecting to see surprise or maybe even disgust on Grace's face, but she saw nothing but sympathy and kindness.

"Your mother is an alcoholic?"

Miserable, Audrey nodded. "I feel bad saying it. I do love her, honest. But it's hard. I've never told anyone before." She grabbed a tissue from the box Grace had left close to her and blew her nose hard. "I probably shouldn't have told you. Don't ever tell anyone, will you? Not a living soul."

"I promise." Grace hugged her. "A moment ago you said you were just like her, but you know that's not true, don't you?"

Audrey scrubbed her face with her hand. "That's how it starts, isn't it? Every alcoholic starts by having one drink. And then another."

"Is that why you're upset? Because now you think you're one, too?"

It probably sounded ridiculous to someone else. No one was going to get how it
felt.

Defensive, vulnerable, she pulled away
from Grace. "Forget it. I don't expect you
to understand."

"I understand perfectly."

"Yeah, right." She picked up the glass of
water next to her and finished it. "You're
just trying to make me feel better. How
could you possibly understand how I feel?"

Grace took the empty glass from her.
"Because my mother was an alcoholic, too.
I understand exactly how you feel."

Grace beat the eggs in a bowl. She added herbs from the pots on her balcony, a twist of salt and pepper and then tipped the mixture into a skillet. They sizzled and she nudged the edges, juggling the pan until the base of the omelet was golden brown. It was a routine that calmed her.

She slid it onto a plate, and added toasted slices of sourdough bread and a dollop of ketchup.

Audrey was sitting at the table on the balcony, wearing dark glasses and nursing an appalling hangover. Her hair was still wet from the shower and she was wearing one of Grace's shirts. Her legs and feet were bare.

She looked young and vulnerable, and Grace ached for her.

She understood everything Audrey was feeling. All of it, including the shameful agony of sharing the truth with someone outside the family.

"Here." Grace put the plate of eggs in front of her. "The first thing you need to do is eat properly. It will make you feel better."

Audrey looked at the eggs dubiously. "I don't want to be sick again."

"You won't be." Grace handed her a fork, and Audrey used it to poke at the food on her plate.

"Did you used to do this for your mother?"

"All the time. Do you do it for yours?"

"Yeah, when there's food in the house. Mostly I make toast." She took a small mouthful and then another. She ate like a bird, tiny delicate mouthfuls that she chewed slowly. "I always said I was never going to be like her. No way was I drinking. I had more control than that."

Grace understood her fear. "You're not like her, Audrey."

"Doesn't feel that way right now." She fiddled with her food. "You don't drink, either, do you? I noticed that, but I never thought that there might be a reason."

Grace sat down opposite her, nursing her coffee in her hands. "I haven't touched a drop of alcohol for decades. Like you, I was afraid that I wouldn't be able to control it. And drinking was just one of many things I tried to control. I thought that was the only way to live safely. I didn't trust myself. I thought that the only thing stopping me being like her was one little slip. Miss a parent teacher conference, leave dirty washing on the floor, run out of milk —"

Audrey put her fork down. "I slipped."

"You had a few drinks. A few drinks doesn't make you an alcoholic." But she'd worried about the same thing herself. "I had a glass of wine last night with dinner. I had one the night before, too. While I was here on my own."

Audrey lifted her eyebrow. "I'm guessing you don't exactly feel peer pressure, so why? Did you want it, or were you proving something?"

"Both." Grace shifted in her seat. "I've been so rigid and inflexible with myself and with my family. I knew in theory that enjoying a glass of wine wouldn't turn me into an alcoholic, but I was afraid to do it. I've been afraid for a lot of my life. Since my marriage ended, I've thought about a lot of things. The truth is, I was so busy proving to myself that I could live a controlled, ordered life that I didn't stop to think about whether it was a good life. A life I was enjoying. I think in my head I confused spontaneity with chaos."

"You grew up with chaos?" The food in front of Audrey lay forgotten. "I'm the same. In my house the rules change from one day to the next. Promises are never kept. I stopped inviting my mum to school stuff because I never knew if she'd show up or not, or if she'd show up drunk."

"Yes. I understand that." Grace heard her mother's voice. *I promise we're going to do something special for your birthday, Gracie.*

"So your mum — when did it start? And you had a dad, right? So why didn't he just fix it?"

She never talked about it, not even to Sophie.

But Sophie was her child, and there was always the instinct to protect your child no matter how old she was. Audrey was her friend.

There was a difference.

She didn't have to worry about what Audrey would think, or how it might affect them as a family. She and Audrey had become incredibly close.

"I don't remember a time when my mother didn't drink." Hopefully it might help Audrey a little if she shared her experience, even if only to make her feel less alone. "She was the perfect hostess. The life and soul of the party." She had an image of

385

her mother whirling through the house in a new dress. *Look at me!*

"Sounds exactly like my mum."

"When I was young I assumed that was how people lived, that it was normal, but then I realized other mothers didn't drink like her. I tried talking to my father, but he always told me there was nothing wrong. *Your mother is fine, Grace.*" The feelings of hurt and confusion were still there and she saw the same reflected in Audrey's eyes.

"Yeah, that's the hard part. You start to think there's something wrong with you."

"As I grew up I realized she wasn't fine at all. I couldn't understand why my father couldn't see it. Then I realized he did see it, but chose to ignore it. That was the biggest mystery of all. I thought that if he loved her, he'd want her to be well. He was a doctor —"

"Crap. Well, if he couldn't fix it, what hope is there for the rest of us?"

"Exactly. I still don't really understand it." She stared out onto the balcony, her mind back in that time. "He loved her very much. I suppose he thought he was protecting her. She was an important member of the local community. She was at every fundraising event and committee meeting. I guess that's where the drinking started. But because no one in my house would ever acknowledge it was a problem, it never stopped. He never got her help. He made excuses for her. It's called enabling. And when I mentioned it, worried about her health, he became angry. I was told that we never discuss our family business outside the family so I learned that not only did I have to live in this awful situation, but I couldn't ever talk about it with anyone."

Audrey looked shocked. "I always felt kind of sorry for myself, dealing with it on my own, but you had it even tougher. You had an adult there and he didn't deal with it, either. So it was like you were dealing with both of them."

Talking to Audrey was so easy.

"How did you get to be so smart?"

Audrey gave a faint smile. "Born that way, I guess. I try to hide it, though. I don't want to make the people around me feel inferior."

Grace laughed. "You're right, though. That kind of situation creates a special kind of isolation. I just wanted a normal family. The worst times were when we socialized. Because she was good at disguising her problem, everyone thought she was just loud and fun, but I could never relax because I was terrified that she'd cross the line."

"Did you have to do all the stuff in the house?"

"Yes, because Dad was always working. My grades slipped."

Audrey leaned back. "What happened? You're a teacher, so you can't have crashed out."

"My grandmother came for a visit. She and my mother had a difficult relationship. My grandmother was a very independent woman." Where would she be if Mimi hadn't descended on them all those years ago? "She was a single parent, which was unusual for those times, I guess. My mother blamed her for not being around much when she was growing up. I think my grandmother blamed herself for that, too. That's why she was determined to help. She moved in with us and took over the house. Things changed then. Mimi is like a force of nature. She took on the burden of my mother and encouraged me to get on with life. She was the reason I came to Paris at eighteen. I think she was hoping I'd stay here."

"But you didn't."

Grace stood up and stared across the rooftops. "I was on my way to meet Philippe when I had a phone call telling me my parents had been killed on the way back

388

from a party. Their car went into a tree."

There was silence. "I'm so sorry, Grace." Audrey whispered the words. "Were they — Was your mother —"

"Drunk? Almost definitely. Was she driving? No one knows. They spun off the road, hit a tree and were both flung through the windscreen. Neither of them were wearing a seat belt. I've asked myself over and over again whether my father would have let her drive. I hope not, but he lived his life pretending none of it was happening so it's not impossible. And I felt so guilty. I thought that maybe I should have tried harder to get help for her. That maybe if I hadn't left for Paris, it wouldn't have happened."

"It wasn't your fault."

Grace nodded. "Over the years I came to understand that, but it took a long time and a small part of me still wonders if I could have done more."

"The only person who knew about the drinking was your grandmother?"

"And David." Grace thought back to that time. "David was my best friend. We went to kindergarten together. Then high school. We ran the school newspaper, although we weren't involved at that point. He was the only person I talked to. When I got the call, I flew back from Paris, and he was at the airport. The whole thing was a blur. David stayed with me the whole time." She sat down. "There was something else — something I've never told anyone, not even Mimi."

"You don't have to tell me anything you don't want to."

"I want to." It felt like a relief to share it. "David was working for the local newspaper at the time. A summer job before going to college. He was working the night my parents had the accident and because his bosses knew he had a personal connection with me, they sent him to the scene. They wanted him to find the human story. Dig a little."

Audrey's mouth tightened. "You mean they wanted him to dish the dirt."

"And he could have done. David knew my mother was an alcoholic. He could easily have told them that, but he didn't." Remembering it brought a lump to her throat. David had always prided himself on reporting the truth, but in this case he'd turned away from it. He'd done it for her. Because he loved her. "It was reported as being a tragic accident, and I was always so grateful to him for that."

"But it was a tragic accident."

Grace looked at her. "Yes, it was."

"And what good would it have done if people had known? None. That's not in the public interest, it's ghoulish interest, like when there's an accident and people stop and stare. I've never got that."

"Me neither."

The shared honesty had brought them closer.

"I won't ever say anything, Grace, so don't worry about that." At that moment Audrey seemed at least a decade older than her eighteen years. "And I totally get why you'd feel guilty, even though none of it was your fault. I feel guilty a lot of the time. And angry."

"You think to yourself that if they loved you enough, they'd stop. But they don't stop, so you assume that means they don't love you."

Audrey stared at her. "That's it. That's it exactly."

Grace felt a tug of compassion. "Believe me, I felt all those things, too. It's helpful to remember that it's an illness, not a choice. It's not as simple as that. Who have you talked to about it?"

"You."

"That's it? You've been carrying this on your own all these years?"

Audrey shrugged. "You know how it is.

You don't want people to know. It's embarrassing. And also you feel bad. Disloyal. And you think if she can keep up this charade, then you should, too. But I feel responsible for her, you know? And that's awful. That's the worst part."

Grace had carried that same feeling for years. "She's not your responsibility, though. You know that, don't you? She's the adult."

"Easy to say."

Grace nodded, thinking about the times she'd had to turn her mother into the recovery position. Still, at least she'd had her father even if he'd been about as much use as a log fire in a heat wave.

Your mother isn't feeling well, Grace.

"What about your friend? The one you've mentioned a few times?"

"Meena? I love her, but I can't tell her about my mum."

"Why not?"

"I don't know. Maybe because her family is perfect. Maybe because when I'm with her I get to pretend things are normal." Audrey paused. "My mother got married last month. My stepdad's name is Ron."

"You don't like him?"

"I like him a lot. That's the problem." Audrey shifted in the chair. "I'm worried that he'll leave. And that might destroy her.

She's been with men before. She's actually been married a few times, but it never lasted. Ron is different."

"You don't think he knows?"

"He knows she drinks, but he doesn't know how big the problem is. And I haven't said anything. Every day I expect to get a crisis call." Audrey swallowed. "Is it wrong to have my own dreams? Is that selfish? Sometimes I lie there thinking *please, please don't let me have to leave Paris.*"

Grace had a lump in her throat. How had she survived? Grace had at least had her father and Mimi. Her opinion of Audrey had been high from that first day when she'd rescued her bag, but now it was off the scale. She had nothing but admiration for this brave, fierce, warm, loving young woman. "You have a right to more than dreams. You have a right to live the life you want." A tear spilled down her cheek and Audrey look appalled.

"Shit. I made you cry."

"That word didn't add anything to the sentence." Grace wiped her eyes, embarrassed by her inability to control her emotions.

"Okay, *darn,* I made you cry." Audrey pulled a face. "Sorry, but it just doesn't work for me. Is there an alternative?"

Despite everything, Grace laughed. "You could try not swearing at all?"

"I'd burst. All these words would build up inside and then eventually they'd come out. It wouldn't be pretty. Probably even worse than when I'm drunk." But Audrey was smiling, too. "Why did I make you cry?"

"Because I think you're a very special person." Grace blew her nose. "And through it all you keep smiling and laughing."

Audrey turned pink. "Life just seems easier when you joke about it. And you're pretty special, too. You were a good friend to me last night. I didn't know who to call."

"I'm so glad you called me." She'd thought that good friendships were formed over time. That the length of the relationship was what gave it depth. She'd been wrong. She'd known Monica for almost two decades and considered her a good friend, but she'd never once felt as close to her as she did to Audrey who she'd known for a matter of weeks.

It was heartening to think that new friendships could form at any stage of your life, and a reminder that stepping out of the safe, predictable circle of your life almost always reaped rewards.

Audrey gasped and slapped her hand over her mouth. "OMG your *date*! How could I have forgotten? How did it go?"

"It went well."

"Yeah? Did you have wild, amazing sex?" Audrey's face went from animated to anxious. "Please tell me I didn't text when you were in the middle of —"

"You didn't." Although there was no doubt in her mind that had Audrey not texted when she did, the outcome would have been exactly that. "We were on our way back to his place when you texted."

Audrey groaned. "So I *did* ruin your evening."

"No. I had a great evening."

"Are you seeing him again?"

Grace thought about the chemistry. The easy flow of conversation. The looks they'd exchanged. The subtle touches. "I'm sure I will see him again. He's invited me to a concert he's playing in."

"Cool." Audrey picked up her fork and took a mouthful of her now cold breakfast. "I take full credit. It was the hair that did it. And the dress, of course."

"I have a ticket for you, too, if you'd like to come."

"Me? A classical concert? What if I don't like it? I don't know a single thing about music. Will you hate me?"

"Of course not. As long as you don't make

sick noises during the performance. You don't have to know anything about it to enjoy it. How about you? Are you going to call Etienne?"

"No way. It's embarrassing. I'm so mad at myself." Audrey picked up her plate. "Why did I let them pressure me last night? Why didn't I just say *I don't drink?*"

"I'm guessing it's because you really like him."

"Yeah, there's that. And people judge you if you don't drink. They think you're weird, or no fun. I don't get it. I don't get why you have to drink to be cool. Anyway, obviously he doesn't think I'm cool because I didn't even see him after he went to get a drink. He never came back. So this blinding headache and all that throwing up was for nothing. He probably did a runner with someone who speaks perfect French and can hold her drink." She stood up and carried her plate through to the kitchen.

Seeing the tension in Audrey's shoulders, Grace followed.

"You don't know that's what happened."

"It's what men do, isn't it? They run when things get tough. I mean, technically your guy didn't actually run, but he did leave. It's easier than sticking."

Grace sifted through the words and tried

to find the deeper meaning. "You've seen it happen often?"

"Yes." Audrey rinsed her plate. "I don't blame them. My mum isn't easy to live with. Love isn't always a rosy, shiny thing, is it?"

"No." Grace made more coffee. "It isn't. How's the headache?"

"Almost gone. You're a genius." Audrey glanced around her. "Shit — I mean, darn, I lost my purse last night."

"I have it safe." Grace put the coffee in front of her and toasted slices of French bread. She put it on the table along with creamy butter and a small bowl of apricot jam. "You barely touched your eggs. Eat a little more if you can."

"You found my purse?"

"It was on the bathroom floor."

"I have no recollection, but thanks." Audrey sat back down at the table and spread butter and jam on the toast. "I guess that makes us even. A purse for a purse. Hey, I sound like Shakespeare!"

Grace laughed and handed over the purse. "It didn't look as if anyone had tampered with it."

"This toast is delicious, by the way." Audrey ate toast with one hand and pulled the phone out of her purse with the other.

"Woah, I have sixteen missed calls. Shit. *Sixteen?*" She caught Grace's eye. "Sorry. Absolutely did *not* need to swear then, but it kind of slipped out. What can I say? I'm a work in progress and probably not about to rival Shakespeare any day soon. I hope it's not my mum."

"Is it?"

Audrey checked and shook her head. "They're all Etienne. Sixteen missed calls."

"I guess he didn't do a runner, then." As she said it, there was a knock on the door.

Grace stared at Audrey.

Audrey stared back and then swallowed. "Do you think it's him?"

"If he has an ounce of decency, then it will be him. And if it is him, I might even forgive him for leaving you. Do you want me to answer?"

"You'd ignore the door for me?"

Grace discovered she'd do just about anything for Audrey. "If that's what you want."

"Yeah?" Audrey grinned. "Would you rob a bank?"

"I have limits."

"Good to know. Well, it's probably better to get this over with." Audrey rubbed her cheeks and swept her fingers through her hair. "How do I look?"

"Stunning, which is actually annoying given the night you had." Grace walked to the door and opened it. Etienne stood there looking like he'd had a worse night than Audrey. His hair was messy and his skin was pale.

"Mrs. Porter." He spoke in French, desperately trying to be formal. "I'm sorry for disturbing you, but I'm looking for Audrey. She's not in her apartment, and she's not answering her phone. I don't know where she is. I'm worried about her, and it's all my fault —" He looked so anxious Grace almost felt sorry for him, and then she thought about Audrey lying on the floor of the bathroom. Vulnerable. Alone.

What if she'd dropped her phone or hadn't wanted to bother Grace?

What if she'd been too drunk to make the call?

She gave him the same look she used on her class of eleven-year-olds when they were misbehaving. "How can you not know where she is? Weren't you together?"

He flushed awkwardly. "I went to fetch her a drink and bumped into someone I knew. I was only a minute and when I came back, Audrey had disappeared."

"A minute?"

He eyed her. "It might have been longer

than a minute. I'm worried, Mrs. Porter. When I came back she was gone. Someone said they'd seen her with an older woman. I know you and Audrey are close, so I thought maybe it was you —" His face drained of color. "If she's not with you, then I need to call the police." He looked so traumatized that Grace felt herself soften.

"She's with me." She opened the door. "You can come in, but — oh —" Her words were cut off as Etienne hugged her. She felt his gangly body and was reminded that he was barely more than a teenager himself. It was such a complicated age.

"Thank you for taking care of her." He released her, clumsy, embarrassed. "Sorry, it's just that I've been imagining —"

"Hi, Etienne." Audrey stood there, her riot of russet curls emphasizing the pallor of her skin and the dark hollows under her eyes.

"Audie!" Etienne took two steps toward her and then stopped, unsure of his reception. "I'm so sorry. I went to get a drink, and when I came back you'd gone."

"You were ages."

"I know." He looked mortified. "I got talking to some friends. I lost track of time."

Grace gave him marks for honesty.

Knowing that she shouldn't be listening, she cleared the table, took the breakfast things into the kitchen and closed the door.

A moment later the door opened. Audrey stood there, looking awkward and uncomfortable.

"I'm going back to mine to change, and then Etienne and I are going for a quick walk before he opens up the bookshop."

Grace suppressed the urge to tell her to be careful. "Have fun. Is your phone charged? Take it with you."

Audrey hesitated. "Will you be okay? It's just that we talked about a lot of stuff, and —"

"I'll be fine." But she was touched that Audrey would think to ask.

"You're not upset? What are you going to do today?"

"I don't know." And that, she realized, was nowhere near as scary a feeling as she would have thought. An idea came to her. "Why don't I cover the bookshop this afternoon? Then you and Etienne can spend the afternoon together."

Audrey shook her head. "You can't do that."

"I'd like to. I can carry on sorting through those boxes of books that have been gathering dust for centuries. I enjoy it."

Audrey swallowed. "You're the kindest person I've ever met. Seriously. I didn't

401

think people like you existed in real life."

There was no sign of the prickly, defensive young woman she'd met on her first day in Paris.

Grace gathered her up and hugged her. "You're going to be fine."

She felt Audrey's arms tighten around her. "You're the best. I'm so glad I met you. And I'm so glad we're friends."

"I'm glad we're friends, too."

Audrey sniffed and stepped back. "Shit — I mean, darn, you're making my eyes red."

Grace nodded. "Mine, too. The difference is that you look great when you cry and I look like an overripe tomato."

She watched the two of them leave, hand in hand.

Without Audrey, the apartment seemed quiet.

Grace carried her coffee back to the balcony.

Opening up with Audrey had been therapeutic in a way she hadn't expected. To begin with, she'd done it because she'd wanted to encourage Audrey to talk about her own mother, but in the end she'd been doing it for herself. It had made her feel lighter. Like having a massive clear-out of things you'd been hoarding for far too long. Things that used to fit you but didn't now.

Things you'd never wear in a million years.

It felt like a mental decluttering.

She finished her coffee and checked her emails.

Sophie had messaged her some photos of Sienna, and Mimi had emailed her with more pictures of the garden.

Grace replied to both and stared at the screen for a moment.

Nothing from David. No email. No call. He seemed to have cut her out of his life.

She flipped the lid of her laptop shut and stood up.

She should probably be relieved that he wasn't in touch. It made it easier to move on.

She locked her apartment and went downstairs to the bookshop. There was something about the still silence that seeped into her. Beyond the walls of the bookshop Paris was in the grip of a heat wave, but the thickness of the walls kept the rooms cool.

The moment she opened up the bell rang, and Toni walked through the door. On Sundays the store only opened for a few hours in the afternoon, but he never missed a day.

Grace was pleased to see him. She liked his old-fashioned manners and the kindness of his smile.

Did he live alone? Was that why he spent so much time in the bookshop? Maybe he was widowed and filling his time.

So much of life was habit, wasn't it? You got used to living a certain way, with a certain person, and when it ended you had to find a new way. Form new habits.

"I was just about to make a cup of tea," she said. "Would you join me?"

"If you have the time, I'd like that."

"Sundays are usually quiet." Grace stepped into the tiny kitchen at the back and made tea, talking through the open doorway. "I plan to sort through more of the books in the back. There are boxes and boxes. Elodie says that some of them go back decades."

"On your own? Where is Audrey? She is out with Etienne?"

Toni obviously saw a lot more than he let on.

"Yes."

"And you're worried."

"Crazy, isn't it?" She set two cups of tea down on the old leather desk that Elodie used for paperwork. "I worry about her as much as I would about my own daughter."

"You have a daughter?"

"Sophie. She's eighteen. Traveling in Europe at the moment."

404

"So you worry, but you still let her go."

"You can't hold on to people." She'd tried to hold on to David, and that hadn't worked out, either. "Do you live nearby, Toni?"

He told her where he lived and she did a quick calculation. "It must take you at least half an hour to walk here."

"Twenty-five minutes."

"That seems quite a distance."

Why here? Why this bookshop when Paris was stuffed with so many alternatives?

He focused on his tea. "I like the walk."

She had a feeling there was more to it than that. "Well, we love seeing you every day."

He smiled at her. "You are looking better, Grace."

"Better?"

"The first day I saw you, you had ghosts in your eyes." He took a sip of tea. "Those ghosts have gone."

"My life was a little complicated." The understatement almost made her laugh. She had a sudden urge to tell him everything but managed to stop herself. There was opening up, and then there was oversharing. Toni was delightful and caring, but that didn't mean he wanted to hear the sordid details of her life. "Fortunately, things have settled down. How about you, Toni? Do you have family?"

"I'm widowed. And you have no idea how much I dislike that word. It's an invitation for pity, and I hate that." He stood up. "Thank you for the tea. I'll leave you to sort the books while I browse for a little while." With a gentle smile, he walked into one of the small rooms at the back of the shop and picked a shelf.

Grace couldn't help herself. "Are you looking for something specific, Toni? Is it something I can help with? Two pairs of eyes are better than one."

His gaze softened. "Thank you, but I'm better doing this alone."

Did a person pick up every book from every shelf if they were browsing? What he did didn't seem like browsing to her. It looked as if he was searching methodically for something specific.

Still, it wasn't her business. If he wanted her help, he'd ask for it.

She walked into the back room where all the boxes were stacked and started working her way through.

She checked each book, sorted them into piles for shelving, making sure there was nothing that might be of particular value. Elodie had told her that she'd found at least two first editions in the past few years.

After half an hour Toni said goodbye and

left. The shop was empty, and her mind wandered to Philippe. If Audrey hadn't called when she did, would Grace have slept with him?

She rocked back on her heels and stared at the book in her hands.

Yes. She probably would. She'd enjoyed the evening, the chemistry between them was off the charts and she had to move on sometime. Maybe Philippe was exactly what she needed.

Would she have felt guilty? There was only one way to find out.

Pausing in her book-sorting efforts, she leaned across and grabbed her bag. She was too old for games. Just because he hadn't called her, didn't mean she couldn't call him.

Before she could change her mind, she sent him a text.

Had a good time last night. Sorry to leave early. Had to help Audrey, but all good now. Looking forward to concert.

There. Done.
His reply came almost instantly.

I had a good time, too. Will leave concert

tickets at the ticket office. Bring your friends.

Feeling light-headed, she lifted another book from the box. As she added it to the pile for shelving, a photograph fluttered to the floor. She picked it up, dusted it off with her fingers and studied it. A couple were locked together. It was taken in black-and-white and there were a couple of cracks on the surface as if it had been folded into someone's pocket. There was something familiar about the woman. Grace held it closer and her heart skipped like a child in the playground.

She carried it to the front of the shop, where the light was better.

It was her grandmother. She'd seen photos of Mimi taken when she was in her early twenties, and she'd recognize her anywhere. She had the elegant, willowy form of a dancer.

In the photo she was holding tightly to the hand of the man by her side. There was no doubt at all that they were in love.

But her grandmother had never been in love, had she?

Grace stared hard at the photograph. The woman in the picture was definitely in love.

Who was the man in the picture, and why

was it hidden inside a book?

She walked to the back of the shop and retrieved the book, but there didn't seem to be anything significant about it. It was a nonfiction book about the geography of the Alps. There were no clues as to why the photograph would be inside that particular book.

She put it down and stared at the photograph for a long time.

Who was this man her grandmother was looking at with such devotion? And why hadn't she ever mentioned him?

AUDREY

She'd never felt more awkward in her life.

She'd wanted to impress Etienne, and she'd totally and utterly blown it. What must he think of her?

As they took the steps that led down to the river, she shoved her hands into her pockets and decided to get the conversation over with.

"Look, about last night. I'm sorry, okay?"

"*You're* sorry?" Etienne stopped walking and caught her arm. "I'm the one who is sorry. I'm the one who left you. I didn't mean to be so long, I swear."

"Your job wasn't to look after me. I can look after myself." Technically, it had been Grace who had looked after her, but she wasn't going to broadcast that fact.

"You were my guest. Also —" he shrugged "— I know what Marc is like. He doesn't understand boundaries. Never knows when to stop."

"He kept topping up my glass —" She broke off in midsentence. That was what her mother did, wasn't it? Made excuses. *You don't understand. I've had a bad day.* As if the bottle of wine had opened itself and jumped into her hand without any collusion on her part.

Marc had topped up her glass, but he hadn't poured it down her throat, had he? She was the one who had drunk it. She could have said no. Blaming Marc was the easy way out, but the truth was all she'd needed to do was say the words *I don't drink.* But she hadn't. She'd been trying to fit in. To look cool.

She'd been cowardly.

"I don't know what happens next, Etienne, but if we go on another date, I won't be drinking. I need you to know that."

"I understand. Your head hurts, it is the morning after —" he waved a hand expressively "— you're never drinking again."

He didn't get it. And why would he? He wasn't a mind reader, and she hadn't shared anything personal about herself. And that was part of the reason she was in this mess now.

If she didn't fix it, this would keep happening and she didn't want it to keep happening.

"You don't understand. I don't drink." She spoke firmly and clearly. "Not alcohol."

He frowned. "But last night — you said vodka was your favorite."

"Last night I was stupid. I should have said no when Marc offered it to me, but —" Oh, this was so *awkward.* "I really like you, but I can't do that again even for you. Next time I'll be saying no. So if that's going to bother you, then you'd better say now."

He looked confused. "You did it for me?"

"Everyone was drinking! It's the cool thing to do at parties. If you don't drink, people assume you're boring or a killjoy. They were your friends. I wanted to make a good impression. I wanted them to like me. Pathetic, huh?" Her eyes filled, and she blinked rapidly. Great. On top of everything, she was going to cry. She never should have gone for a walk with him. "I'd better get back."

"Wait —" He grabbed her arm. "Are you saying you drank because of me?"

"I didn't want to embarrass you in front of your friends."

It sounded incredibly stupid when she said it out loud.

He was silent for so long she assumed he was thinking she was stupid, too. Probably working out what he could possibly say to that.

She tugged at her arm. "Like I said, I should go."

"No." He let go of her arm, but only so that he could pull her into a hug. "There are so many things I want to say, I don't know where to start." He held her tightly for a moment and then eased her away from him and took her face in his hands. "First, how could anyone not like you? You're funny, smart, beautiful and really interesting —"

"I'm not smart. I can't believe I'm going to tell you this, but you should probably know that I don't really like books. I'm dyslexic."

"I know."

"How can you possibly know?"

"Because my younger sister is dyslexic. You remind me of her. And I saw the way you looked all panicked when I talked about books. She does the same."

He *knew*? "Why didn't you say something?"

"Because you didn't say anything! I thought if you'd wanted to talk about it, you would have talked about it. I like you, too. I was afraid of messing up and driving you away."

"That's why you stopped talking about books?"

"Yes. I figured it made you uncomfortable."

"But you love books."

"I love plenty of other things, too. The point is, you're not the only one that's afraid of messing up. Let's sit down. We're blocking the path." He took her hand and they sat down on the riverbank. "My friends really liked you, but even if they didn't it wouldn't matter because *I* like you. A lot."

"Right." She'd gone to all that trouble not to embarrass him, and he didn't even care what his friends thought? She felt like throwing herself into the Seine. She was so stupid.

"I'm sorry I took so long to come back to you last night. I feel terrible about it."

"Forget it."

"Was last night the first time you've been drunk?"

"It was the first time I've ever had a drink." And she told him then. All of it. She started clumsily, telling him about her mum. About the drinking. The moods. The fact that at home her whole life revolved around the alcohol.

Etienne listened carefully, absorbing every word.

414

At one point he took her hand, as if by holding on to her he could stop her sliding back into that dark, terrifying place.

The words tumbled out unfiltered, and she knew she should probably shut up, but now she'd started talking she somehow couldn't stop. When she stammered out an apology, he simply tightened his grip on her hand and urged her to keep talking. So she did. She told him even more than she'd told Grace. She told him about the time she'd found her mother unconscious on the bathroom floor and thought she was dead. She told him about the chaotic conversations where nothing seemed to make sense and which left her feeling as if she was the one with the problem. She told him about how responsible she felt, and how lonely that was, and that now there was Ron but how terrified she was it might all go wrong and things would end up worse.

And at some point she must have started crying again but she didn't even realize until she felt him tug her into his arms and hug her. His touch felt safe and kind. She'd never had a boyfriend who cared before. Feelings had never been involved. Being able to tell him made the relationship feel special. She'd never thought that telling people could make her feel better.

"Shh." He stroked her hair with his hand and pulled her onto his lap. He spoke in French, soft words that she didn't understand but that made her feel better anyway.

Deep down she knew it was over now. If there was one thing a guy hated more than a girl spilling her guts, it was a girl sobbing all over him. Who was going to want a relationship with someone as complicated as her? It was summer in Paris. This was meant to be something light and fun and she'd just deluged him with her whole life story. It was like spilling the trash. She could have just given him a few of the lowlights, but no, she'd drenched him in sordid details.

She lay with her head nestled in the curve of his neck, horribly embarrassed. She didn't know what to say. Given that she'd already said more than enough, she kept quiet. She could feel the warmth of his suntanned skin, and the roughness of his jaw where he hadn't shaved. She breathed in, keeping her eyes closed. Etienne always smelled so good. She wished she could stay here forever.

People strolled past, enjoying the Paris sunshine, but Etienne didn't seem to care.

He shifted slightly, but instead of nudging her off his lap, he held her closer.

"Do you want to go back to my place?"

She'd expected him to dump her. Maybe he was going to dump her, but he didn't want to do it on the riverbank in public in case she turned into a water feature.

She lifted her head and looked at him.

His expression was serious. With his ruffled dark hair and incredible cheekbones, he looked like a moody actor. It was no wonder all the girls had been looking at him at the party. He was seriously good-looking.

"It's okay." She choked on the word. "You don't have to be tactful. Just say it, I'll be fine."

"Say what?"

"You don't think this is going to work. You don't think we should see each other again." She tried to wriggle off his lap then but he tightened his arms.

"Is that what you want? Do you want to end it?"

"No! But I just showered you with my personal crap and drenched your shirt, so I'm guessing you're plotting the fastest route out of here. A relationship should be simple and fun. You're probably thinking I'm too complicated."

"That's not what I'm thinking. To have dealt with all that —" He slid his hand over her cheek and turned her face to his. "And you got this job by yourself, and traveled here — I think you're amazing."

"Really?" She sniffed. "You think I'm amazing?" Apart from Grace, no one thought she was amazing. Not even her mother, and mothers were supposed to be programmed to think it, weren't they? "You like my legs. And my butt."

"That, too. But I also like you." He smiled and lowered his mouth to hers. "I think you're incredible."

"I'm really not."

He did tip her off his lap then, but only so they could both stand up. "We're going back to my place so that I can show you how incredible you are."

Audrey saw a couple give them a disapproving look. "I think you just told the whole of Paris."

"I don't care. I don't care about anyone except you." He locked her hand in his, and they walked the short distance to his apartment.

Inside, it was cool and quiet, and Audrey suddenly felt awkward. "I'm sorry about — well, all of it. I'm a bit messed-up, to be honest."

"Stop apologizing. We're all a bit messed-up." He gave a funny crooked smile that did weird things to her insides. "What? You think you're the only one with a complicated

418

family?"

"Yours isn't. You have this perfect family and it's kind of embarrassing to admit that mine is all screwed-up."

"I don't have the perfect family. Not that it's a competition but I'm willing to bet that my family is way more messed-up than yours. Or maybe just messed-up in different ways." He walked through to the kitchen and found a couple of glasses.

"What? Are you kidding? You have this apartment that's like something out of a magazine, and they're away at their house on the Côte de wherever."

"My mum is there, but she's with my two little sisters. I don't know where my dad is, but it's a safe bet that he's with a woman somewhere." There was a bitterness to his voice that she hadn't heard before.

"Your parents aren't together?"

"In public they're together. They are great at keeping up appearances, but behind the scenes it's a different picture. I wish they actually did live apart because the things they say to each other are terrible. They close the doors, as if that makes a difference." He opened the fridge and pulled out a jug of iced water. "They hate each other so much it makes me wonder how they ever got together in the first place. I mean, did they even love each other once or was it always a mistake?"

Audrey gaped at him. She'd had no idea. And surely she, of all people, should know that what you saw on the surface didn't always reflect what was going on underneath.

She saw now that he was hurting, too. That underneath that easy smile, he had his own problems that he didn't usually talk about. She knew all about that.

"I'm sorry." Audrey touched his arm. "Why didn't you tell me that first night in your apartment?"

"Probably the same reason you didn't tell me about your mum. It's not the first thing you tell someone, is it? It's heavy stuff, and we weren't doing heavy stuff."

"It doesn't feel heavy. It feels —" Audrey tried to work it out. How did it feel? "It feels good to be honest with someone, that's all. To have it all out there. To be able to properly share. It's a relief."

She took the glass of water he handed her.

"My mum wanted me to join them this summer, but I couldn't face it. That's why I took the job in the bookshop. This was my escape."

"It was my escape, too. The difference is that I don't like books."

420

He laughed. "We're going to fix that."

Her heart sank. "You can't fix me."

"I don't want to fix *you.* You're fine just as you are. I want to fix the fact that you think you don't like books. Why are you eyeing the door?"

"I'm plotting my escape route. That's what happens when you know someone plans to torture you."

He leaned in to kiss her neck. "Give me one hour. That's all. One hour to prove to you that you *do* like books. Just not necessarily reading them yourself. One hour. Is it a deal?"

"I guess so."

She would rather have done something else with that hour, but she wasn't about to argue.

He led her into the bedroom and grabbed a book from the bookshelf that lined one of the walls. "Lie down and close your eyes."

She slid off her shoes and lay down, watching him. "Now what?"

"You haven't closed your eyes."

"I like to see what's happening."

"Everything that is going to happen is going to happen in your head. Close your eyes."

She sighed and squeezed her eyes shut. "Okay. Now what?" She felt the mattress

421

move as he lay down next to her, the rustle of pages and then his voice, deep and velvet smooth as he read to her.

To begin with she found it impossible to relax. It felt totally weird. But then something happened and instead of hearing him reading and feeling self-conscious, she slid into the story and found herself living the action along with the characters. She lost track of time and when he finally stopped reading she opened her eyes, annoyed.

"Why are you stopping? I want to know what happens next."

"That's why I'm stopping." He put the book down and shifted closer. "Am I allowed to say I told you so?"

"No."

He swooped down and kissed her. "You might not like reading, but you like books and stories."

"So what? You're going to read every book ever written aloud to me? That's going to take a while."

His mouth hovered close to hers. "Are you in a hurry?"

"No."

She could have spent the rest of her life lying here listening to him read, but she was desperate for him to kiss her.

She squirmed with anticipation. Her heart

was pounding. When he looked into her eyes she saw something different there, and was breathlessly aware that he knew everything there was to know about her. She no longer had anything left to hide.

She'd always thought intimacy was a physical thing, but now she realized it was so much more complicated than that. It was about knowing someone. *Really* knowing them. Not just their body, but what was inside their head.

He lowered his head and kissed her gently and she kissed him back, tasting, breathing, holding, exploring. He eased off her clothes and she did the same with his. His shoulders were broad and bronzed and she wondered if it was shallow of her to like the way he looked so much.

"I love your body." He slid his mouth over her skin and she was glad she was lying down otherwise she would definitely have lost her balance. When he touched her it made her head swim, not in the way alcohol did but in a dizzying way that it was impossible to describe. He made her feel delicate even though she'd been convinced for years that she was unbreakable. She thought of herself as tough, and yet Etienne turned her to jelly. Her thoughts slid away from her until she was aware only of the slide of his mouth on hers, the touch of his hands and the words he whispered in her ear.

Being with him made her feel something she'd never felt before.

It was perfect, not just because he was skilled and clever, but because he was Etienne. She wrapped her arms around him, opening not just her body but her heart. For the first time in her life she was with someone who really knew her, who cared about her.

For the first time in her life she felt truly happy.

If only this feeling could last forever.

GRACE

"I've never been to a concert before. I mean, apart from school concerts, but those don't count." Audrey shifted in her seat, and Etienne handed her a bottle of water.

Grace noticed that they couldn't stop touching each other. Shoulders, arms, fingertips. It was as if they had to be in physical contact at all times. Something had changed, she could see that.

"When you said his name was Philippe, I didn't realize he was *the* Philippe." Etienne slid glasses onto his nose and read the program. "I heard him play in Paris a few years ago. My mother loves him. I bought her his Mozart recordings for Christmas."

"Who knew you were such a culture vulture?" Audrey took a swig of her water. "Grace loves him, too, don't you, Grace?"

Grace ignored her cheeky grin. "I love his playing."

"That's not what I meant."

"I know that's not what you meant." She glanced up as the orchestra took their seats. She'd seen Philippe play as a student and he'd been good then, but she knew this was going to be an entirely different experience.

"Are you sure you don't love more than his playing? Because you've been smiling a lot since you had dinner. And I notice you're wearing the blue dress again." Audrey nudged her and craned her neck. "Is that him? Why is he last? He's late. Will they fire him?"

"He's not late. He's the soloist so he comes on last."

"Oh, I get it, so he gets the attention. A bit like rocking up late to a party and making an entrance. One of the girls in my year does that. It's *super* annoying, in fact. Can we wave?"

"No." Grace joined the audience in applause as Philippe strode to the piano, gave a brief bow to acknowledge the audience and then sat down.

"He's seriously hot." Audrey spoke in a whisper and caught Etienne's eye. "I mean, for an older guy, *obviously.* What are you doing? You can't kiss me here. This is not the back row of the movies."

"I'm stopping you talking."

"I'll stop talking once the music starts."

Despite the disapproving murmurings of the people behind her, Grace couldn't help smiling. They were so completely enchanted by one another that it almost hurt to watch.

Had she and David ever been like that? Yes, they had. She remembered a concert where they'd left in the interval because they'd both found it impossible to keep their hands off each other.

What did the future hold for Audrey and Etienne?

Grace breathed deeply.

She wasn't going to do that. She wasn't going to turn into a bitter, twisted divorcée who thought all relationships were doomed. You had to approach life with optimism and hope, otherwise where was the pleasure? Where was the fun? Better to hope for the best and deal with the worst, than expect the worst and miss the best.

Philippe's fingers flew over the keys, stroking, coaxing, seducing each note from the piano. She knew he wasn't thinking about her. He wasn't thinking about anything. He was lost in the music, unaware of his surroundings, and she was lost, too.

Her mind wandered along with the notes. She'd listened to this concerto a thousand times in her kitchen but she'd forgotten how different it was to hear music live. Suddenly she couldn't bear the thought of returning to her little town in Connecticut. It no longer felt safe and secure, it felt stifling. The place was tied up with a life that was in the past. It no longer felt like hers. The idea of leaving and living somewhere else had never entered her head, but it did now. Why not? Once she and David sold the house she could do what she liked. Sophie was off to college and she knew Mimi would be excited to know Grace was moving on with her life. She'd miss her friends at the school, but she could teach anywhere. Maybe even here, in Paris.

She straightened her shoulders, invigorated by the music.

Why was she waiting for David to mention divorce? Why couldn't she be the one to do it?

The concert passed in a flash and when applause exploded across the auditorium, Audrey leaned toward Grace.

"That sounded like the music you play when you're cooking."

"It is the music I play when I'm cooking."

Still clapping, Audrey winked at her. "So you hadn't altogether forgotten about Philippe, then, even though you were married to David."

All around them people were standing and

stamping their feet and Audrey stood up and tugged Grace up, too.

"This is fun. And I actually like this Mozart guy. Color me shocked. It's a shame they don't let you dance, because I could have totally danced to that. His music is pretty cool. I like the rhythm and it's kind of happy."

"I'm sure Mozart would be thrilled and proud to know he'd won you over."

Audrey chortled with laughter. "Yeah, well, he should be because I'm a tough audience when it comes to brainy stuff."

"Don't put yourself down. It's just music, that's all. You can enjoy it the same way you enjoy other types of music."

"No kidding. If I told the people in my school I liked Mozart, do you know what they'd do to me? It's bad enough having red hair and not drinking. Red hair, not drinking *and* Mozart? That's social suicide, right there." Audrey clapped harder. "He's looking for you, Grace. See him searching the audience? There — She's here —" She stopped clapping and waved her arms, just as Philippe flashed Grace a smile. His gaze locked on hers and he gave a small bow in her direction before walking off the stage ahead of the orchestra.

Heat spread through her.

"Okay, that's enough. My hands are sore." Audrey stopped clapping and flapped her hands to cool them down. "Now what? It's super early. Most rock concerts are only getting started around now. Do we go on to a club or something?"

Grace grabbed her wrap and her purse. "Philippe and I are going to dinner. You and Etienne are welcome to join us."

"No way. We don't want to intrude, do we, Etienne?"

Etienne was more respectful. "Are you meeting him at the restaurant, Mrs. Porter? We could take you there first, before we go back to my parents' place."

"Thank you, but I'm meeting him by one of the quiet entrances at the back. He has a driver."

"Okay, well, in that case we're out of here." Audrey leaned across and kissed her on the cheek. "This is one of those times when you do *not* need company. Have fun, although I already know you will because that man really does know what to do with his hands."

"Audrey!"

"What? Tell me you didn't want to be that piano. Of course you did." Audrey hugged her, but only so that she could whisper in Grace's ear. "Go for it."

430

"I don't know what you're talking about."

Audrey pulled away, grinning. "I love you, Grace. I especially love you when you're being all stiff and prim, but I've seen you without your tights, remember?"

Grace gave her a gentle push. "You're going back to Etienne's?"

"Yeah, I need to know what happens next to that girl in the book. Her whole life was going to shit — darn. I tell you, it almost made my life feel straightforward."

"You're reading?" She must have looked surprised because Audrey shrugged.

"He knows I'm dyslexic. He knows all of it. All my dirty little secrets. Technically I'm not *actually* reading, I'm being read to. I never thought that sounded like a fun thing to do in bed, but you'd be surprised."

Grace glanced at Etienne, who was red-faced and embarrassed.

Really, the man was adorable.

"You're reading to her?"

"I like reading aloud. I take a drama module."

"See?" Audrey nudged her. "Story *with actions.* I'm going to make him read erotica next just to see if he can do it without blushing. Now go and write your own story, and don't forget the actions." She and Etienne melted into the throng of people, leaving

431

Grace to fight her way to the entrance.

The crowd had thinned by the time Philippe appeared.

He pulled her to him and kissed her, ignoring everyone around them. "Well? Did you enjoy it?"

"You have to ask? Didn't you hear the applause?"

"I'm not talking about the audience," he murmured against her lips, "I'm talking about you. I was playing for you."

"It was exquisite. You were brilliant." They slid into the car that was waiting. Philippe shrugged out of his jacket and tugged at his bow tie. Without shifting his gaze from hers, he pushed it into his pocket.

"You look beautiful. And you wore the dress."

"You asked me to."

And why not? She couldn't imagine ever wearing it again once she arrived home.

She could imagine Clemmie's face if she walked into the store wearing the blue dress and gold strappy sandals.

Here in Paris, she was New Grace. She liked being New Grace. New Grace didn't feel intimidated about walking around Paris alone. New Grace was happy not to plan every second of her day. New Grace occasionally left shoes on the floor where she'd kicked them off, and tonight New Grace was on a date with a man.

New Grace had punched Old Grace in the jaw and knocked her unconscious.

And she had Audrey to thank for it. Who would have thought that an eighteen-year-old girl would have been her inspiration to challenge herself?

The car prowled silently through the streets, and she gazed out of the window.

Paris at night sparkled like a woman all dressed up for a night out. She thought how pretty it was and how much she was going to miss it when she returned home.

Finally, they pulled in near the river.

"Are we going to another of your favorite restaurants?"

"No restaurant."

"I thought we were eating?"

"We are, but I wanted something a little more intimate. How do you feel about picnics?"

She started to laugh. "It's late. It's dark —"

"And there is no view like this one."

His driver produced a hamper of food, and they ate by the river with their legs dangling over the edge, enjoying a perfect view of Notre Dame. Here in the heart of the city, they were surrounded by both tour-

433

ists and locals.

And a picnic with Philippe turned out not to be a few slices of packaged ham from the supermarket, but food bought fresh from the finest shops in Paris.

"I'm guessing you didn't put this together yourself."

"I might have had a little help." He opened the basket and unwrapped the food. "I was playing the piano, so I delegated."

She wasn't about to complain, because the food was delicious.

They ate savory tarts, charcuterie, cheese and plump olives. The bread was crusty and fresh and the view was unbeatable.

It was more romantic than any dinner she'd eaten in a restaurant.

Or maybe it was the way she was feeling.

It was a perfect night for seduction, and Grace was ready to be seduced. She was also ready to do the seducing.

She tested herself by trying to think about David, but she couldn't even conjure up his face. It was like pressing on an old bruise and discovering it didn't hurt anymore.

When Philippe put his arm around her, she leaned into him.

All around them were groups of young people, shoulders bare, legs bronzed from the sun. The soft lap of the water against the banks was all but drowned out by the sounds of laughter and conversation. Someone near to them was quietly playing a guitar.

It occurred to Grace that she missed out on this part of being young.

She thought of her life in two parts — before the death of her parents, and after. Neither part had featured picnics on riverbanks with nothing to think about but the perfection of the moment.

And it was perfection.

When she turned to Philippe it was inevitable that he would kiss her. Or maybe she'd kissed him. She wasn't sure.

When he stood up and tugged at her hand, she followed him, and they walked along the river toward his apartment.

It had been so hot that the first drops of rain took them by surprise. The few damp spots turned into a steady patter and then a downpour that soaked the sunbaked streets. He tightened his grip on her hand, laughing as they sprinted the short distance to his apartment.

Breathless, they tumbled through the door.

Her hair was plastered to her head and her dress was soaked.

His white dress shirt clung damply to his

chest and shoulders and his dark lashes were clumped together by rain.

Her stomach felt hollow. She thought it wasn't possible to want him more than she already did.

And then he smiled. "Paris needed cooling down."

She'd needed cooling down, too, but nothing seemed to be working.

She stroked her damp hair away from her face. "We're dripping on your floor. Do you have a towel?"

"Of course. More importantly I have champagne in the fridge."

Champagne.

The first and last time Grace drank champagne had been with this man.

And now here she was doing it again.

He vanished and returned a few minutes later with a bottle and two glasses. "The towel can wait."

He handed her a glass, and she watched as the bubbles rose. She took a sip and closed her eyes. It was cool, dry and utterly delicious.

His apartment was impressive, with large shuttered windows and polished wood floors. The walls were lined with books and impressive artwork, but the main focus of the living room was the grand piano.

It stood in polished grandeur, and she was left with the feeling that the apartment had been chosen especially for this one single piece.

"How long have you lived here?"

"Ten years." He flung open the doors to a terrace to let in the cooler air. Rain splashed the tiles and the wrought-iron table. It clung to leaves and soaked parched plants.

She heard the distant rumble of thunder and rubbed her damp arms. "It's fabulous."

He glanced around, as if verifying her statement. "I spend less than a hundred nights a year in this apartment. I'd lived here for eighteen months before I even unpacked the boxes."

She tried to imagine a life where you spent more time in hotels than your own place.

"You must miss your own bed."

He gave her a devilish smile. "I do. In fact, I think we should go and say hello to it right now." He put his glass down and scooped her up, and she gasped with shock and muttered something about weighing too much for romantic gestures, but he carried her anyway, executing a smooth turn so that he didn't smack her legs against the door.

He lowered her to the floor, and she saw that his bedroom overlooked the river. Through the windows she could see the slow curves of the Seine, the river stippling under the force of the rain, light bouncing along the surface.

She thought to herself *this is romantic,* and then he kissed her.

There was nothing tentative about it. Nothing questioning or cautious. This was a kiss that was only ever going to have one ending.

His mouth was hot on hers, and his hands moved straight to the zipper of her dress. The fabric was damp and clung to her, but he peeled it down, leaving her standing in her underwear.

She'd wondered if she might feel self-conscious when the moment came, but as it turned out it was the last thing on her mind. Her blue dress landed on the floor along with his shirt and the rest of his clothes.

He hadn't opened the windows in this room, and the rain thundered against the glass, increasing the feeling of intimacy. It was just the two of them, cocooned in this room, protected from the weather. From the world.

He kept kissing her, deeper, harder, as if he was determined to make up for all the time they'd missed. The heat of it almost burned her up. He kept one hand behind her head, the other on her lower back, lock-

438

ing her against him. She felt the heat of his skin and the intimate pressure of his body, and then he lowered her to the bed, and she wrapped her arms around him, feeling the ripple and flex of muscle as he took his weight on his arms.

Finally, his mouth left hers, but only so that he could kiss her in other places. Her jaw, the curve of her neck, her shoulder. And all the time he was murmuring soft words in French, telling her how much he wanted her, how she was beautiful, how she tasted incredible.

He explored her in so many intimate ways she lost count. She felt the silken stroke of his tongue and the skilled slide of his fingers. She squirmed and shifted, but every movement brought him closer and simply fed her hunger. It was intensely erotic and she suspected that whatever he was doing, playing the piano or making love, he gave it his whole self. He wasn't someone who dealt in half measures, but it turned out neither was she. Her desperation matched his, and when he finally sank into her she cried out. He paused for a moment, giving her time to adjust, his breathing unsteady as he held back. She was the one who urged him on, driven by a ferocious need that she didn't recognize, and then he was kissing her again and thrusting deeper, until sensation made her mind blank. She couldn't hold on to a single thought, she could only feel. Hard against soft, silk against steel. Her body tightened around his and she heard his raw, fractured groan and felt sensation explode around her. Her orgasm triggered his and they kissed their way through it, sharing each spasm, each thrust, each gasp. It was the most intimate, all-consuming experience, and afterward she lay limp in his arms, listening to the rain splashing onto the roof. He'd left the bedroom door open and a breeze wafted through, cooling her heated skin.

They made love again and again, and finally she drifted off to sleep. When she woke the air felt cooler. The rain had stopped and the sun was out.

Philippe stirred and looked at her, his eyes sleepy. "What time is it?"

She checked. "Just after six."

He groaned and rolled onto his back. "I have an early rehearsal. But you don't need to leave."

"I'll make you coffee. Can I use your shower?"

"That depends." He turned to look at her. "Are you going to let me join you?"

"I thought you were in a hurry."

"Today I'll be late." He tugged her out of bed and into the shower.

She closed her eyes as water rained down on her and gasped as he worked his way down her body.

It was another half an hour before he finally left the apartment, and he was back five minutes later because he'd forgotten something. "Being with you has fried my brain."

"Are you going straight to the concert after your practice?"

"No. I'll come back here. Will you stay?"

"I have to go to the bookshop. Why don't you call me later?"

"I will. And maybe tonight you should bring a change of clothes with you, that way if it rains again you won't have to walk home in a damp dress."

He wanted her to bring a change of clothes.

The suggestion made her ridiculously happy. She was pleased it wasn't just one night.

He leaned down and kissed her, taking his time. "I'm sorry to leave. There's nothing I'd like more than to spend the day with you."

"It's not a problem." And really it wasn't. She wasn't used to missing an entire night of sleep and planned to go back to bed the moment he left. "I could cook for you this evening if you like."

"Do you want to come to the concert again or meet me here afterward?"

"Do you have tickets?"

"Of course." He flashed her a smile. "I'm the star."

"In that case, yes. I never get tired of hearing Mozart."

"Ouch." He put his hand on his chest. "And there was me thinking it was me you wanted to watch."

"Why would you think that?"

He leaned down to kiss her. "Go back to sleep. I'll call you later."

She heard the door shut and leaned back against the pillow, smiling.

She liked New Grace. New Grace had fun.

She made herself coffee and took it back to bed. The rain had cleared. The sky was blue again. After work, she'd wander to the market and buy something special for dinner. And she needed to decide what to wear tonight because she couldn't wear the blue dress again.

Contemplating the life story of that dress so far made her smile, and she was still smiling when the phone rang.

She didn't recognize the number, but assumed it was Philippe.

"Hi. I already miss you." She spoke in a smoky, suggestive voice and then paused when there was no response. "Hello?"

"Grace?"

It wasn't Philippe.

"David?"

"Hi, Grace. I'm in Paris."

MIMI

"So? What did she say?" Mimi paced the hotel room, trying to ease the stiffness in her joints. She'd made some bad choices in her time, but this might be the worst. Would Grace ever forgive her for interfering? For not warning her? "Did she sound angry?"

"She said she already missed me. But as she didn't know it was me on the phone, it's obvious I'm not the one she is missing." His tone was light but his voice shook a little. "I should have called her sooner. I shouldn't have waited this long."

"I seem to remember suggesting that." She was too old for this. Her head ached, her bones ached and her heart ached.

"After everything that has happened — what I did — I thought the only way I would stand a chance of putting it right was to see her face-to-face. I would have waited until she was back from Paris, but then she started to talk about that Philippe guy, and

444

—" He ran his hand over his face and gave her a desperate look. "I'm going to fix this, Mimi. I'm going to find a way."

Mimi swayed, suddenly dizzy. It had been a long time since she'd flown anywhere.

David was by her side in an instant. "Are you feeling unwell?"

"Worry about yourself."

"Right now I'm worrying about you. I never should have let you do that long flight. Grace will kill me for that alone."

His kindness was one of the many qualities that made it hard to hate him despite everything.

"I don't remember asking your opinion on whether I should come or not." There was no way she would have allowed him to come without her. She wanted to be here to support Grace, if that became necessary. "I'm fine. You worry about how you're going to handle this." She felt David's arm come around her, firm and reassuring.

"You need to lie down, Mimi. Close your eyes." He helped her to the bed and pulled off her shoes. "There's an interconnecting door between our rooms. I'm going to leave it open a crack. If you need me, call. I'll be listening out for you." He adjusted pillows behind her and pulled the cover over her.

For the last few months he'd been conflicted and confused. She'd been the strong one, but not today. Today he was the one showing strength and determination. It was as if he knew, finally, exactly what he wanted. She was the one who felt wobbly and uncertain.

Maybe it wasn't only the flight and the journey. It was being here, in Paris.

She'd firmly closed the lid on her past, but now it was open again.

"Is she coming here?"

"Yes." David poured water into a glass. "But not because of me. Because of you. She was furious that I'd brought you here. She's on her way. She wants to check on you." He lifted the glass, and she noticed that his hand shook a little. He was nowhere near as steady as he pretended to be.

"You're nervous."

"I'll handle it."

She grabbed his hand. "Don't make her unhappy, David."

"I already did. What I'm trying to do next is put it right, and I'll keep working on that even if it takes me the rest of my life." He handed her the water. "I don't expect you to understand. You've never done something and then looked back afterward and realized you were a total and utter fool."

"We all make bad decisions, David."

446

Perhaps that was why she was so willing to forgive him. She knew what it was like to question a decision.

"What if Grace won't listen to you?"

"I'll keep trying. I don't want you to worry."

"I'm officially worried." What worried her most was that Grace might already be involved with another man. What if it was too late?

Mimi took a few sips of water and then handed the glass back to David. Anxiety had formed a solid lump in her chest. She really was too old for all this.

She'd thought being back in Paris would be exciting, but it simply felt exhausting.

Maybe it was being in this stifling hotel room.

"Do me a favor, David. Open the windows."

"Are you sure?" He frowned. "It's pretty noisy out there. It will stop you resting."

"I like the noise." She heard the persistent honking of car horns and her eyes drifted shut. "It takes me back."

He poured her another glass of water and put it on the nightstand, close to her. "Close your eyes and I'll wake you when Grace is here."

She knew she should probably question

him more about what he intended to do, but she didn't have the energy. She needed to sleep for just a little bit.

She woke to the sound of knocking and then voices.

David's voice, deep and level and then Grace's softer tones.

Mimi opened her eyes. For a moment she couldn't remember where she was. She'd been dreaming, and in her dreams she'd made different decisions. If only life were that easy.

"Grace?"

The door between the rooms opened, and Grace appeared.

Mimi almost didn't recognize her.

Her hair was short and curved inward in a sleek bob and she was wearing a white summer dress that made her look decades younger.

The only time Mimi had seen Grace wear white was on her wedding day. It wasn't a practical color, and her granddaughter was nothing if not practical.

At least, that had always been the case in the past.

There was nothing practical about the outfit Grace was wearing today. It shrieked confident woman, and there was a glow in her cheeks that Mimi hadn't expected to see.

Oh, David, David, Mimi thought. *You are in trouble.*

"Mimi." Grace crossed the room in a swirl of perfume and smiles, her eyes alight with happiness. "I can't believe you're here!" She sat on the edge of the bed and wrapped her arms around Mimi, rocking her gently. "I missed you so much." There was strength in her hug, and an energy that had been missing in the few months before she'd gone away.

Mimi felt relieved and afraid at the same time.

This wasn't a vulnerable, pliable Grace.

How was she going to react to what David had to say?

"I missed you, too." She closed her eyes. "You smell amazing and you look wonderful. Paris suits you."

Grace laughed and pulled away. "I'm loving Paris."

Was it Paris, or something more? Someone more?

Mimi studied her. "I think you look better than I've ever seen you. I love your hair. You've never worn it short before."

"I decided it was time for a change. My friend Audrey did it. Remember I men-

449

tioned her? Why are you here? I tried to persuade you to come to Paris so many times. You always said there was no reason to come."

"You gave me a reason."

"You should at least have told me you were coming."

"That was my fault." David spoke from the doorway. "I wanted to see you. I need to talk to you." His voice was firm and steady, but Mimi saw desperation in his eyes.

Had Grace seen it, too?

"You came all the way here for a conversation?" Grace's tone went from warm to polite, bordering on chilly. "You couldn't have just picked up the phone or sent an email?"

"What I need to say is better said face-to-face."

Grace's smile disappeared. "So for that reason alone you dragged my grandmother halfway across the world?"

"No one has ever dragged me anywhere in my life." Mimi shifted on the bed. She had no idea what was going to happen, but she didn't want to be in the middle. "I'm here because I wanted to come."

She'd thought she might be able to support Grace, but her granddaughter didn't look like a woman who needed support. Where was the woman who had sobbed into her lap a few months before?

Grace took her hand, ignoring David. "Are you feeling unwell? Should I fetch you a doctor?"

"I don't need a doctor. I just need a little time to recover from the flight, that's all. If you could order me some tea, I'll drink it here while you two have a chat."

"I'm not leaving you, Mimi. Whatever it is David wants to say can wait." The strength in her made Mimi both relieved and scared. Relieved for Grace. Scared for David.

Mimi didn't know this version of Grace.

She had a feeling David didn't know her, either, which could only mean trouble ahead.

GRACE

Grace stared at David across the hotel room, derailed by her emotions. She hadn't expected to feel like this. She didn't *want* to feel like this.

She'd missed him. She'd missed him so much.

Hearing him on the end of the phone had been a shock. Seeing him in person was an even greater shock. She'd managed to push him out of her mind, or at least shrink him, and now here he was, broad shouldered and solid, legs spread as he watched her across the calm, neutral decor of his hotel room.

Seeing him brought everything rushing back, and she braced herself against it, determined not to be swept away. It was like navigating in rough seas only to find yourself being dragged toward the rocks. Her feelings for him were the rocks. She didn't dare go there again.

She opened her mouth to ask how he was

feeling and whether he was remembering to go to his doctor appointments, but then remembered it wasn't her place anymore.

For her own sake she needed to keep this as brief and clinical as possible.

"You look —" His gaze slid over her. "Different. Stunning."

Did he think she'd done it for him? Maybe, and that irritated her, but still she was glad that she'd taken the time to sweep her new lipstick over her lips and slip on the cool white dress Audrey had picked out from a trendy boutique near her salon. "What did you want to say, David?"

The atmosphere crackled with tension. Being in a room with him felt awkward. If someone had told her a year before that she'd feel awkward with David, she would have laughed. You couldn't feel awkward with someone who knew you as well as you knew yourself. Someone who knew all your secrets. Except he no longer knew all her secrets. There were things, intimate things, that he didn't know.

Philippe.

Guilt tapped her on the shoulder, and she brushed it away. David was the one who had ended their marriage, not her. She was simply rebuilding her life.

"I'm sorry to call without warning." He

thrust his hands into his pockets awkwardly. "I've probably ruined your plans for the day."

"I have no plans today." She could tell he didn't believe her. And why would he? The version of Grace that he knew planned every second of every day. He'd never met the version who lounged in bed watching the sun rise over Paris or wandered to the market on impulse.

She only checked the time when she was working in the bookshop or meeting Philippe.

"So you moved into an apartment. You didn't like the hotel you chose for us?"

"The hotel was fine." She wasn't in the mood for small talk. She'd figured out why he was here. He wanted a divorce. It was typical of David to want to do it face-to-face. Ironic, really. He probably thought this was the most painless, decent way of hurting her. For once, she wished he'd taken the easy option and said what needed to be said in a phone call or even an email.

Seeing him was unsettling, and she didn't want to be unsettled.

"I spent the last month and every moment of the flight trying to figure out how to say this." He breathed out. "I've tried a million different ways and it never comes out right."

There it was again, the kindness. Once, she'd loved that about him but now it seemed like torture.

"Don't waste time trying to find a tactful way to say what you came here to say. I agree we should get a divorce. Go ahead and put it all in motion. I'll sign whatever it is you need me to sign." She was proud of how brisk and unemotional she sounded even though her insides were churning. This was an aftershock, that was all. The earthquake in her life had happened months before. "I'll instruct a lawyer when I'm back. Or I suppose I could do it from here if you want to move quickly."

"Instruct a lawyer?" His head jerked back as if she'd slapped him. "You want a divorce?"

"So do you. That's why you're here."

"No! Why would you think I'd want a divorce?" He looked panicked and confused, and she felt equally confused.

"Er — because generally speaking when the woman you're living with isn't your wife, it indicates that the marriage is over. Is Lissa here with you?"

"Of course not. I would never — How can you even think I'd do that?"

Grace almost backed down, but then she imagined what Audrey would do in the same situation. There was no way she'd be backing down.

"How can I think it? Maybe it's because you wanted to use our tickets to bring her to Paris. She has never been, as I recall." Her tone was sharp, and a little sarcastic. Not like her at all. She was a little in awe of herself. She could almost hear Audrey saying, *Go, Grace.*

David seemed as surprised as she was.

"You're angry with me."

"I'm not angry. I *was* angry, it's true. Angry and sad. But I moved past that and now I barely think about you if I'm honest. I was shocked to get your call. I still don't understand why you're here if it isn't about the divorce."

"I came here with Mimi. I checked on her while you were away." He gave a half smile. "Fixed that damn cupboard door that always sticks. You know the one?"

Don't do that, David. Don't remind me of all the reasons I love you.

"You didn't have to do that. I was in regular contact."

He took a deep breath. "It's over, Grace."

"I know it's over. You told me that six months ago." She couldn't believe he'd flown all this way just to dig the knife in personally.

456

"I mean it's over with Lissa. We're not together anymore. I moved out a while ago."

Of all the things she'd thought he might be about to say, that hadn't even made the list.

Grace felt the earth rock beneath her feet. "You're —"

"I ended it, Gracie."

She wished he wouldn't call her that. It added another layer of intimacy when she was struggling hard to be detached.

"I — There's so much I want to say to you." He walked toward her, and she took several steps backward.

He'd had an affair. He'd slept with Lissa. There was no coming back from that.

"You told me you loved her."

"For a little while, I thought I did. I was crazy. I don't know —" He jammed his fingers into his hair. "I made a stupid, horrible mistake for all those clichéd reasons you read about. The thought of Sophie leaving home. End of an era. I felt old. Redundant. Isolated. You didn't seem to be feeling it the way I did."

Grace swallowed. She'd felt it, but she hadn't talked about it. She'd been so determined that Sophie would leave the nest happily, without feeling any sense of responsibility toward her parents. "You've already made it clear that you think this is all my fault."

"I never thought that."

"You think the idea of Sophie leaving home didn't affect me?" Surely he knew her better than that?

"You handled it so well. You were always so positive, talking about the future — you didn't have the slightest wobble about our daughter leaving."

She'd wobbled more than a plate of jelly, but she'd done it on her own. She'd tried to be strong.

Why hadn't she shared her inner thoughts with him?

Because part of her had been afraid that if she acknowledged her feelings out loud, they'd grow.

"I had feelings, too, David, but I chose to focus on the future."

"You make it look effortless. You're so capable, you organize everything and I didn't feel needed — not that I'm blaming you," he added hastily, "and then one day there was Lissa —"

Lissa, whose father had walked out when she was seven. Lissa, who had never had an adult male in her life that she could depend on.

Grace was shocked by her own thought

458

process. Was she making excuses for her? No! She wasn't going to do that. Lissa was old enough to know what she was doing. David was certainly old enough.

She lifted her chin. "I'm not interested in the details. I can't imagine why you'd think I would be."

Her phone rang and she checked it, thinking it might be Sophie.

It was Philippe.

Never in a million years did she think she'd ever have to take a call from her lover while standing in front of her husband.

New Grace having a face-off with Old Grace.

Her life was turning into a farce.

David watched her steadily. "If you need to take that, then take it."

She thought about what a conversation with Philippe would be like with David listening.

"I'll call back." She rejected the call. "I still don't understand why you're here. You flew all the way to Paris to tell me you and Lissa have broken up?" It hurt that Mimi hadn't warned her. For her whole life, Mimi was the one Grace had been able to depend on. And she knew she could still depend on her, but still it felt like a tiny bit of a betrayal that Mimi had accompanied David and not contacted Grace first.

"I made her promise not to tell you. I wanted to tell you in person. And I wanted to tell you that I —" his voice was rough and ragged "— I miss you, Gracie. I miss you so much."

At the beginning she'd wanted to hear those words so badly but he hadn't said them. And he was saying them now, when she'd finally managed to take a few strides forward?

Did he think she was just going to fling herself into his arms and forgive him?

The cruelty of it almost shredded her. "You broke my heart, David. You almost broke *me*."

"I know, and I will never be able to make that up to you but I'm going to try anyway."

She took a step backward and almost fell over a chair. "What are you saying?"

"I'm saying — I'm asking — if you think there is any way you might be able to forgive me. If there are any circumstances in which you might consider —" He swallowed. Licked his lips. "Trying again."

Grace felt as if she'd stepped into an alternate universe.

This morning she'd been in bed with Philippe. And now David was asking if they could try again.

"You slept with someone else." She ignored the little voice that told her she'd slept with someone else, too. "You said our marriage was over."

"It was madness. You're my best friend, Grace. I don't know how I could have lost sight of that."

"Lissa's long legs probably had something to do with it." Grace glanced at the door, wondering if Mimi was listening. Had her grandmother known what David was going to say? If she'd known his relationship with Lissa had ended, why hadn't she warned her?

He ran his hand over the back of his neck. "Will you at least have dinner with me tonight? So that we can talk."

"I can't. I have plans."

"I thought you didn't have any plans."

"You asked me about the day. Tonight I have plans." Was that why Philippe was calling? She felt awkward being with David, which was ridiculous because Philippe had never shown the slightest interest in the domestic details of her life.

Philippe didn't do domestic details. He flew from country to country, from city to city, indulging his one big love, which was the piano. He'd never wanted anything that kept him rooted in one place.

David put his hands on the back of the chair. His knuckles whitened. "What *are* you doing tonight?"

"Not that it's any of your business, but I'm going to a concert." She told him because she didn't want him thinking even for a moment that she was sitting indoors crying over him.

His gaze held hers. "On your own?"

"No. Not on my own." She reached for her bag and started to walk toward the interconnecting door, but he caught up with her and turned her to face him.

She could feel his fingers gripping her arms and smell the familiar scent of him.

"Is it Philippe? Sorry —" He let go of her, raising his hands by way of apology. "I know I have no right to ask."

"You're right. You have no right to ask." She didn't ask how he knew about Philippe. Mimi, presumably. Maybe she should feel guilty, but she didn't. Right now she felt angry. She'd loved David. Adored him. Maybe she still did, but he'd carelessly destroyed what they had and now he expected her to just take him back?

She looked away so that she didn't meet those blue eyes that had always made her feel weak at the knees. She wasn't that woman anymore.

"Don't worry about Mimi." She tugged open the interconnecting door so violently she almost lost her balance. "I'll take her out with me tonight. I'm sure you'll find a way to entertain yourself."

"How about lunch tomorrow?"

He sounded so calm and reasonable, so totally like the old David that for a moment she was tempted. Just a conversation. Why not hear what he had to say?

Even as the thought entered her head, she could imagine Audrey's jaw dropping.

You said yes? What, are you a doormat or something?

No, she wasn't a doormat. And she was so mad at herself for even *considering* saying yes that her anger levels trebled and she hurled the whole burning coal of emotion that had built up inside her in his direction.

"I don't want to eat lunch with you, David. I don't want to get back together. This wasn't some adolescent row. You ended our relationship on our twenty-fifth wedding anniversary, and you did it in public! You *left* me. You left Sophie. Our daughter." She dug out all the reasons she had to be angry with him and stuck them right in front of her where she could see them. She almost heard Audrey cheering. "Right now I don't want you in my life in any shape or form. Go

463

home." Before she could change her mind and do something she regretted, she walked away from him and back into Mimi's room.

She'd spent the past six months trying to learn to live a life that didn't have David in it, and now he was muscling his way in again?

She was furious and also a little afraid because part of her missed him, too, and that made her vulnerable to making bad decisions. They'd been friends for most of her life. You didn't just turn that off.

Maybe, one day, they'd be friends again but right now she couldn't even entertain it. She didn't dare.

She closed the interconnecting door and kept her back to it.

Mimi looked anxious and maybe also a little guilty. "Well?"

Grace felt torn. She adored her grand-mother, but why hadn't she warned her that David was coming or that he'd broken up with Lissa? Still, this wasn't the place to have that conversation with David standing just the other side of the door.

"How would you like to go to a concert tonight? Mozart."

"The three of us?"

"Two of us." Grace let go of the door handle. "You and me. I have two tickets. All you need is a dress."

"I have a dress. What I don't have is the energy." Mimi reached out her hand, and Grace crossed the room in a flash, her anger with David spilling over.

"He shouldn't have dragged you here, and you shouldn't have let him."

"You know me better than that. You know him better, too. I wanted to see you. I wanted to see Paris. And I will enjoy Paris all the more if I rest tonight. I'll have a little dinner in my room, an early night and then perhaps tomorrow you can show me your apartment. You go to the concert. If you have a spare ticket you could invite David."

Grace tried to imagine Philippe's face if she turned up with David. Awkward wouldn't begin to describe it.

"I'm not inviting David."

Mimi held her hand tightly. "He was desperate to see you and talk to you."

"Why didn't you warn me?"

"Because he asked me not to. He thought if he arrived in Paris, it would be harder for you to say no. You're upset." Mimi stroked her hand. "And you're angry. I've never seen you this angry."

"I don't like being manipulated. He used you, Mimi. He knew I'd come if you were here."

"I was the one who insisted on coming. He still loves you, Grace."

"Are you defending him?"

"No." Mimi sounded tired. "But I want to make sure you know what you're doing. Would it hurt to talk to him?"

"I just did. That's it." She came here expecting him to end their marriage. The last thing she'd expected was that he'd be trying to save it.

She kissed Mimi. "Do you want to come back and stay in my apartment? I'd love you to meet Audrey. She's so much fun."

"Do you have air-conditioning?"

Grace smiled. "No."

"In that case I'll stay here. But I'd like to see your apartment tomorrow. And the bookstore. And I'd like to meet Audrey. Perhaps she could do my hair, too."

"I'm sure she would." Grace stood up. "I work in the mornings, so have a lie-in and I'll come over at lunchtime and pick you up."

Mimi reached out and grabbed her hand. "Spend some time with David."

"I can't promise to do that." She couldn't believe her grandmother seemed to be taking David's side in this. Did she really think there was hope their relationship could be fixed?

He'd had an affair, for goodness sake. And maybe it was over, but that didn't change the fact that it had happened. That he'd thrown out what they had like a disposable napkin.

Was she expected to forget that?

What exactly could you forgive in a marriage?

AUDREY

Audrey hammered on the door of Grace's apartment. They had an hour until they had to open up the bookstore. Once they started work Grace insisted on speaking French, and there was no way Audrey could tell Grace everything she wanted to tell her in French. She wasn't even sure she'd get it right in English. "Hey, Grace? You there? I bought breakfast. *Petit dejeuner.*"

Grace opened the door, clutching the neck of her robe.

Audrey grinned. "*Ça va? Vous allez bien?* Look at me. I'm virtually fluent." She was so excited to show off all the phrases Etienne had taught her the night before it took her a minute to realize that Grace didn't seem like herself.

Her hair was messy and she looked exhausted.

Audrey froze. She'd once walked in on her mother having sex and the memory hadn't left her. "Have you got company? I should have thought —"

"I don't have company." Grace opened the door wider. "I didn't have a great night so I'm running late this morning. Make some coffee and I'll take a quick shower."

Audrey tried to figure out what was wrong. "I went to the bakery." She waggled the bag she was carrying. "And not only did I ask for everything in French, I was actually given what I asked for. Result! Not like last week when I asked for bread and ended up with some totally weird cheesy thing. Are you impressed?"

"I'm impressed." Grace gave a wan smile, and Audrey narrowed her eyes.

"Okay. Enough. What's wrong?"

"Nothing."

Audrey put the bag down on the table. "I know that's not true."

"I'm fine. Why don't you get some plates and as soon as I'm out of the shower we can eat? It's a gorgeous day. We'll have breakfast on the balcony."

"Woah, wait a minute." Audrey caught Grace by the arm. "We don't do that, do we?"

"We don't do what?"

"We don't say 'I'm fine' when we're not fine. Not to each other. We have a proper

469

friendship. The sort where you don't have to say you're fine when you're not. When I arrived in Paris I was so stressed. Sometimes I feel like I've been stressed for my whole life, but sharing stuff has made that feeling go away. Now if I feel myself panicking about something I just think *I can talk to Grace,* and it calms me down. Do you have any idea how that feels? I don't want that to stop, but it has to work both ways or I'll just end up being this annoying person who loads you with problems. What's up, Grace? And don't say nothing again or you'll offend me." She saw Grace's eyes glisten.

"That's a lovely thing to say."

"Well, it's all true. So tell me."

Grace sniffed. "It's complicated."

"Complicated is my specialist subject." Audrey propelled Grace onto the balcony. "Sit. The shower can wait, but I know you can't function without coffee, so I'll make the coffee and you can tell me what happened."

"I can't sit on the balcony in my nightdress. Someone might see me."

"Who cares? Live a little, Grace."

Grace hesitated and then sat. Audrey had a feeling she was too tired to protest.

She swiftly made coffee and then returned with plates and warm croissants.

"Is this about Philippe? Here, drink." She poured coffee into a cup and put it in front of Grace. "Did you go back to his place after the concert?"

"I didn't go to the concert." Grace took a sip of coffee but didn't touch the croissant. "Something came up."

Audrey bit back the rude joke that came to mind. *Not the right time, Aud.* "But you loved that concert. Hearing him play." She ripped a corner off the croissant. "What could have stopped you going?"

"My ex-husband."

"What?" Audrey paused with the croissant halfway to her mouth. "Did he email you or something?"

"He called. He's here in Paris."

"Well, shit — I mean, darn." She put the croissant down. "Why? I mean, are you going to see him?"

"I saw him yesterday afternoon. I went to his hotel. My grandmother is with him. I wanted to see her. I was angry that he'd brought her here, but if I'm honest no one ever made Mimi do anything she didn't want to do, so it probably wasn't his fault."

"Let's pretend it's his fault. It will help us to pile on the mad. So what happened?" Audrey picked her way carefully over the broken fragments of Grace's emotions. "Did

471

he want a divorce? No, it couldn't be that."

Grace took another sip of her coffee. "How do you figure that?"

"Because he would have called or sent an email." She ate the piece of croissant. "He flew all the way here, so I'm guessing that means he had something important to say. Something he thought you wouldn't listen to unless he was face-to-face." She stopped chewing. "He wants you to get back together, doesn't he?"

"Yes." Grace sat slumped in the chair. "It was . . . unexpected."

"No shit. What did you say?"

"I can't even remember. I think I told him he was deluded and walked out."

"But it made you feel like crap. And that's why you canceled Philippe. Because you couldn't have lighthearted fun after seeing your cheating ex."

"How do you know so much?"

"Because hairdressers are like priests and psychologists. We're very experienced." Audrey leaned forward. "Are you going to forgive him?"

"No! Definitely not. I mean, I don't think so. No." Grace stared miserably at her plate. "I thought I was doing so well. I thought I'd moved on. And when I saw him standing there all I wanted to do was run to him and hug him."

Audrey thought about her mother. About how she still loved her despite everything. "Love isn't that simple. At least, that's what you told me and I believe every word you say." She was rewarded by a glimmer of a smile.

"Of course you do. In particular when I tell you about fashion and street smarts."

"It's weird, though, isn't it? You can hate some things about someone, and still love them. That's the way I feel about my mum. I hate that she drinks. I hate what that does to her and the things she says and does when she's drunk. But it doesn't stop me loving her. You can hate a person's actions without hating *them.* And that's the hard bit. If you could just switch it off, then it would be easy, wouldn't it?"

Grace managed a smile. "How are you so wise?"

"Because although I look eighteen on the outside, inside I'm, like, a thousand and fifty." Audrey pushed the croissants toward Grace. "I asked for these in French. You'd better eat one or I'll be offended."

"I'm not hungry."

"When I'm upset you always make me eat, so eat."

Grace put a croissant on her plate. "How

could he think I'd forgive him that easily? I never thought he was that insensitive."

"Maybe he's desperate. Maybe he wants you back so badly he is willing to try anything. Let's face it, that's not a conversation that would have gone well on the phone." Audrey leaned forward, broke off some of Grace's croissant and held it toward her mouth. "Open and chomp."

Grace sighed and ate. "How can he love me one minute and not the next?"

"Maybe he always loved you and he had, like, a mind explosion or something." Audrey made a gesture with her hands. "I mean, people fuck up — I mean, mess up — all the time, don't they?"

"I suppose so."

Audrey glanced at the clock. "I need to go and open up the bookshop."

Grace gasped and sprang to her feet. "I had no idea it was so late."

"Take your time. I've got this. I'll get down there now so that Elodie doesn't try to fire you. I don't mind saving your butt again —" Audrey winked at her "— but this is your final warning." She kept it light, but she didn't like the way Grace looked. Lost and vulnerable. "Why don't you forget about him for the rest of the day? Come and sort some dusty books, have a cup of

474

tea with Toni and give yourself a day off from thinking."

"Philippe asked me to dinner tonight. At his apartment."

"Great. I'll do your hair and makeup."

"It feels wrong all of a sudden."

"It's not wrong, Grace. David walked away. You picked up the pieces of your life. Are you supposed to just drop them again because he's changed his mind?"

"Maybe I should go and see Philippe as planned. You don't think I'm awful?"

"I think you're brilliant in every way." She hugged Grace and was hugged back.

"Thank you. You are a wonderful person and a great friend."

Audrey felt her throat thicken. Grace was so smart, wise and kind. To be loved by someone like her made her feel like she'd got top grades in everything. And Grace was an inspiration. She'd been badly hurt, but she still didn't hold anything back. "Hey," she said as she patted Grace on the back, "what's all this talking in English? That's not allowed."

Grace pulled away. "I didn't even ask you about Etienne! What happened?"

"I'll tell you later."

"Tell me now. You look happy, so I assume you had a good talk."

"We did. I told him everything. Turns out his family isn't all perfect, either." She didn't say more because that would have been betraying a confidence. "We went for a long walk along the river and bought a baguette and some cheese. It was cool. Then we went back to his place. But I set three alarms so I wasn't late this morning."

"You came here to tell me all about it, and all I've done is talk about myself."

"Yeah, well, the friend who gets priority is the one whose crisis is bigger, right? And yours is bigger. Next time my life falls apart, I'm shoving you right to the bottom of the pile. Now I have to go or Elodie will give me her frowning look."

Audrey kissed Grace on the cheek, picked up her bag and clomped down the stairs to open up the bookshop.

Although she was worried about Grace, Audrey was also relieved that David obviously hadn't found it easy to throw away twenty-five years of marriage. She didn't know why she kept linking it to her own situation, but she did. It was all about hope. If you could see something existed for someone else, then you could believe it might exist for you.

There was no sign of Elodie, and Grace joined her thirty minutes later, her hair freshly washed and her makeup immaculate. She was wearing a cool linen dress and her arms were bare.

"You look great." Audrey handed her a glass of iced water. "Much too good to mess around with dusty books."

"We've made good progress. Let's go and see what needs to be done today."

They walked into the back room. The number of boxes piled high was slowly reducing.

Grace picked up a book and gasped. "Oh!"

"What?"

"When I was sorting through the books, I found a photograph of my grandmother. I intended to show Mimi, but I totally forgot all about it when I was there yesterday. It's still in my bag."

"You found a photo of her in a book?"

"Yes."

"That is weird and a little spooky, frankly. Not sure I want to think about it. Maybe a ghost put it there or something."

Audrey knelt down and finished emptying the open box on the floor.

The doorbell clanged, making them both jump out of their skin.

"That darn bell is a health and safety risk." Audrey levered herself to her feet. "It's going to give someone a heart attack. Or maybe you're carrying hot tea and you scald yourself and all your skin peels off. Or maybe you jump and bang your head on a beam. There are any number of ways to die in this store, and none of them are glamorous. You stay here. I'll go and do the whole customer service thing and if I need you, I'll call."

She walked into the shop.

The man standing in front of the desk was a stranger.

The touches of gray at his temples suggested he was nudging fifty, but that didn't stop him being handsome. He had intense blue eyes and a few lines that suggested he smiled a lot.

She delivered her warmest French greeting. *"Bonjour. Je peux vous aidez, monsieur?"*

"I'm looking for Grace."

David.

Shit. What was she supposed to do? Should she pretend Grace was out? Would Grace want to see him? Why hadn't they planned for this scenario?

"Er —"

"Do you speak English?"

Audrey tried to look vacant and French and in the meantime David gave her a warm friendly smile. His smile was so compelling and attractive, Audrey almost smiled back and then she remembered he'd been a total shit to Grace and that she absolutely wasn't on his side.

She gave him a cool look, modeling it on the look Elodie had given her when she'd fired her. To tell the truth, she was a little shaken.

David was nothing like Audrey had imagined him.

She'd imagined some desperate, aging middle-aged guy and David probably *was* middle-aged, but he didn't look like some cheating, no-good rat bastard. He looked solid and dependable, a bit like Meena's dad. The sort of person who could easily shoulder any number of people's problems at once without struggling under the weight.

"David." Grace appeared from behind her. "What are you doing here?"

He thrust his hands into his pockets, looking self-conscious. "Can I buy you a coffee?"

"I'm working."

"Just half an hour, that's all." He turned to Audrey. "Would you be able to cover?"

"No, she wouldn't." Grace straightened her shoulders. "We work here together. That's the deal."

Audrey felt like a sandwich being toasted between two hot plates.

She opened her mouth, but then David took a step toward Grace.

"Please. Just half an hour." His voice was soft and he looked at Grace as if she was the only woman on the planet.

Audrey swallowed, and reminded herself that he hadn't treated her like the only woman on the planet.

Grace glanced toward her, and Audrey gave a helpless shrug.

She was still in that toaster with her edges burning.

"Fifteen minutes," Grace said. "And we'll go to the coffee shop down the street. Audrey, if you need me, then call."

"Sure." Did that mean Grace wanted her to call anyway and rescue her? Or was she only supposed to call in a crisis?

Oh, darn, darny, darn. If they were going to use a code, then they could at least have agreed on it first.

Audrey watched them go and slumped on the chair.

Was she supposed to throw Grace a rope? Right now, she felt like hanging herself from it.

Five minutes later Toni walked in.

Audrey was so relieved to see a friendly face she almost hugged him. "Hi there, handsome. How's the big bad world treating you today? Can I tempt you to a little Earl Grey? Or something stronger? I think we have some Darjeeling if you're feeling daring."

His eyes twinkled. "Sounds perfect. Grace not here?"

"Oh, you know —" Audrey made the tea. "She just popped out." To have a conversation with her almost ex-husband. As you do.

She made herself a tea, too. Thinking about what the kids at school would say if they could see her sipping Earl Grey in a bookshop made her grin to herself.

"How are you, Audrey? How are things going with Etienne?"

She sat cross-legged on one of the chairs and told him about her date and he listened closely.

She decided he would make a perfect grandpa. He'd be patient, kind and he'd probably read to his grandchildren. He certainly loved books.

She'd gotten used to it now, the way he spent half an hour browsing through every book on a shelf. Maybe he was memorizing them.

They chatted, and then he left and she washed up the cups.

It was almost an hour before Grace returned and when she did Audrey almost jumped on her.

"Well? What happened?" She searched for clues but Grace looked as cool and elegant as she had when she'd left. Her lipstick wasn't smudged.

Obviously hasn't been kissed, Audrey thought.

"Nothing happened."

"You're still seeing Philippe tonight?"

"Of course." Grace put her bag down. "What do you think I should wear?"

If she was asking that question, then presumably she wasn't getting back together with David.

Audrey had a thousand questions she wanted to ask but managed to keep them to herself. "Wear the pale green dress with the little shell buttons."

"You think so?"

"Definitely. I'll do your hair."

"Would you like to come and meet my grandmother? I'm going to see her this afternoon and I know she'd love you. You could practice your French."

"I'm sure your grandmother doesn't want to talk about things like condoms."

"Don't you believe it." Grace gave a half smile. "My grandmother doesn't fit any of the stereotypes."

482

"In that case I should definitely meet her. She sounds like fun. I've never had a grandmother." The more Audrey thought about it, the more she realized she was seriously short of reliable family. It wasn't that she didn't like Ron because she did, but he wasn't related to her so there was nothing at all stopping him from walking out the door when he discovered the secret her mother was hiding. Audrey didn't want to let herself love him in case he decided it was all too much and left. By holding back, she was cutting out months of being upset.

Still, she decided she would meet Mimi because Grace had talked about her all the time.

"She was amazing," she told Etienne later when they were curled up on the creaky bed in her tiny apartment. The windows were open and a light breeze wafted through the room. "So alive and enthusiastic about everything. And she was interesting. She'd done so much. I hope I'm like that when I'm ninety."

It was so easy being with him now. Not having anything to hide meant that she didn't have to be careful what she said, and that meant she could completely relax.

And he'd been honest with her, too.

They'd talked a lot about his situation at home.

"Family is a weird, complicated thing." She snuggled closer. "Do you think your parents will get a divorce?"

"I truly hope so. In the meantime, I feel bad for my two sisters who are still living there. Adults think that their problems don't affect us, as if somehow their lives are separate from ours." He spoke quietly. "They think all they have to do is close a door, or speak in a whisper, and we won't know what's going on. But all that does is stop us from feeling we can talk to them, because we're not supposed to know and we're playing along with that. And we can't tell anyone else because that feels like a betrayal, so we're stuck handling it by ourselves and that sucks."

She slid her hand over his chest. "It does suck, but right now it doesn't suck anywhere near as much as it did before because we can share it."

"That's true. And because of that I am going to the villa tonight, to spend two days with my mother and sisters. I want to check on them. I've asked Elodie, and she is going to cover afternoons at the bookstore. I'll be back on Friday." He shifted so that he could look at her. "I'm sorry, Audie. Are you okay with it?"

"Of course." She'd miss him, of course, but she wasn't going to be selfish. And she liked the fact he wanted to be there for his family. "I wish I could come with you, but there is no way Elodie would give me time off, and anyway I don't want to leave Grace right now. What time are you leaving?"

"I'll get the last flight out tonight. I have another two hours before I need to leave for the airport."

"I have a good idea how we could use those two hours."

He grinned and leaned down to kiss her. She kissed him back and wrapped her arms around his neck. It was only a couple of days. That was nothing. And in that time maybe she'd learn some more French. Surprise him.

"Call me. Tell me how you are. All of it, not just the good stuff."

That was what a real relationship was, wasn't it? Sharing all of it. Good and bad.

She'd felt alone for most of her life, but now she had Etienne and also Grace.

And she knew she was lucky. Maybe that was one positive thing about going through bad stuff. You knew good stuff when you saw it.

She thought it again when she waved him

off to get the last flight, and savored the good stuff as she lay down on top of the bed and listened to the sounds of Paris at night.

The bad stuff came at three in the morning when her phone rang.

It was Ron.

GRACE

"Grace?"

Grace blinked and realized she hadn't heard a word Philippe was saying. She'd been thinking about David. "I'm sorry. What did you say?"

She'd met him in his apartment after the concert, and he was still wearing his white dress shirt although the sleeves were rolled back and the neck was undone. His formal black trousers skimmed his lean hips and his feet were bare.

He looked handsome and lethally sexy.

A few nights ago she would have grabbed him and suggested they forget about food, but everything was different now.

"I was telling you about my concert tour in Budapest and Prague. I was inviting you to join me. Are you going to dress that salad or just stare at it?"

Salad?

She'd forgotten she was supposed to be

487

dressing the salad. "Sorry. I was miles away."

"Yes. I see that." He studied her for a moment and then turned his attention back to the steaks. "You can come to the concerts, of course, and during the day when I'm not practicing I can show you the cities."

Budapest. Prague.

As she made a vinaigrette dressing she tried to picture it, but David kept nudging his way into her thoughts.

She pushed him out again and instead thought about being with Philippe, strolling across the Charles Bridge.

It sounded idyllic, and maybe it was the right thing to do. And if David could arrive without warning, she could certainly leave. Maybe it was exactly what she needed to do. It would give her space to think. "When are you leaving?"

"Tomorrow."

"Seriously? That's the notice you give me?"

He turned the heat off under the steaks, took her face in his hands and kissed her, smiling against her lips. "My Grace. Such a planner."

His kiss made her dizzy but at the back of her mind she was wondering why all the men in her life thought planning was such a sin.

"Without planning you wouldn't have a flight ticket and a hotel."

He shrugged, and plated up the food. "That is all done for me by other people."

Grace resisted the temptation to roll her eyes. Couldn't he see the irony?

"I'll think about it."

"Think fast."

They ate on the balcony overlooking the tiny private garden at the back of the apartments.

She noticed others doing the same thing.

"Your neighbors probably sell tickets when you practice the piano."

He cut into his steak. "I'm not here enough to annoy them."

She couldn't imagine never being home. "Don't you miss being settled in one place? It must be tough."

He shrugged. "Not for me. For me 'tough' is being in one place without change."

They were so different. Maybe that was part of the attraction. He represented an alternate existence.

They ate and flirted, skimming over the surface of life, never dipping down into anything serious or important.

He talked about a young pianist he was mentoring who he thought had a brilliant future. After they'd finished eating, he played her some pieces he desperately wanted her to hear because he thought she'd love them. And she did, but mostly she loved the passion he poured into everything.

It would have been a lovely evening if she could have stopped thinking about David.

Was she being unfair not giving him another chance? Or would she be foolish to even consider it?

And did she really mean what she said or was she punishing him just a little bit?

Philippe lifted his glass. "Tonight your mind is somewhere else. Do you want to tell me where?"

She could hardly tell him she was thinking about her husband so she simply smiled. "I'm thinking what fun this is. The food was delicious, thank you."

He put his glass down, drew her to her feet and kissed her. His touch was practiced, skilled, but somehow he didn't have the same effect on her as the last time. It was as if a part of her was determined to remain detached.

No matter how much she wanted to deny it, a part of her would always belong to David.

And she was furious with herself. Why

couldn't she just move on? Why wasn't it easy?

Philippe led her to the bedroom and kissed her again, gently at first and then with more and more passion.

Without breaking the kiss, he slid the straps of her dress over her shoulders and pushed it down to her hips. His mouth moved from her lips to her jaw, and then to her neck.

Grace closed her eyes and tried to relax.

What was she doing? Was she here because of the attraction she felt toward Philippe, or was it something more? Deep down she was afraid her reasons might be more complicated than that. Was she proving something to herself?

Last time they'd been together she'd felt excited and a little reckless. She'd managed to push David out of her head, but now he'd crept back in and she couldn't shift him.

And it wasn't just that she felt a little guilty, although she did, it was more than that.

She didn't really *know* Philippe, did she?

They'd been intimate, but they weren't close.

When she'd met him at eighteen, it hadn't mattered. Her family had felt like handcuffs, chaining her to a life she'd hated. The last thing she'd wanted to do was talk about them. But now?

Somehow the chemistry alone wasn't enough.

They'd talked about art, music, travel, literature but every time she tried to talk about anything more personal he'd closed the conversation down. Audrey would no doubt laugh at her and tease her for being old-fashioned and maybe she was, but if that was the person she was, then what was wrong with that?

Philippe lifted his head reluctantly. "Somehow I don't think I have your full attention."

Grace rested her hand on his chest. If she was seriously considering going with him to Budapest and Prague, then they needed to have an honest relationship, surely? "Could we talk?"

Philippe raised an eyebrow. "Talking wasn't what I had in mind," he drawled, "but if that's what you want to do, then of course, let's talk. What do you want to talk about?"

"I want to know more about you. Tell me about your family. Your parents. Your sister."

"I don't think they come under the heading of erotic conversation."

"I don't feel as if I *know* you."

492

He slid his hand into her hair and kissed her gently. "After the other night? You know me, Grace."

She thought about the first time she'd had sex with David. It had been after her parents' funeral, which sounded dreadful when you thought about it, but in fact hadn't been dreadful at all. David had been living in a one-bedroom apartment in the town where they'd both grown up, and he'd taken her there afterward, nurturing her like a wounded animal.

He'd tucked her up on his old battered sofa, made her a cup of tea and listened while everything she'd been thinking and feeling had spilled out of her mouth.

David was a good listener, of course. Always had been. It was one of the things that made him a good journalist. Most people listened and then jumped in the moment there was a pause in the conversation, but David listened because he was truly interested in what you were saying.

They'd talked all night, about everything and anything and even in the middle of the heartbreak she'd found herself laughing. They'd made love as dawn was breaking and it had felt like the beginning of something rather than the end.

She'd moved in with him the same day.

At first it had seemed like an unusually impulsive move for her, but then she'd realized that this moment had been coming for a long time. She and David had been friends since childhood. Their whole lives had been intertwined. She'd loved him for a long time, although it had taken a tragedy for her to realize that her love went much deeper than friendship.

It was that friendship and closeness that she'd missed most. Waking up next to someone who really knew her.

She felt an ache behind her ribs.

Philippe stroked his finger across her cheek. "You look tired."

"I haven't been sleeping." She didn't tell him why, of course, because she knew he wouldn't be interested.

He smiled. "Lie down."

"Philippe —"

"I'm going to give you a foot massage, that's all."

She lay down and closed her eyes. She'd worry about everything tomorrow. Make decisions tomorrow. For now she just needed to rest. She was completely exhausted.

She fell asleep within minutes and was woken by bells. At first she thought it was her alarm, but then she realized it was her phone.

Next to her, Philippe muttered something in French and pulled her into his arms. "Leave it. You can call them back."

She almost did. Whoever it was could leave a message.

But what if it was Mimi? Or Sophie?

She slid out of his arms, feeling guilty even though they hadn't actually done anything. At some point in the night they'd both fallen asleep. "I have to check. It could be important."

He slid his hand over her hip. "More important than this?"

"Possibly." This wasn't the time to point out that not everyone lived in the moment all the time. That some people had ties and responsibilities.

She rummaged for her phone and by the time she found it, it had stopped ringing.

She saw a missed call from Sophie.

Just a chat or something more?

Her question was answered when her phone rang again.

She sent Philippe a look of apology. "I really need to take this."

"It can't wait?"

She almost explained that it was her daughter, and then she realized there was no point. He didn't have family. He wouldn't understand the urge that made her put family above everything else.

And she was at least partly responsible for that. She'd broken his heart.

"It can't wait. But it will probably only take a minute. And after that I'll make up for the fact that I fell asleep on you last night."

Philippe gave her a slow smile and she smiled back, making a decision.

When she'd finished talking to Sophie she was going to tell him that yes, she'd join him in Budapest and Prague. Just for a couple of nights. Audrey could manage for a couple of days now, surely? She had enough words and phrases and she could always call Grace if there was a problem.

Already making a mental packing list in her head, she answered the phone.

"Hi, honey."

"Mom?" Sophie's voice came down the phone, high-pitched and tearful.

The clouds of sleep vanished. "What's wrong?"

"Mom." Sophie was crying so hard she couldn't get the words out, and Grace fought to stay calm.

"Honey, you need to slow down. I can't hear what you're saying." She pressed the phone to her ear and turned away from Philippe. "Tell me slowly."

"It's Chrissie." Sophie gulped and sobbed, and Grace made out the words *hospital, sick* and *taken drugs.*

Chrissie had taken drugs? Chrissie, who had been raised on a diet of organic vegetables and had never swallowed so much as an antibiotic? No, that wasn't possible.

Her heart was thudding. "Did someone spike your drink or something?"

"No." Sophie was almost incoherent. "Chrissie's gone crazy wild since we've been traveling. Parties, boys and stuff. She said she wanted to try drugs, just once, because her mom would never let her do anything like that."

Grace felt a rush of nausea. "Were you there with her?"

"Yes. She wanted me to do it, too, and I said no, but then she said I was the most boring person ever, so I took it. I'm sorry." Sophie choked. "I'm *so* sorry. It was stupid, but she kept telling me I was spoiling her fun. She's my friend and I didn't know how to say no. I didn't want to ruin her trip."

Grace felt as if she'd been dunked in ice.

She remembered Chrissie at six years old, playing with Sophie, her hair in a ponytail.

Chrissie splashing in a paddling pool in the garden.

Chrissie, refusing chocolate cake because her mother wouldn't want her to eat it.

And now Chrissie had pushed Sophie into taking drugs. And Sophie hadn't said no.

Focus, focus.

Grace breathed through her anger. "First of all, tell me how you are. Are you all right? Did you suffer any ill effects?"

"I spat it out when she wasn't looking."

Relief flooded through her. "And Chrissie? How bad is she? What was the drug, do you know? Did —" she was almost afraid to ask the question "— anything else happen? Did anyone take advantage?" She thought about Audrey, alone at the party in the bathroom.

"No, n-nothing like that." Sophie's voice was jerky. "I called an ambulance and went with her to the hospital."

"Good girl." Forcing herself to stay calm, Grace closed her eyes. "Have you called Monica?" She sat on the edge of the bed, remembering how worried Monica had been. She'd been the one to reassure her. She'd said that she'd be around to help if anything went wrong, but she hadn't really thought it would happen. How would her friend react to the news that her clean-eating daughter had been filling her body with chemicals? Grace felt a rush of anger that Chrissie had not only done that, but that she'd pressured Sophie into doing it, too.

"I called you first. I haven't rung Monica yet. Mom, what if Chrissie *dies*? Monica will blame me for not trying to stop her —" Sophie carried on talking, but the rest of what she said was mostly incoherent.

Grace was shaking. She felt a little sick.

"You are not to blame."

"Could you call Monica, Mom? I don't know what to say."

"Of course. Leave that with me, honey." It felt good to be able to do something to help.

Behind her, she felt the bed move and heard Philippe leave the room.

She couldn't help thinking that if David was here he'd be sitting on the bed right by her, giving her support. He'd be as worried as she was. He'd definitely have his arm around her.

She missed him so badly it was like a physical ache in her chest.

He'd wanted to talk to her. And what had she done?

She'd rebuffed him. Twice.

She hadn't even listened to him. She hadn't given him a chance. Wasn't that what he'd done to her? And she'd criticized him.

"I need you to calm down and give me the details of the hospital. I'll meet you there as soon as I can get a flight. I'll text you details as soon as I have them. And I'll call Monica now."

"Okay. Thank you. And I'm sorry, Mom. I'm so, so sorry. I've been so messed-up since Dad left, and with the whole Sam thing —" her breathing juddered "— I didn't want to lose my best friend, too. I know that's not an excuse, I know I made a bad decision. Are you mad at me?"

Was she mad? Maybe she was a little. Mostly she was stunned. And scared.

I've been so messed-up since Dad left.

Was this her and David's fault? Were they the ones who had indirectly caused this? Was their daughter now so emotionally needy that she'd do anything to keep a friend?

This wasn't the right time to think about that. "I'm not mad, Sophie. I'm just glad you told me. We'll find a way through this, I promise."

"I tried calling Dad, too, but he didn't answer."

"He's here, in Paris. He brought Mimi."

There was a soft gasp on the end of the phone. "Are you guys back together? Oh, my God, that would be the best thing ever. Can you call him, Mom? Can you tell Daddy? Will he come with you?"

Daddy.

When had Sophie last called him Daddy?

Not since she was very young.

Grace stared straight ahead. She hadn't planned on contacting David, but she knew he'd be horrified when he found out about this and discovered she'd known and hadn't told him.

They'd always handled everything together.

It was a shock to discover that she *wanted* to call him.

"I'll call Dad. Go and splash your face, then go back to Chrissie. I'll be there as soon as I can." She ended the call and turned to find Philippe standing there.

He handed her a cup of coffee. "I'm guessing this means you're not coming to Budapest."

Budapest? The one thing she hadn't given a single thought to during the conversation was Philippe.

"No, I won't be coming. I have a family crisis. My daughter —" She stopped as Philippe held up his hand.

"You don't need to explain."

She felt so tired and emotional it was hard

501

to speak. "I'm sorry."

"Why? It's been fun, Grace."

That was all he was going to say?

"These last few days —" she swallowed. "I thought maybe —"

"That we could be more?" He shook his head. "I don't want more. We could have extended the fun, but it would never have been more than that. Not for me."

"And that's my fault." She realized that she had tears on her cheeks. "I feel terrible that I'm the reason you don't have anyone special in your life. That you prefer to be alone. I hurt you so badly —"

"That's not true."

"You said —"

"You're not understanding me, Grace. I am happy with this life. This is exactly the life I want. It's not a compromise for me. I'm not living this way because I'm wounded. I'm living this way because I like to be free."

"But what about family? Love?"

"Music is my love, Grace. I travel for her. I live for her. That's it."

He hadn't even asked about her call. He could see she was upset and anxious, but he hadn't made any attempt to comfort her.

That wasn't what their relationship was.

And she saw then that what they had

wasn't real at all. It never would have been anything other than a dizzying fling. It was like dining out in a fancy restaurant. An amazing occasional experience, something you'd always remember, but not something you wanted to do every day.

She'd thought she was in love with him at eighteen, but perhaps she'd really been in love with the contrast he'd offered to her own life. At the time, she'd been desperate to step out of her world and into his.

But now his world held no appeal for her at all.

She put her coffee down and dressed quickly. "Do you know how quickly I can get a flight to Rome?" Should she have said something when Sophie had mentioned partying? She'd been afraid of being a killjoy. What else had the girls been doing that Grace didn't know about?

"You're forgetting I never make my own travel plans."

She felt a flash of irritation. The man didn't live in the real world. What she'd seen as glamorous and exciting, she now saw as immature. "Don't worry. I'll figure it out by myself."

She gathered up her things and walked across to him. "Thank you for dinner, and for the concert tickets, and for a wonderful few days."

She was grateful to him for the distraction, and for making her feel good about herself, but mostly she was grateful to him for reminding her what was important.

"My Grace." He gave a half smile. "Always making the safe, sensible choice."

Grace thought about her family. About David.

"You're wrong," she said. "There's nothing safe about love. Commitment takes bravery because there is every chance you'll be badly hurt. Not ever getting involved, just moving from one experience to the next — *that's* the safe choice." She reached up and kissed him softly on the cheek. "Take care, Philippe. If you're ever playing a concert in New York, let me know."

She grabbed a cab back to her apartment and on the way she dialed David's number.

His phone might be switched off, but she knew where he was staying.

He answered after a couple of rings, and sounded sleepy and disoriented.

"David, it's me." As they pulled up outside the bookstore, Grace paid the cabdriver in cash and stumbled out of the car. "Sophie's in trouble. You need to come."

He responded exactly the way she'd known he would respond. He was calm, supportive and strong. He didn't ask needless questions. Didn't panic or waste time.

Instead, he said the words she'd hoped he'd say.

"I'll be right there."

Audrey crammed her clothes into her backpack. Did she need to take everything? Yes, she probably did. Paris, Etienne, her apartment, the bookshop — it already seemed like a dream and she hadn't even left yet.

She'd been so happy.

How could her life have turned to crap so quickly?

She wanted to call Etienne and tell him, but she didn't want to be selfish. He had his own family issues. That was why he was flying down to the South of France. He didn't need to deal with hers, too.

As soon as she was packed, she'd talk to Grace.

Grace would understand. She'd probably have some good advice.

In the meantime, she called Elodie. Not that there was any way she could be talked into staying, but she didn't want to behave unprofessionally. Elodie had given her a second chance, so Audrey needed to tell her that she was leaving and why.

She was braced for a difficult conversation but Elodie was warm and caring, which made Audrey feel even worse.

Having cleared everything into her bag, she took a last look around the little apartment.

She pulled out her phone and took a few photos. Not that she was ever going to forget this place, but when she was feeling low the photos might give her hope that someday she might have a place of her own again.

With a sniff, she locked the apartment and took the stairs down to the bookstore for the last time.

She'd go direct to the station and get the first train to London. Hopefully she'd have enough money for a one-way ticket.

The last thing she expected to see when she walked into the bookshop was Grace, wrapped in David's arms.

Audrey froze on the spot. Bad timing.

And then she saw that he wasn't kissing her. It didn't look passionate or anything.

It looked as if he was comforting her.

Grace's head was buried in his shoulder and he was hugging her tightly and speaking in a calm, confident voice.

"It's going to be fine, honey. The flight takes two hours. We'll be there by lunch-time."

Audrey dropped her backpack behind the desk. "Where? What's wrong?"

Grace turned, and Audrey saw that her eyes were red. "Oh, Audrey, I'm so glad you're here. Sophie, our daughter, called. The friend she's traveling with is in the hospital in Rome. We're going right away. I don't know how long we'll be gone, but hopefully I'll be back tomorrow. I'm so sorry to leave you with the bookstore. Will you be okay?"

Audrey felt a solid lump in her chest. She held back the words she'd been about to say. "Sure. I'll be fine."

Sophie was Grace's daughter. She was going to take priority over Audrey, and quite right, too. Grace was everything a mother should be.

She noticed the way Grace leaned into David, taking the support he was offering, and felt a pang of loneliness.

She wished someone was hugging and holding her like that. She wished someone would tell her everything was going to be okay.

Grace looked at her. "Is something wrong?"

"No. Nothing." She'd lied a million times about how she was. Why did it seem so hard this time? "Is there anything I can do? What's happened to Sophie?"

She listened as Grace told her the details.

It wasn't that unusual a story, but Grace was obviously devastated, and David seemed surprised that she was being so open with Audrey.

"She'll be okay." Audrey focused on Grace. "So, she was pressured in trying drugs. It happens."

"I always thought she'd say no. She knows the dangers."

"Never underestimate peer pressure." Audrey thought about all the times she'd pretended to drink alcohol, and the one time she *had* drunk alcohol. She sympathized with Sophie.

David still had his arm around Grace. "Audrey is right. This is all going to be okay, Grace, I promise. We'll figure it out together. And maybe it means she won't be so easily pressured when she gets to college."

There was a calmness about him that was contagious. Although David had behaved like a total shit, Audrey could see why Grace loved him.

He had kind eyes and solid shoulders.

She couldn't imagine him freaking out

509

about anything.

She shrugged. "Bad choices are part of life, aren't they? Doesn't mean your next choice can't be a good one."

Grace sniffed. "You're right. I'll see you tomorrow." She pulled away from David and hugged Audrey.

Audrey hugged her back tightly. She didn't want to let go.

This was probably the last time they'd see each other. She didn't have Grace's address, and she didn't have the money to travel to the US. She felt as if part of her was being wrenched away.

She thought about Grace stepping in and saving her job. Grace teaching her French. Grace rescuing her when she was drunk. *Grace listening while she talked about her mother for the first time in her life.*

Trying not to cry, she pulled away. "Take care."

She wanted to tell her what a difference she'd made to her life, how she felt as if Grace had actually saved her, but she couldn't say any of that without revealing that something was wrong, so she said nothing else and within minutes Grace and David had left.

She flinched as the door closed.

The breath left her lungs in a whoosh.

So that was it, then.

Audrey stared after them for a moment and then picked up her backpack and made her way to Gare du Nord to get the Eurostar. It was hard to imagine she'd be back in London in a few hours. Her old life had felt like a million miles away, but now it was getting closer again.

She called Ron again, but his phone went to voice mail.

She had no idea how her mother was.

At the station, she bought a ticket and sat down to wait for the next train. Etienne called twice but she didn't take his call. She didn't want to dump more crap on him and she didn't trust herself to say "I'm fine" convincingly.

She was on her own with this.

She blinked. She'd been on her own with things her whole life, so why did this suddenly feel different?

She twisted the ring on her finger and thought of Grace.

She thought of the conversations they'd had, the long hours they'd spent in the bookshop. Remembering Grace acting out French words should have made her laugh, but instead it made her want to cry.

She'd never felt lonelier in her life.

Having friends and losing them was worse

than not having them in the first place. But she still didn't wish for anything different. These last few weeks with Grace and Etienne had been the happiest of her life.

She'd had someone to share her thoughts and problems with and it had somehow made them easier to handle.

She'd had friends she trusted. Friends who knew the truth.

She should have taken more photographs so that she would always have the memory.

Crap. She rubbed her face with her fingers and glared at a man who was looking at her with concern.

She was a survivor. She'd get through this. So it was harder than usual. So what?

She was tough. Bring it on.

To distract herself, she put her headphones on and listened to an audiobook, but it made her think of Grace and Etienne so she took it off and stared into space instead.

Finally, they boarded the train and she elbowed her way to a seat by the window and slumped there.

Two minutes before the train doors closed someone sat down next to her. Audrey kept her face averted. The last thing she wanted was to make polite conversation with some stranger.

"We don't do this, do we?" The woman spoke, and Audrey whirled around and there was Grace, sitting in the seat next to her.

"What are you talking about? What are you doing here?"

"We don't say 'I'm fine' when we're not fine. Not to each other. We have a proper friendship. The sort where you don't have to say you're fine when you're not. What's happened, Audrey? Why are you on this train?"

Audrey was swamped by emotion and also panic.

"Shit, Grace, the train leaves in, like, thirty seconds! You need to get off or you'll be in London next and you have to be in Rome with Sophie."

"You could have said, 'Grace, the train leaves in thirty seconds.' The swearing didn't add anything to that sentence."

Audrey felt a rush of frustration. "Don't you get it? You're going to be trapped on here."

"Did I ever teach you the French word for train? I hope you bought your ticket in French."

The doors closed, sealing them inside and Audrey sagged against her seat.

"Well, now you're doomed. You're going

513

on a trip to London where, by the way, it is raining. How did you know I was here anyway?"

"I knew there was something wrong, but I was so wrapped up in my own problems it took me a few minutes to work it out. I was halfway to the airport when I thought to ring Elodie and sure enough she told me you'd called her and explained you had to go home because there was a family emergency. She was worried about you. What's the emergency, honey?" Her voice was gentle. "Did something happen to your mom?"

Audrey's eyes filled. She tried to hold back the tears, but then she remembered that this was Grace, and she didn't have to put on an act with Grace.

"Ron called me in the middle of the night." Ron, who had spoken in that impossibly kind voice people only used when they were delivering seriously bad news. "My mum is in hospital. She was hit by a car. She's in surgery."

"Oh, Audrey —" Grace took her hand. "You poor thing. You must be so worried."

"What if she dies?" And then she remembered Grace's parents had died and she felt terrible. "I'm sorry. That was so tactless."

"Don't apologize. You don't have to be

careful what you say. Remember I know exactly what you're going through."

"I feel like I've been such a terrible daughter."

"No!" Grace's hand tightened on hers. "You are a wonderful daughter. You're caring, loving and strong."

"But I get so frustrated with her."

"Of course you do! That doesn't make you a bad daughter, honey. You're frustrated because you love her, and you hate to watch her doing this to herself. She understands all that, I'm sure."

Grace always, always made her feel better.

"I can't believe you're here with me."

"That's what friends do."

"What?" Audrey blew her nose. "Make sacrifices?"

"They show up in times of trouble."

"David must be mad that you've left him to deal with Sophie."

"He doesn't get mad. He's very even tempered. He understands about putting someone you love first. He did it for me more times than I can count."

"Yeah. I was ready to hate him for what he did to you, but he's not that easy to hate. You still love him, don't you?"

"Unfortunately, yes. Love isn't something you can switch on and off that easily."

"I know." Audrey thought of her mum. "What if she dies and she doesn't know I really love her? I get so mad at her sometimes. Once, I told her I hated her." Tears spilled down her cheeks. "But it wasn't true. It wasn't true."

"Oh, Audrey." Grace put her arm around her and pulled her close. "For a start, I can tell you that your mom definitely knows you love her."

"You don't know that. I don't even know if I've ever said it aloud."

"Love isn't what you say aloud, honey. It's what you do. You've been there for your mom the whole time. You check on her, care for her and try to persuade her to care for herself. Your feelings for her are virtually written all over you."

Audrey sniffed. "Are they?"

"Yes. And as for telling her you hated her — that's a normal, heat of the moment teenage thing."

"I bet Sophie never told you she hated you."

"In fact, she did. She'd found what she thought was a stray dog, and she brought it home but it turned out it belonged to someone. When I made her give it back, she was devastated. She didn't speak to me for two whole days."

"And you remember it, so it must have hurt your feelings."

"It did, but it didn't make me doubt her love for me. She was showing me that she was upset, that's all." Grace hugged her. "And you should have told me you were upset. You should have called me right away."

"I was in a bit of a state to be honest. I packed my things and I thought I'd talk to you before I left, but then it turned out you were having traumas, too. Sophie needs you, and she should be your priority. I don't know why you're here."

"I'm here because I'm your friend," Grace said. "And the moment Elodie told me there had been a family emergency, I thought you might need a friend. David can handle Sophie."

Audrey gave a wobbly smile. "You're delegating?"

"I prefer to call it sharing. It's what you do when you're a couple."

Audrey shifted in her seat so she could look at Grace. "Are you a couple?"

Grace sighed and withdrew her arm from Audrey's shoulders. "In the sense you mean? I don't know. But we have a daughter together, so we'll always share that no matter what happens. David has gone to Sophie, and we had another call telling us that her friend Chrissie is recovering. I spoke to Monica, Chrissie's mother, and she is flying over so she'll be there soon, too. David is going to bring Sophie back to Paris. I'll meet up with them there in a few days, whenever we decide to go back."

"I don't think I'll be going back."

"Let's see what happens. Elodie is covering the bookstore for a few days, and she's holding both the apartments for us. We can make a decision when we know more. That's your phone ringing. Aren't you going to answer it?"

"I can't. It's Etienne. He's gone to stay with his family for a few days. I don't want to lie to him, so I'm ignoring his calls."

"There's an alternative," Grace said, "and that's that you take his call and tell him the truth."

"I'll think about it."

"I called you, too, but your phone kept going to voice mail."

"I was probably trying to call Ron."

"So what do you know? What details?"

"Not much. I mean, I know the hospital, but not much else." She felt an ache spread across her chest. "She probably fell because she was drunk. You do get that, don't you? This isn't going to be pretty."

518

"Life isn't always pretty, but friendship gets us through the ugly bits. I'll be there with you. And if you don't want me to come with you to see your mother because she doesn't know me, I'll wait in the corridor and you can come and talk to me whenever you need to."

The fact that Grace was willing to stand in a cold, impersonal hospital corridor for Audrey almost tipped her over the edge.

"I can't believe you did this. No one has ever put me first before."

"We're friends. And in the spirit of friendship I'm pointing out that you could do with putting on some makeup or your mom will be the one worrying about you. You look like an extra in a ghost movie." Grace reached for her bag. "Did you eat before you left? If not, I'm going to pay a visit to the buffet car."

Audrey hadn't even thought about food. "I don't think they sell anything green in the buffet car. Unless it's mold on bread."

"That doesn't sound appetizing. Maybe I'll buy chocolate bars."

"Grace Porter, that doesn't sound like a good choice."

"It doesn't, but I know you love chocolate and we can't all make good choices all of the time." Grace squeezed her hand. "Stay there. I'll be back in a few minutes."

Audrey watched her go. She was still anxious about her mum, but now she had Grace there she felt stronger. She'd been worried she wouldn't be able to cope, but now she thought she probably would.

The train arrived in London and she was so glad to have Grace there because she took over. It was raining, but somehow Grace managed to get a cab. Audrey texted Ron to say they were nearly there and when they arrived at the hospital there he was, waiting for them at the entrance dodging the flow of people going in and out of the hospital.

He hugged Audrey awkwardly and shook hands with Grace after Audrey introduced them.

"Thanks for coming with her, Grace. Decent of you. I didn't expect you to get here so quickly, Aud."

"I jumped on the first train." Audrey hauled her bag onto her shoulder. "How is she?"

"She's out of surgery. The operation went well, although she'll be out of action for a while because she broke her leg and her arm." Ron scratched his head. "She was sleeping, but I know she'll be pleased to see you. I thought you might like a cup of coffee first. Then we can have a bit of a chat."

A chat?

He was going to tell her he was leaving.

Audrey's pulse rocketed. Her heart skipped in her chest and she couldn't breathe properly.

"Okay. Coffee. Whatever." She grabbed Grace's hand as they walked to the small coffee shop on the ground floor of the hospital.

Ron found a table and then went to buy drinks.

Audrey felt sicker than she did when she waited for exam results. "This is it, then. He's going to tell me he's leaving."

Grace frowned. "I don't think so, honey."

"Why did he bring me here, then?"

"I'm guessing it's because he wants to tell you more about your mom before you see her."

There was no time to reply because Ron returned with a tray, three coffees and two prewrapped slices of brownie.

The coffee was murky and looked like nothing anyone would want to drink unless they were desperate.

"Okay, so I thought I could tell you a few things so we don't have to talk in front of your mum." He ripped open three mini packets of sugar and tipped them into his coffee. "Don't judge. It's the only way I can keep this stuff down. Oh, and I got you these because I know you like them." He stuck his hand into his pocket and pulled out two of her favorite chocolate bars.

Audrey was touched. She didn't want to hurt his feelings by admitting she was already full of chocolate, so she ate one and thought that if there was a way of curing her chocolate habit it might be eating it in bulk.

Her hands shook under the table. "You're leaving, aren't you?"

Ron blinked. "No, although I've been here since midnight and I could probably use a shower, but it can wait."

"I meant, you're leaving my mum." Audrey's throat thickened and she felt a flash of horror. Before Paris she'd never cried. Never. Now she seemed to have turned into a water feature.

Ron looked bemused. "Why would I leave her? I just married her."

Audrey thought about Grace and David. "Marriage doesn't mean anything."

"Yes, it does. It means I wanted to be with her. I didn't marry her on a whim, Aud." Ron stirred his coffee, took a sip and pulled a face. "Shit, that's bad." He glanced at Grace. "Excuse my language."

Grace smiled. "No problem."

Audrey would have gaped if her jaws hadn't been welded together by chocolate. Why was Ron allowed to swear when she would have been lectured? Grace obviously liked him enough to give him a free pass.

She swallowed the last of the chocolate. "What happened to my mum?"

"I don't exactly know. She stayed late for drinks at work. Sometimes she does that, as you know." His gaze skidded to Grace, and Audrey shook her head.

"Grace is my friend. She knows everything."

"Right." Ron gave Grace a quick nod. "Well, like I was saying, she stayed for drinks. Then I got a call from the police. Must have been around midnight. I'd been calling her phone and I was worried. They told me she'd been hit by a car and was in hospital."

"Was the driver drunk?" Was it crazy that she was almost hoping that was the case?

"No, love." Ron's voice was gentle. "It was your mum who was drunk. The driver was in shock. He said she just stepped out with no warning. He didn't even have time to swerve."

Audrey could picture it, and the picture was shocking.

"She could have been killed."

"Yes." Ron took another sip of coffee. "So we have to talk about what happens next."

"B-but you're not leaving? I thought, maybe if you knew — I mean, she does drink too much —" Audrey couldn't get the words to come out properly, and Ron patted her hand awkwardly.

"I know what she is, Audie. I know she drinks. I've always known. I love her anyway. I had a few issues myself in that direction. I'm ten years sober. Still go to meetings."

The noise around her faded. She forgot Grace was sitting there. She forgot everything.

Ron?

Audrey stared at him. "I didn't know."

"First time I met her, all she did was talk about you." Ron pushed one of the brownies toward her. "She loves you a hell of a lot, but I guess you know that."

She hadn't known that. Not really.

Audrey ignored the brownie. If she ate any more sugar she'd end up being admitted to this hospital herself. "I — I love her, too."

"I told her that, but when you're drinking your brain can play tricks on you."

Audrey still couldn't believe it. "You still go to meetings after ten years?"

"Yes. And your mum has already promised

to come to a meeting with me."

"She has?" Hope blossomed. "I hope that happens."

"I feel bad you came rushing back. Maybe I shouldn't have called you. Did I do the wrong thing?" He finished his coffee and scrunched the cup in his hand. "I've never had a daughter. Not that I'm pretending I'm your dad or anything. That's why I called. I didn't think it was my place to keep it from you."

"I'm glad you called." Audrey gave up on her coffee. It tasted like poison, especially after Grace's coffee. Ron's stomach must be lined with lead or something. "And I'm glad you told me everything. Shall we go and see her now?"

"If you're up to it." Ron stood up. "Just to warn you, she doesn't look too good. She's a bit bruised. I don't want you to freak."

Audrey made a mental vow to keep her freaking internal. "I'm okay."

Ron squeezed her arm. "That's my girl. I know it doesn't seem like it right now, but everything is going to work out. We'll figure it out. You know what I always say —"

"*— as long as no one is dead, it will be fine.*"

"Exactly. If everyone is still alive, then there are things we can do."

Audrey choked on a laugh. That response

was totally Ron. He was so laid-back he was practically horizontal. He was perfect for her mother. Why hadn't she seen that before?

They took the lift up to the ward, and Grace chatted to Ron. *Did he need fresh clothes? Could she fetch him something? Was there anything practical she could do while he and Audrey visited Linda?*

"I like your friend," Ron said as Grace vanished to call David.

Audrey nodded. "She's the kindest person I've ever met." It occurred to her that he must be exhausted. "If you've been here all night, you should have a break. Go home, get some sleep or something."

"Plenty of time for sleep later." Ron paused outside the entrance to the ward. "I'll stick around, if that's all right with you. We're a family now, aren't we?"

"Yes. Yes, we are." Audrey felt a pressure in her chest. Family. It was surprising how good that one word sounded. How good it *felt.*

A nurse showed them where her mother was, and Audrey was grateful that Ron had given her warning because the bruising on her face was scary.

"Hi, Mum." She leaned down to kiss her, and when her mother started to cry, Audrey's stomach knotted. At first it felt like every time before, and then it became clear that this time was different. This wasn't a drunken sobfest, these were genuine tears of regret and hopelessness. And although seeing her mother cry broke her heart, Audrey no longer felt that horrible guilt that the whole thing was somehow her fault. It was one of the many things Grace had taught her. She wasn't a bad daughter. She hadn't done anything to cause this. The only person responsible for her mother's problems was her mother.

"Don't cry, Mum." She hugged her mother gently. "Don't cry."

"I'm so ashamed." Linda clutched her. "I only meant to have one drink, but then it turned into two and then three."

"It's okay, Mum. You don't have to explain." Audrey eased away and sat down on the bed. "I'm just pleased you're going to try to do something about it."

A look of panic crossed Linda's face and she turned to Ron. "You told her?"

"Yeah, I told her. She needs to know what we're doing. We shouldn't have secrets."

"But what if I fail?" Linda gave a strangled sob, and Audrey took her hand.

"It's not all or nothing. You just have to keep trying. Like me and those stupid exams. It's not failure until you stop trying. Don't give up."

"I've been such a bad mother. I'm truly sorry, Audie." She'd said the same words before, but only when she was drunk and upset. This was the first time Audrey had heard genuine remorse.

"You're not a bad mother. You're not well, that's all."

"So many times you looked after me, when I should have been the one looking after you. I feel so guilty about that. I can't change the past, but I can change the future. I'm going to do better." Her mother took a tissue from Ron and blew her nose. "I'm going to make it up to you. I'm going to be a mother to you, not a burden. I want you to be proud of me."

"I am proud. I'm proud that you're trying to stop." And relieved. Oh, so relieved that her mother had at last admitted she had a problem.

"When you're out of here and recovered, we'll figure out a program," Ron said.

"I've already talked to the doctors here." Linda looked thin and pale. "I'm sorry I dragged you back from Paris, Audie. You didn't have to come."

"Of course I did. You're my family." Audrey swallowed. "What about your job?"

528

"My bosses have been very supportive. There will be a job waiting for me when I'm back on my feet. And the doctors say I can probably go home tomorrow or the next day. I'll have to come back to clinic, of course, but that's not as bad as being in a hospital bed. And that's enough about me. Tell us about Paris. I want to know everything."

It was the first time her mother had shown interest in how she was spending her summer.

Audrey talked about the bookshop and her apartment with its views of the rooftops. She told them about Etienne, and she told them about Grace. Her mother asked questions, and even laughed a little at the stories Audrey told. For the first time Audrey felt there was a connection there.

The more she talked, the more she realized just how much she missed Paris. She missed the city and the people. She even missed the dusty smell of books. Most of all, she missed Etienne.

She wondered how he was getting on with his mother and sisters. She wanted to talk to him and tell him everything that had happened.

Families messed with your head, but at the same time they were the very best thing.

When Grace appeared in the doorway, Audrey and Ron introduced her and Grace was wonderful with Linda, saying exactly the right things.

Audrey wondered if it was hard for Grace, seeing Linda reach for a second chance knowing that there was none for her own mother.

It was Grace who encouraged her to call Meena once they'd left Linda to sleep. Grace who encouraged her to tell Meena the truth.

Audrey did, and Meena arrived at the hospital an hour later with food sent by her mother and offers of help from her whole family.

At first Audrey felt awkward, but then Meena hugged her and all she felt was relief.

"So now you know," she croaked. "Welcome to my real life. Bit of a shocker."

"Not really." Meena squeezed her tightly. "I always knew something was wrong."

"Yeah?" Audrey pulled away, horrified by the lump in her throat. "Why didn't you say something?"

"If you'd wanted to tell me, you would have told me. I didn't want to push. I spent hours trying to work out how to let you know I was there for you if you needed me, but I couldn't find a way to do it without scaring you away."

She'd felt so alone, but it seemed that she hadn't been as alone as she'd thought.

Part of her wished she'd confided in Meena sooner, but knew she was only doing it now because of Grace. If they hadn't met and become friends, she'd probably still be keeping everything to herself.

Grace had intended to book a hotel room for herself, but in the end Meena's mother insisted she stay with them, and Meena's dad picked them up from the hospital.

Word spread that Grace spoke French and two of Meena's cousins joined them for dinner so that Grace could check their homework and help them with their French.

Meena was mortified, but Grace seemed delighted to help.

"Don't teach them the word for *condom,*" Audrey muttered to Grace as she carried what felt like a banquet to the table. Meena's mother always catered on a large scale.

Instead of going home, she shared Meena's room and they talked into the night.

Audrey discovered that trusting someone and letting them close pushed away that horrible feeling of loneliness that she'd lived with for so long.

The following day Linda was discharged home.

She was the one who insisted Audrey go straight back to Paris.

"You have a job."

"Two jobs actually. I work in the bookshop in the morning and the salon in the afternoon."

"Then that's where you should be." Linda lay on the sofa, a cup of tea in her hand. "You have a responsibility to them. It's going to take me a while to recover, but I'll get there."

"I should be here to look after you."

"That's what I'm here for." Ron patted her shoulder. "Grace is planning on going back to Paris tomorrow because her daughter and husband are there. You should go with her."

Meena's mother had promised to keep an eye on things, too, and Meena was going to keep Audrey posted.

"I've missed you this summer." Her friend hugged her tightly as they waited for Meena's dad to arrive to drive them to the station to get the train back to Paris. "Come and stay with me in Oxford."

"I will. And don't forget to be meaner-Meena."

Meena giggled. "I've been working on it, I

promise. I only apologized once to the woman who complained about me yesterday. A few weeks ago I would have apologized at least six times."

Back on the train Audrey was so exhausted she slept most of the way with her head on Grace's shoulder.

She woke as the train came to a halt. "Where are we?"

"Just outside Paris. Ten more minutes."

Audrey yawned. "I'm sorry I slept. Great company I am."

"I was glad to see you sleep. You were exhausted. Emotionally and physically. But you must be feeling better about it all."

"I am." And if it did all go wrong again, at least now she had proper support. She had friends she could be honest with. People who would help her. She wasn't on her own with it. That felt like the best thing of all.

It occurred to her that Grace must be exhausted, too, even though she hadn't said anything. All she'd thought about was Audrey.

"Thank you." Audrey put her head back on Grace's shoulder. "I never could have survived that trip without you. Having you there made all the difference."

"Well, I wouldn't have survived my time in Paris without you. You're a very special person."

Audrey felt her eyes sting. "You're making my mascara run."

"In that case don't rub your face in my new white shirt."

Audrey sniffed and lifted her head. "I'm going to miss you so much when you leave. Can we stay in touch?"

"What sort of a question is that? Of course we're going to stay in touch. You'll come and visit, and I'll come back and visit you in Paris, or London or wherever you are. We can chat online and I can carry on teaching you French." Grace dug in her bag and handed Audrey a tissue. "Here."

Audrey blew her nose and pretended to be irritated. "French? Don't I get time off for good behavior?"

"No."

"I'm glad I have a friend like you. It's nice having someone who cares about you."

The train was slowing down as it pulled into the station. A few people were already standing up and grabbing their bags.

"There are plenty of people who care about you. Including your mom. She really loves you, Audrey."

"I know. I didn't used to know, but I do now."

"And she's not the only one." Grace

nudged her. "This would be a good time to look out of the window."

Audrey turned her head and saw Etienne standing on the platform, scanning the train. Her heart lifted and excitement shot through her, closely followed by horror.

"Oh, my God." She shrank against the seat. "What is he doing here?"

"I expect he was bored and thought he'd hang out at the train station."

"Ha ha." But she couldn't summon a laugh. "Seriously? Why is he here? I mean, how does he even know I'm on this train?"

"He texted me," Grace said, "and I told him this was the train we were catching, although I admit I didn't know he actually planned to meet you."

Audrey gaped at her. "He texted you?"

"I probably should have told you, but you had a lot going on and he asked me not to." Grace looked at her steadily. "He's here for you, Audrey. Aren't you pleased?"

"Yes! No — I mean, I want to see him, of course. I've missed him horribly, but the timing is bad." Audrey wiped her cheeks with her hand. "I look like crap."

"Language."

"Sorry, but *darn* just doesn't work here. You can't look like *darn*."

"You look gorgeous. But we should get

535

rid of the streaked mascara." Grace opened her purse and pulled out her makeup bag. "Sit still."

"What are you doing?"

"Your makeup." She quickly wiped under Audrey's eyes with a cleansing pad. "That's better. And now blusher."

"Don't make me look like a granny." Audrey closed her eyes as Grace swept a brush over her cheeks. "Aren't you going to use lip gloss?"

"No, because Etienne will just kiss it off. It's a waste."

Audrey felt something flutter in her stomach. "Grace, how do you know when you love someone? I mean, really love them, and not just want to get naked with them the whole time."

"That's a hard question." Grace dropped the makeup back in her bag. "It's probably different for everyone, but I think when that person is the one you want to be with more than anyone, that's a pretty good sign. And caring about their happiness. That's important, too. I'm guessing Etienne is here because he was worried about you and cares about you."

"I think about him all the time. And I feel like I'm on a high. Like I've drunk a ton of diet cola, or eaten six bars of chocolate. It feels great, but also a bit scary. A bit too good to be true, you know? It's so easy. We talk all the time, and we have fun, and I never expected a relationship to be this easy." Watching her mother's experiences, and also her own, had left her thinking relationships were awkward and hard work. It was a surprise to discover it didn't have to be that way. "I can be myself with him."

"Well, that's the best thing, of course. Because being someone else doesn't work in the long-term."

"He knows I love animated movies. He even watched one with me, but don't let on that I told you that. I don't think he likes them, but he did it for me."

Grace laughed. "That's definitely love." She stood up. "Time to put him out of his misery. Let's go." She lifted Audrey's bag down and retrieved her own.

Audrey hugged Grace tightly. "I love you. And I don't mean that in a weird way, and all I've drunk is water so I'm not under the influence of anything except gratitude." She felt Grace hug her back.

"I love you, too. And you're going to let me know what happens with your mom, and with Etienne. And if you need me, I'm always here."

"And I'm here if you need me." Audrey

stepped back and swung her backpack onto her shoulders. "Anytime you need fashion advice, or a new haircut, or some fresh new ways to curse —"

The train had stopped, and she saw Etienne catch sight of her.

His face brightened.

Grace gave her a push. "Go. I'll give you five minutes to get the sloppy stuff out of the way."

Audrey stumbled on her way out of the train, and then Grace called after her.

"Audrey?"

"What?"

"Poulpe."

Audrey frowned. "Excuse me?"

"The French word for *octopus*. In case you ever want to order one from a menu."

Audrey laughed and hitched her bag onto her shoulder.

She gave a final wave and stepped down from the train, and then Etienne was grabbing her, kissing her and talking all at the same time. She loved the way he was holding her — as if she was something precious that he'd almost lost.

"Elodie told me about your mum being in hospital." He lifted his mouth from hers just long enough to speak. "Why didn't you answer my calls? I've been going mad."

"I didn't want to bother you with it. How was your family?"

"The same as ever. And don't ever, ever keep things from me again. When you're in trouble, I want to know." He kissed her again. "I love you, Audie. I really love you."

"I love you, too." Audrey decided that love was the most exciting, intoxicating thing she'd ever experienced. It was like a drug, with none of the side effects. But it was also comforting. That hollow feeling of loneliness that had been with her for so long had vanished. "I love you so much."

She flung her arms around him and then felt Grace tap her on the shoulder.

"En francais," Grace said, and Audrey rolled her eyes at Etienne.

"What's the French for *get off my back?*"

GRACE

Grace headed straight to the hotel, leaving Etienne and Audrey to cover the bookshop. She was desperate to see Sophie. Choosing to support Audrey over her own daughter had been one of the hardest decisions of her life, but following her maternal instinct and going to Sophie would have meant abandoning Audrey when she most needed a friend. Grace hadn't been able to do it, especially knowing that David was equally capable of supporting their daughter.

She'd had a text from him earlier saying they were having lunch in the restaurant, so she headed there but before she reached the restaurant her phone rang.

Lissa's name showed on her caller ID.

Oh, you have to be kidding me.

Grace stared at the phone. Was she really going to take a call from her husband's lover just before she walked into the restaurant? There had been a time when she'd loved

Lissa like a daughter, but that feeling was long gone.

She could ignore the call, but if she ignored it, she'd simply think about it all day. It would be like a stone in her shoe. She needed to get rid of it now.

With a sigh, she answered the call and stepped into a quiet corner of the reception area. "Lissa."

"Mrs. Porter? Gr-Grace?" Lissa sounded impossibly young, and Grace almost rolled her eyes.

She wasn't going to let a little wobble in the voice soften her.

The girl had been old enough to seduce David. Old enough to be at least 50 percent responsible for threatening a marriage.

"What do you want, Lissa?"

"I wanted to talk to you. I wanted to say —" there was a hitch in her breathing "— I wanted to say I'm sorry."

Sorry? *Sorry!*

Grace gripped the phone like a weapon. She was angry and also bemused. Did the girl really think that this could be fixed and forgiven in a phone call?

"You didn't dent my car or run over my flower beds. You slept with my husband. This isn't one of those things you get to say sorry for."

Lissa was crying. "I'm so ashamed. You've always been so kind to me, Mrs. Porter. And after my dad left —"

"Enough. I don't want to hear this." Mostly because she knew that if Lissa carried on, she might start to feel sorry for her. She didn't want to feel sorry for her.

"I loved babysitting for you. I love Sophie. I always wanted a family just like yours. You and David still kiss when he gets home from work, and you eat dinner around the table and laugh a lot —"

"And? You decided you wanted to wreck that?"

"No! I just liked the way I felt when I was with you all."

"So you thought you could move in and join the family?" She knew her tone was bitingly sarcastic, but she couldn't help it. She wasn't in a gentle mood. Audrey's influence showing again.

"I don't know what I thought. I was stupid and selfish and —" Lissa sniffed. "It's just that your family was so warm and perfect, and David always made me feel safe."

Grace stared across the lobby.

David had always made her feel safe, too.

He'd sheltered her from the harsh winds of life. Except that he was responsible for a hurricane-strength wind that had all but

542

flattened her. So much for strength and solidity. She saw now that you needed to build your own walls.

But she could easily see how someone like Lissa, whose father had never even bothered to fight for custody, might be attracted to that strength and solidity. David never panicked about anything. His approach to a problem was simply to find the best solution. As someone who had grown up alongside chaos, Grace had found his pragmatism soothing. She could see how Lissa might have found it irresistible.

She frowned. She was doing it again. Making excuses for something that was inexcusable.

Oh, what a mess.

"You don't get to make excuses for this, Lissa," she said. "Part of being an adult is taking responsibility." And she needed to take responsibility, too, of course.

It hadn't all been David's fault.

"That's what I'm doing." Lissa spoke in a quiet, tired voice. "I'm taking responsibility. I'm moving away. But before I leave, I wanted to tell you something. David never loved me, Grace. He was looking for something, sure, but it wasn't me personally. And yeah, it hurts to admit that in the end I wasn't special. I think being with me made him feel young, but the affair could have been with anyone. I was nothing more than an adrenaline rush. It's like when you go on a roller coaster, knowing that for a few breathless minutes you're going feel terrified and truly alive."

"I don't —"

"Please let me just say this and then I promise I will never bother you again. David stepped out of his life for a little while, and who hasn't sometimes wanted to do that? But it's you he loves. It's always been you. Even when we moved in together, he couldn't stop missing you. He was miserable. In the end we spent more time talking about how he could rescue his marriage and make it all up to you than we ever did about our own relationship."

He'd stepped out of his life for a little while . . .

Hadn't she done the same?

"I don't understand why you're telling me this."

"Because I'm doing what I can to put right a wrong before I leave."

"Where are you going?"

"I'm going to stay with my aunt in Seattle. I'll try to find a job there."

Lissa was moving to Seattle? So she

wouldn't be there when Grace finally went home.

There would be no awkward encounters in the supermarket. Grace wouldn't have to stifle the temptation to hurl melons at her in public or smack her over the head with a skillet.

Lissa spoke again. "I'm making a fresh start. I envy you, Grace. Having a man love you the way David loves you —" Her voice thickened. "You're lucky."

Lucky? *Lucky?*

Grace stared across the foyer of the hotel. David had humiliated her. He'd left her. How did that make her lucky?

"Goodbye, Lissa." She ended the call, her hands and legs shaking.

She took a moment to calm down and then walked into the restaurant.

David and Sophie were seated at a table by the window.

Sophie looked more subdued than usual, but she sprang to her feet when Grace arrived.

"Mom." She gaped at Grace. "Your *hair*! And your dress — you look so different. You look amazing. Doesn't she, Dad? Beautiful."

Color streaked across David's face. "She

does. But your mother always looks beautiful."

But not beautiful enough to stop him choosing Lissa.

Oh, stop it, Grace.

Bitterness could eat you alive and she wasn't going to let that happen.

"A change of circumstances called for a change in look." She hugged Sophie. "Are you doing okay?"

Sophie clung to her. "I'm so sorry."

Grace stroked her back, aware that David was looking at her searchingly.

"Is everything all right?"

"Everything is fine." Had he known Lissa would call? No, probably not. And maybe she'd tell him at some point, but not right now.

Sophie pulled away. "Is Monica mad at me?"

"No. She's grateful to you for handling everything in such an adult way."

Truthfully, Grace had been afraid that Monica might blame Sophie, but that hadn't been the case at all. Monica had bravely digested the facts and looked honestly at her relationship with her daughter without shifting blame.

Grace decided not to relay the details of the conversation where poor Monica had blamed herself and her parenting for Chrissie's sudden rebellion.

It's my fault, Grace. I held on to her too tightly.

Grace could sympathize, because to some extent she'd done the same with David. She glanced briefly at her husband, who was talking quietly to Sophie. Had she looked honestly at *their* relationship? Was she willing to admit that she was at least partly responsible? It was so much easier to wholly shift the blame onto another person than to take responsibility oneself.

She sat down on the opposite side of the table, facing David and Sophie.

"I was so stupid." Sophie's eyes were swimming. "Chrissie went totally crazy and I didn't want to say no to her. When she collapsed, it was terrifying. And I couldn't speak Italian so no one understood me."

"Don't be so hard on yourself. You stuck with your friend," Grace said, "and that's important. If you hadn't been there, maybe Chrissie wouldn't be alive and flying home with her mother."

A waiter appeared by her chair. "Would madame like to order?"

"Just coffee, please."

David ordered the same for himself. "How was London? How is Audrey's mother?"

547

"Recovering. Audrey is back in Paris."

"Will I get to meet Audrey?" Sophie looked curious. "You've talked about her a lot. Will you stay in touch when you come home? She's obviously important to you."

Grace thought about what the last month would have looked like without Audrey.

She would have lost her purse and all her valuables on day one for a start.

Would she have had the courage to contact Philippe if Audrey hadn't pushed her? Probably not. She certainly wouldn't have changed her hair. Audrey had made her question everything. Inspired her.

"Yes, you'll get to meet her. We'll be staying in touch."

They talked a little about Sophie's travels and when David excused himself to use the bathroom, Sophie leaned forward.

"You really do look *great,* Mom. When you told me you were doing okay, I thought you were probably being brave, but you weren't. You seem to have really enjoyed yourself."

"I have."

If David hadn't left her, her summer in Paris would have looked very different. She wouldn't have worked in the bookshop. She wouldn't have met Audrey.

She thought about Audrey and Etienne

and smiled.

Would their relationship work out? It was impossible to say, but it was obviously good right now. When it came to relationships there were no guarantees. Not after twenty-five days, and not after twenty-five years. Sometimes good right now was enough.

Sophie fiddled with her cup. "Do you think you and Dad might get back together?"

"I don't know. It's much too soon to even think about that."

"He loves you, Mom. He really loves you. He did a stupid thing, just like Chrissie. And me."

"Taking a single Ecstasy isn't quite the same as having an affair after twenty-five years of marriage." On the other hand maybe it wasn't so far removed. Each offered the promise of adventure. A moment away from the routine of daily life. Excitement. What had Lissa called it?

A few breathless minutes on a roller coaster.

Sophie looked pleading. "You're the one who always says that everyone does stupid things sometimes. You can hate the action, but not the person, right?"

"I don't hate your father. But that doesn't mean I'm ready to trust him again."

David arrived at the table at the same time

as Grace's coffee.

A woman at the table nearest to them sent him a lingering glance and for a moment Grace saw him as another woman might.

Dark hair. Strong shoulders. That knockout smile.

He really was good-looking, but that wasn't what had attracted her to him in the first place. What had drawn her were his values. His sense of responsibility. His kindness. He was a man who stood by his word and would never let you down, or so she'd thought.

Was she willing to move past that one mistake? Was she *able* to move past it or would she always feel suspicious? She didn't want to be in a marriage where she didn't trust her husband.

On the other hand, when had he ever let her down before this? Never. And when she'd called him about Sophie, he'd come immediately, even though she'd been pretty rude to him in their two encounters before that.

He'd given her comfort and reassurance but hadn't tried to take advantage of her vulnerability by addressing their own personal issues. He'd kept the focus on Sophie.

Underneath it all, he was still a kind person.

And she did believe that he loved her.

Grace noticed the woman sent David another lingering glance and felt suddenly possessive. Was that ridiculous? Yes, it probably was in the circumstances.

He used to be all hers. He could be all hers again if that was what she wanted.

But was it what she wanted?

Could she see what he'd done as human rather than unforgivable?

She sipped her coffee and listened while Sophie told them about an amazing pizza they'd eaten in Florence, and how the gelato was the best anywhere.

David was mildly amused that Sophie's focus was on food when Florence was all about art and culture. They all reminisced about a vacation they'd had in New York where all Sophie remembered was the pizza.

They were a family again. It had been such a long time since they'd sat around a table and laughed together like this.

She'd missed it.

"Did Mimi have lunch in her room?"

"Yes. And she has gone to the bookshop to see it for herself."

Grace put her cup down. "I was going to take her! I would have taken her today."

"I told her that, but she insisted."

"It's true," Sophie said, jumping to her

father's defense. "You know what Mimi is like. When she wants to do something, she does it. She doesn't care what anyone thinks."

Why had Mimi gone to the bookshop alone?

Why hadn't she waited for Grace?

"I don't like to think of my elderly grandmother traveling alone in a cab, that's all."

"She wasn't alone," David said. "I went with her to make sure she arrived safely and that the place was open. I waited in the cab until she went inside, then I came back here and met Sophie in the restaurant. I'm going back to pick her up in two hours."

He'd gone with her grandmother in the cab.

That was so typical of David. Grace felt a pressure in her chest and a thickening in her throat.

"Thank you." Her voice sounded husky. "Thank you for doing that."

She'd been working so hard to find a way to stop loving him, and now she realized she never had. Even hurt and angry, she hadn't stopped loving him.

But could she ever trust him again? Could she trust *anyone* again?

She didn't know.

MIMI

The bookshop hadn't changed at all. It was like stepping back in time. There was the same smell of dust and leather and the cool shade that offered respite from the relentless Paris heat.

She knew every nook and cranny.

"Bonjour." An elegant woman stepped forward with a smile, and Mimi assumed this must be Elodie.

She introduced herself in French and explained that she used to come here when she lived in Paris and would like to look around a little.

Elodie was gracious and charming and offered to make tea, but Mimi wasn't in the mood to chat.

She wanted to see the place that had stayed in her mind all her life.

It was time to admit that she hadn't made this trip for David. She hadn't even done it for Grace. She'd done it for herself.

She walked slowly from room to room, remembering.

It was where they'd met, although ironically, she hadn't come here for the books. She'd been taking photos of Paris, trying to capture the reality of daily life.

She'd been perched on a ladder, angling her camera at one of the high shelves, trying to capture the spirit of this bookstore. It was like a time capsule, an oasis of calm in a world of chaos. She'd leaned a little too far and would have fallen if it hadn't been for him.

He'd caught her, his hands on her waist, and lifted her down as if she'd weighed nothing.

Her bulky camera had swung and hit him in the jaw, but he'd laughed as he set her on her feet.

She'd had many affairs, but only one love affair. It had been the single most terrifying thing she'd ever experienced.

She'd had plans. So many plans, and she'd known right from the first touch of his hands that this was something that could stop all of them. If she let it continue, there would be no more adventures.

The clanging of the bell signaled another visitor and yanked her from the past.

Mimi blinked and almost lost her balance.

Why had she come here? What had she been thinking? It was like sticking a knife in a wound.

There had been so many times when she'd wondered how her life might have looked if she'd made different choices.

She turned, intending to leave. And there he was. Standing there.

For a moment she assumed her mind had conjured him up. That her memories were so vivid they seemed real.

But then he took a step toward her. "Mimi?" His voice was hoarse. "Mimi?"

Dizziness swamped her. She reached out and clutched the nearest bookshelf.

"Antoine."

She wasn't even sure how she got there, but somehow she was in his arms and it was as if they'd never been parted. He still hugged the same way. He even smelled the same.

Her cheeks were wet. She might have been crying, or maybe it was him.

"I'm sorry." She pressed her lips to his cheek, speaking in French. "I'm sorry for hurting you. I wanted so many things. I had so much ambition, it burned inside me like rocket fuel and I knew that if we —"

"Hush." He covered her lips with his fingers. "I knew what you wanted. And I always knew who you were."

"If I'd been a different type of woman —"

"— then maybe I wouldn't have loved you. You needed to leave. You needed to do all those things you wanted to do. Why would I have stopped you from becoming who you wanted to be?"

Her eyes filled. "You're so unselfish, and I'm so selfish."

"No. I loved who you were, Mimi. You were fierce and fearless, in love with the possibilities of life. Just tell me one thing —" he searched her gaze with his "— has your life been everything you wanted it to be?"

She thought of all the adventures she'd had. And then she thought about the bad times. Judy's addiction. Judy's death. Those moments where you were sucked so deep into darkness you thought you'd never surface.

But that was life, wasn't it? If her work as a photographer had taught her anything, it was that pain was part of being human.

"My life has been interesting," she said finally. She should tell him, of course. And she would, but first she wanted to enjoy this moment.

He cupped her face in his hands and she gazed up at him, thinking how strange it was that age didn't change a person inside.

The packaging might change, but the product was the same.

He was still handsome. Even with gray hair and weathered skin, he was handsome. Strong bones. Calm, kind eyes. That slow smile.

The bell clanged again, but Mimi didn't pay attention until she heard Grace's voice.

A moment later her granddaughter appeared and she looked at Mimi and Antoine in astonishment.

"Mimi? *Toni?*"

Mimi swallowed and eased out of Antoine's arms. It had to be now.

"Antoine, I'd like you to meet my granddaughter, Grace."

"We know each other well." Grace stepped forward, smiling, but puzzled. "How do you two — ?"

"She was the love of my life," Antoine said. His hand gripped Mimi's tightly. "This was where we met. We spent a glorious summer together."

One summer in Paris, Mimi thought. The best summer of her life.

Grace looked bemused. "And what happened?"

Antoine gave a tired smile. "If you know your grandmother well, you'll know she has an adventurous spirit. Committing to one man felt like securing herself with a padlock, am I right, Mimi?"

Mimi nodded. She couldn't speak.

Should she make excuses? Should she apologize for the person she'd been then?

No. A person should never have to apologize for who they were.

"I wasn't ready," she said. "I wasn't ready for the life we would have made together. I needed something different. So I ended it."

"She left me a note and a photograph." His mouth twisted. "I carried that photograph with me for years. I put it inside a book for safekeeping. I had hundreds of books. About six months ago I moved from my house to a small apartment. An old friend helped me move and clear some of the books. He brought them here. When I went to look for the photograph, it wasn't there. I realized I'd muddled up the book. My memory isn't what it was. Or maybe it fell out when my cleaner was dusting and she put it back in a different book. I don't know what happened, but I couldn't find it. I've been looking for the photo ever since."

Grace looked stunned. "Every day, you go through each book on every shelf. That's why?"

"It's lost."

"What? No! No, it isn't." Grace opened

her purse and scrabbled around in it. "How could I have forgotten something so important? Oh, where *is* it? I know it's here —" She tugged out a map of the Louvre, followed by some stray receipts and a printed email. "Aha! Here it is." She pulled out a photograph and waved it, triumphant. "I found it when I was sorting through the books. I meant to give it to Mimi the other day, but I forgot. I think I was a little distracted."

Mimi had no doubt David was the cause of the distraction.

She took the photograph and felt a sudden pressure in her chest.

She remembered the day it was taken. They'd been standing on Pont Neuf with the sun blinding them. She'd known then that she had to make a choice. The most difficult choice of her life.

"This was all I had left of you." Antoine took the photo from Grace. "This and the note. This was the end of it."

Now. She had to tell him now.

"It wasn't the end." Mimi swallowed. "I had a daughter. *We* had a daughter. Judy. I was already in New York when I discovered I was pregnant."

Antoine was silent for a moment. "And you had no way of contacting me."

559

She could lie, but that time was past. "I didn't try to contact you. You would have wanted to marry me and I couldn't be a stay-at-home wife, Antoine. I just couldn't. I wasn't ready for any of that. I made the choice that was right for me at the time."

He was silent. There was a sheen in his eyes. "A daughter?"

"Wait —" Grace put her hand on Mimi's arm. "You're saying Toni — Antoine — is my grandfather?"

"Yes."

Antoine looked stunned. "And Judy — ?"

"She died." Mimi felt Grace's hand on her arm. Comforting. "I'll tell you all about it. I'll tell you everything." Everything? Would she tell him about the dark times when she'd doubted her decision? When she'd questioned everything about her life?

Grace squeezed her arm. "Mimi, why don't you and Antoine go and talk in private? You can use my apartment. It's just up the stairs." She handed over a key. "I think you need some time together."

Would he want that?

She'd just confessed that she'd had a child and hadn't told him.

Maybe that was something he wouldn't be able to forgive.

She felt lost and vulnerable and it was Antoine who took the key from Grace.

"Now I know we're related, you will be forced to keep in touch when you return home." He kissed Grace on the cheek, warm and gracious, and Grace hugged him.

"I've always wondered about the identity of my grandfather. I'm so very happy it's you."

Antoine turned to Mimi. "We have a lot to talk about. So much to catch up on. I have things to tell you, too."

She looked at his face, nervous of seeing condemnation or anger, but all she saw there was love.

Grace was watching her anxiously and she knew she would have so much explaining to do, but for now she was content just to be with Antoine.

She'd assumed she was too old for a new adventure, but maybe she'd been wrong about that.

GRACE

"I leave you alone for five minutes and you gain a whole new family member." Audrey rummaged for the key to the bookstore. "I can't believe Toni is your grandfather. That's both weird and very cool. Honestly, I'm a bit jealous. I've never had a grandpa. Or not one that's present in my life that I can hug."

"It is romantic." Grace's head was still reeling. What a day. She couldn't even begin to imagine what Mimi and Toni were talking about upstairs in the apartment. After revelations like that, where did you start?

Audrey locked the bookstore and turned the sign on the door to Closed. "Mimi never mentioned him?"

"Not once. She led me to believe she'd never been in love. I had no idea she had a secret like that."

"Everyone has secrets." Audrey grinned at her. "Except us, of course. You pretty much know everything there is to know about me. And I know where all your bodies are buried."

"Don't ever say that in public. You make me sound like a serial killer."

"I just mean we have a great friendship. So was Toni mad? I mean, it must have been a shocker finding out you had a kid, and then she died —" Audrey pulled a face. "Sorry."

"Don't be. You're right, it must have been a shocker, but he didn't seem mad. He didn't even seem surprised. It was as if he knew Mimi so well, and loved her so much, nothing needed explaining. As if everything she did, he was willing to accept as part of who she was."

Audrey dropped the key on the desk. "Well, that's what everyone wants, I guess. Someone who loves you even when you fu— mess up. Did you see what I did there? No swearing. Are you proud of me?"

Grace smiled. "Very."

"Ron seems to have forgiven my mum, and Toni has forgiven Mimi, so all that's left is for you to decide if you're going to forgive David." Audrey nibbled the corner of her nail, her eyes on Grace. "So what do you think?"

"I really don't know. I'm meeting him on

the bridge in half an hour, and I have no idea what to say."

"Well, if you want to talk it through —" Audrey shrugged "— you can call me anytime. Because I'm an expert on relationships, in case you hadn't noticed."

Grace laughed. "You are?"

"Yeah, I mean, I'm the reason you got in touch with Philippe, right? And okay, maybe that didn't exactly work out, but you had some fun and you got concert tickets. And I got concert tickets, too. And right now my family feels as close to normal as it has ever been. That's not saying much, of course."

"And Etienne?"

Audrey blushed. "He is whisking me away to the South of France to meet his mum and sisters. Not sure if that's exciting or scary, but it sounds a bit jet-set, don't you think? I'm thinking of a suitable hashtag. And Elodie says it's fine for me to have some days off, so don't worry. I'm not about to be fired a second time. Her niece is staying with her for the next week and she is going to be working here, so we're all good."

"That is good." Grace felt a pang. "I'm going to miss you."

Audrey's smile faded. "I'm going to miss you, too. But I'm going to be emailing you the whole time, and texting, and calling, and showing up on your doorstep until you're tempted to swear at me."

"That day is never going to come." Grace hugged her. "Thank you. These last few weeks have been — well, I think you saved me."

"I think we saved each other." Audrey squeezed her and then pulled away. "Go, or you'll be late and then he might think you're not coming and throw himself in the river or something."

Grace sniffed and smoothed her hair. "How do I look?"

"You look like a woman who knows what she wants out of life, so go and grab it."

"He was the love of her life, and I didn't even know." Grace leaned on the bridge, staring down at the water. David stood next to her, his arm brushing against hers. He'd been waiting for her, his eyes scanning the throngs of tourists, clearly worried that she wouldn't come. She'd seen the relief in his face when he'd caught sight of her.

"Everyone has their secrets."

"But why didn't she tell me?"

"Perhaps it hurt too much to talk about it. Perhaps she regretted her choice. Who knows? Not every choice is easy and obvious. And what can seem right at the time might not seem right when you look back."

She could feel his gaze on her. Knew he was talking about himself as well as Mimi.

"I can't believe I have a grandfather. And not only that, I love him. He comes into the bookshop every day. We've had tea. Chatted."

"I'm happy you've had a good time here." She tilted her head and looked at him. "Really?"

"Yes. I thought about you all the time. I worried about you. I kept wondering if you were all right on your own."

Grace thought about Audrey and smiled. "I wasn't on my own much. And being here has been good for me. I've done things I wouldn't have done if we'd been together. I've made some changes."

"I'm thinking of making some, too." He took a breath. "I've decided to resign from my job."

"You've resigned?" She couldn't have been more surprised.

"No, not yet. I wanted to talk to you about it first."

"What's it got to do with me?"

"I hope a lot." He stroked her face gently. "I've had a lot of time to think lately, and I realized that all those things I said — well, I was wrong, Gracie. I was in a bad place and

566

it was easier to blame you than take responsibility. It was never about you. It was about me. The man I felt I'd become. The life I was living. Sophie leaving made me question all of it. I felt weighed down by responsibility. There was no surprise, no mystery, every day was mapped out and I could see all the way to old age. It terrified me."

"And Lissa offered surprise and excitement." The lure of the forbidden, she thought, wondering why she was suddenly able to be so analytical. "It's human nature, isn't it? The thing we can't have always seems more attractive than the thing we already have."

David gave a rueful smile. "I wish I'd had your clarity of thinking. Life seemed hard, and for a time it was easier to step out of it than step up. The excitement of being with Lissa wore off once we were together all the time. When I was still married to you, I had the security of our marriage and the excitement of an affair. Turns out an affair isn't so exciting when it becomes the main relationship."

"Why didn't you talk to me? Why didn't you tell me you found it hard?"

"Because you were relentlessly upbeat about Sophie leaving. It made me feel inadequate that I couldn't be as positive about it as you were. Your approach was so healthy and mature. You were fine about it."

"No, I wasn't. I didn't feel that way at all. Inside I was heartbroken, devastated, but I thought if I kept up an act and said all the right things eventually I might start to feel the way I wanted to feel." She took a deep breath. "And I could pretend that I didn't realize you felt differently and needed to talk, but the truth is I did sense that. I was afraid to open that conversation because what I was feeling was so huge, I was afraid I wouldn't be able to bottle it again. And I didn't want Sophie to feel the guilt and responsibility that I felt at her age."

"I was faithful to you for more than two decades. I never in a million years thought I'd have an affair. It goes against my values, and everything I feel for you. I don't know what made me step over that line, but it wasn't anything you did."

"She gave you something that I wasn't able to at that time. She made you feel young. It was my fault, too." She could see it so clearly now, and her brief but intense experience with Philippe had given her more sympathy for David. His affair had little to do with sex or love, and everything to do with a need for the unpredictable, the unfamiliar, the exciting. For a short time

he'd thrown off the responsibility of adult-
hood. And what about her own brief fling?
Hers had been mostly driven by a need for
attention. A need to reinstate some of the
confidence that David's actions had destroyed. "Some of what you said about our
life together was right. I confused chaos
with spontaneity. I held so tight to life I
almost strangled it."

"It's understandable."

"Maybe, but not excusable. As you say, it
was my life. If I let it get boring and predictable that was my fault."

His gaze lingered on hers. "It doesn't look
as if the last few weeks have been predictable. I barely recognize you." He hesitated.
"Was the makeover for Philippe?"

"No. It was for me. I haven't made enough
changes in my life and that was one of
them." How much should she say? "About
Philippe —"

"Don't tell me." He covered her lips with
his fingers.

Her heart thudded. "But —"

"Can we forget the past, Gracie?" He slid
his hand behind her head and looked deep
into her eyes, searching for the truth. "If I
met you for the first time today, you'd still
be the woman I want to spend the rest of
my life with. Are you able to forgive me? If

you give me another chance, I swear I'll never again give you reason not to trust me."

Her heart bumped hard against her chest. Forgive him?

Could she do that? If someone had asked her before this if she could forgive an affair she would have definitely said no, but now she knew choices weren't as easy as that. It was impossible to know what you'd do until you were in that situation. Life was messy and complicated. And what was love if it wasn't hanging on when things were tough? If a person meant enough to you, then surely love was worth fighting for?

"What if you have another midlife crisis?"

"Then I'll have it with you."

"You're suggesting we join a gym and buy a sports car?"

"I wasn't, but when you put it like that it doesn't sound so bad." He smiled down at her, but there was a wariness in his eyes as if he didn't quite dare let himself think this might have a positive ending. "What do you say? Can we forget the past or will it always be a barrier between us?"

She thought about Mimi spending all those years alone, thinking of her lost love.

And she thought about David.

She saw their life in slow motion. Working on the school magazine. The first time they'd kissed. The death of her parents. The death of his parents. Scraping money together. Buying their first house. The night they'd found out she was pregnant. Sophie's delivery where David had driven like a maniac to get her to the hospital. David dancing with Mimi and fixing things around the house. The way he calmed every storm. His Happy Memory Project. Niagara. Florence. Rome. Highs and lows. Didn't every marriage have highs and lows?

Yes, there had been a bad patch. Worse than bad. But bad didn't have to mean over, did it? And sometimes the bad made you appreciate the good.

"I don't think we should forget the past, David." She rested her hand on his chest. "I think we should use it to make what we have stronger. Treat it as a foundation, not a barrier. We should look at what was missing, and somehow fill the gap between us."

"So — we have a future?"

"We have a future." She'd barely said the words before he was crushing her against him, his lips against her hair as he murmured that he loved her, that he would spend the rest of his life making her happy.

Eventually, he pulled away and in his eyes she saw relief and respect. She saw love.

"Monica, other people at home —" he

cupped her face in his hands "— they'll think you're crazy giving me a second chance. They'll tell you not to."

She knew he was right. She also knew that marriage and happiness weren't so easy to judge from the outside. She'd been angry with her father for enabling her mother, but she knew now she had no right to judge. Her father had loved her mother. He'd done what he thought was best, even if from the outside it hadn't seemed that way. A marriage was as individual as a person. What kept two people together was different for every couple. There was no blueprint.

"It doesn't matter what they think. It only matters what we think." She leaned her head against his chest and felt his arms come around her again.

"I love you, Gracie."

Warmth spread through her. "I love you, too." She really did. Yes, she was hurt. Yes, part of her was still angry. But all through the whole terrible nightmare she'd never stopped loving him. It wouldn't have felt like a nightmare if she hadn't loved him.

No one made the right decisions all the time, although she'd tried hard. She'd controlled every aspect of her life and David's life.

That was going to change.

She lifted her head to look at him. "So if you resign, what will you do instead?"

"I'll do some freelance writing. And I finally finished my novel, so I'm sending that off to a few agents although I doubt anything will happen. I'm braced for rejection."

"You finished it?"

"I thought it was time I stopped talking about it and did it. I wrote at night. It was better than lying there wide-awake, missing you. I thought maybe we could travel for a while. Go to California and help Sophie settle in. Maybe take a car down the coast. Monterey. Carmel. Maybe stop off in wine country." He paused. "But of course if you'd rather stay home and stick with the routine —"

Her old routine held no appeal. She'd found comfort in knowing what was going to happen next, but that was no longer the case.

"I have a question — is this car a sexy little sports car?"

He smiled. "Definitely."

"And we should drink champagne together. We've never done that."

"You want to drink champagne?" He raised an eyebrow. "Who are you and what have you done with my Grace?"

573

My Grace.

"I'm ready to live a little, that's all."

"Does that mean you're saying yes to the trip?"

"I think as a midlife crisis goes, this sounds like a good one. I'm happy to join you in it."

She'd wanted this summer to be something they'd always remember, and she knew they would. There had been bad, but there had also been good and there would be more good to come. And she had new people in her life, too. Antoine, her grandfather. Audrey, who would be a friend for life.

A summer in Paris had taught her so much about herself and now she was on the edge of renewing her relationship with David.

And what they built together moving forward would be better and stronger. Perhaps it would feel all the more precious because what they shared had been threatened.

David pulled her into his arms. "We can plan the trip carefully if you like. Every last detail."

Grace slid her arms around his neck and smiled. "We don't need to do that. Why don't we just see what happens?"

ACKNOWLEDGMENTS

Setting plays an important part in every book I write, so my first thank-you is to Paris for providing exactly what I needed to tell this story, and for the many happy hours spent exploring what must surely be one of the most romantic cities in the world. Also, thank you Paris for the wine, and all the delicious cheese, for the macarons (eaten for research purposes, obviously), the art galleries and the bistros.

Writing is a fairly solitary process, but publishing isn't and I'm lucky to work with the best publishing teams on both sides of the water — HQN in the US and HQ Stories in the UK. They work hard to make sure my books reach as many readers as possible and I'm massively grateful. I think they know that, but I'm putting it in writing.

It's always nerve-racking picking out individual people because publishing is like a massive jigsaw and every piece of the puzzle is important, but still I'm going to thank Loriana Sacilotto, Dianne Moggy and Susan Swinwood. Also, extra big thanks to my fabulous editor, Flo Nicoll, and to Manpreet Grewal and Lisa Milton for guiding my career in the UK with such enthusiasm and dedication. My agent, Susan Ginsburg, is simply the best, and I'm so lucky to work with her.

Thank you to the many wonderful bloggers who tirelessly read and review my books, and to my publicity dream team, particularly Sophie Calder, Lucy Richardson, Lisa Wray and Anna Robinson.

I'm grateful to my international publishers for their enthusiasm and commitment. Connecting with readers from around the globe is one of the highlights of the job for me.

Thanks to my nonwriter friends who patiently answer questions like "what would you do if . . .", to my writer friends who sustain me through the ups and downs of writing a book, and to my family, who are wonderful in every way.

As always, my biggest thank-you goes to my readers, who brighten each day with their kind messages, their book recommendations and their enthusiasm for my stories. Thank you for picking up another book of mine. I'm honored to be on your shelves. If you can't take a trip to Paris this summer, I hope this book will feel like the next best thing.

ABOUT THE AUTHOR

USA Today bestselling author **Sarah Morgan** writes lively, sexy contemporary stories for Harlequin.

Romantic Times has described her as "a magician with words" and nominated her books for their Reviewers' Choice Awards and their "Top Pick" slot. In 2012 Sarah received the prestigious RITA® Award from the Romance Writers of America. She lives near London with her family. Find out more at www.sarahmorgan.com.

The employees of Thorndike Press hope you have enjoyed this Large Print book. All our Thorndike, Wheeler, and Kennebec Large Print titles are designed for easy reading, and all our books are made to last. Other Thorndike Press Large Print books are available at your library, through selected bookstores, or directly from us.

For information about titles, please call:
(800) 223-1244

or visit our website at:
gale.com/thorndike

To share your comments, please write:

Publisher
Thorndike Press
10 Water St., Suite 310
Waterville, ME 04901